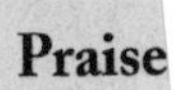

Praise ... or

NORA ROBERTS

"Nora Roberts is among the best." —*Washington Post*

"Roberts has a warm feel for her characters and an eye for the evocative detail." —*Chicago Tribune*

"Her stories have fueled the dreams of twenty-five million readers." —*Entertainment Weekly*

"Some estimates have [Nora Roberts] selling 12 books an hour, 24 hours a day, 7 days a week, 52 weeks a year." —*New York Times*

"With clear-eyed, concise vision and a sure pen, Roberts nails her characters and settings with awesome precision, drawing readers into a vividly rendered world of family-centered warmth and unquestionable magic." —*Library Journal*

"Romance will never die as long as the megaselling Roberts keeps writing it." —*Kirkus Reviews*

Also available from Silhouette Books and Harlequin by

NORA ROBERTS

THE BRIGHTEST OF STARS
Their love shines brightest on the darkest of nights

ALL MY STARS
A cosmic trio: bounty hunters, jewel thieves and memory loss

SUMMER ALL ALONG
A captivating Calhoun tale of charm, faith and rich family history

THE DARKEST OF NIGHTS
The darkest of nights are rife with desire and danger

SOMETHING ABOUT TOMORROW
Daring, passionate and full of heart

JUST BETWEEN US
Two sizzling MacKade romances

For a full list of titles by Nora Roberts, please visit www.noraroberts.com.

NORA ROBERTS

Love and Other Stars

Includes *Night Shield* & *Secret Star*

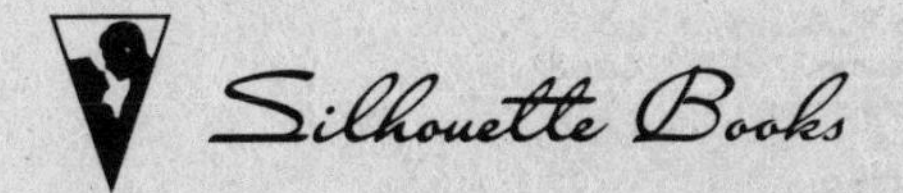

Recycling programs for this product may not exist in your area.

Love and Other Stars

ISBN-13: 978-1-335-08046-2

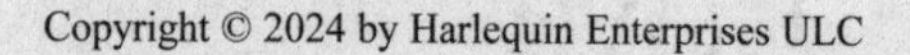

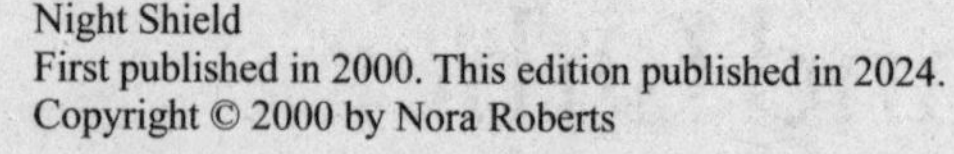

For questions and comments about the quality of this book, please contact us at CustomerService@Harlequin.com.

Silhouette
22 Adelaide St. West, 41st Floor
Toronto, Ontario M5H 4E3, Canada
www.Harlequin.com

Printed in U.S.A.

CONTENTS

NIGHT SHIELD

For tough guys with soft hearts

Chapter 1

He didn't like cops.

His attitude had deep roots, and stemmed from spending his formative years dodging them, outrunning them—usually—or being hassled by them when his feet weren't fast enough.

He'd picked his share of pockets by the time he'd turned twelve and knew the best and most lucrative channels for turning a hot watch into cold cash.

He'd learned back then that knowing what time it was couldn't buy happiness, but the twenty bucks the watch brought in paid for a nice slice of the happiness pie. And twenty bucks cannily wagered swelled into sixty at three-to-one.

The same year he'd turned twelve, he'd invested his carefully hoarded takes and winnings in a small gambling enterprise that centered around point spreads and indulged his interest in sports.

He was a businessman at heart.

He hadn't run with gangs. First of all he'd never had the urge to join groups, and more importantly he didn't care for the pecking order such organizations required. Someone had to be in charge—and he preferred it to be himself.

Some people might say Jonah Blackhawk had a problem with authority.

They would be right.

He supposed the tide had turned right after he'd turned thirteen. His gambling interests had grown nicely—a little too nicely to suit certain more established syndicates.

He'd been warned off in the accepted way—he'd had the hell beat out of him. Jonah acknowledged the bruised kidneys, split lip and blackened eyes as a business risk. But before he could make his decision to move territories or dig in, he'd been busted. And busted solid.

Cops were a great deal more of an annoyance than business rivals.

But the cop who'd hauled his arrogant butt in had been different. Jonah had never pinned down what exactly separated this cop from the others in the line of shields and rule books. So, instead of being tossed into juvie—to which he was no stranger—he'd found himself yanked into programs, youth centers, counseling.

Oh, he'd squirmed and snapped in his own cold-blooded way, but this cop had a grip like a bear trap and hadn't let go. The sheer tenacity had been a shock. No one had held on to him before. Jonah had found himself rehabilitated almost despite himself, at least enough to see there were certain advantages to, if not working in the system, at least working the system.

Now, at thirty, no one would call him a pillar of Denver's community, but he was a legitimate businessman whose enterprises turned a solid profit and allowed him a lifestyle the hustling street kid couldn't have dreamed of.

He owed the cop, and he always paid his debts.

Otherwise, he'd have chosen to be chained naked and honey-smeared to a hill of fire ants rather than sit tamely in the outer office of the commissioner of police of Denver.

Even if the commissioner was Boyd Fletcher.

Jonah didn't pace. Nervous motion was wasted motion and gave too much away. The woman manning the station outside the commissioner's double doors was young, attractive with a very interesting and wanton mass of curling red hair. But he didn't flirt. It wasn't the wedding ring on her finger that stopped him as much as her proximity to Boyd, and through him, the long blue line.

He sat, patient and still, in one of the hunter-green chairs in the waiting area, a tall man with a long-legged, tough build wearing a three-thousand-dollar jacket over a twenty-dollar T-shirt. His hair was raven-black, rain straight and thick. That and the pale gold of his skin, the whiplash of cheekbones were gifts from his Apache great-grandfather.

The cool, clear green eyes might have been a legacy from his Irish great-grandmother, who'd given the Apache man three sons.

Jonah knew little of his family history. His own parents had been more interested in fighting with each other over the last beer in the six-pack than tucking their only son in with bedtime stories. Occasionally Jonah's father had boasted about his lineage, but Jonah had never been sure what was fact and what was convenient fiction.

And didn't really give a damn.

You were what you made yourself.

That was a lesson Boyd Fletcher had taught him. For that alone, Jonah would have walked on hot coals for him.

"Mr. Blackhawk? The commissioner will see you now."

She offered a polite smile as she rose to get the door. And she'd taken a good, long look at the commissioner's ten o'clock appointment—a wedding ring didn't strike a woman blind, after all. Something about him made her tongue want to hang out, and at the same time made her want to run for cover.

His eyes warned a woman he'd be dangerous. He had a dangerous way of moving as well, she mused. Graceful and sleek as a cat. A woman could weave some very interesting fantasies about a man like that—and fantasies were probably the safest way to be involved with him.

Then he flicked her a smile, so full of power and charm she wanted to sigh like a teenager.

"Thanks."

She rolled her eyes as she shut the door behind him. "Oh boy, are you welcome."

"Jonah." Boyd was already up and coming around his desk. One hand gripped Jonah's while the other gave Jonah's shoulder a hard squeeze in a kind of male hug. "Thanks for coming."

"Hard to refuse a request from the commissioner."

The first time Jonah had met Boyd, Boyd had been a

lieutenant. His hair had been a dark, streaked gold, and his office small, cramped and glass walled.

Now Boyd's hair was deep, solid silver, and his office spacious. The glass wall was a wide window that looked out on Denver and the mountains that ringed it.

Some things change, Jonah thought, then looked into Boyd's steady bottle-green eyes. And some don't.

"Black coffee suit you?"

"Always did."

"Have a seat." Boyd gestured to a chair then walked over to his coffee machine. He'd insisted on one of his own to save himself the annoyance of buzzing an assistant every time he wanted a hit. "Sorry I kept you waiting. I had a call to finish up. Politics," he muttered as he poured two mugs with rich black coffee. "Can't stand them."

Jonah said nothing, but the corner of his lips quirked.

"And no smart remarks about me being a damn politician at this stage of my game."

"Never crossed my mind." Jonah accepted the coffee. "To say it."

"You always were a sharp kid." Boyd sat on a chair beside Jonah's rather than behind the desk. He let out a long sigh. "Never used to think I'd ride a desk."

"Miss the streets?"

"Every day. But you do what you do, then you do the next thing. How's the new club?"

"It's good. We draw a respectable crowd. Lots of gold cards. They need them," Jonah added as he sipped his coffee. "We hose them on the designer drinks."

"That so? And here I was thinking of bringing Cilla by for an evening out."

"You bring your wife, you get drinks and dinner on the house—is that allowed?"

Boyd hesitated, tapped his finger against his mug. "We'll see. I have a little problem, Jonah, I think you might be able to help me with."

"If I can."

"We've had a series of burglaries the last couple of months. Mostly high dollar, easily liquidated stuff. Jewelry, small electronics, cash."

"Same area?"

"No, across the board. Single-family homes out in the burbs, downtown apartments, condos. We've had six hits in just under eight weeks. Very slick, very clean."

"Well, what can I do for you?" Jonah rested his mug on his knee. "B and E was never my thing." His smile flashed. "According to my record."

"I always wondered about that." But Boyd lifted a hand, waved it away. "The marks are as varied as the locations of the hits. Young couples, older couples, singles. But they all have one thing in common. They were all at a club on the night of the burglary."

Jonah's eyes narrowed, the only change of expression. "One of mine?"

"In five out of the six, yours."

Jonah drank his coffee, looked out the wide window at the hard blue sky. The tone of his voice remained pleasant, casual. But his eyes had gone cold. "Are you asking me if I'm involved?"

"No, Jonah, I'm not asking you if you're involved. We've been beyond that for a long time." Boyd waited a beat. The boy was—always had been—touchy. "Or I have."

With a nod, Jonah rose. He walked back to the coffeemaker, set down his cup. There weren't many people who mattered enough to him that he cared what they thought of him. Boyd mattered.

"Someone's using my place to scope marks," he said with his back to Boyd. "I don't like it."

"I didn't think you would."

"Which place?"

"The new one. Blackhawk's."

He nodded again. "Higher-end clientele. Likely a bigger disposable income than the crowd at a sports bar like Fast Break." He turned back. "What do you want from me, Fletch?"

"I'd like your cooperation. And I'd like you to agree to work with the investigating team. Most specifically with the detective in charge."

Jonah swore, and in a rare show of agitation, raked his fingers through his hair. "You want me to rub shoulders with cops, set them loose in my place?"

Boyd didn't bother to hide his amusement. "Jonah, they've already been in your place."

"Not while I was there." Of that, he could be sure. He could sense cop at half a mile, while he was running in the other direction in the dark.

And had.

"No, apparently not. Some of us work during daylight hours."

"Why?"

With a half laugh, Boyd stretched out his legs. "Did I ever tell you I met Cilla when we were both on night shift?"

"No more than twenty or thirty times."

"Same smart mouth. I always liked that about you."

"That's not what you said when you threatened to staple it shut."

"Nothing wrong with your memory, either. I could use your help, Jonah." Boyd's voice went soft, serious. "I'd appreciate it."

He'd avoided prisons all his life, Jonah thought. Until Boyd. The man had built a prison around him of loyalty and trust and affection. "You've got it—for what it's worth."

"It's worth a great deal to me." He rose, offered his hand to Jonah again. "Right on time," he said as his phone rang. "Get yourself some more coffee. I want you to meet the detective in charge of the case."

He rounded the desk, picked up the receiver. "Yes, Paula. Good. We're ready." This time he sat at the desk. "I have a lot of faith in this particular cop. The detective shield's fairly new, but it was well earned."

"A rookie detective. Perfect." Resigned, Jonah poured more coffee. He didn't bobble the pot when the door opened, but his mind jumped. He supposed it was a pleasant thing to realize he could still be surprised.

She was a long-legged, lanky blonde with eyes like prime whiskey. She wore her hair in a straight, sleek tail down the middle of her back over a trim, well-cut jacket the color of steel.

When she flicked those eyes over him, her wide, pretty mouth stayed serious and unsmiling.

Jonah realized he'd have noticed the face first, so classy and fine-boned, then he'd have noticed the cop. The package might have been distracting, but he'd have made her.

"Commissioner." She had a voice like her eyes, deep and dark and potent.

"Detective. You're prompt. Jonah, this is—"

"You don't have to introduce her." Casually Jonah sipped fresh coffee. "She has your wife's eyes and your jaw. Nice to meet you, Detective Fletcher."

"Mr. Blackhawk."

She'd seen him before. Once, she recalled, when her father had gone to one of his high school baseball games and she'd tagged along. She remembered being impressed by his gutsy, nearly violent, base running.

She also knew his history and wasn't quite as trusting of former delinquents as her father. And, though she hated to admit it, she was a little jealous of their relationship.

"Do you want some coffee, Ally?"

"No, sir." He was her father, but she didn't sit until the commissioner gestured to a chair.

Boyd spread his hands. "I thought we'd be more comfortable having this meeting here. Ally, Jonah's agreed to cooperate with the investigation. I've given him the overview. I leave it to you to fill in the necessary details."

"Six burglaries in a period of under eight weeks. Estimated cumulative loss in the ballpark of eight hundred thousand dollars. They go for easily fenced items, heavy on the jewelry. However, in one case a victim's Porsche was stolen from the garage. Three of the homes had security systems. They were disengaged. There have been no signs of break-in. In each case the residence was empty at the time of the burglary."

Jonah crossed the room, sat. "I've already got that much—except for the Porsche. So, you've got someone who can boost cars as well as lift locks, and likely has a channel to turn over a variety of merchandise."

"None of the goods have turned up through any of the known channels in Denver. The operation's well organized and efficient. We suspect there are at least two, probably three or more people involved. Your club's been the main source."

"And?"

"Two of your employees at Blackhawk's have criminal records. William Sloan and Frances Cummings."

Jonah's eyes went cold, but didn't flicker. "Will ran numbers, and did his time. He's been out and clean for five years. Frannie worked the stroll, and it's her business why. Now she tends bar instead of johns. Don't you believe in rehabilitation, Detective Fletcher?"

"I believe your club is being used as a pool to hook fish, and I intend to check all the lines. Logic indicates someone on the inside's baiting the hook."

"I know the people who work for me." He shot Boyd a furious look. "Damn it, Fletch."

"Jonah, hear us out."

"I don't want my people hassled because they tripped over the law at some point in their lives."

"No one's going to hassle your people. Or you," Ally added. Though you did plenty of tripping of your own, she thought. "If we'd wanted to interview them, we would have. We don't need your permission or your cooperation to question potential suspects."

"You move them from my people to suspects very smoothly."

"If you believe they're innocent, why worry?"

"Okay, simmer down." Boyd stayed behind the desk, rubbed the back of his neck. "You're in an awkward and difficult position, Jonah. We appreciate that," he said pointedly with a subtle lift of his eyebrows for his daughter. "The goal is to root out whoever's in charge of this organization and put an end to it. They're using you."

"I don't want Will and Frannie yanked down into interrogation."

"That's not our intention." So he had a hot button, Ally mused. Friendship? Loyalty? Or maybe he had a thing going with the ex-hooker. It would be part of the job to find out. "We don't want to alert anyone on the inside to the investigation. We need to find out who's targeting the marks, and how. We want you to put a cop on the inside."

"I'm on the inside," he reminded her.

"Then you should be able to make room for another waitress. I can start tonight."

Jonah let out a short laugh, turned to Boyd. "You want your daughter working tables in my club?"

Ally got to her feet, slowly. "The commissioner wants one of his detectives undercover at your club. And this is my case."

Jonah rose, as well. "Let's clear this up. I don't give a damn whose case it is. Your father asked me to co-operate, so I will. Is this what you want me to do?" he asked Boyd.

"It is, for now."

"Fine. She can start tonight. Five o'clock, my office at Blackhawk's. We'll go over what you need to know."

"I owe you for this, Jonah."

"You'll never owe me for anything." He walked to the door, stopped, shot a glance over his shoulder. "Oh, Detective? Waitresses at Blackhawk's wear black. Black shirt or sweater, black skirt. Short black skirt," he added, then let himself out.

Ally pursed her lips, and for the first time since she'd come into the room relaxed enough to slip her hands casually into her pockets. "I don't think I like your friend, Dad."

"He'll grow on you."

"What, like mold? No," she corrected. "He's too cool for that. I might end up with a little skin of ice, though. You're sure of him?"

"As sure as I am of you."

And that, she thought, said it all. "Whoever's set up these B and E's has brains, connections and guts. I'd say your pal there has all three." She lifted her shoulders. "Still, if I can't trust your judgment, whose can I trust?"

Boyd grinned. "Your mother always liked him."

"Well then, I'm half in love already." That wiped the grin off his face, she noted with amusement. "I'm still going to have a couple of men under as customers."

"That's your call."

"It's been five days since the last hit. They're working too well not to want to move again soon."

She strode toward the coffeepot, changed her mind and strode away again. "They might not use his club next time, it's not a given. We can't cover every damn club in the city."

"So, you focus your energy on Blackhawk's. That's smart, and it's logical. One step at a time, Allison."

"I know. I learned that from the best. I guess the first step is to go dig up a short black skirt."

Boyd winced as she walked to the door. "Not too short."

Ally had the eight-to-four shift at the precinct, and even if she left on the dot and sprinted the four blocks from the station to her apartment, she couldn't get home before 4:10 p.m.

She knew. She'd timed it.

And leaving at exactly four was as rare as finding diamonds in the mud. But damned if she wanted to be late for her next meeting with Blackhawk.

It was a matter of pride and principle.

She slammed into her apartment at 4:11 p.m.—thanks to the delay of a last-minute briefing by her lieutenant—and peeled off her jacket as she raced to the bedroom.

Blackhawk's was a good twenty minutes away at a brisk jog—and half again that much if she attempted to drive in rush-hour traffic.

It was only her second undercover assignment behind her detective's shield. She had no intention of screwing it up.

She released her shoulder harness and tossed it onto the bed. Her apartment was simple and uncluttered, mostly because she wasn't there long enough for it to be otherwise. The house where she'd grown up was still home, the station house was second on that list of priorities, and the apartment where she slept, occasionally ate and even more rarely loitered, was a far down third.

She'd always wanted to be a cop. She hadn't made a big deal of it. It simply was her dream.

She yanked open her closet door and pushed through a selection of clothes—designer dresses, tailored jackets and basketball jerseys—in search of a suitable black skirt.

If she could manage a quick change, she might actually have time to slap together a sandwich or stuff a handful of cookies into her mouth before she raced out again.

She pulled out a skirt, winced at the length when she held it up, then tossed that on the bed as well to dig through her dresser for a pair of black hose.

If she was going to wear a skirt that barely covered her butt, she would damn well cover the rest with solid, opaque black.

Tonight could be the night, she thought as she stripped off her trousers. She had to stay calm about it, cool, controlled.

She would use Jonah Blackhawk, but she would not be distracted by him.

She knew a great deal about him through her father, and she'd made it her business to find out more. As a kid he'd had light fingers, quick feet and a nimble brain. She could almost admire a boy with barely twelve years under his belt who'd managed to organize a sports' betting syndicate. Almost.

And she supposed she could come close to admiring someone who'd turned those beginnings around—at least on the surface—and made himself into a successful businessman.

The fact was she'd been in his sports' bar and had enjoyed the atmosphere, the service and the truly superior margaritas Fast Break provided.

The place had a terrific selection of pinball machines, she recalled. Unless someone had broken her record in the last six months, her initials were still in the number one slot on Double Play.

She really should make time to get back there and defend her championship status.

But that was beside the point, she reminded herself. Right now the point was Jonah Blackhawk.

Maybe his feathers were ruffled because she'd made

it clear that two of his employees were on her short list of suspects. Well, that was too bad. Her father wanted her to trust the man, so she'd do her best to trust him.

As far as she could throw him.

By 4:20 p.m., she was dressed in black—turtleneck, skirt, hose. She shoved through the shoes on the floor of her closet and found a suitable pair of low heels.

With a nod to vanity, she dragged the clip out of her hair, brushed it, clipped it back again. Then she closed her eyes and tried to think like a waitress in an upscale club.

Lipstick, perfume, earrings. An attractive waitress made more tips, and tips had to be a goal. She took the time for them, then studied the results in the mirror.

Sexy, she supposed, certainly feminine and in a satisfactory way, practical. And there was no place to hide her weapon.

Damn it. She hissed out a breath, and settled on stuffing her nine millimeter in an oversize shoulder bag. She tossed on a black leather jacket as a concession to the brisk spring evening, then bolted for the door.

There was enough time to drive to the club if she got straight down to the garage and hit all the lights on green.

She pulled open the door. Swore.

"Dennis, what are you doing?"

Dennis Overton held up a bottle of California Chardonnay and offered a big, cheerful smile. "Just in the neighborhood. Thought we could have a drink."

"I'm on my way out."

"Fine." He shifted the bottle, tried to take her hand. "I'll go with you."

"Dennis." She didn't want to hurt him. Not again.

He'd been so devastated when she'd broken things off two months before. And all his phone calls, pop-ins, run-intos since then had ended badly. "We've been through all this."

"Come on, Ally. Just a couple of hours. I miss you."

He had that sad, basset hound look in his eyes, that pleading smile on his lips. It had worked once, she reminded herself. More than once. But she remembered how those same eyes could blaze with wild and misplaced jealousy, snap with barely controlled fury.

She'd cared for him once, enough to forgive him his accusations, to try to work through his mood swings, enough to feel guilty over ending it.

She cared enough now to strap her temper at this last invasion of her time and her space. "I'm sorry, Dennis. I'm in a hurry."

Still smiling, he blocked her way. "Give me five minutes. One drink for old times' sake, Ally?"

"I don't have five minutes."

The smile vanished, and that old, dark gleam leaped into his eyes. "You never had time for me when I needed it. It was always what you wanted and when you wanted it."

"That's right. You're well rid of me."

"You're going to see someone else, aren't you? Brushing me off so you can run off to be with another man."

"What if I am." Enough, she thought, was way past enough. "It's no business of yours where I go, what I do, whom I see. That's what you can't seem to get straight. But you're going to have to work harder at it, Dennis, because I'm sick of this. Stop coming here."

He grabbed her arm before she could walk by. "I want to talk to you."

She didn't jerk free, only stared down at his hand, then shifted her gaze, icy as February, to his eyes. "Don't push it. Now step back."

"What're you going to do? Shoot me? Arrest me? Call your daddy, the saint of the police, to lock me up?"

"I'm going to ask you, one more time, to step back. Step way back, Dennis, and do it now."

His mood swung again, fast and smooth as a revolving door. "I'm sorry. Ally, I'm sorry." His eyes went damp and his mouth trembled. "I'm upset, that's all. Just give me another chance. I just need another chance. I'll make it work this time."

She pried his fingers off her arm. "It never worked. Go home, Dennis. I've got nothing for you."

She walked away without looking back, bleeding inside because she had to. Bleeding inside because she could.

Chapter 2

Ally hit the doors of Blackhawk's at 5:05 p.m. One strike against her, she thought and took an extra minute to smooth down her hair, catch her breath. She'd decided against the drive after all and had run the ten blocks. Not such a distance, she thought, but the heels she wore were a far cry from track shoes.

She stepped inside, took stock.

The bar was a long, gleaming black slab that curved into a snug semicircle and offered plenty of room for a troop of chrome stools with thick, black leather cushions. Mirrored panels of black and silver ran down the rear wall, tossed back reflections and shapes.

Comfort, she decided, as well as style. It said, sit down, relax and plunk down your money.

There were plenty of people to do so. Apparently happy hour was under way, and every stool was occupied. Those who sat at the bar, or kicked back at the chrome tables, drank and nibbled to the tune of recorded music kept low enough to encourage conversation.

Most of the patrons were the suit-and-tie crowd with briefcases dumped at their feet. The business brigade, she concluded, who'd managed to slip out of the office a little early, or were using the club as a meeting arena to discuss deals or close them.

Two waitresses worked the tables. Both wore black, but she noted with a hiss through her teeth that they wore slacks rather than skirts.

A man was working the bar—young, handsome and openly flirting with the trio of women on stools at the far end. She wondered when Frances Cummings came on shift. She'd need to get work schedules from Blackhawk.

"You look a little lost."

Ally shifted her gaze and studied the man who approached her with an easy smile. Brown hair, brown eyes, trim beard. Five-ten, maybe one-fifty. His dark suit was well cut, his gray tie neatly knotted.

William Sloan looked a great deal more presentable tonight than he had for his last mug shot.

"I hope not." Deciding a little agitation fit the role, Ally shifted her shoulder bag and offered a nervous smile. "I'm Allison. I'm supposed to see Mr. Blackhawk at five. I guess I'm late."

"Couple of minutes. Don't worry about it. Will Sloan." He offered a hand, gave hers a quick, brotherly squeeze. "The man told me to keep an eye out for you. I'll take you up."

"Thanks. Great place," she commented.

"You bet. The man's in charge, and he wants the best.

I'll give you a quick go-through." With a hand on her back, Will led her through the bar area, into a wide room with more tables, a two-level stage and a dance floor.

Silver ceilings, she mused, glancing up, set with pinpoint lights that blinked and shimmered. The tables were black squares on pedestals that rose out of a smoky silver floor with those same little lights twinkling under the surface, like stars behind clouds.

The art was modern, towering canvases splashed or streaked with wild colors, odd, intriguing wall sculptures fashioned from metals or textiles.

The tables were bare but for a slim metal cylindrical lamp with cut-outs in the shape of crescent moons.

Deco meets the third millennium, she decided. Jonah Blackhawk had built himself a very classy joint.

"You work clubs before?"

She'd already decided how to play it and rolled her eyes. "Nothing like this. Pretty fancy."

"The man wanted class. The man gets class." He turned down a corridor, then punched a code into a control panel. "Watch this."

When a panel in the wall slid open, he wiggled his eyebrows. "Cool, huh?"

"Major." She stepped in with him, watched him reenter the code.

"Any of us who've got to do business on the second level get a code. You won't have to worry about it. So, you new in Denver?"

"No, actually I grew up here."

"No bull? Me, too. I've been hanging with the man since we were kids. Life sure was different then."

The door opened again, directly into Jonah's office. It was a large space, split into business and pleasure.

with an area to one side devoted to a long leather sofa in his signature color, two sink-into-me armchairs and a wide-screen TV where a night baseball game was being battled out in silence.

Automatically she checked the stats in the top corner of the screen. Yankees at home against Toronto. Bottom of the first. Two out, one on. No score.

The focus on sports didn't surprise her, but the floor-to-ceiling shelves of books did.

She shifted her attention to the business area. It appeared to be as ruthlessly efficient as the rest of the room was indulgent. The workstation held a computer and phone. Across from it stood a monitor that showed the club area. The single window was shielded with blinds, and the blinds were tightly shut. The carpet was cozily thick and stone-gray.

Jonah sat at the desk, his back to the wall, and held up a hand as he completed a call. "I'll get back to you on that. No, not before tomorrow." He lifted a brow as if amused by what was said to him. "You'll just have to wait."

He hung up, sat back in his chair. "Hello, Allison. Thanks, Will."

"No problem. Catch you later, Allison."

"Thanks a lot."

Jonah waited until the elevator door shut. "You're late."

"I know. It was unavoidable." She turned to the monitor giving him an opportunity to skim his gaze down her back, over those long legs.

Very nice, he thought. Very nice indeed.

"You have security cameras throughout the public areas?"

"I like to know what's going on in my place."

She just bet he did. "Do you keep the tapes?"

"We turn them over every three days."

"I'd like to see what you've got." Because her back was to him, she allowed her gaze to slide over and check the action in Yankee Stadium. Toronto brought one home on a line drive bullet. "It'll help to study the tapes."

"For that you'll need a warrant."

She glanced back over her shoulder. He'd changed into a suit—black and, to her expert eye, of Italian cut. "I thought you'd agreed to cooperate."

"To a point. You're here, aren't you?" His phone rang and was ignored. "Why don't you sit down? We'll work out a game plan."

"The game plan's simple." And she didn't sit. "I pose as a waitress, talk to customers and staff. I keep my eyes open and do my job. You keep out of my way and do yours."

"Wrong plan. I don't have to keep out of anyone's way in my place. Now, ever worked a club?"

"No."

"Ever waited tables?"

"No." His cool, patient look irked. "What's the big deal. You take the order, you put in the order, you serve the order. I'm not a moron."

He smiled now, that quick, powerful strike. "I imagine it seems that way when you've spent your life on the other side of it. You're about to get an education, Detective. Head waitress on your shift is Beth. She'll help train you. Until you've got a handle on it, you'll bus tables. That means—"

"I know what busing tables involves."

"Fine, I've put you on six to two. You get a fifteen-minute break every two hours. No drinking during shift. Any of the customers get overly friendly or out of line, you report to me or to Will."

"I can handle myself."

"You're not a cop here. Somebody puts hands on you in an inappropriate way, you report to me or to Will."

"You get a lot of that?"

"Only from the women. They can't keep their hands off me."

"Ha-ha."

Out of the corner of his eye, he noted the Yankees ended the inning on a strikeout. "No, we don't get a lot of it, but it happens. Some guys cross lines when they drink. They only cross them in my place once. The crowd starts getting thick after eight. Entertainment starts at nine. You'll be busy."

He got to his feet, walked to her, walked around her. "You've got a nice cover over the cop in you. You have to look hard to see it. I like the skirt."

She waited until he'd come around and they were face-to-face. "I'll need work schedules for all employees. Or do I need a warrant?"

"No, I can help you out there." He liked the scent of her. Cool and clearly female. "I'll have printouts for you by closing. Anyone I hire who I don't know personally—and even some I do—goes through a full background check. Not everyone here's been lucky enough to come from a nice, tidy family and live a nice, tidy life."

Jonah picked up a remote, switched the angle of the cameras so the bar area popped on screen. "Kid just coming off shift at the bar? Grew up with his grandparents when his mother ran off. Got into a little trouble when he was fifteen."

"And what kind of trouble was that?"

"Got tagged with a joint in his pocket. He straightened out, they sealed the records, but he was up front with me when he wanted the job. He's putting himself through night school."

At the moment she wasn't interested in the young man going off shift at the bar. She kept her eyes on Jonah. "Is everyone up front with you?"

"The smart ones are. That's Beth." He tapped the screen.

Ally saw a little brunette, about thirty, come in through a door behind the bar.

"Bastard she was married to used to kick her around. She can't weigh a hundred pounds. She's got three kids at home. Sixteen, twelve and ten. She's been working for me on and off about five years, used to come in every couple weeks with a black eye or split lip. She took the kids and left him two years ago."

"Is he leaving her alone?"

Jonah shifted his gaze to Ally's. "He was persuaded to relocate."

"I see." And she did. Jonah Blackhawk looked after his own. She couldn't fault him for it. "Did he relocate in one piece?"

"Mostly. I'll take you down. You can leave your bag up here if you want."

"No, thanks."

He pushed the button for the elevator. "I assume you've got your gun in there. Keep it in there. There's a secure employee area off the bar. You can lock it up in there. This shift Beth and Frannie have keys. Will and I have keys or codes for all areas at all times."

"Tight ship, Blackhawk."

"That's right. What's the cover?" he asked as they stepped into the elevator. "How'd I meet you?"

"I needed a job, you gave me a job." She shrugged. "Keep it simple. I caught you at your sports bar."

"Know anything about sports?"

She sent him a smile. "Anything that takes place off a field, a court or outside an arena is just marking time."

"Where have you been all my life?" He took her arm as they stepped out on the main floor. "So, Jays or Yankees?"

"Yankees have stronger bats this season and rule the long ball, but their gloves are sloppy. The Jays chip away with reliable base hits, and their infield's a ballet of guts and efficiency. I go for guts and efficiency over the power stroke every time."

"Is that a baseball statement, or a life statement?"

"Blackhawk, baseball is life."

"Now you've done it. We have to get married."

"My heart's all aflutter," she said dryly and turned to scan the bar area. The noise level had bumped up several notches. They were two and three deep at the curved black slab now, the after-work, before-dinner crowd.

For some it was unwind time, she thought, for others a casual mating ritual. But for someone, it was a hunt.

People were so careless, she mused. She saw men leaning on the bar, back pockets ripe for picking. More than one handbag hung vulnerable on the back of a stool or chair. Coats and jackets, some likely to have car or house keys in their pockets, were tossed aside.

"Nobody ever thinks it can happen to them," Ally murmured, then tapped Jonah's arm, inclined her head. "Check out the guy at the bar—six down, with the news anchor hair and teeth."

Amused, Jonah tagged the guy from Ally's description and watched him flash his wallet, choked with bills and credit cards.

"He's trying to lure the redhead there, or her pretty blond friend. Doesn't matter which. Odds are he hits with the blonde," Jonah concluded.

"Why?"

"Call it a hunch." He looked down at Ally. "Wanna bet?"

"You don't have a license for gambling on the premises." As she watched, the blonde sidled over and batted her lashes at the man with the wallet. "Good call."

"It was easy. And so's the blonde." He steered Ally back toward the club area where Beth and Will huddled over the reservation book at a black podium.

"Hey, boss." Beth plucked the pencil out of her thick curls and made a note in the book. "Looks like we're turning most tables over twice tonight. Big dinner crowd for midweek."

"Good thing I brought you some help. Beth Dickerman, Allison Fletcher. She needs training."

"Ah, another victim." Beth shot out a hand. "Nice to meet you, Allison."

"Ally. Thanks."

"You show her the ropes, Beth. She'll bus tables until you figure she can wait them."

"We'll whip her into shape. Come on with me, Ally. I'll get you set up. Got any experience in food services?" she asked as she plowed through the crowd.

"Well, I eat."

Beth let out a bright cackle of a laugh. "Welcome to my world. Frannie, this is Ally, new waitress in training. Frannie's captain of the bar here."

"Nice to meetcha," Frannie called out, flipped a smile, dumping ice into a blender with one hand and shooting soda into a glass with the other.

"And that gorgeous specimen down the other end of the bar's Pete."

The big-shouldered black man sent them a wink as he measured Kahlúa into a short glass.

"Now, no flirting with Pete, 'cause he's my man and nobody else's. That right, Pete?"

"You're the one for me, sugar lips."

With another laugh, Beth unlocked a door marked Employees Only. "Pete's got a beautiful wife and a baby on the way. We just tease. Now, if you need to get in here for any reason—hey, Jan."

"Hey, Beth." The curvy brunette on the other side of the door had her waist-length hair pulled back with combs from a lovely, heart-shaped face. Ally gauged her as mid-twenties, and a fashion plate. She'd gone for a skirt the approximate size of a table napkin, and a clingy shirt with small silver buttons. Silver winked at her wrists, ears and throat as she freshened her lipstick in a mirror.

"This is Ally. Fresh meat."

"Oh, yeah." The smile when she turned was friendly enough, but there was a measuring gleam in her eye. One female sizing up another, and the competition.

"Jan works the bar area," Beth explained. "But she'll pinch hit in the club if we need her." There was a wild burst of laughter from outside the door. "Tom-toms are beating."

"I'd better get out there." Jan tied a short, many-pocketed black apron at her waist. "Good luck, Ally, and welcome aboard."

"Thanks. Everybody's so friendly," Ally said to Beth when Jan strolled out.

"You get to be kind of a family when you work for Jonah. He's a good boss." She pulled an apron out of a closet. "You work your butt off for him, but he lets you know he notices and that he appreciates. Makes a difference. Here, you'll need this."

"Have you worked for him long?"

"About six years, give or take. I handled tables at Fast Break, his sports bar. And when he opened the club here, he asked me if I wanted to switch. It's a classy place, and closer to home. You can leave your purse in here." She opened a narrow locker. "You reset the combination by spinning around zero twice."

"Great." Ally set her purse inside, palming her beeper out of it and hooking it on the waist of her skirt under the apron. She shut the locker, set the combination. "I guess that's it."

"You want to freshen up or anything?"

"No, I'm fine. A little nervous, I guess."

"Don't worry. In a few hours your feet are going to ache so bad you won't think about nerves."

Beth was right. About the feet anyway. By ten, Ally felt she'd hiked twenty miles in the wrong shoes, and lifted approximately three tons of trays loaded with dirty dishes.

She could have marched the trail from table to kitchen in her sleep.

The live band was considerably louder than the recorded music that had played until just after nine. The crowd shouted above it, crammed the dance floor and jammed together at the tables.

Ally piled dishes on trays and watched the crowd. There were plenty of designer clothes, expensive watches, cell phones and leather briefcases. She saw a woman flash a lightning bolt diamond engagement ring for three friends.

Plenty of money here, she noted. And plenty of marks.

Hefting the loaded tray, she headed off for the kitchen, detouring toward an attractive couple when the man signaled her.

"Sweetheart, can you get me and my lovely companion a refill here?"

She leaned closer, pasted on her sweetest smile and made a quiet and crude suggestion.

The man only grinned. "Cops have such filthy mouths."

"Next case I'm going to be the one sitting on my butt, Hickman, while you work out," Ally replied. "See anything I should know about?"

"Nothing's popped yet." He grabbed the hand of the woman sitting next to him. "But Carson and I are in love."

Lydia Carson gave Hickman's hand a vicious squeeze. "In your dreams."

"Just keep your eyes open." She aimed a stare at Hickman's glass. "And that'd better be club soda."

"She's so strict," she heard Hickman murmur as she walked away.

"Beth, table…ah, sixteen's looking for a refill."

"I'm on it. You're doing good, Ally. Go dump those and take your break."

"You don't have to tell me twice."

The kitchen was a madhouse, full of noise and shouted orders and heat. Gratefully Ally set down her tray, then lifted her eyebrows as she spotted Frannie slipping out the back door.

Ally stalled for ten seconds, then followed.

Frannie was already leaning against the outside wall and taking her first drag from a cigarette. She blew out smoke with a long, relieved sigh. "Break time?"

"Yeah. I thought I'd grab some air."

"Zoo in there tonight. Blackhawk's really packs them in." She pulled the cigarettes out of her pocket, offered them.

"No, thanks. I don't smoke."

"Good for you. I can't kick it. No smoking in the employee lounge. Jonah gives me a break and lets me use his office if the weather's lousy. So how's your first night?"

"My feet are killing me."

"Occupational hazard. First paycheck you buy yourself one of those bubbling footbath things. Put some eucalyptus in it and go straight to heaven."

"I'll do that."

An attractive woman, Ally noted, though the lines around Frannie's eyes made her look older than twenty-eight. She kept her dark red hair cut short and the makeup subtle. Her nails were short and unpainted, her hands ringless. Like the rest of the staff, she wore black, and finished off the simple shirt and slacks with sturdy yet trendy black shoes.

The only touch of flash was the silver hoops that swung at her ears.

"How'd you get into tending bar?" Ally asked her.

Frannie hesitated, then puffed on her cigarette. "I guess I hung out at bars a lot, and when there came a time I was looking for what you could call gainful employment, Jonah asked me if I wanted a job. Trained me over at Fast Break. It's good work. You need a decent memory and people skills. You interested?"

"I'd better see if I make it through one shift busing before I start raising my sights."

"You look like you can handle whatever comes along."

Ally smiled into Frannie's considering eyes. "You think so?"

"Observation's one of those people skills. And on short observation you don't strike me as the type who expects to make waiting tables her life's work."

"Gotta start somewhere. And paying the rent's a priority."

"Don't I know it." Though Frannie had already calculated that Ally's shoes equaled half a month's rent on her own apartment. "Well, if you want to climb the ladder, Jonah's the one to give you a boost. You'd have figured that."

Frannie dropped the cigarette, crushed out the butt. "Gotta get back. Pete pouts if I go over break."

The ex-hooker, Ally decided, was proprietary when it came to Jonah. They were probably lovers, she thought as she went back inside. When you factored in his defensive attitude toward her, it added up.

As lover, as trusted employee, Frannie was in a prime position to cull out marks, to pass the information along. The bar faced the entrance. Whoever went in or out passed by her station.

People handed her credit cards, and the name and account number led to addresses.

It would pay to look at her most closely.

Jonah was doing his own looking. From his office, from the floor. He knew enough about cons, short and long, to calculate who the targets might be. He pegged three possibilities that would have topped his list if he'd been running the game. And since he'd also spotted the cops at table sixteen, he wandered over.

"Everything all right tonight?"

The woman beamed up at him, swept back her short swing of streaky blond hair with one hand. "Everything's terrific. It's the first night on the town Bob and I have managed in weeks with work keeping both of us so busy."

"I'm glad you picked my place." Jonah laid a friendly hand on Bob's shoulder, leaned down. "Next time ditch the cop shoes. Dead giveaway. Enjoy your evening."

He thought he heard the woman snort out a laugh as he walked away.

He headed for the table Ally was busy cleaning. "How you holding up?"

"I haven't broken any of your dishes yet."

"And now you want a raise?"

"I'm going to stick with my day job, thanks all the same. I'd rather clean up the streets than tables." Absently she pressed a hand to the ache in the small of her back.

"We go back to bar food at eleven, so the busing slows down."

"Hallelujah."

He laid a hand on her arm before she could lift the tray. "You corner Frannie outside?"

"Excuse me?"

"She went out, you went out, she came in, you came in."

"I'm doing my job. However, I resisted shining a light in her eyes and smacking her in the face with my rubber hose. Now let me get on with it."

She hefted the tray, shoved past him.

"By the way, Allison."

She stopped, a snarl working up her throat. "What?"

"The power ball trounced your guts and efficiency. Eight to two."

"One game doesn't a season make." She jerked up her chin and strode off. On her way by the dance floor, a man reached out and gave her butt a hopeful pat. As Jonah watched she stopped dead in her tracks, turned slowly and gave him one, long icy look. The man stepped back, lifted his hands in apology and quickly melted into the dancers.

"Handles herself," Beth said from beside him.

"Yeah. Yeah, she does."

"Pulls her weight, too, and doesn't whine about it. I like your girlfriend, Jonah."

He was too surprised to comment and only stared when Beth hustled away.

He let out a short laugh and shook his head. Oh, that one had slipped by him. Right on by him.

Last call was enough to make Ally all but weep with gratitude. She'd been on her feet since eight that morning. Her fondest wish was to go home, fall into bed and sleep for the precious five hours she had before starting it all over again.

"Go on home," Beth ordered. "We'll go over closing tomorrow night. You did fine."

"Thanks. I mean it."

"Will, let Ally into the lounge, will you?"

"No problem. Nice crowd tonight. Nothing I like better than a crowded club. Want a drink before you head out?"

"Not unless I can stick my feet in it."

He chuckled, patted her back. "Frannie, pour me one, will you?"

"Already on it."

"I like a brandy at the end of a shift. One glass of the good stuff. You change your mind," he said as he unlocked the door. "Just pull up a stool. The man, he doesn't charge employees for an end of shift drink."

He went off, whistling through his teeth.

Ally shoved her apron into her locker, pulled out her bag and jacket. She was just putting the jacket on when Jan breezed in. "Heading out? You look beat. Me, I'm just hitting stride this time of night."

"My stride hit me about an hour ago." Ally paused at the door. "Don't your feet hurt?"

"Nah. I got arches of steel. And most guys tip better if you walk around on skinny heels." She bent to run a hand up her leg. "I believe in using what works."

"Yeah. Well, good night."

Ally stepped out of the lounge, shutting the door behind her, and bumped solidly into Jonah.

"Where'd you park?" he asked her.

"I didn't. I walked." Ran, she remembered, but it came to the same thing.

"I'll drive you home."

"I can walk. It's not far."

"It's two in the morning. A block is too far."

"For heaven's sake, Blackhawk, I'm a cop."

"So naturally, bullets bounce off you."

Before she could argue, he caught her chin in his hand. The gesture, the firm grip of his fingers, shocked her to silence. "You're not a cop at the moment," he murmured. "You're a female employee and the daughter of a friend. I'll drive you home."

"Fine. Dandy. My feet hurt anyway."

She started to shove his hand away, but he beat her to it and shifted his grip to her arm.

"Night, boss," Beth called out, grinning at them as they passed. "Get that girl off her feet."

"That's my plan. Later, Will. Night, Frannie."

Suspicion was buzzing in Ally's brain as Will lifted his brandy snifter and Frannie watched her with quiet and serious eyes.

"What was that?" Ally demanded when they stepped out in the cool air. "What exactly was that?"

"That was me saying good-night to friends and employees. I'm parked across the street."

"Excuse me, my feet have gone numb, not my brain. You gave those people the very distinct impression that we have a thing here."

"That's right. I didn't consider it, either, until Beth made some remark earlier. It simplifies things."

She stopped beside a sleek black Jaguar. "Just how do you figure that having people think there's a personal thing between us simplifies anything?"

"And you call yourself a detective." He unlocked the passenger door, opened it. "You're a beautiful blonde with legs up to your ears. I hire you, out of the blue, when you have basically no experience. The first assumption from people who know me is I'm attracted to you. The second would be you're attracted to me. Add all those together and you end up with romance. Or at least sex. Are you going to get in?"

"You haven't explained how those deductions equal simple."

"If people think we're involved they won't think twice if I give you a little leeway, if you come up to my office. They'll be friendlier."

Ally said nothing while she let it run through her head. Then she nodded. "All right. There's an advantage to it."

Going with impulse he shifted, boxed her in between his body and the car door. There was a light breeze, just enough to stir her scent. There was a three-quarter moon, bright enough to sprinkle silver into her eyes. The moment, he decided, seemed to call for it.

"Could be more than one advantage to it."

The thrill that sprinted straight up her spine irritated her. "Oh, you're going to want to step back, Blackhawk."

"Beth's at the window of the bar, and she's got a romantic heart despite everything that's happened to her. She's hoping for a moment here. A long, slow kiss, the kind that slides over melting sighs and heats the blood."

His hands came to her hips as he spoke, rode up to just under her breasts. Her mouth went dry and the ache in her belly was a wide stretch of longing.

"You're going to have to disappoint her."

Jonah skimmed his gaze down to her mouth. "She's not the only one." But he released her, stepped back. "Don't worry, Detective. I never hit on cops, or daughters of friends."

"Then I guess I've got a double shield against your wild and irresistible charms."

"Good thing for both of us, because I sure as hell like the look of you. You getting in?"

"Yeah, I'm getting in." She got into the car and waited until the door shut before letting out the long, painful breath she'd been holding.

Wherever that spurt of lust inside her had come from, it would just have to go away again. Cool off, she ordered herself, but her heart was bumping madly against her rib cage. Cool off and focus on the job.

Jonah slid in beside her, annoyed that his pulse wasn't quite steady. "Where to?" When she rattled off the address, he shoved the key into the ignition and aimed one hot look at her. "That's a damn mile. Why the hell did you walk?"

"Because it was rush hour. It's quicker. And it's ten blocks."

"That's just stupid."

She had a response for that. The venom of it scalded her tongue as she rounded on him. She didn't even recognize the vibration of her beeper for several seconds, mistaking it for the vibration of rage.

She yanked it from her skirt, checked the number. "Damn it. Damn it." From her purse she pulled out her cell phone and quickly dialed. "Detective Fletcher. Yeah, I got it. I'm on my way."

Calming herself, she shoved the phone back into her

purse. "Since you're determined to play cabdriver, let's get going. I've got another B and E."

"Give me the address."

"Just take me home so I can get my car."

"Give me the address, Allison. Why waste time?"

Chapter 3

Jonah dropped her off in front of an attractive, ranch-style home in an upscale development convenient to the freeway. In reasonable traffic, the commute to downtown would take under twenty minutes.

The Chamberses, Ally discovered, were an attractive, upscale couple, both lawyers in their early thirties, childless professionals, who spent their comfortable income on the good life.

Wine, wardrobe, jewelry, art and music.

"They got my diamond earrings, and my Cartier tank watch." Maggie Chambers rubbed her eyes as she sat in what was left of her sprawling great room. "We haven't gone through everything, but there were Dalí and Picasso lithographs on that wall there. And in that niche there was an Erté sculpture we bought at an auction two years ago. Joe collected cuff links. I don't know how many pairs he had offhand, but he had diamond ones, and ruby for his birthstone and several antique pairs."

"They're insured." Her husband reached out to take her hand, squeeze it.

"It doesn't matter. It's not the same. Those thugs were in our house. In our house, Joe, and they've taken our things. Damn it, they stole my car. My brand-new BMW, and it didn't have five thousand miles on it. I loved that stupid car."

"Mrs. Chambers, I know it's hard."

Maggie Chambers whipped her gaze toward Ally. "Have you ever been robbed, Detective?"

"No." Ally set her notebook on her knee a moment. "But I've worked plenty of burglaries, robberies, muggings."

"It's not the same."

"Maggie, she's just doing her job."

"I know. I'm sorry. I know." She covered her face with her hands, drew air in, slowly let it out. "I've got the shakes, that's all. I don't want to stay here tonight."

"We don't have to. We'll go to a hotel. How much more do you need, Detective...was it Fletcher?"

"Yes. Just a few more questions. You said both of you were out all evening."

"Yeah, Maggie won a case today, and we decided to go out and celebrate. She's been piled under for more than a month. We went to the Starfire club with some friends." As he spoke, he rubbed soothing circles over his wife's back. "Drinks, dinner, a little dancing. Like we told the other policeman, we didn't get home until nearly two."

"Does anyone other than the two of you have a key?"

"Our housekeeper."

"Would she also have the security code?"

"Sure." Joe started to speak, then blinked, stuttered. "Oh, listen, Carol's been cleaning for us for nearly ten years. She's practically family."

"It's just procedure, Mr. Chambers. Could I have her full name and address, for the record?"

She took them through the entire evening, looking for a connection, a contact, anything that struck a chord. But for the Chamberses it had been nothing more than an entertaining evening out, until they'd walked back in their own front door.

When Ally left them, she had a partial list of stolen items, with a promise for the complete as well as the insurance information. The crime scene unit was still working, but she'd gone over the scene herself. She didn't expect the miracle of fingerprints or dropped clues.

The moon had set, but the stars were out and brilliant. The wind had picked up to dance down the street in little whirls and gusts. The neighborhood was hushed, the houses dark. Those who lived here had long since been tucked in for the night.

She doubted the canvass was going to turn up any handy eyewitnesses.

Jonah was leaning against the hood of his car, drinking what appeared to be a cup of takeout coffee with one of the uniforms.

When she approached the car, Jonah held out the half cup he had left. "Thanks."

"You can have a whole one. There's a twenty-four-hour place a few blocks down."

"This is fine," she replied, taking the cup. "Officer, you and your partner were first on scene?"

"Yes, ma'am."

"I'll need your report on my desk by eleven hundred." With a brisk nod, the officer headed for his car. Ally sipped the coffee, then turned to Jonah and handed him the cup. "You didn't have to wait. I can get a ride home in one of the radio cars."

"I have a stake here." He opened the car door. "Were they at my place?"

"Now why would you ask me when we both know you just got finished pumping that uniform?"

"Hey, I bought the coffee." He handed it back to her, then walked around to the driver's side. "So, the perps picked their marks at the Starfire tonight. Have they hit there before?"

"No, you're still the only repeater. They'll come back to you." She shut her exhausted eyes. "It's just a matter of time."

"Well, that makes me feel lots better. What kind of take did they get?"

"BMW roadster out of the garage, some art, high-end electronics and heavy on the jewelry."

"Don't these people have safes?"

"These did, a small one in the walk-in closet of the master suite. Of course they had the combination for it written down on a piece of paper in the desk."

"That'll discourage the criminal element."

"They had a security system, which they swear they engaged when they left—though the wife didn't look quite so sure of that. Anyway, the point is they felt secure. Nice house, nice neighborhood. People get sloppy." Eyes still closed, she circled her head, cracking out the tension. "They're both lawyers."

"Well, hell then, what do we care?"

She was tired enough to laugh. "Watch it, ace. My aunt is district attorney in Urbana."

"You going to drink that coffee or just hold on to it?"

"What? Oh, no, here, I don't want anymore. It'll just keep me awake."

He doubted a tanker truck of coffee could keep her awake much longer. Her voice was going thick, adding, he thought, to the in-the-gut sexiness of it. Fatigue had her unguarded enough to tilt her face toward him as she tried to find a comfortable resting spot. Her eyes were shut, her lips soft and just parted.

He had a feeling he knew exactly how they'd taste. Warm and soft. Ripe with sleep.

At a stop sign, he put the car in neutral, engaged the emergency brake, then leaned over her to press the mechanism that lowered her seat back.

She jerked up, rapped her head smartly against his. Even as he swore she slapped a hand on his chest.

"Back off!"

"Relax, Fletcher, I'm not jumping you. I like my women awake when we make love. I'm putting your seat back. If you're going to sleep, you might as well get as close to horizontal as we can manage."

"I'm all right." Mortified, but all right, she thought. "I wasn't sleeping."

He put a hand on her forehead, shoved her back. "Shut up, Allison."

"I wasn't sleeping. I was thinking."

"Think tomorrow. You're brain-dead." He glanced over at her as he started to drive again. "How many hours have you been on duty?"

"That's math, I can't do math if I'm brain-dead." She gave up and yawned. "I'm on eight to fours."

"It's closing in on 4:00 a.m., that gives you twenty hours. Why don't you put in for night shift until this is over, or do you have a death wish?"

"It's not my only case." She'd already decided to talk to her lieutenant. She couldn't give her best to the job on a couple of hours sleep a night. But it wasn't any of Jonah's business how she ran her life.

"I guess Denver's not safe without you on the job."

She might have been tired, but she still had a pretty good ear for sarcasm. "That's right, Blackhawk. Without my watchful eye, the city's in chaos. It's a heavy burden but, well, somebody's got to shoulder it. Just pull up at the corner. My building's only a half a block down."

He ignored her, drove through the light and pulled smoothly to the curb in front of her building. "Okay. Thanks." She reached down to retrieve her bag from the floor.

He was already out of the car, skirting around the hood. Maybe it was fatigue that had her reacting so slowly, as if she were moving through syrup instead of air. But he had the outside handle of the door seconds before she had the inside handle.

For about five seconds they battled for control. Then with a halfhearted snarl, Ally let him open the door for her. "What are you, from another century? Do I look incapable of operating the complex mechanism of a car door?"

"No. You look tired."

"Well, I am. So good night."

"I'll walk you up."

"Get a grip."

But he fell into step beside her, and damn him, reached

the door one pace ahead of her. Saying nothing, merely watching her with those impossibly clear green eyes, he held it open for her.

"I'll have to curtsy in a minute," she muttered under her breath.

He grinned at her back, then crossed to the lobby elevators with her, sliding his hands into his pockets.

"I can make it from here."

"I'll take you to your door."

"It's not a damn date."

"Lack of sleep's making you irritable." He stepped into the elevator with her. "No, wait, you're always irritable. My mistake."

"I don't like you." She jabbed the button for the fourth floor.

"Thank God you cleared that up. I was afraid you were falling for me."

The movement of the elevator tipped her already shaky balance. She swayed, and he closed a hand over her arm.

"Cut it out."

"No."

She jerked at her arm. He tightened his grip. "Don't embarrass yourself, Fletcher. You're asleep on your feet. What's your apartment number?"

He was right, and it was stupid to pretend otherwise, and foolish to take it out on him. "Four-oh-nine. Let me go, will you? I'll be all right after a couple hours' sleep."

"I don't doubt it." But he held on to her when the elevator opened.

"You're not coming in."

"Well, there go my plans to toss you over my shoulder, dump you in bed and have my wicked way with you. Next time. Key?"

"What?"

Her burnt-honey eyes were blurry, the delicate skin beneath them bruised. The wave of tenderness that swept inside him was a complete surprise, and far from comfortable. "Honey, give me your key."

"Oh. I'm punchy." She dug it out of her jacket pocket. "And don't call me honey."

"I meant Detective Honey." He heard her snicker as he unlocked her door. He pulled the key back out of the lock, took her hand, dropped it in and closed her fingers around it. "Good night."

"Yeah. Thanks for the lift." Because it seemed the thing to do, she closed the door in his face.

Hell of a face, she thought as she stumbled toward the bedroom. Face that dangerous ought to be registered as a weapon. A woman who trusted a face like that got exactly what she deserved.

And probably enjoyed every minute of it.

Ally stripped off her jacket, whimpering a little as she pried off her shoes. She set her alarm, then fell facedown and fully clothed on the bed. And was instantly asleep.

Four and a half hours later, she was finishing up her morning meeting in the conference room at her station house. And her fourth cup of coffee.

"We'll canvass the neighborhood," Ally said. "We could get lucky. In that kind of development, people tend to look out for each other. Some sort of vehicle was necessary to get the perpetrators to the Chamberses', and to transport at least some of the stolen goods.

The sports car they boosted wouldn't hold that much. We have a full description of the car, and the APB's out on it."

Lieutenant Kiniki nodded. He was a toughly built man in his mid-forties who enjoyed the way command sat on his shoulders. "The Starfire's a new pool for them. I want two men over there to check out the setup. Soft clothes," he added, indicating he wanted his detectives to dress casually rather than in suit jackets. "Let's keep it low-key."

"Hickman and Carson are canvassing pawn shops, pressuring known fences." Ally glanced toward her two associates.

"Nothing there." Hickman lifted his hands. "Lydia and I've got a couple of good sources, and we've put the heat on. Nobody knows anything. My take is that whoever's running this has an outside channel."

"Keep the heat on," Kiniki ordered. "What about the insurance angle?"

"It doesn't play out," Ally told him. "We've got nine hits and five different insurance companies. We're still trying to find a connection, but so far that's a dead end. We've got no common links between the victims that carry through," she went on. "Out of the nine, we've got four different banks, three different brokerage houses, nine different doctors, nine different places of employment."

She rubbed the ache at the back of her neck and went down her list. "Two of the women go to the same hair salon—different operators, different schedules. They use different cleaning services, different mechanics. Now two of the targets used the same caterer in the last six months, and we're running that. But it doesn't look like a hook. The only common link so far is a night on the town."

"Give me the rundown on Blackhawk's," Kiniki ordered.

"The place does a hell of a business," Ally began. "Pulls in a big crowd, and the crowd varies, though it's heavy on the upwardly mobile. Couples, singles on the prowl, groups. He's got good security."

Absently Ally rubbed her eyes, then remembered herself and lowered them. "He's got cameras, and I'm working on getting the security tapes. Sloan is the floater. He works the public areas, has access to everything. There are six tables in the bar area and thirty-two in the club. People push them together if they get friendly. There's a coat check but not everybody bothers with it. I couldn't count the number of handbags left on tables when the dancing started."

"People mill," Lydia added. "Especially the younger customers. It's a regular meeting ground for them, and they tend to table hop. Lots of sex vibes." She gave Hickman a bland look when he chortled. "It's a sexy place. People get careless when their blood's hot. There's a ripple when Blackhawk comes through."

"A ripple?" Hickman repeated. "Is that a technical term?"

"The women watch him. They don't watch their bags."

"That's accurate." Ally walked over to the board where the list of victims and stolen items were posted. "Every hit involved a woman. There are no single men on the list. The female's the prime target. What's a woman carry in her purse?"

"That," Hickman said, "is one of life's most complex mysteries."

"Her keys," Ally continued. "Her wallet—with ID, credit cards. Pictures of her kids if she has them. None of the victims had children at home. If we break this down to its basic element, we're looking first for a pickpocket. Somebody with good fingers who can get what he needs out of a bag, then put it back before the victim knows she's been hit. Do an imprint of the key, make a copy."

"If you pick the pocket, why put the stuff back?" Hickman asked.

"Keep the victim unaware, buy more time. A woman goes into the bathroom, she takes her purse. If she reaches in for her lipstick and doesn't find her wallet, she's going to send up an alarm. This way, the house is hit and the perpetrators are out before the victims get home. Whatever time they get home."

She turned back to the board. "Twelve-thirty, one-fifteen, twelve-ten, and so on. Somebody at the club alerts the burglars when the victims call for their check. Somebody's on the inside, or a regular and repeat customer. At Blackhawk's the average time between calling for the check and leaving the club was about twenty minutes."

"We have two other clubs involved now, besides Blackhawk's." Kiniki's brow furrowed. "We'll need stakeouts on all of them."

"Yes, sir. But Blackhawk's is where they'll come back. That's the money tree."

"Find a way to cut down the tree, Fletcher." He got to his feet. "And take some personal time today. Get some sleep."

* * *

She took him up on it and curled up on the small sofa in the coffee room, leaving word that she was to be notified when the reports she was waiting for came in.

She got ninety minutes and felt very close to human when Hickman shook her shoulder.

"Did you steal my cheese bagel?"

"What?" She pushed herself up, shoved back her hair.

"You like cheese bagels. I had one. It's gone. I'm detecting."

Shaking off sleep, she dug her clip out of her pocket and pulled back her hair. "It didn't have your name on it."

"Did, too."

She circled her shoulders. "Is your name Pineview Bakery? Besides I only ate half of it." She checked her watch. "The first-on-scene reports in yet?"

"Yeah, and so's your warrant."

"Great." She swung to her feet, adjusted her weapon harness. "I'll be in the field."

"I want a cheese bagel back in that box by end of shift."

"I only ate half of it," she called out and stopped by her desk for the paperwork. Scanning it, ignoring the backwash of noise from the detectives' bull pen, she hitched her harness into a more comfortable position, then shrugged into her jacket.

She glanced up when the noise became a murmur, and watched her father walk in. Like Blackhawk, she thought, this was a man who created ripples.

She knew a few of her fellow officers harbored some resentment over her rapid rise to detective. There were mutters now and then, just loud enough for her to hear, about favoritism and oiling the ranks.

She'd earned her badge and knew it. Ally was too proud of her father and too secure in her own abilities to let mutters worry her.

"Commissioner."

"Detective. Got a minute?"

"A couple." She pulled her shoulder bag from her bottom desk drawer. "Can we walk and talk? I'm on my way out. Got a warrant to serve on Jonah Blackhawk."

"Ah." He stepped back to let her pass, and his eyes scanned the room. If there were any mutters, they would wait until he was well out of range.

"Stairs okay with you?" she asked. "I didn't have time to work out this morning."

"I think I can keep up with you. What's the warrant?"

"To confiscate and view Blackhawk's security tapes. He got pissy about it yesterday. I seem to put his back up."

Boyd pushed open the door to the stairwell, then angled his head to study his daughter's back as she passed through. "I seem to detect a few ruffled feathers on yours."

"Okay, good eye. We put each other's backs up."

"I figured you would. You both like to do things your own way."

"Why would I want to do them someone else's way?"

"Exactly." Boyd skimmed a hand down the long, sleek tail of her hair. His little girl had always had a mind of her own, and a very hard head around it. "Speaking of ruffled feathers, I have a meeting with the mayor in an hour."

"Better you than me," Ally said cheerfully as she jogged down the stairs.

"What can you tell me about last night's break-in?"

"Same M.O. They hit a real treasure trove with the Chamberses. Mrs. Chambers got me the loss list this morning. The woman's efficient. They were fully insured—value of stolen items comes to a solid two hundred and twenty-five thousand."

"That's the biggest haul so far."

"Yeah. I'm hoping it makes them cocky. They took some art this time. I don't know if it was dumb luck or somebody knew what they had when they saw it. They have to have somewhere to keep the goods before they turn them. Big enough for a car."

"A decent chop shop could have a car dismantled and turned in a couple hours."

"Yeah, but…" She started to push open the next door herself, but her father beat her to it. It reminded her oddly, and not entirely happily, of Jonah.

"But?" he prompted as they crossed the lobby.

"I don't think that's the route. Somebody likes nice things. Somebody has really good taste. At the second hit, they took a collection of rare books, but they left an antique clock. It was appraised at five thousand, but it was dead ugly. It's like they said, please, don't insult us. There've been other cars at other scenes, but they've only taken two. Cool cars."

"Burglars with standards."

"Yeah, I think so." When they stepped outside she blinked against the brilliant sunlight until she pulled out her shaded glasses. "And a kind of arrogance. Arrogance is a mistake. That's going to turn it my way."

"I hope so. The pressure's on, Ally." He walked her

to her car, opened the door for her in a way that made her frown and think of Jonah again. "We're getting press, the kind that makes the mayor uncomfortable."

"In my best judgment they won't wait more than a week. They're rolling now. They'll come back to Blackhawk's."

"They got a bigger slice of pie from the new place."

"Blackhawk's is reliable. Once I spend a few nights under there, I'll start recognizing faces. I'll pin him, Dad."

"I believe it." He bent down to kiss her cheek. "And I'll handle the mayor."

"I believe it." She slid behind the wheel. "Question."

"Ask it."

"You've known Jonah Blackhawk for what, like fifteen years?"

"Seventeen."

"How come you never had him over to the house? You know, for dinner or football afternoons or one of your world-famous cookouts?"

"He wouldn't come. Always acknowledged the invitation, thanked me and said he was busy."

"Seventeen years." Idly she tapped her fingers on the steering wheel. "That's a lot of busy. Well, some people don't like socializing with cops."

"Some people," Boyd told her, "draw lines and never believe they have the right to cross them. He'd meet me at the station house." The memory made Boyd grin. "He didn't like it, but he'd do it. He'd meet me for coffee or a beer, at the gym. But he'd never come to my home. He'd consider that crossing the line. I've never convinced him otherwise."

"Funny, he strikes me as being a man who considers himself good enough for anything, or anyone."

"There are a lot of twists and pockets in Jonah. And very little about him that's simple."

Chapter 4

She called ahead, and had to admit she was surprised when Jonah answered the phone in his office.

"It's Fletcher. I didn't think you were much on daylight hours."

"I'm not. Some days are exceptions. What can I do for you, Detective?"

"You can come downstairs and let me in. I'll be there in ten minutes."

"I'm not going anywhere." He waited a beat. "So, what are you wearing?"

She hated herself for laughing, and hoped she managed to smother most of it. "My badge," she told him and flicked the phone off.

Jonah hung up, sat back and entertained himself by imagining Allison Fletcher wearing her badge, and nothing else. The image came through, entirely too clear, entirely too appealing, and had him shoving back from the desk.

He had no business imagining Boyd's daughter naked. No business, he reminded himself, fantasizing about Boyd's daughter in any way whatsoever. Or wondering how her mouth would taste. Or what scent he'd find on the flesh just under the line of that very stubborn jaw.

God, he wanted to sink his teeth there, right there. Just once.

Forbidden fruit, he told himself and paced since there was no one to see. She was forbidden fruit and therefore all the more alluring. She wasn't even his type. Maybe he liked leggy blondes. Maybe he liked leggy blondes with brains and a strong backbone. But he preferred friendlier women.

Friendlier, unarmed women, he thought, amusing himself.

He hadn't been able to get her out of his head, and the clearest most compelling picture had been the yielding and temporary, he was certain, fragility of her when she'd fallen asleep in his car.

Well, he'd always been a sucker for the needy, he reminded himself, as he pulled up the blinds on his office window. Which should solve his problem over Allison. Despite that short interlude of vulnerability early that morning, needy was one thing the gorgeous detective wasn't.

She had a use for him, again temporary. And when the job was done, they'd both go back to their separate corners in their separate worlds. And that would be the end of that.

He saw her pull up in front of the club. At least she'd

had the sense to drive, he noted, and wasn't hiking all over Denver today.

He took his time going down to let her in.

"Good morning, Detective." He looked around her, studied the flashy lines of the classic red-and-white Stingray. "Nice car. Is that the new police issue? Oh wait, what was I thinking? Your daddy's loaded."

"If you think you can razz me over a car, you're going to be disappointed. Nobody razzes like a precinct full of cops."

"I'll practice. Nice threads," he commented and rubbed the lapel of her subtly patterned brown jacket between his thumb and forefinger. "Very nice."

"So we both like Italian designers. We can compare wardrobes later."

Because he knew it would irritate her, because he enjoyed the way the gold highlighted her eyes when he irritated her, he shifted, blocking her before she could step inside. "Let me see the badge."

"Come off it, Blackhawk."

"No. Let's see it."

Eyes narrowed behind her sunglasses, she pulled her badge out of her pocket, pushed it close to his face. "See it?"

"Yes. Badge number 31628. I'll buy myself a lottery ticket and play your numbers."

"Here's something else you might want to look at." She took out the warrant, held it up.

"Fast work." He'd expected no less. "Come on up. I've been reviewing the tapes. You look rested," he said as they walked to his elevator.

"I am."

"Any progress?"

"The investigation is ongoing."

"Hmm, policy line." He gestured her into the elevator. "We seem to be spending a lot of time in these. Close quarters."

"You could do your heart a favor and take the stairs."

"My heart's never caused me any problems. How about yours?"

"Whole and healthy, thanks." She walked out when the doors opened. "Wow, you actually let the sunlight in here. I'm shocked. Let's have the tapes. I'll give a receipt."

She wasn't wearing perfume today, he noted. Just soap and skin. Odd how erotic that simplicity could be. "In a hurry?"

"Clock's ticking."

He strolled into an adjoining room. After a small internal battle, Ally walked over to the doorway. It was a small bedroom. Small, she noted, because it was two-thirds bed. A black pool of bed, unframed and on a raised platform.

Curious, she looked up and was mildly disappointed there wasn't a mirror on the ceiling.

"It would be too obvious," Jonah told her when her gaze skimmed back to his.

"The bed's already a statement. An obvious one."

"But not vain."

"Hmm." To amuse herself she poked around the room. On the walls were a number of framed black-and-white photographs. Arty, interesting, and all stark or shadowy night scenes.

She recognized a couple of the artists, pursed her lips. So the man had a good eye for art, and decent taste, she admitted.

"I've got this print." She tapped a finger against a study of an ancient man in a ragged straw hat sleeping on a cracked concrete stoop, a paper bag still clutched in his hand. "Shade Colby. I like his work."

"So do I. And his wife's. Bryan Mitchell. That's one of hers beside it. The old couple holding hands on the bench at the bus stop."

"Quite a contrast, despair and hope."

"Life's full of both."

"Apparently."

She wandered. There was a closet, closed, an exit door, securely locked, and what she assumed was a bath or washroom just beyond. She thought of the sex vibes Lydia Carson had referred to. Oh, yeah, this room had plenty of them. It all but smoked with them.

"So, what's through there?" She jerked a thumb at another door. Instead of answering he gestured, inviting her to see for herself.

She opened the door, let out a long sigh of pleasure. "Now we're talking." The fully equipped gym was a great deal more appealing to her than a lake-size bed.

He watched as she trailed her fingers over machines, picked up free weights, doing a few absent curls as she roamed. Very telling, he thought, that she'd given the bed a sneer, and was all but dewy-eyed over his Nautilus.

"You got a sauna?" Envy curled inside her as she pressed her nose to a little window of a wooden door and peered into the room beyond.

"Want to try it out?"

She turned her head enough to slide her gaze in his direction. And the sneer was back. "This is pretty elaborate when you could be at a full-service health club in two minutes."

"Health clubs have members—that's the first strike. They also have regular hours. Strike two. And I don't like using someone else's equipment."

"Strike three. You're a very particular man, Blackhawk."

"That's right." He took a bottle of water out of a clear-fronted bar fridge. "Want one?"

"No." She replaced the free weight, moved back to the doorway. "Well, thanks for the tour. Now, the tapes, Blackhawk."

"Yeah, clock's ticking." He unscrewed the top of the bottle, took a casual sip. "You know what I like about night work, Detective Fletcher?"

She looked deliberately toward the bed, then back at him. "Oh, I think I can figure it out."

"Well, there's that, but what I really like about night work is that it's always whatever time you want it to be. My favorite's the three o'clock hour. For most people, that's the hard time. If they don't sleep through it, that's the time the mind wakes up and starts worrying about what they did or didn't do that day, or what they'll do or not do the next. And the next, and right up until life's over."

"And you don't worry about yesterday or tomorrow."

"You miss a lot of the now doing that. There's only so much now to go around."

"I don't have a lot of the now to stand around philosophizing with you."

"Take a minute." He crossed to her, leaning on one jamb as she leaned on the other. "A lot of people who come into my place are night people—or those who want to remember when they were. Most have jobs now, the kind of jobs that pay well and make them responsible citizens."

She took the water bottle from his hand, drank. "Your job pays well."

He grinned. That quick jab was just one of the things that attracted him to her. "You saying I'm not a responsible citizen? My lawyers and accountants would disagree. However, my point is that people come in here to forget about their responsibilities for a while. To forget the clock's ticking and they have to punch in at 9:00 a.m. I give them a place without clocks—at least till last call."

"And this means?" She passed the bottle back to him.

"Forget about the facts a minute. Look at the shadows. You're hunting night people."

And he was one of them, she thought. Very much one of the night people, with his black mane of hair and cool, cat's eyes. "I'm not arguing with that."

"But are you thinking like them? They've picked their prey, and when they move, they move fast. It would be less risky, give them more time to study the lay of the land, if they waited to make the hit during the day. Stake out the mark, learn their patterns—when do they leave for the office, when do they get back? These guys could probably nail it down in a couple of days."

He lifted the bottle, drank. "That would be more efficient. Why don't they play it that way?"

"Because they're arrogant."

"Yeah, but that's only the top layer. Go down."

"They like the kick, the rush."

"Exactly. They're hungry, and they like the thrill of working in the dark."

It irked almost as much as it intrigued her that his thought process so closely followed her own. "You think that hasn't occurred to me before?"

"I figure it has, but I wonder if you've factored in that people who live at night are always more dangerous than people who live during the day."

"Does that include you?"

"Damn right."

"So warned." She started to turn away, then stopped, stared down at the hand he'd shot out to grip her arm. "What's your problem, Blackhawk?"

"I haven't figured it out yet. Why didn't you send a uniform over here to pick up the tapes?"

"Because it's my case."

"No."

"No, it's not my case?"

"No, that's not the reason. I'm crowding you." He edged forward to prove it. "Why haven't you decked me?"

"I don't make a habit of punching out civilians." She angled her chin when he nudged her back against the doorjamb. "But I can make an exception."

"Your pulse is jumping."

"It tends to when I'm irritated." Aroused, she'd nearly said aroused because that was the word that came into her head. That was the sensation sliding through her body. And enough was enough.

She shifted, a smooth move that should have planted her elbow in his gut and moved him aside. But he countered, just as smoothly, and changed his grip so that his fingers wrapped tight around her wrist. Instinctively she pivoted, started to hook her foot behind his to take him down.

He adjusted his weight, used it to plaster her back against the door. She told herself it was annoyance that quickened her breathing, and not the way the lines of his body pressed against the lines of hers.

She bunched the hand at her side into a fist, calculated the wisdom of using it for one short-armed punch to the face, and decided sarcasm was a more potent weapon against him.

"Next time, ask me if I want to dance. I'm not in the mood to—" She broke off when she saw something sharp come into his eyes, something reckless that had her already rapid pulse tripping to a faster rate.

She forgot self-defense, forgot the fist she still held ready. "Damn it, Blackhawk, back off. What do you want from me?"

"The hell with it." He forgot the rules, forgot the consequences of breaking them. All he could see was her. "The hell with it, let's find out."

He let the bottle drop, and the water that remained in it spilled unnoticed on the bedroom rug. He wanted his hands on her, both his hands, and used them to hold her arms over her head as his mouth came down on hers.

He felt her body jerk against his. Protest or invitation, he didn't care. One way or the other, he was bound to be damned for this single outrageous act. So he might as well make the most of it.

He used his teeth on her, the way he'd already imagined, scraping them along the long line of her lower lip. Freeing the warmth, the softness of it to him, then absorbing it. She made some sound, something that seemed to claw up from her throat and was every bit as primitive as the need that raged through him.

The scent of her—cool soap and skin—the flavor of

her, such a contrast of ripeness and heat, overwhelmed him, stirred every hunger he'd ever known.

When his hands took her, fingers sliding down, gripping her hips, he was ready to feed those hungers, to take what he craved without a second thought.

Then his hand bumped over her weapon.

He jerked back as if she'd drawn it and shot him.

What was he doing? What in God's name was he doing?

She said nothing, only stared at him with eyes that had gone blurry at the edges. Her arms remained over her head, as if his hands still pinned them there.

Her body quaked.

"That was a mistake," she managed to say.

"I know it."

"A really serious mistake."

With her eyes open, she fisted her hands in his hair and dragged his mouth back to hers.

This time it was his body that jerked, and the shock of it vibrated through her, down to the bone. He'd savaged her mouth with that first mad kiss, and she wanted him to do it again. He would damn well do it again until her system stopped screaming.

She couldn't breathe without breathing him, and every desperate gulp of air was like the pump of a drug. The power of it charged through her while their lips and tongues warred.

With one violent move, he yanked her shirt out of the waistband of her slacks, then snaked his hand beneath until it closed over her breast.

The groan came from both of them.

"The minute I saw you." He tore his mouth from hers to feast on her throat. "The first minute I saw you."

"I know." She wanted his mouth again, had to have it. "I know."

He started to drag her jacket off, had it halfway down her arms when sanity began to pound against madness. The madness urged him to take her—why shouldn't he?—fast and hard. To take what he needed, the way he needed it, and please himself.

"Ally." He said her name, and the old-fashioned sweetness of it clicked reality back into place.

She saw him step back—though he didn't move, she saw the deliberate distance he built between them by the change in his eyes. Those fascinating and clear green eyes.

"Okay." She sucked in a breath. "Okay, okay." In an almost absent move she patted his shoulder until he did indeed step back. "That was…whoa." She sidestepped, paced away into his office. "Okay, that was… something."

"Something or other."

"I need a minute for my mind to clear." She'd never had passion slam into her with a force that blanked the mind. But she'd have to worry about that, deal with that later. Right now it was essential she find her balance.

"We probably both knew that was in there. And it's probably best we got it out," she said.

To give himself a moment he bent down, picked up the empty water bottle, set it aside. Then he dipped his hands into his pockets because they weren't altogether steady, and followed her into the office.

"I'll agree with the first part and reserve judgment on the second. What do we do now?"

"Now we…get over it."

Just like that? he thought. She'd cut him off at the

knees, and now he was supposed to just hobble away and get over it?

"Fine." Pride iced his voice. He walked over, took three tapes out of his desk drawer. "I believe these satisfy your warrant."

Her palms were sweaty, but she couldn't sacrifice the dignity she was trying to rebuild by wiping them off. She took the tapes, slipped them into her shoulder bag. "I'll give you a receipt."

"Forget it."

"I'll give you a receipt," she repeated, and took out a pad. "It's procedure."

"We wouldn't want to tamper with procedure." He held out his hand, accepting the copy she offered. "Don't let me keep you, Fletcher. Clock's ticking."

She strode to the door, yanked it open. Dignity be damned, she decided and spun back. "You can save the attitude. You made the first move, I made the second. That's an even slate to me, and now it's done."

"Honey—make that Detective Honey, if we were done, we'd both be feeling a lot better right now."

"Yeah, well. We'll live with it," she muttered and sacrificed dignity for satisfaction by slamming the door.

Ally wasn't cut out to be a waitress. She was sure of it when, during her second shift at Blackhawk's, she poured the drink Beth had allowed her to serve over the head of the idiot customer who grabbed her butt and invited her to engage in a sexual act that was illegal in several states.

The customer had objected, rather strongly, to her response, but before she could flatten him, Will had appeared like smoke between them. She'd had to stand passively and be rescued.

It had grated for hours.

But if she was sure of her lack of waitress potential after her second shift, she was desperate to shed her cover by the third.

She wanted action. And not the kind that required her to serve wild wings in demon sauce and take orders for drinks called tornadoes to young executives on the make.

Twenty minutes into her third night at Blackhawk's had given her a profound respect for those who served and cleared and tolerated impatience, lousy tips and lewd propositions.

"I hate people." Ally waited for her drink order at the bar while Pete drew a beer off tap.

"Ah, no, you don't."

"Yes. Yes, I do. I really do. They're rude, annoying, oblivious. And all of them are jammed into Blackhawk's."

"And it's only six-thirty."

"Please. Six thirty-five. Every minute counts." She glanced back at Jan who worked the bar area, all but dancing between tables as she cleared, served and played up her assets. "How does she do it?"

"Some are born for it, Blondie. You'll excuse my saying so, but you're not. Not that you don't do the job, but you don't have the passion."

She rolled her eyes. "I don't have the arches, either." She started to lift the tray, eyes tracking the room as always, then she let it drop again when she spotted the man coming in the front door.

"Oh, hell. Pete, ask Jan to get this order to table eight club side. I have to do something."

"Ally, what're you doing here?"

It was all Dennis got out of his mouth before Ally grabbed his arm and hauled him through the bar, into the kitchen and out the back door. "Damn it, Dennis. Damn it!"

"What's the matter? What did you drag me out here for?" He put on his best baffled look, but she'd seen it before. She'd seen the whole routine before.

"I'm on the job. You'll blow my cover, for God's sake. I told you what would happen if you started following me again."

"I don't know what you're talking about." His injured air had worked on her once. More than once.

"You listen to me." She stepped close, jabbed a finger in his chest. "Listen hard, Dennis. We're done. We have been done for months. There's no chance that's going to change, and every chance, if you keep hassling me, I'll slap a restraining order on your butt and make your life a living hell."

His mouth thinned, his eyebrows lowered, the way she knew they did when he was backed into a corner. "This is a public place. All I did was walk into a public place. I'm entitled to buy a drink in a bar when I'm in the mood."

"You're not entitled to follow me, or to jeopardize my cover in a police investigation. You crossed the line, and I'm calling the D.A.'s office in the morning."

"You don't have to do that. Come on, Ally. How was I supposed to know you were on the job here? I just happened to pass by and—"

"Don't lie to me." She balled her hand into a fist, then in frustration tapped it against her own temple as she turned away. "Don't lie."

"I just miss you so much. I think about you all the time. I can't help it. I know I shouldn't have followed you. I didn't mean to. I was just hoping we could talk, that's all. Come on, baby." He took her shoulders, buried his face in her hair in a way that made her skin crawl. "If we could just talk."

"Don't…touch me." She hunched her shoulders, started to pull away, but he wrapped his arms around her, one hard squeeze of possession.

"Don't pull away. You know it makes me crazy when you go cold like that."

She could have had him flat on his back with her foot on his throat in two moves. She didn't want it to come to that. "Dennis, don't make me hurt you. Just leave me alone. Take your hands off me and leave me alone or it's going to be so much worse than it already is."

"No. It'll be better. I swear, it'll be better. You just have to take me back, and things'll be the way they used to be."

"No. They won't." She stiffened, braced to break the hold. "Let me go."

Light spilled out of the kitchen door as it opened. "I'd advise you to do what the lady asked," Jonah warned. "And do it fast."

She closed her eyes, felt temper and embarrassment rise up under the frustration. "I can handle this."

"Maybe, but you won't. This is my place. Take your hands off her."

"We're having a private conversation." Dennis turned, but pulled Ally with him.

"Not anymore. Go inside, Ally."

"This is none of your business." Dennis's voice rose, cracked. It was a tenor she'd heard before. "Just butt out."

"That wasn't the right response."

She moved now, breaking free and stepping between the men when Jonah moved forward. There was a gleam in his eye that worried her, like a flash of lightning against thin ice. "Don't. Please."

Anger wouldn't have stopped him, nor would an order. But the plea in her eyes, the weariness in them, did. "Go back inside," he said again, but quietly as he laid a hand on her shoulder.

"So that's the way it is." Dennis lifted bunched fists. "There's nobody else. That's what you told me. No, there was nobody else. Just another lie. Just one more of your lies. You've been sleeping with him all along, haven't you? Lying bitch."

Jonah moved like a snake. She'd seen street fights before. Had broken up her share while in uniform. She only had time to swear and leap forward, but Jonah already had Dennis up against the wall.

"Stop it," she said again and grabbed his arm to try to pull him off. She might as well have tried to shove aside a mountain.

He shot her one steely look. "No." He said it casually, like a shrug. Then he plowed his fist into Dennis's belly. "I don't like men who push women around or call them names." His voice stayed cool and steady as he delivered a second blow. "I won't tolerate it in my place. You got that?"

He let go, stepped back, and Dennis collapsed in a heap at his feet. "I think he got it."

"Great. Wonderful." While Dennis moaned, Ally pressed her fingers to her eyes. "You just gut-punched an assistant district attorney."

"And your point would be?"

"Help me get him up."

"No." Before she could try to haul Dennis to his feet, Jonah took her arm. "He walked in on his own, he'll walk away on his own."

"I can't leave him here, curled up like a damn shrimp on the pavement."

"He'll get up. Right, Dennis?" Elegant and unruffled in black, Jonah crouched down beside the groaning man. "You're going to get up, you're going to walk away. And you're not going to come back here in this lifetime. You're going to stay very far away from Allison. In fact, if you find out that by some mischance you're breathing the same air, you'll hold your breath and run in the opposite direction."

Dennis struggled to his hands and knees, retched. Tears swam in his eyes, but behind them was a rage that drilled in his head like a diamond bit. "You're welcome to her." Pain radiated through him as he stumbled to his feet. "She'll use you, then toss you aside. Just like she did me. You're welcome to her," he repeated, then limped away.

"Looks like you're all mine now." Jonah straightened, flicked fingers down his shirt as if removing some pesky lint. "But if you're going to start using me, I'd prefer we do it inside."

"It's not funny."

"No." He studied her face, the shadowed eyes and the pity in them. "I can see that. I'm sorry. Why don't you come inside, take a few minutes up in my office until you're feeling steadier."

"I'm okay." But she turned away, dragged the clip out of her hair as if it were suddenly too tight. "I don't want to talk about it now."

"All right." He put his hands on her shoulders, used his thumbs to press at the tension. "Take a minute anyway."

"I hate having him touch me, and I feel lousy because I hate it. I don't think it jeopardized the cover."

"No. According to Pete, some dude walked in, you flipped and dragged him out."

"Anybody asks, I'll keep it close to the truth. Ex-boyfriend who's hassling me."

"Then stop worrying." He turned her around. "And stop feeling guilty. You're not responsible for other people's feelings."

"Sure you are, when you help make them. Anyway." She lifted a hand to the one he still rested on her shoulder, patted it. "Thanks. I could have handled him, but thanks."

"You're welcome."

He couldn't stop himself from leaning into her, drawing her close. He watched her lashes lower, her mouth lift to his. And was a breath away from tasting her when the light spilled over them.

"Oh. Sorry." Frannie stood, framed in the door where kitchen noise clattered, a lighter in one hand, a cigarette at the ready in the other.

"No." Ally broke away, furious with herself for forgetting her priorities. "I was just going back in. I'm already late." She flicked one look at Jonah then hurried back inside.

Frannie waited until the door swung shut, then stepped over to lean back against the wall. She flicked on her lighter. "Well," she said.

"Well."

She blew out smoke on a sigh. "She's beautiful."

"Yes, she is."

"Smart, too. It comes across."

"Yeah."

"Just your type."

This time he angled his head. "You think so?"

"Sure." The tip of her cigarette glowed as she lifted it to her lips. "Classy. Class shows. She suits you."

It troubled him, more than he'd imagined it would, to dance around the truth with an old friend. "We'll see how well we fit."

Frannie moved a shoulder. But she'd already seen. They fit like lock and key. "Was there trouble with that suit?"

Jonah glanced in the direction Dennis had taken. "Nothing major. An ex who doesn't like being an ex."

"Figured it was something like that. Well, if it matters, I like her."

"It matters, Frannie." He walked to her, touched a hand to her cheek. "You matter, and always have."

Chapter 5

Six days after the Chamberses' burglary, Ally stood in her lieutenant's office. To save time, she'd already changed into her waitress gear for the evening. She had her badge in the pocket of her trousers and her clutch piece strapped just above her ankle.

"We haven't been able to trace one single piece of stolen property." She knew it wasn't what he wanted to hear. "There's no news on the street. Even Hickman's bottomless sources are dry. Whoever's pushing the buttons on this is smart, private and patient."

"You've been inside Blackhawk's for a week."

"Yes, sir. I can't tell you any more than I could the first day. Between the security tapes and my own in-the-field observations I've tagged several regulars. But nobody pops. On the upside, my cover's secure."

"Fortunately. Shut the door, Detective."

Her stomach sank a little, but she did so and stood in the glass box of his office with the noise from the bull pen humming behind the clear wall.

"On the matter of Dennis Overton."

She'd known it was coming. Once she'd made the complaint to the D.A.'s office, it was inevitable that some of the flak would scatter into her own house.

"I regret the incident, Lieutenant. However, the way it ultimately played out added to my cover rather than detracting from it."

"That's not my concern. Why didn't you report his behavior previously to the D.A.? To me?"

They both heard the unspoken *To your father.*

"It was personal business, and until this last incident, on my personal time. I believed I could handle it without involving my superiors or Dennis's."

He understood the defensive stance, because he understood her. "I've spoken with the district attorney. In your complaint to him you state that Overton has, over a period of time beginning the first week of April, harassed you with phone calls both here and at home, has staked out your apartment, followed you on and off duty."

"He didn't interfere with the job," she began, then wisely closed her mouth when her lieutenant stared at her.

Kiniki set aside a copy of her written statement, folded his hands on it. "Contacting you against your stated wishes when you're on duty, as well as when you're off, interferes. Are you unaware of the stalking laws, Detective?"

"No, sir. When it became apparent that the subject would not desist in his behavior, could not be discouraged and could potentially interfere with this investigation, I reported his behavior to his superior."

"You haven't filed charges."

"No, sir."

"Nor have you, as yet, requested a restraining order."

"I believe a reprimand from his superior is sufficient."

"That, or being knocked back by Jonah Blackhawk?"

She opened her mouth, closed it again. She hadn't mentioned that part of the incident to the D.A.

"Overton claims that Blackhawk attacked him, unprovoked, in a fit of jealous rage."

"Oh, for God's sake." The words, and the disgust in them, were out before she could stop them. She yanked at her hair once, then bit down on control. "That is completely inaccurate. I didn't detail the incident, Lieutenant. It didn't seem necessary. But if Dennis insists on making trouble here, I'll write out a full report."

"Do it. I want a copy on my desk by tomorrow afternoon."

"He could lose his job."

"Is that your problem?"

"No." She blew out a breath. "No, sir. Lieutenant, Dennis and I dated for a period of three months." She hated this, bringing her personal life into her superior's office. "We were…intimate, briefly. He began to display—hell."

She dropped the copspeak, approached the desk. "He got possessive, jealous, irrational. If I was late or had to cancel, he'd accuse me of being with another man. It got way out of hand, and when I broke things off he'd come by or call. Full of apologies and promises to be different. When I didn't go for it, he'd either get nasty or fall apart. Lieutenant, I slept with him. Part of this situation is my doing."

Kiniki waited a moment, pulling on his bottom lip while he studied her. "That's one of the few stupid remarks I've ever heard you make. If a victim came to you describing this situation, would you tell her it was her doing?" When she didn't answer, he nodded. "I didn't think so. You would follow procedure. Follow it now."

"Yes, sir."

"Ally…" He'd known her since she was five. He tried to keep the personal separate as religiously as she. But there were times… "Have you told your father about this?"

"I don't want to bring him into it. Respectfully, sir, I'd prefer you didn't discuss it with him."

"That's your choice. The wrong one, but yours. I'll agree to it if I have your word that if Overton so much as breathes within ten feet of you, you report it to me." He cocked his head when her lips quivered. "That's amusing?"

"No, sir. Yes." She let go of the cop-to-cop stand. "Jonah made nearly the same statement, Uncle Lou. I guess it's…sweet. In a manly sort of way, of course."

"Always had the smartest mouth. Go on, get out of here. And get me something on these burglaries."

Since most waitresses-in-training didn't drive classic Corvettes, Ally was in the habit of parking two blocks away and walking the rest of the distance to Blackhawk's.

It gave her time to shift gears, to appreciate what spring brought to Denver. She'd always loved the city, the way the buildings, silver towers, rode into the sky.

She loved seeing the mountains go from winter-white to those steely jags laced by snow and forest.

And though she enjoyed the mountains, had spent many wonderful days in her parents' cabin, she preferred to view them from city streets. Her city.

Her city had scarred-booted cowboys walking down the same streets with Armani-clad executives. It was about cattle and commerce and nightlife. It was about the wild, coated with a sheen or polish but not quite tamed.

The East would never hold the same appeal for her.

And when spring was in full, balmy life, when the sun beamed on the white-tipped peaks that guarded Denver, when the air was thin and bright, there was no place like it in the world.

She stepped out of the city, and into Blackhawk's.

Jonah was at the bar, the far end, leaning casually, sipping what she knew was his habitual sparkling water and listening to one of his regular customers complain about his day.

Those light and beautiful green eyes pinned her the minute she walked in, stayed steady, stayed level and gave away nothing.

He hadn't touched her since the night behind the club, and had said little. It was best that way, she told herself. Mix duty and lust and you end up compromising one and being burnt by the other.

But it was frustrating to see him night after night, to remain just close enough to maintain illusions and not be able to take a complete step forward or back.

And to want him, the way she'd never wanted anyone else.

She shrugged out of her jacket and got to work.

* * *

It was killing him, by inches. Jonah knew what it was to want a woman, to have one stir blood and loins and spin images in the mind. It could be a kind of hunger that slowly churned in the belly, gnawing there until it was finally satisfied.

This was a hunger, his desire for Ally. But there was nothing of the slow churning in it. This was sharp, constant and painful.

No other woman had ever caused him pain.

He carried the taste of her inside him. He couldn't rid himself of it. That alone was infuriating. It gave her an advantage he'd never allowed another to have over him. The fact that she didn't appear to know it didn't negate the weakness.

Where you were weak, you were vulnerable.

He wanted the investigation over. He wanted her back in her own life, her own world so he could regain his balance in his.

Then he remembered the way she'd erupted against him, the way her mouth had scorched over his, and her hands fisted in his hair. And he began to worry he'd never find his feet firmly planted again.

"Good thing we don't have a cop around."

Jonah's fingers tightened on his glass, but his eyes were mild as he turned to Frannie. "What?"

She pulled a beer, poured a bump, then served it. "A guy could get arrested for looking at a woman that way. I think it's called intent or something. What you intend is pretty clear, at least when she's not looking."

"Really?" And that, he realized, was another worry. "Then I'd better watch myself."

"She's doing plenty of watching," Frannie murmured as he walked away.

"The man's got trouble on the brain," Will commented. He liked coming over to Frannie's end of the bar so he could get a whiff of her hair or maybe work a smile out of her.

"He's got woman on the brain. And he's not altogether easy with this one." She winked at him and squirted a glass of the soft drink Will drank by the gallon during working hours.

"Women never trouble the man."

"This one does."

"Well." He sipped his drink, scanned the bar crowd. "She's a looker."

"That's not it. Looks are surface stuff. This one's got him down in the gut."

"You think?" Will tugged on his little beard. He didn't understand women, and didn't pretend to. To him they were simply amazing creatures of staggering power and wonderful shapes.

"I know." She patted Will's hand and had his heart throbbing in his throat.

"Two margaritas, frozen with salt, two house drafts and a club soda with lime." Jan set down her tray and walked her fingers up Will's arm in a teasing, tickling motion. "Hey, big guy."

He blushed. He always did. "Hey, Jan. I better do a round in the club."

He hurried off and had Frannie shaking her head at Jan. "You shouldn't tease him like that."

"I can't help it. He's so sweet." She flipped her hair back. "Listen, there's this party tonight. I'm going by after closing. Want to tag along?"

"After closing I'm going to be home, in my own little bed, dreaming of Brad Pitt."

"Dreaming never gets you anywhere."

"Don't I know it," Frannie muttered and sent the blender whirling.

Allison carried a full tray of empties, and had two tables worth of drink orders in the pad tucked in her bar apron. Only thirty minutes into shift, she thought. It was going to be a long night. Longer, she realized when she spotted Jonah coming toward her.

"Allison, I'd like to speak with you." About something, anything. Five minutes alone with you might do it. Pitiful. "Would you come up to my office on your break?"

"Problem?"

"No," he lied. "No problem."

"Fine, but you'd better tell Will. He guards your cave like a wolf."

"Take your break now. Come up with me."

"Can't, thirsty people waiting. But I'll shake loose as soon as I can if it's important." She walked away quickly because she'd heard it, that underlying heat that told her what he wanted with her had nothing to do with duty.

She stopped at her station beside Pete and ordered herself to settle down. Since he was in the middle of entertaining three of the stool-sitters with a long, complicated joke, she took the time to rest her feet and study the people scattered at table and bar.

A twentysomething couple who looked like they were on the leading edge of an argument. Three suits with ties loosened arguing baseball. A flirtation, in its early stages, starting to cook between a lone woman and the better-looking of a pair of guys at the bar. Lots of eye contact and smiles.

Another couple at a table laughing together over some private joke, holding hands, she noted, flirting some even though the hands wore wedding rings. Well married, happy and financially secure if the designer handbag on the back of the woman's chair and the matching shoes were any indication.

At the next table another couple sat having a quiet conversation that seemed to please them both. There was an intimacy there as well, Ally noted. Body language, gestures, the smiling looks over sips of wine.

She envied that...comfort, she supposed, of having someone who could sit across the table in a crowded place and focus on her, care about what she said, or what she didn't have to say.

It was what her parents had—that innate rhythm and respect that added real dimension to love and attraction.

If it was lovely to watch, she wondered, how much more lovely must it be to experience?

Brooding over it, she listened to the laughter break out at Pete's punch line. She placed her orders, listening absently to the chatter around her, scanning, always scanning the movements, the faces.

She watched the hand-holding couple signal Jan, and the woman pointing to an item on the bar menu when the waitress moved to the table to take the order. Bending down, Jan waved a hand in front of her mouth, rolled her eyes and made the woman laugh.

"The hotter the better," the woman claimed. "We don't have a club table until eight, so there's plenty of time to cool down."

When Jan had scribbled down the order and moved

off, Ally found herself smiling at the way the man brought the woman's hand to his mouth and nipped at her knuckles.

If it hadn't been for that kernel of envy that kept her attention focused on them, she might have missed it. As it was, it took her several seconds to note the picture had changed.

The woman's bag still hung over the back of her chair, but at a different angle, and the outside zipper pocket wasn't quite closed.

Ally came to attention, her first thought to focus on Jan. Then she saw it. The second woman sitting with her back to the first, still smiling at her companion. While under the table, smooth and unhurried, she slipped a set of keys into the purse she held on her lap.

Bingo.

"You gone to the moon, Ally?" Pete tapped a finger on her shoulder. "I don't think anybody's waiting for vodka tonics up there."

"No, I'm right here."

As the woman rose, tucked her purse under her arm, Ally lifted her tray.

Five-four, she thought. A hundred and twenty. Brown hair, brown eyes. Late thirties with an olive complexion and strong features. And just now heading toward the ladies' room.

Rather than break cover, she hurried into the club, spotted Will and shoved the tray at him. "Sorry, table eight's waiting for these. Tell Jonah I need to speak with him. I have to do something."

"But hey."

"I have to do something," she repeated and walked briskly toward the restrooms.

Inside, she scanned the bottom of the stalls, located the right shoes. Making a wax mold of the keys, Ally concluded and turned to one of the sinks. She ran water while she watched the shoes. It would only take a few minutes, but she'd need privacy.

Satisfied, Ally walked out.

"Ally? I got tables filling up here. Where's your tray?"

"Sorry." She shot Beth an apologetic smile. "Little emergency. I'll get on it."

She moved quickly, catching the eye of one of her team members and pausing by the table. "White female, late thirties. Brown and brown. She'll be coming out of the ladies' room in a minute. Navy jacket and slacks. She's sitting in the bar area with a white male, early forties, gray and blue in a green sweater. Keep them in sight, but don't move in. We handle it just like we outlined."

She walked back to the bar to pick up another tray as a prop. The man in the green sweater was paying the tab. Cash. He looked relaxed, but Ally noted he checked his watch and glanced back toward the restrooms.

The woman came back in, but rather than taking her seat, stood between the tables and reached down for the short, black cape she'd draped over the chair. For a matter of seconds, her body blocked the view, then she straightened, beamed at her companion and handed him the cape.

Smart hands, Ally thought. Very smart hands.

When Jonah turned the corner of the bar, she inclined her head and let her gaze slide over to the couple preparing to leave, then back to him.

Casually she crossed over and ran a hand affectionately up and down Jonah's arm. "I've got two officers to tag them. We want them to get through the setup, all the way through. I want to give it some time before I alert the targets. When I do, I need your office."

"All right."

"We need to keep business as usual down here. If you'll hang around, I can let you know when I want to move. You can tell Beth you need me for something so she can juggle tables. I don't want any alarms going off."

"Just let me know. I'll take care of it."

"Let me have the code for your elevator. In case I need to take them up without you." She leaned in, her face tilted to his.

"Two, seven…" He leaned down, brushed his lips over hers. "Five, eight, five. Got it?"

"Yeah, I got it. See if you can keep attention off me until I move the targets out of the bar."

Her energy was up, but her mind was cool. She waited fifteen minutes. When the female target rose to use the restroom, Ally slipped in with her.

"Excuse me." After a quick check of the stalls, Ally pulled her badge out of her pocket. "I'm Detective Fletcher, Denver P.D."

The woman took a quick, instinctive step in retreat. "What's this about?"

"I need your help with an investigation. I'd like to speak with you and your husband. If you'd come with me."

"I haven't done anything."

"No, ma'am. I'll explain it all to you. There's a private office upstairs. If we could move up there as quietly as possible? I'd appreciate your cooperation."

"I'm not going anywhere without Don."

"I'll get your husband. If you'd walk back out, turn to the left, and wait in the corridor."

"I want to know what this is about."

"I'll explain it to both of you." Ally took the woman's arm to hurry her along. "Please. Just a few moments of your time."

"I don't want any trouble."

"Please wait here. I'll get your husband." Because she didn't trust the woman to stay put long, Ally moved fast. She paused at the couple's table, picked up empty glasses.

"Sir? Your wife's back there. She asked if you could come back for a minute."

"Sure. Is she okay?"

"She's fine."

Ally crossed to the bar, set down the empties. Then ducked quickly back into the corridor.

"Detective Fletcher," she said with a quick flash of her badge as the man joined her. "I need to speak with you and your wife in private." She was already keying in the code.

"She won't say what it's about. Don, I don't see why—"

"I appreciate your cooperation," Ally said again and all but shoved them both into the elevator.

"I don't appreciate being bullied by the police," the woman said with an edge of nerves in her voice.

"Lynn, calm down. It's okay."

"I'm sorry to be abrupt." Ally stepped into Jonah's office, gestured to the chairs. "If you'd have a seat, I'll fill you in."

Lynn crossed her arms, hugged her elbows tight. "I don't want to sit down."

Have it your way, sister, Ally thought. "I'm investigating a series of burglaries in and around Denver during the last several weeks."

The woman sniffed. "Do we look like burglars?"

"No, ma'am. You look like a nice, well-established, upper-class couple. Which has been, to date, the main target of this burglary ring. And less than twenty minutes ago, a woman we suspect is part of that ring lifted your keys out of your purse."

"That's impossible. My purse has been right with me all night." As if to prove it, she started to unzip the pocket. Ally snagged her wrist.

"Please don't touch your keys."

"How can I touch them if they're not there?" the woman argued.

"Lynn, shut up. Come on." He squeezed his wife's shoulder. "What's going on?" he asked Ally.

"We believe molds are made of the keys. They're replaced and the targeted victim remains unaware. Then their house is broken into and their belongings are stolen. We'd like to prevent that from happening to you. Now sit down."

Authority snapped in her voice this time. Visibly shaken, the woman lowered herself into a chair.

"If I could have your names please."

"Don and Lynn—Mr. and Mrs. Barnes."

"Mr. Barnes, would you give me your address?"

He swallowed, sat on the arm of his wife's chair and rattled it off while Ally noted it down. "Do you mean someone's in our house right now? Robbing us right now?"

"I don't believe they can move quite that quickly." In

her mind she was calculating the drive time. "Is there anyone at that address right now?"

"No. It's just us. Man." Barnes ran a hand through his hair. "Man, this is weird."

"I'm going to call in your address and begin setting up a stakeout. Give me a second."

She picked up the phone as the elevator doors opened, and Jonah walked it. "I've got it covered here," she told him.

"I'm sure you do. Mr. and Mrs....?"

"Barnes," the man answered. "Don and Lynn Barnes."

"Don, can I offer you and your wife something to drink? I realize this is very inconvenient and upsetting for you."

"I could use a shot. A good stiff bourbon, I think."

"Can't blame you. And Lynn?"

"I..." She lifted a hand, dropped it. "I just can't... I don't understand."

"Maybe a little brandy." Jonah turned away, opened a panel in the wall to reveal a small, well-stocked bar. "You can put yourselves in Detective Fletcher's capable hands," he continued and he chose bottles and glasses. "And meanwhile, we'll try to keep you as comfortable as possible."

"Thanks." Lynn took the brandy from him. "Thank you so much."

"Mr. Barnes." A little miffed at how smoothly Jonah had settled ruffled feathers, she yanked the man's attention back to her. "We have units on the way to your house right now. Can you describe your house for me? The layout, doors, windows?"

"Sure." He laughed, a little shakily. "Hell, I'm an architect."

He gave her a clear picture, which she relayed to the team before she began to set up the coordinates for the stakeout.

"You have dinner reservations here tonight?" Ally asked them.

"Yeah. Eight o'clock. We're making a night of it," he said with a sour smile.

Ally checked her watch. "They'll think they have plenty of time." She wanted them to go back down, to finish their time at the bar, go into dinner and present the appearance of normality. And one look at the woman's face told her it was a long shot.

"Mrs. Barnes. Lynn." Ally came back around the desk, sat on the edge of it. "We're going to stop these people. They won't take your things or damage your home. But I need you to help me out here. I need you and your husband to go back down, to try to get through the evening as if nothing was wrong. If you could hold on for another hour, I think we could wrap this up."

"I want to go home."

"We'll get you there. Give me an hour. It's possible that a member of the organization is assigned to keep an eye on you. You've already been away from your table nearly twenty minutes. We'll cover that, but we can't cover another hour. We don't want to scare these people off."

"If they're scared off, they won't break into my house."

"No, just into someone else's the next time."

"Give me a minute with her, okay." Barnes got up, took his wife's hands. "Come on, Lynn. Hell, it's an adventure. We'll eat out on the story for years. Come on, let's go—let's just go downstairs and get drunk."

"Jonah, go with them. Ah, pass the word that those—what was it—the wild wings you ordered didn't sit too well after all. You're fine now, but you were feeling a little sick. Blackhawk's will cover your bar bill, right?"

"Naturally." Jonah offered Lynn his hand to help her to her feet. "And the dinner tab. I'll take you down. You just needed to stretch out for a few minutes, and I offered to take you and your husband up to my office until you felt better. Good enough?" he asked Ally as he pressed for the elevator.

"Perfect. I need to make a couple more calls, then I'll be down. I'm going to have to cut out before end of shift. I've had a family emergency."

"Good luck with it," he told her, and led the Barneses away.

Chapter 6

She got the key from Jonah and went straight to the employee lounge for her bag. She ran straight out, doing no more than waving a hand when Frannie called out to her from behind the bar.

She was trusting Jonah to answer any questions. No one could do it better, she thought as she raced the blocks to her car. A simple word, a shrug from him and that would be that. No one pumped a man like Jonah Blackhawk.

She had to get to Federal Heights before everything went down.

At first she thought she was seeing things. But the night was clear and cool and her vision excellent. There was no mistaking the fact that all four of her tires were slashed.

She swore, kicked viciously at the mangled rubber. A

hell of a time, she thought, one hell of a time for Dennis Overton to get nasty. Digging into her bag she pulled out her cell phone and called for a radio car.

Time wasted, was all she could think. Two minutes, five minutes ticking away while she paced the sidewalk and waited. She had her badge out and her teeth clenched when the patrol car pulled up.

"Got some trouble, Detective?"

"Yeah. Hit the sirens, head north on 25. I'll tell you when to go silent."

"You got it. What's going down?"

She settled into the back behind the two uniforms, itching to have her hands on the wheel and her foot on the gas. "I'll fill you in." She took her weapon and harness out of her bag, and felt more herself the minute she strapped it on.

"Call for a tow truck, will you? I don't want to leave my car on the street like that."

"Shame about that. Nice car."

"Yeah." She forgot about it as they screamed up the interstate.

A block from the Barneses' address, she hopped out of the car, and arrowed straight to Hickman. "Give me the story."

"They took their time getting here. Balou and Dietz had the first leg of the tail and said they drove like solid citizens, kept under the speed limit, signaled for turns. Woman riding shotgun, made a call on a cell phone. He turned over the tail to me and Carson when they got on 36. They stopped for gas. The woman gets in the back. They're driving a nice, suburban minivan. She's doing something back there, but I couldn't get close enough to see."

"Making the keys. I bet you two weeks' pay she's got the works for it in the van."

"Do I look like I take sucker bets?" He glanced down the quiet street. "Anyhow, we had a unit here, waiting. The suspects were observed parking the van a block down from the target address. They strolled up the street, walked right up to the door, unlocked it and went in like they owned the place."

"Barnes said they have a security system."

"Alarm didn't trip. They've been inside about ten minutes now. Lieutenant's waiting for you. We've got the area blocked off, the house surrounded."

"Then let's move in and wrap this up."

He grinned, handed her a walkie-talkie. "Saddle up."

"God, I love cowboy talk."

They moved fast, kept low. She spotted the cops positioned on the street, behind trees, in shadows, hunched in cars.

"Glad you could join the party, Detective." Kiniki nodded toward the house. "Ballsy, aren't they?"

Lights gleamed, a homey glow against windows on the first and second floor. While Ally watched, she saw a faint shadow move behind the lower window.

"Dietz and Balou are covering the back. We've got them closed in. What's your play?"

Ally reached in her pocket, pulled out keys. "We move in on all sides, and go in the front. When we move, pull one of the radio cars across the driveway. Let's block that route."

"Call it."

She lifted the walkie-talkie, to establish positioning and give the orders. And all hell broke loose.

Three gunshots blasted the air, the return fire slamming into the echoes. Even as Ally drew her own weapon, voices shouted through the walkie-talkies.

"Dietz is down! Officer down! Shooter's male, heading east on foot. Officer down!"

Cops rushed the house. Ally hit the door first, went in low. Blood pounded in her ears as she swept the area with her weapon. Hickman took her back, and at her signal headed up the stairs while she turned right.

Someone was shouting. She heard it like a buzz in the brain. Lights flashed on.

The house opened out like a fan. She brought the layout Barnes had described into her mind as she and the rest of the team spread out. At each doorway she led with eyes and weapon, following training while her breath came short and shallow.

There was more gunfire from outside, muffled pops. She started to turn in that direction and saw the sliding door on what looked like a small solarium wasn't quite shut.

She caught a scent, very female, and following instinct turned away from the shouts and bolted for the door.

She saw the woman, just the silhouette of her, running hard toward a line of ornamental trees. "Police! Stop where you are!"

She would replay it a dozen times. The woman continued to run. Weapon drawn, Ally raced after her, calling out the warning, shouting her position and situation into her hand unit.

She heard calls from behind her, running feet.

They'd cut her off, Ally thought. Cut her off even before she reached the six-foot fence that closed in the property.

Nowhere to go.

She gained ground, caught both the scent of perfume and panic sweat the woman left on the air. Moonlight picked her out of the shadows, the swing of her dark hair, the stream of the short, black cape.

And when, on the run, the woman turned, the moonlight bounced off the chrome plating of the revolver in her hand.

Ally saw her lift it, felt with a kind of detached shock the heat of the bullet that whined past her own head.

"Drop your weapon! Drop it now!"

And as the woman pivoted, and the gun jerked in her hand, Ally fired.

Ally saw the woman stagger, heard the thud as the gun fell from her hand, and heard a kind of sighing gasp. But what she would remember, what seemed to burn on her brain like acid on glass, was the dark stain that bloomed between the woman's breasts even as she dropped.

It was bone-deep training that had her rushing forward, stepping on the woman's gun. "Suspect down," she said into her hand unit as she crouched to check for a pulse. Her voice didn't shake, and neither did she. Not yet.

It was Hickman who got to her first. She heard his voice like something carried on the crest of a wave of churning water. Her head was full of sound, a rushing liquid sound.

"Are you hit? Ally, are you hit?"

His hands were already moving over her, tugging at her jacket to check for injury.

"Call an ambulance." Her lips were stiff, they felt wooden, splintered. She reached forward, crossing her hands over each other, pressing the heels of them on the woman's chest.

"On the way. Come on. Get up."

"She needs pressure on this wound. She needs an ambulance."

"Ally." He holstered his own weapon. "You can't do anything for her. She's dead."

She didn't let herself be sick. She made herself stand and watch as the wounded officer and the woman's partner were loaded into ambulances. She made herself watch when the woman was zipped into a thick black bag.

"Detective Fletcher."

And she made herself turn, face her lieutenant. "Sir. Can you tell me Dietz's condition?"

"I'm on my way to the hospital. We'll know more later."

She rubbed the back of her hand over her mouth. "The suspect?"

"Paramedics said he'll make it. It'll be a couple of hours at least before we can question him."

"Am I…will I be allowed to be in on the interrogation?"

"It's still your case." He took her arm to draw her away. "Ally, listen to me. I know what it feels like. Ask yourself now, right now, if you could have done anything differently."

"I don't know."

"Hickman was behind you, and Carson was coming in from the left. I haven't spoken with her as yet, but Hickman's report is you identified yourself, ordered her to stop. She turned and fired. You ordered her to drop her weapon, and she prepared to fire again. You had no choice. That's what I expect to hear from you during the standard inquiry tomorrow morning. Do you want me to call your father?"

"No. Please. I'll talk to him tomorrow, after the inquiry."

"Then go home, get some rest. I'll let you know about Dietz."

"Sir, unless I'm relieved of duty, I'd rather go to the hospital. Stand by for Dietz, and be on hand to question the suspect when we're cleared to do so."

It would be better for her, he thought, to do what came next. "You can ride with me."

Panic was like an animal clawing at his throat. He'd never felt anything like it before. Jonah told himself it was just hospitals that did it to him. He'd always detested them. The smell of them brought back the last hideous months of his father's life, and made him all too aware that a turn here, a turn there in a different direction might have damned him to experience the same fate his father had at fifty years old.

His source had assured him that Ally wasn't hurt. But all he knew for certain was that something had gone very wrong at the bust and she was at the hospital. That had been enough to have him heading straight out. Just to see for himself, he thought.

He found her, slumped in a chair, in the hallway of Intensive Care. The panic digging into his throat released.

She'd taken the clip out of her hair as he knew she did when she was tense or tired. The gilt curtain of hair fanned down the side of her face, concealing it. But the tired slouch, the hands she gripped together on her knees, told him what to expect.

He stepped in front of her, crouched down and saw, as he'd known he would, pale skin and dark, bruised eyes.

"Hey." He gave in to the need to lay his hand over hers. "Bad day?"

"Pretty bad." It seemed like wires were crossed in her brain. She didn't think to wonder why he was there. "One of my team's in critical condition. They don't know if he'll make it till morning."

"I'm sorry."

"Yeah, me, too. The doctors won't let us talk to the son of a bitch who shot him. Male suspect identified as Richard Fricks. He's sleeping comfortably under a nice haze of drugs while Dietz fights for his life, and his wife's down in the chapel praying for it."

She wanted to close her eyes, to go into the dark, but kept them open and on his. "And for a bonus, I killed a woman tonight. One shot through the heart. Like she was a target I aced at practice."

Her hands trembled once under his, then fisted.

"Yeah, that's a pretty bad day. Come on."

"Come where?"

"Home, I'm taking you home." When she looked at him blankly, he pulled her to her feet. She felt featherlight, her hands fragile as glass. "There's nothing you can do here now, Ally."

She closed her eyes, groped for a breath. "That's

what Hickman said at the scene. There's nothing you can do. Looks like you're both right."

She let him lead her to the elevator. There was no point in staying, or arguing or pretending she wanted to be alone. "I can…get a ride."

"You've got one."

No, she thought, no point in arguing, or in resisting the supporting arm he slipped around her waist. "How did you know to come here?"

"A cop came by to take the Barneses home. I got enough out of him to know there'd been trouble, and where you were. Why isn't your father with you?"

"He doesn't know. I'll tell him about it tomorrow."

"What the hell's wrong with you?"

She blinked, like a woman coming out of a dark room into the light. "What?"

He pulled her out of the elevator, across the hospital lobby. "Do you want him to hear about this from someone else? To not hear your voice, hear you tell him you're not hurt? What are you thinking?"

"I… I wasn't thinking. You're right." She fumbled in her purse for her phone as they crossed the lot. "I need a minute. I just need a minute."

She got into the car, steadying herself, steadying her breathing. "Okay," she whispered it to herself as Jonah started the car. She punched in the number, waited through the first ring, then heard her mother's voice.

"Mom." Her breath hitched. She bore down, holding a hand over the phone until she was sure her voice would be normal. "I'm fine. Everything okay there? Uh-huh. Listen, I'm on my way home, and I need to speak to Dad a minute. Yeah, that's right. Cop talk. Thanks."

Now she closed her eyes, listened to her mother call

out, heard the warm mix of their laughter before her father's voice sounded in her ear.

"Ally? What's up?"

"Dad." Her voice wanted to crack but she refused to let it. "Don't say anything to upset Mom."

There was a pause. "All right."

"I'm okay. I'm not hurt, and I'm on my way home. It went down tonight, and things went wrong. Ah, one of the team was wounded, and he's in the hospital. One of the suspects is in there, too. We'll know more tomorrow on both."

"You're all right? Allison?"

"Yes, I wasn't hurt. Dad. Dad, I had to fire my weapon. They were armed. Both suspects were armed and opened fire. She wouldn't… I killed her."

"I'll be there in ten minutes."

"No, please. Stay with Mom. You'll have to tell her and she's going to be upset. I need to… I just need to go home and—tomorrow, okay? Can we talk about it tomorrow? I'm so tired now."

"If that's what you want."

"It is. I promise, I'm all right."

"Ally, who went down?"

"Dietz. Len Dietz." She lifted her free hand, pressed her fingers to her lips. They didn't feel stiff now, but soft. Painfully soft. "He's critical. The lieutenant's still at the hospital."

"I'll contact him. Try to get some sleep. But you call, anytime, if you change your mind. I can be there. We both can."

"I know. I'll call you in the morning. I think it'll be easier in the morning. I love you."

She broke the connection, let the phone slide into her

purse. She opened her eyes and saw they were already in front of her apartment. "Thanks for..."

Jonah said nothing, simply got out, came around to her door. Opening it, he held out a hand for hers. "I can't seem to get my thoughts lined up. What time is it?"

"It doesn't matter. Give me your key."

"Oh, yeah, the traditionalist." She dug it out, unaware her other hand was clutching his like a lifeline. "I'm going to start expecting flowers next."

She walked through the lobby, to the elevator. "It seems like there's something I have to do. I can't get a rope around what it is, though. There should be something I have to do. We identified her. She had ID anyway. Madeline Fricks. Madeline Ellen Fricks," she murmured, floating like a dream out of the elevator. "Age thirty-seven. She had an address in... Englewood. Somebody's checking it out. I should be checking it out."

He unlocked the door, drew her inside. "Sit down, Ally."

"Yeah, I could sit down." She looked blankly around the living room. It was just the way she'd left it that morning. Nothing had changed. Why did it seem as if everything had changed?

Jonah solved the matter by picking her up and carrying her toward the bedroom.

"Where are we going?"

"You're going to lie down. Got anything to drink around here?"

"Stuff."

"Fine. I'll go find some stuff." He laid her on the bed.

"I'll be okay."

"That's right." He left her to hunt through the kitchen. In a narrow cupboard he found an unopened bottle of brandy. He broke the seal, poured three fingers. When he brought it back, she was sitting up in the bed, her knees rammed into her chest, her arms roped around them.

"I've got the shakes." She kept her face pressed to her knees. "If I had something to do, I wouldn't have the shakes."

"Here's what you need to do." He sat on the bed, cupped a hand under her chin and lifted it. "Drink this."

She took the first sip obediently when he lifted the glass to her lips. Then she coughed and turned her head away. "I hate brandy. Somebody gave me that last Christmas, God knows why. I meant to..." She trailed off, began to rock.

"Have some more. Come on, Fletcher, take your medicine."

He gave her little choice but to gulp down another swallow. Her eyes watered and color flooded her cheeks. "We had the place closed in, surrounded the house, cordoned off the area in a three-block radius. They couldn't have gotten through. They had no place to run."

She needed to talk through it. Jonah set the brandy aside. "But they ran anyway."

"We were just about to move in, and he—Fricks—came out the back, already firing. He hit Dietz with two rounds. Some of us went around the back, covering both sides. Some of us went in the front. I was first in, Hickman was behind me. We spread out, started the sweep."

She could still see it in her head. Moving through, fast and steady, the lights blazing.

"I could hear more gunfire, and shouting from outside. I nearly turned back, thinking they were both out of the house and running—that they were together. But I saw—there's this bump-out sunroom deal on the house, and the sliding door leading out wasn't closed, not all the way closed. I spotted her as soon as I stepped out. Going in the opposite direction as her partner. Splitting us up, I guess. I called out, told her to stop. I was in pursuit and she fired a round. Sloppy shot. I ordered her to stop, to drop her weapon. I didn't see she had a choice. Where the hell could she go? But she spun around.

"She spun around," Ally repeated. "The moon was very bright, very bright and it was on her face, in her eyes, shining on the gun. And I shot her."

"Did you have a choice?"

Her lips trembled open. "No. In my head that's clear. Jonah, that's so clear. I've gone over it, step after step, a dozen times already. But they don't prepare you for what it's like. They can't. They can't tell you how it feels."

The first tear spilled over and she wiped it impatiently away. "I don't even know what I'm crying for. Or who."

"It doesn't matter." He put his arms around her, drew her head down on his shoulder and held her while she wept.

And while she wept he went back over what she'd told him.

Sloppy shot, she'd said, almost skimming over the fact that someone had tried to kill her. Yet she wept because she'd had no choice but to take a life.

Cops. He turned his cheek against her hair. He'd never understand cops.

She slept for two hours, dropping into oblivion like a stone in a pool, and staying deep at the bottom. When she woke, she was wrapped around him in the dark.

She lay still a moment, orienting herself, while his heart beat strong and steady under her palm. With her eyes open and her mind clearing she went through a mental checklist. She had a vague headache, but nothing major—just a hangover from the crying jag. There was a stronger feeling of embarrassment, but she thought she could live with that, too.

She wiggled her toes and discovered she was barefoot. And her ankle holster was gone.

So, she realized, was her shoulder harness.

He'd disarmed her, she thought, in more ways than one. She'd blubbered out her story, cried on his shoulder and was now wrapped around him in the dark. Worse than all of that was realizing she wanted to stay there.

Believing him asleep she started to inch away.

"Feel any better?"

She didn't jolt, but it was close. "Yeah. Considerably. I guess I owe you."

"I guess you do."

In the dark he found her mouth with his and sank in.

Soft, unexpectedly soft. Warm, deliciously warm. Yes, she wanted to stay there, and so she opened for him, sliding her hand from his heart to his face, yielding when he turned his body to press hers into the mattress.

The good solid weight of him, the hard lines of his body, the drugging heat of his mouth was exactly what she wanted. Her arms came around him, holding him there as he had held her in tears and in sleep.

He gave himself the moment, the dark taste of her mouth, the sleepy sigh she made, the feminine give of her beneath him. He'd lain beside her, his body alert, his mind restless while hers slept. Wanting her, wanting her so it was like a fever in the blood.

Yet when she woke, he found himself drowning in tenderness.

Yet when she surrendered, he found himself unwilling, unable, to take.

He drew back, skimmed a thumb over the curve of her cheek. "Bad timing," he said and rolled off the bed.

"I..." She cleared her throat. Her body had just started to ache, her mind had just started to float. Now she floundered free. "Look, if you have some weird idea that you were taking advantage, you're wrong."

"Am I?"

"I know how to say yes or no. And while I appreciate you bringing me home, hearing me out and not leaving me alone, I'm not grateful enough for any of that to pay you back with sex. I think too much of myself. Hell, I think too much of sex."

He laughed, sat on the edge of the bed again. "You do feel better."

"I said I did. So." She slid over, tossing her hair back and nuzzling his throat.

His pulse tripped and a fireball burst in his belly. "That's tempting." He was lucky to be able to breathe, and still casually patted her hand and got to his feet. "But no thanks."

Insult came first, and something vile nearly spilled off her tongue. Because it made her think of Dennis, she yanked herself back. "Okay. Mind if I ask why? Under the current circumstances, that seems like a reasonable question."

"Two reasons."

He switched on the bedside light, watched her eyes narrow in defense. And the look of her slammed into him like a fist in the throat.

"God. You're beautiful."

A little thrill jumped up her spine. "And that's why you don't want to make love with me?"

"I want you. Enough that it's starting to hurt. That ticks me off."

Idly he took the ends of her hair, wrapped a length of it around his hand, released it. "You're on my mind, Ally, too often for comfort. I like to be comfortable. So reason one is that I haven't decided if I want to get tangled up with you. If I do half of the very interesting things I have in mind to do with you, I'm going to be tangled."

She sat back on her heels. "I imagine you know how to cut line when you want to."

"I've never had any trouble before. You're trouble. It's that simple."

Insult and annoyance had vanished. "This is fascinating. Here I had you pegged as somebody who took what he wanted when he wanted it, and the hell with the consequences."

"No. I prefer calculating, then eliminating consequences. Then I take what I want."

"In other words, I make you nervous."

"Oh, yeah. Go ahead and grin," he said with a nod. "I can't blame you."

She laughed, lifted her eyebrows. "You said there were two reasons. What's the second?"

"That's easy." He stepped to the bed, bent down and caught her chin in his hand. "I don't like cops," he said, and brushed his lips lightly over hers.

When he would have leaned away from the kiss, she leaned in, sliding up so that her body rubbed over his.

She felt his body quiver, and nothing had ever been more satisfying.

"Yeah, you're trouble," he muttered. "I'm leaving."

"Coward."

"Okay, that stings, but I'll get over it." He walked over to shrug on the jacket he'd tossed onto a chair, slip his feet back into his shoes.

She didn't just feel better, Ally realized. She felt fabulous. Invincible. "Why don't you come on back here and fight like a man."

He glanced at her. She knelt on the side of the bed, her eyes dark and challenging, her hair a tumble of gold around her face and shoulders.

The taste of her was still sizzling on his tongue.

But he shook his head, walked to the door. Tormented himself with one last look. "I'm going to hate both of us in the morning," he told her, then strode away while her laughter followed him.

Chapter 7

Ally was up at six and ready to roll out the door at seven. She nearly rolled right over her parents, who were at her front door.

"Mom." She flicked her eyes up to her father, started to speak, but her mother already had her caught in a hard hug. "Mom," she said again. "I'm all right."

"Indulge me." Cilla held on, tight, heart pressed to heart, cheek pressed to cheek.

Stupid, Cilla thought, so stupid to have kept it together all night and to feel herself falling apart now that her child was in her arms.

She couldn't, wouldn't allow it.

"Okay." She laid her lips on Ally's temple for a moment, then drew back far enough to study her daughter's face.

"I had to see for myself. You're lucky your father held me off this long."

"I didn't want you to worry."

"It's my job to worry. And I believe in doing a job well."

Ally watched her mother's lips curve, saw the tears willed away. And knew it cost her. "You do everything well."

Cilla O'Roarke Fletcher's eyes were the same golden-brown as her daughter's, her short sweep of hair a luxuriant black that suited her angular features and smoky voice.

"But I've got worry down to a science," she said.

Since they were almost of identical heights, Ally had only to shift closer to kiss Cilla's cheek. "Well, you can take a break. I'm fine. Really."

"I suppose you look it."

"Come on inside. I can make some more coffee."

"No, you're on your way out. I just needed to see you." To touch you, Cilla thought. My baby. "I'm heading into work. I'm interviewing a new sales manager at KHIP. Your dad's dropping me off. You can use my car today."

"How did you know I needed a car?"

"I have connections," Boyd told her. "You should have yours back by midafternoon."

"I would've handled it." Ally shut the door behind her, frowned.

"Meaning you would have handled the car, and Overton and the tangle of bureaucracy," Cilla put in. "I hope I didn't raise a daughter who's ungrateful, and who expects her father to stand back with his hands in his pockets when something happens to her." Cilla tilted her head, lifted her brows. "I'd be very disappointed if I had."

Boyd grinned, slipped an arm around Cilla's shoulders and pressed his lips to her hair.

"Good one," Ally muttered, properly chastised. "Thank you, Dad."

"You're welcome, Allison."

"Now, which one of us is going to go beat the tar out of Dennis Overton?" Cilla rubbed her hands together. "Or can we all do it? In which case, I get to go first."

"She has violent tendencies," Ally pointed out.

"Tell me about it. Down, girl," he told Cilla. "Let the system work. Now… Detective." Boyd draped his arm around his daughter's shoulders as they walked to the elevator. "You're to report to the hospital first. There's a suspect who needs to be questioned."

"The inquiry into the shooting?"

"Will proceed this morning. You'll need to give your statement and file your report. By ten hundred. Detective Hickman filed his last night, which gives a very clear picture. You don't have anything to worry about."

"I'm not worried. I know I did what I had to do. It gave me some bad moments last night." She blew out a breath. "Some pretty bad ones. But I'm okay with it now. As okay as it gets, I guess."

"You shouldn't have been alone last night," Cilla said.

"Actually I had…a friend with me for a while."

Boyd opened his mouth, shut it again. After Ally's call the night before, he'd contacted Kiniki immediately. He knew that Jonah had driven Ally home from the hospital, so he had a good idea just who the friend was.

But he had no idea how he felt about it.

Ally pulled into the hospital visitors' lot, circled until she found a space. She spotted Hickman as she set the locks and alarm.

"Nice ride," he commented, hands in pockets, eyes squinted into slits against the brilliant sunshine. "Not every cop's got herself a Mercedes as a backup vehicle."

"It's my mother's."

"You've got some mother." He'd seen Cilla, so he knew it was true. "So, how's it going?"

"Okay." She fell into step beside him. "Look, I know you already filed your report on last night's incident. I appreciate you getting it in so fast and backing me up."

"It happened the way it happened. If it smooths any edges for you, you should know that you fired about a split hair before I did. If I'd been in the lead instead of you, I'd've been the one to take her out."

"Thanks. Any word on Dietz?"

"Still critical." Hickman's expression darkened. "He made it through the night, so that's hopeful. I want a round with the son of a bitch who put him here."

"Get in line."

"You know how you want to play it?"

"I've been thinking about it." They moved together across the lobby to the bank of elevators. "She made a call from her cell phone—that puts at least one other person in on the deal. I say two. Whoever's inside the club, and somebody pushing the buttons, organizing. Our guy here shot a cop, so he knows he's going down hard. His wife's dead, his operation's broken and he's looking at death row."

"Doesn't give him much incentive to talk. You going to deal him a life sentence?"

"That's the road. Let's make sure he walks it."

She showed her badge to the uniform on guard at Fricks's door, walked through.

Fricks lay in bed, his skin pale, slightly gray. His

eyes were blurred, but open. His gaze passed over Ally and Hickman, then returned to contemplate the ceiling.

"I have nothing to say. I want a lawyer."

"Well, that makes our job easier." Hickman walked over to the bed, pursed his lips. "Doesn't look like a cop killer, does he, Fletcher?"

"He's not. Yet. Dietz might make it. Of course, this guy here's still looking at being strapped to a table and being put down like a sick dog. Nighttime B and E, burglary, possession of an unregistered weapon, assault with a deadly, attempted murder of a police officer." She moved her shoulders. "And plenty more where that came from."

"I have nothing to say."

"Then shut up," she suggested. "Why try to help yourself? Trust a lawyer to take care of everything. But… I'm not in the mood to make deals with lawyers. How about you, Hickman?"

"Nope, can't say that's my mood at this time."

"We're not in the mood," Ally repeated. "Not when we have a fellow officer fighting for his life up in Intensive Care. That really puts us off lawyers who look for ways to wiggle cop killers out of the noose. Right, Hickman?"

"Yeah, puts me right off. I don't see any reason we should give this guy any kind of a break. I say let him hang for it all by himself."

"Well, we ought to look at the big picture, though. Show a little compassion. He lost his wife last night." She watched the ripple of pain run over Fricks's face before he closed his eyes.

There, she thought, was the key to him.

"That's rough. His wife's dead, and he's lying here

shot up and looking at a death sentence." Ally lifted her shoulders, let them fall. "Maybe he's not thinking how other people, people who helped put him in this situation could walk away clean. Clean, and rich, while he's twisting in the wind on a very short rope. And his wife gets put in the ground."

She leaned over the bed. "But he ought to be thinking about it. Of course maybe he didn't love his wife."

"Don't talk to me about Madeline." His voice wavered. "She was my heart."

"Really. I'm touched. That touches me. Now that might not hold any weight with Hickman here, but me, I've got a soft spot for true love. Since I do, I'm going to tell you you ought to be thinking how you can help yourself now, because if you were her heart, she wouldn't want you to go down for this alone."

His eyes flickered, then closed.

"You ought to be thinking that if you cooperate and tell us what we want to know, we'll go to the D.A. and press for a little leniency. Show some remorse now, Richard, reach out. That'll go a long way toward keeping you off a table in a little room a few years down the road."

"I talk, I'm already dead."

Ally shot Hickman a glance. "You'll get protection."

Fricks's eyes were still closed, but tears began to leak out of them. "I loved my wife."

"I know you did." Ally lowered the bed guard so she could sit beside him.

Intimacy now, she thought. Sympathy. And infused her voice with both. "I saw you together at Blackhawk's. The way you looked at each other tells me you had something special between you."

"She—she's gone."

"But you tried to save her, didn't you, Richard? You ran out of the house first, to cover for her. That's why you're in this jam. She loved you. She'd want you to help yourself. She'd want you to go on living, to do whatever you had to do to go on. Richard, you tried to save her last night, drawing the cops off her so she could get away. You did what you could. Now you've got to save yourself."

"No one was supposed to get hurt. The guns were just a precaution, to scare anybody off if something went wrong."

"That's right. You didn't plan on this. I believe that. That'll make a difference how this all comes out for you. Things just got out of control."

"Nothing ever went wrong before. She panicked. That's all. She just panicked, and I couldn't think of anything else to do."

"You didn't mean to hurt anybody." Ally kept her voice quiet, compassionate, even while the image of Dietz, bleeding on the ground, ran through her mind. "You just wanted to give her time to get away." She took a moment while he wept.

"How'd you get past the alarm systems?"

"I've got a knack for electronics." He took the tissues she handed him, wiped his eyes. "I worked in security. People don't always remember to set their alarms anyway. But when they did, I could usually disarm them. If I couldn't, it was a wash and we walked away. Where have they put Madeline? Where is she?"

"We'll talk about that. Help me out here, and I'll do what I can to arrange for you to see her. Who called you from the club, Richard, to tell you something was wrong with the Barneses? Was it the same person Madeline called from the car?"

He let out a sobbing breath, shook his head. "I want immunity."

Hickman let out a snort, made a move to draw Ally off the bed, make her the protector. "The son of a bitch wants immunity. You're bending over backward to help him out, and he wants a walk. Screw him. Let him hang."

"Hold on. Just hold on. Can't you see the man's upset? Lying here like this, he can't even make arrangements for his wife's funeral."

"She—" Fricks turned his head away, and his chest heaved once. "She wanted to be cremated. It was important to her."

"We can help you arrange that. We can help you give her what she wanted. You have to give us something back."

"Immunity."

"Listen, Richard. You can't ask for the moon and stars on this one. Now I could make you promises, but I'm being straight with you. Best I can do is leniency."

"We don't need him, Ally." Hickman picked up the chart at the foot of the bed, scanned it. "We got him cold, and we'll pick up the rest of the pieces within a couple of days."

"He's right." Ally let out a sigh, looked back at Fricks. "A couple of days, maybe less, we'll have all the answers. But if you save us some time, some trouble, prove you're remorseful over shooting that cop, I can promise to go to bat for you. We know there are other people involved. It's just a matter of time before we get to them. Help me out, I'll help you. I'll help you do what you need to do for Madeline. That's fair."

"It was her brother." He said it between his teeth, then opened his eyes. They were no longer blurry, no longer wet, but burning dry with hate. "He talked her into it. He could talk her into anything. It was going to be an adventure, exciting. He set it up, all of it. He's the reason she's dead."

"Where is he?"

"He has a house down in Littleton. Big house on the lake. His name's Matthew Lyle, and he'll be coming after me for what happened to Madeline. He's crazy. I tell you he's crazy, and he's obsessed with her. He'll kill me."

"Okay, don't worry. He won't get near you." Ally took out her notebook. "Tell me more about Matthew Lyle."

At four that afternoon, Jonah was settled behind his desk, trying to work. He was furious with himself for calling Ally three times, twice at home, once at the station. And equally furious she'd made no attempt to get back to him.

He'd decided he'd made a very big mistake by walking out of her apartment instead of staying with her in the dark, in the bed, instead of taking what he wanted.

It was a mistake he'd have to live with, and he was certain he could live with it more comfortably than live with the options.

All he wanted now was the simple courtesy of information. Damn it, she owed him that. He'd let her into his life, into his business, let her work side by side with his friends while she deceived them. While he deceived them.

Now, by God, he wanted answers.

He snatched the phone up again just as the elevator doors slid open. And Ally walked through.

"I still had your code."

Saying nothing, he replaced the receiver. She was dressed for work, he noted. Cop work. "I'll make a note to have it changed."

Her eyebrows rose but she continued across the room and dropped comfortably into the chair across from his desk. "I figured you'd want an update."

"You figured correctly."

Something was in his craw, she noted. They'd get to that later. "Fricks rolled over on his brother-in-law. Matthew Lyle, aka Lyle Matthews, aka Lyle Delaney. Computer crimes mostly, with some assaults. He's got a long sheet, but most of the charges were dumped. Insufficient evidence, deals. Did some psych time, though. He's cleared out. We hit his place a couple of hours ago, and he's gone."

She paused long enough to rub her eyes. "Didn't have time to take everything with him. The house was packed with stolen goods. From what it looks like they've turned very little, if anything. Place looked like an auction house. Oh, and you're going to be short a waitress tonight."

"I didn't think you'd be reporting for work tonight."

"No, I didn't mean me. Jan. According to Fricks, she and Lyle are..." She lifted a hand, crossed two fingers. "Very close. She's the inside man. Scanned for the marks, passed the credit card number to Lyle via beeper. The Fricks move in, she helps cover for them while they lift the keys. Then she alerts them with another code when the targets call for their check. Gives the Fricks time to finish up, clear out. Very smooth all in all."

"Have you got her?"

"No, doesn't look like she went home last night. My guess is she went straight to Lyle, and they went under together. We will get her. We'll get them both."

"I don't doubt it. I suppose that ends your association with Blackhawk's."

"Looks like." She rose, wandered to the window. He had the blinds shut today, so she tapped a slat up, looked out. "I'll need to interview your people. I thought they'd feel more comfortable if I did it here. Do you have any problem with me using your office for it?"

"No."

"Great. I'll start with you. Get it out of the way." She came back to sit, took out her notepad. "Tell me what you know about Jan."

"She's worked here about a year. She was good at her job, a favorite with a number of the regulars. Had a knack for remembering names. She was reliable and efficient."

"Did you have a personal relationship with her?"

"No."

"But you're aware she lives in the same apartment building as Frannie?"

"Is that against the law?"

"How did you come to hire her?"

"She applied for the job. Frannie has nothing to do with this."

"I didn't say she did." Ally took a photo out of her bag. "Have you ever seen this man in here?"

Jonah glanced at the police photo of a dark-haired man of about thirty. "No."

"See him anywhere else?"

"No. Is this Lyle?"

"That's right. Why are you angry with me?"

"Irritated," he corrected coolly. "I'd classify it as irritated. I don't care to be interrogated by the police."

"I'm a cop, Jonah. That's a fact." She put the photo back into her bag. "I've got a job to finish. That's another fact. And I'm hung up on you, there's fact number three. Now maybe all of that irritates you, but that's the way it is. I'd like to start the interviews now."

He got to his feet as she did. "You're right. It all irritates me."

"There you go. I'd appreciate it if you'd send Will up now. And stay downstairs. I might need to speak with you again."

He came around the desk. Her eyes narrowed, flashed a cold warning as he approached her. They stayed level and cool when he gripped the lapels of her jacket and hauled her to her toes.

A dozen desires, all of them impossible, ran through his mind. "You push too many of my buttons," he muttered, and releasing her, walked away.

"Same goes." But she said it quietly, after he'd gone.

"So…" Frannie lit a cigarette, peered at Ally through the haze of smoke. "You're a cop. I might've figured it if Jonah hadn't been with you. He doesn't like cops any more than I do."

Frannie had put on an attitude, Ally noted, and nodded. "Now, there's breaking news. Listen, let's make this as painless as possible for everyone. You've got the rundown on the burglary ring, how the club was used, Jan's part in it."

"I've got what you've decided to tell me now that you're wearing your badge."

"That's right. And that's all you need. How long have you known her?"

"About a year and a half, I guess. I ran into her in the laundry room of my apartment building. She was waiting tables in a bar. I worked in a bar." Frannie lifted her shoulders. "We hung out together now and again. I liked her well enough. When Jonah opened this place, I helped get her a job. Does that make me an accessory?"

"No, it makes you a jerk for copping an attitude with me. She ever mention a boyfriend?"

"She liked men, and men liked her."

"Frannie." Ally shifted, decided to play another angle. "Maybe you don't like cops, but there's one on the critical list right now, and he's a friend of mine. They're still not sure he'll make it. He's got two kids and a wife who loves him. Another woman's dead. Somebody loved her, too. You want to go a round with me on personal business, fine. Let's just get this done first."

Frannie made a little shrugging movement again. "She talked about this one guy sometimes. Never told me his name. Liked to be mysterious about it. But she said things like pretty soon she wouldn't be hauling trays and bagging tips."

She got up, crossed over to open the panel to the bar in a way that told Ally she was very at home in Jonah's space. She pulled out a soft drink, twisted off the cap. "I figured it was talk. She liked to talk big about men. Conquests, you know?"

"Did you ever see her with this guy?" Ally nudged the photo across the desk.

Sipping from the bottle, Frannie walked back, studied the photo. "Maybe. Yeah." Frannie scratched her jaw. "I saw them come into the building together a couple of times. Didn't seem like her type is what I thought. He's kinda short, a little pudgy. Ordinary. Jan, she went more for flash. Studs with platinum cards was her usual type."

Catching herself, Frannie shook her head, dropped into a chair. "That sounds hard. I liked her. Look, she's young, maybe a little foolish. But she's not mean."

"You might want to keep in mind that she used you, Jonah, and this place. Now, did she ever mention anyplace they went together? Any plans?"

"No…well, she might've said something about a place on a lake. I didn't pay much attention when she started bragging. Most of it was just air."

Ally questioned her for another fifteen minutes, but didn't jiggle anything loose.

"Okay. If you think of anything, I'd appreciate a call." Rising, Ally offered Frannie a card.

"Sure." Frannie skimmed her eyes over it. "Detective Fletcher."

"Would you ask Beth to come up, please?"

"Why the hell don't you leave her alone? She doesn't know anything."

"But I have such a good time intimidating and threatening potential witnesses." She came around the desk, sat on the corner. "Okay, there's the bell. Go ahead with your personal round."

"I don't like the way you came in here, the way you used us and spied on us. I know how it works. You did a background check on everybody, pried into all our lives and sat in judgment. I guess you're sorry it turned out to be Jan instead of the former hooker."

"You're wrong. I like you."

Off balance, Frannie sat again. "Bull."

"Why shouldn't I like you? You got yourself out of a spiral that only goes down. You've got a legitimate job, and you're good at it. The only problem I have with you is Jonah."

"What do you mean, Jonah?"

"You've got a relationship with him. I'm attracted to him. That makes you a personal problem for me."

Baffled now, Frannie took out another cigarette. "I don't get you. You mean it about Jonah?" she said after a minute. "You've got a thing for him?"

"It looks like. But the problem's mine. Like I said, I like you. In fact, I admire the way you turned your life around. I never had to do that, never had to face those kinds of things, make those kind of choices. I'd like to think I'd do as well as you have if I had."

"Damn it." Frannie pushed to her feet, paced the room. "Damn it," she repeated. "Okay, first. I don't have a relationship with Jonah. Not like you mean. Never did. He never bought me when I was for sale, and he never touched me that way when I was free. Even when I offered."

Though a fine sense of relief ran through her, Ally kept her voice mild. "Is he blind or stupid?"

Frannie stopped pacing, took a long, hard look. "I don't want to like you. You're sure making it tough not to. I love him. A long time ago, I loved him…different than I do now. We grew up together, more or less. I mean we've known each other since we were kids. Me and Jonah and Will, we go back."

"I know. It shows."

"When I was working corners, Jonah'd come by

sometimes, pay me for the night. Then he'd take me for coffee or something to eat. And that was it." Frannie's eyes softened. "He always was a sucker."

"Are we talking about the same man?"

"If he cares about you, that's it. He'll keep pulling you up no matter how many times you fall down again. Bite his hand, he'll just ignore you and haul you up. You can't fight that. You can't fight that kind of thing for long. I didn't make it easy for him."

With a sigh, she walked over to sit again, picked up the soft drink, finished it off. "A few years ago, I was scraping the bottom of the gutter. I'd been on the stroll since I was fifteen. By the time I hit twenty I was used up. So I figured what the hell, let's just get out of this whole mess. I started to slash my wrists. Seemed just dramatic enough."

She held out a hand, turned it over to expose the scar on the inside of her left wrist. "Only got to the one, and didn't do such a hot job on it."

"What stopped you?"

"First? The blood. Really put me off the idea," she said with a surprisingly cheerful laugh. "Anyway, I'm standing there in this filthy bathroom, stoned, bleeding, and I got scared. Really scared. I called Jonah. I don't know what would've happened if I hadn't reached him, if he hadn't come. He got me to the hospital, then he got me into detox."

She sat back, tracing a finger over the scar as if it brought the memory back with more clarity. "Then he asked me something he'd asked me a hundred times before. He asked me if I wanted a life. This time I said yes. Then he helped me make one.

"Along the way, I thought I should pay him back, and I offered what I was used to offering men. It was the only time he ever really got pissed off." She smiled a little. "He thought more of me than I did of myself. Nobody else ever had. If I knew anything about Jan, or this business, I'd tell you. Because he'd want me to, and there's nothing I wouldn't do for him."

"From where I'm standing, you both got a good deal."

"I've never once had a man look at me the way I've seen him look at you."

"Then you've got your eyes shut." It was Ally's turn to smile. "Keep them open tonight when Will asks for his after-closing brandy."

"Will? Come on."

"Keep your eyes open," Ally said again. "Are we square here?"

"Yeah, sure. I guess." Confused, Frannie got to her feet again.

"Ask Beth to come up. Just give me five minutes to find my brass knuckles."

With a half laugh, Frannie went to the elevator. After pushing the button, she glanced back. "Will knows what I was."

"I guess he knows what you are, too."

She wrapped up the last interview by seven, circled her shoulders and wondered if there was a possibility of food anytime in her near future.

The clock told her she was officially off duty, and since she had nothing to add to the current status of the case, her reports and follow-ups could wait till morning.

Still, she helped herself to the use of Jonah's phone,

checking in, giving updates. She was sitting quietly at his desk when he came in.

"Dietz. The cop who was shot last night. They've upgraded his condition from critical to serious." Closing her eyes, she pressed her fingers against them. "It looks like he's going to make it."

"I'm glad to hear it."

"Yeah." She pulled the clip out of her hair, ran her fingers through it. "It sure fills this big hole in my gut. I appreciate the use of your office. I can tell you that the rest of your people aren't suspects, at this time."

"At this time."

"I can't give you more than that, Blackhawk. All evidence points to the fact that Jan and Jan alone worked the inside. It's the best I can do."

She tossed the clip on his desk. "Now, I've got something else to say."

"Which is?"

"I'm off duty. Can I have a drink?"

"I happen to have a club just downstairs."

"I was thinking of a private drink. From your private bar." She gestured toward the panel. "If you could spare a glass of wine. I noticed a nice sauvignon blanc in there."

He turned toward the panel, opened it, selected the bottle.

"Why don't you join me?"

"I'm still on duty. I don't drink during working hours."

"I noticed that. Don't drink, don't smoke, don't hit on the customers. During working hours," she added.

He turned back, the glass of pale gold wine in his hand. And watched her take off her jacket.

"I hope you don't mind," she said, then shrugged out

of her holster. "I find it awkward to seduce men when I'm wearing my weapon."

She laid it on his desk, then walked toward him.

Chapter 8

She might have taken off her gun, Jonah thought, but she wasn't unarmed. A woman with eyes as potent as whiskey and a voice like smoke would never be without a weapon.

Worse, she knew it. That longbow mouth was curved up, just a little, like a cat's when the canary cage was open. He didn't much care for his role as target.

"Your wine." He held out the glass, a deliberate move to keep an arm-span of distance between them. "And though I appreciate the thought, I don't have time for a seduction at the moment."

"Oh, it shouldn't take very long."

She imagined he'd devastated countless women with that careless, almost absent dismissal. For her, it was only a challenge she had every confidence of meeting.

She took the wine, and moved right in, grabbing a

fistful of his shirt to hold him in place. "I really like the look of you, Blackhawk. Hot mouth, cool eyes." She took a sip of wine, watching him over the rim. "I want to see more."

His senses went blade sharp. The muscles of his belly tied themselves into a dozen hard and tangled knots. "You get right to it, don't you?"

"You said you were in a hurry." She rose on her toes to nip her teeth into his bottom lip, and sliced a jagged line of need straight through him. "So I'm picking up the pace."

"I don't like sexually aggressive women."

Her laugh was low, mocking. "You don't like cops, either."

"That's exactly right."

"Then this is going to be very unpleasant for you. That's a shame." She leaned in, skimmed her tongue up the side of his neck. "I want you to touch me. I want you to put your hands on me."

He kept them at his sides, but in his mind they were already ripping at her shirt, already taking. "Like I said, it's a nice offer, but—"

"I can feel your heart pounding." She shook her hair back, and the scent of it slithered into his system. "I can feel the way you want me, the same way I want you."

"Some of us learn to shelve certain wants."

She saw the change in his eyes, the faintest deepening of green. Dead giveaway, she thought. "And some of us don't." She took another sip of wine, then moved forward, walking him backward. "I guess I'm going to have to get rough."

Mortified she'd put him in retreat, he stopped short, nearly groaning when her body bumped his. "You're going to embarrass yourself. Drink your wine, Detective Fletcher, and go home."

She imagined he thought his voice was clipped, dismissive. But it was thick and strained. And his heart was a fury under her fist.

"What is that answer you're always giving me? No. Yes, that's it." She drained her glass so the wine pumped in with the reckless power surging through her. "No," she said again and, tossing the glass aside, hooked a hand in the waistband of his trousers.

Aroused and furious, he retreated again. "Cut it out."

"Make me." She threw her head back, then leaped, arms wrapping around his neck, legs vised around his waist. "Come on and make me. You've got plenty of moves."

Her mouth swooped down to tease his, and she tasted a wild, wonderful mix of desire and temper. "Take me down," she whispered, raking her hands through his hair. "Finish it. Finish me."

His blood was raging. The taste of her, hot and female with the faint zip of wine, was on his tongue. "You're asking for trouble."

"So..." She rubbed her lips over his, as if imprinting her flavor on him. "Give it to me."

Control snapped. He could hear it echo in his head like the violent crack of hammer against stone. He gripped her hair, wrapping it around his hand, yanking it back so that she let out a little gasp as her head flew back.

"The line's crossed." His eyes weren't cool now. They simmered, as if a bolt of lightning had struck a pool. "You'll give me everything I want. What you don't give, I'll take. That's the deal."

Her breath was already quickened. "Done."

His gaze lowered to the long, vulnerable curve of her throat. Then he set his teeth on her.

Her body jerked against his as the shock of that threat of pain, that lance of pleasure stabbed into her. Then she was falling, clinging to him as she tumbled into the shadows, into the dark.

She lost her breath when she hit the bed, lost her grip when his body covered hers. Then, for a moment, when he tore her shirt open, she lost her mind.

Floundering for balance, she threw an arm up. Her knuckles thudded against the bedspread, then her fingers dug in. "Wait."

"No."

His mouth was on her breast, ravaging tender flesh with lips and teeth and tongue. She fought for air, fought to find the power that had been hers just moments before. Instead she found herself spinning past control, past reason.

His hands were on her, as she had demanded. And they were hard and fast, ruthlessly exploiting weakness, secrets she hadn't known she'd possessed.

Then his mouth came back to hers, hot and greedy. The low sound in her throat was equal parts terror and triumph. Leaping recklessly toward the heat, she met demand with demand.

She went wild beneath him. Writhing, bucking, reaching. He'd wanted nothing less. If he was to sin, he would sin fully, and reap all the pleasure before the punishment.

Her skin seemed to burn under his hands, his mouth. He craved. The long, clean lines of her. The taut and ready strength. The delicate give of curves.

He rolled with her over the wide pool of the bed, taking what and how he wanted.

She tugged at his shirt, sending buttons flying, then letting out a sound of feral delight when flesh met flesh. When he dragged her to her knees, she trembled. But there was nothing of fear left in her.

She could see his eyes, the predatory gleam of them, from the backwash of light from the office. She let out a ragged breath as she ran her hands up his chest, into his hair.

"More," she told him, and crushed her mouth to his.

And there was more.

Lightning quick flashes of unbearable ecstasy. Gusts of shuddering desperation. And a flood of needs that swamped them both.

He tugged the slacks down her hips, following the path of exposed flesh with his mouth until she was shuddering and mindlessly murmuring his name in that hoarse, erotic voice he couldn't get out of head.

His teeth scraped her inner thigh, sent the strong muscles quivering. When she arched, opened, he feasted on her.

She cried out as the orgasm ripped through her, fisted her hands in the bedclothes and let each glorious aftershock batter her until her system wept with the pleasure of it. Heat swarmed up her body, through her, and she embraced it, reveled in the breathless power of what they made together.

"Now. Jonah."

"No."

He couldn't get enough of her. Each time he thought desperation would overpower him, he found something new to tantalize him. The subtle flare of her hips, the narrow dip of her waist. He wanted to feel the bite of her nails on him again, hear that choked cry of release when he dragged her over the next edge.

Her breath was sobbing, his own so clogged in his lungs he thought they would burst from it. He moved up her again while her hands raced over him and her body bucked.

He could see her eyes, and nothing else. Just the dark glint of them, watching him as he rose over her. He held back for one quivering instant, then plunged.

Here was everything. The thought stabbed through him then shattered in his brain as she closed hot and tight around him.

She rose to him, fell with him, the slick slide of bodies mating. Sighed with him as pleasure shimmered. Her heart thundered against his, beat for beat. Their breath mixed, drawing him deeper so that his mouth was on hers, another link, as they moved together.

The tempo quickened so that the slide became a slap, and sighs broke into gasps and moans. Her hips pistoned as he pounded into her. As sensations staggered her, she raked her nails down his back, dug them into his hips. Urging him on even as she was swamped by the next crest.

He felt himself slip—a glorious feeling of surrender—and with his face buried in the tumbled mass of her hair, he fell.

It was over for him. He knew it the minute his system leveled and his mind began to work again. He'd never get over her. Never get past her. With one sweep, she'd destroyed a lifetime of careful avoidance.

Now he was stupidly, helplessly, irretrievably in love with her.

Nothing could be more impossible or more dangerous.

She could slice him to pieces. No one had ever been allowed to have that kind of control or power over him. He didn't mean to let that change now.

He needed some sort of defense, and determined to start building it, he rolled away from her.

She simply rolled with him, stretched that long, limber body of hers over his and said, "Mmmmm."

Another time he might have laughed, or at least felt that knee-jerk of pure male satisfaction. Instead he felt a light trip of panic.

"Well, you got what you wanted, Fletcher."

Instead of being insulted, which would have given him a little room to regroup, she just nuzzled his neck. "Damn right."

To please herself she hooked a leg around him, then shifted to straddle him and slick back her hair. "I like your body, Blackhawk. All tough and rangy and taut." She trailed a finger over his chest, admiring the contrast of her skin against his. "It looks good on you."

He twirled a lock of her hair around his finger. "Yours too," he said dryly.

She leaned down until they were nose to nose. "Now that we're all cozy and complimentary, how about doing me a favor?"

"And that would be?"

"Food. I'm starving."

"Want a menu?"

"No. Umm." She tilted her head, teased his mouth with hers. "Just something that's on it. Maybe you could send down for something." She trailed her lips down to his jaw, back up to his mouth. "And we could, you know, fuel up. Mind if I grab a shower?"

"No." He rolled her onto her back. "But you'll have to wait until I'm done with you."

"Oh?" She smiled. "Well, a deal's a deal."

And when he was done with her, she staggered more than walked into the bathroom. She closed the door, leaned back against it and let out a long puff of breath.

She'd never had to work harder to maintain a careless, sophisticated image. Then again, she'd never had anyone turn her inside out and leave her jittering like a mass of jelly before.

Not that she was complaining, Ally told herself as she rubbed the heel of her hand over her heart. But her idea that sex was simply a pleasant occupation between two consenting adults who, hopefully, cared about each other had been forever shattered.

Pleasant didn't begin to describe making love with Jonah Blackhawk.

Waiting for her system to level again, she scanned the bathroom. He'd indulged himself here, she noted, with the deep, why-don't-you-join-me whirlpool tub in his customary jet-black. Though it looked tempting, she thought she'd settle for the separate shower enclosed by seeded glass.

The sink was a wide scoop in a sheer black counter. Nothing stood on it, no pieces of him left out for the casual eye to study. Just as there were no pieces, no odds and ends, memorabilia or personal photographs in his office or bedroom.

She was tempted to poke in the cabinet, rifle through

a couple of the drawers—what kind of shaving cream did he use? What brand of toothpaste?—but it seemed so pitifully obvious.

Instead she crossed the white tiles and studied her own face in the mirror. Her eyes were soft, her mouth still swollen from that wonderful assault of his. There were a number of faint bruises shadowing her skin.

All in all, she decided she looked just the way she felt. Like a woman happily used.

But what did he see when he looked at her? she wondered. When he looked at her in that cool, distant way? He wanted her, she could have no doubts about that. But did he feel nothing else?

Did he think she hadn't noticed the way he'd drawn back from her both times, after passion had been spent? As if his need for…separation was as deep as his desire.

And why was she letting it hurt her? It was such a *female* reaction.

"Well, I am a female, damn it," she muttered and turned to switch on the shower.

If he thought he was going to get away with nudging her back whenever he pleased, he was very much mistaken. The man was not going to rock her to her toes then stroll away while she was still teetering.

She stuck her head under the spray, mumbling to herself.

She expected a lot more give-and-take in a relationship. And if he couldn't trouble himself to give her a little affection along with the heat, well then he could…

She trailed off, winced.

She sounded like Dennis, she thought. Or at least close enough.

At least she could stop that before she dug herself a hole too deep to crawl out of.

The only relationship she had with Jonah was a physical one, and she herself had insisted on it. Both of them knew the ground rules and were smart enough not to need them spelled out.

If she needed to mix emotion in with desire, that was fine. That was okay. But it was also her problem.

Satisfied she'd solved the matter in her own mind, she turned off the taps, turned for a towel.

And let out one wild yelp when she saw Jonah holding one out for her.

"Most people sing in the shower," he commented. "You're the first I've come across who talks to herself in the shower."

"I was not." She snatched the towel.

"Okay, it was more unintelligible mumbling."

"Fine. Most people knock before they come into an occupied bathroom."

"I did, but you couldn't hear me because you were talking to yourself. I thought you might want this." He held up his other hand, and the black silk robe that dangled from his fingers.

"Yeah. Thanks." She wrapped the towel around herself, anchored it with a hand between her breasts.

"Dinner'll be up in a minute." Idly he skimmed a fingertip down her arm, sliding water over flesh.

"Good. I need to get my weapon off your desk."

"I moved it." Frowning now, he traced the curve of her shoulder. "I put it in the bedroom. The door's closed. They'll just leave the tray on my desk."

"Works for me." When she felt the brush of his finger

over her collarbone, she released her hold on the towel, let it fall to her feet. "Is this what you're looking for?"

"I shouldn't want you again already." Eyes on hers, he backed her against the wall. "I shouldn't need you again."

"Then walk away." She tugged down the zipper on the trousers he'd pulled on. "Who's stopping you?"

He closed a hand around her throat. Though the pulse under his fingers jumped, she merely lifted her chin and dared him.

"Tell me you want me," he demanded. "Say my name, and that you want me."

"Jonah." She took the first step onto a bridge she knew could burn away under her feet. "I've never wanted anyone the way I want you." Her breath hitched as she drew it in, but her eyes remained steady. "Give it back to me."

"Allison." He lowered his forehead to hers, in a gesture so weary and sweet, she reached out to comfort him. "I can't think for wanting you. Just you," he murmured, then took her mouth, took her body. Desperately.

"I gotta say," Ally commented as she ate like a starving wolf, "you've got a really good kitchen. A lot of clubs, the food's mediocre at best. But yours, um..." She licked barbecue sauce from her thumb. "It's first-class."

She shook her head when he picked up the wine to top off her glass. "No, uh-uh. I'm driving."

"Stay." Another rule broken, he thought. He never asked a woman to stay.

"I would if I could." Smiling she tugged on the lapel of the borrowed robe. "But I don't have a change for tomorrow, and I'm back on eight-to-fours. As it is I'm going to have to borrow a shirt from you to get home. You did a number on mine."

He did no more than pick up his own glass, but she felt him retreat. "Ask me to come back tomorrow and stay."

He looked back at her. "Come back tomorrow and stay."

"Okay. Look at that! Look at that! That runner was safe."

"Out. By a half step," Jonah corrected, amused that she'd nearly come off the sofa when the play on the wide screen caught her eye.

"Bull. You watch the instant replay. They hit the bag at the same time. Tie goes to the runner. See? Manager's coming out. Give him hell. Anyway—"

Satisfied the requisite argument would proceed over a controversial call, she turned her attention back to Jonah. She smiled, rubbed her bare feet intimately against his hip. "Pretty good deal from my point of view. Good sex, good food and a ball game."

"To some..." He reached down to trace a finger up her instep. "Paradise."

"Since we're in paradise, can I ask you something really important?"

"All right."

"Are you going to eat all those fries?"

He grinned at her, shoved the plate in her direction, then leaned over to answer the phone. "Blackhawk. Yes." He held out the portable receiver. "For you, Detective."

"I left this number when I logged out," she told him, and took the phone. "Fletcher." She straightened on the sofa, and her eyes went flat. "Where? I'm on my way."

She was already on her feet when she tossed the receiver on the hook. "They found Jan."

"Where is she?"

"On her way to the morgue. I have to go."

"I'm going with you."

"There's no point in it."

"She worked for me," he said simply and walked into the bedroom.

Jonah had seen and done a great deal. In the first half of his life, he'd thought he'd seen and done everything. He'd seen death, but he'd never seen it stripped bare in cold, antiseptic surroundings.

He looked through the glass at the young woman and felt nothing but raw pity.

"I can verify ID," Ally said beside him. "But it's cleaner procedure if the visual comes from somebody else who knew her. Is that Janet Norton?"

"Yes."

She nodded to the technician behind the glass, and he lowered the blinds. "I don't know how long I'll be."

"I'll wait."

"There's coffee, down this corridor and to the left. It's crap, but it's usually hot and strong." She reached for the door, hesitated. "Listen, if you change your mind and want to go, just go."

"I'll wait," he said again.

It didn't take her long. When she came out he was sitting in one of the molded plastic chairs at the end of the hallway. Her footsteps clicked on the linoleum, and the clicks echoed.

"Nothing much to do until the autopsy report's in."

"How did she die?" When Ally shook her head he

got to his feet. "How? It can't be that big a dent in the rules to tell me."

"She was stabbed. Multiple wounds, by what appears to be a long bladed knife with a serrated edge. Her body was dumped on the side of the road off southbound 85, just a few miles outside of Denver. He threw her purse out with her. He wanted us to find her and ID her quickly."

"And that's it for you? Just identify her and put another piece in the puzzle?"

She didn't snap back. She recognized the chill in his eyes as temper on a short leash, and her own was straining.

"Let's get out of here." Ally headed out. She wanted to fill her lungs with fresh air. "From the number of wounds, it appears she was killed with considerable rage."

"Where's yours?" He shoved the door open. "Or don't you feel any?"

She strode out ahead of him. "Don't slap at me."

He grabbed her arm, whirled her around. She led with her fist and pulled it an inch from his jaw. "You want rage." She shoved away from him. "I'll give you some rage. From the looks of things she was getting sliced to pieces while I was rolling around on the sheets with you. Now ask how I feel?"

He caught her before she got to the car and wrenched the door open. "I'm sorry."

She tried to shrug him off, then push him away, but when she spun around snarling he just wrapped his arms around her.

"I'm sorry." He said it quietly, pressing his lips to her hair. "I was out of line. We both know it wouldn't have made any difference where we were or what we were doing. This would have happened."

"No, it wouldn't have made any difference. And still, two people are dead." She drew away. "I can't afford rage. Can you understand that?"

"Yes." He took the clip out of her hair, rubbed the back of her neck. "I'd like to go home with you. I'd like to be with you tonight."

"Good, because that's what I'd like, too."

She slid into the car, waiting for him to climb into the passenger seat. They both needed to set aside the rage, she knew, and the guilt. "I have to get up really early."

He smiled at her. "I don't."

"Okay." She pulled out of the lot. "That means you get to make up the bed and do the dishes. That's the deal."

"Does it also mean that you make the coffee?"

"It does."

"I'll take the deal."

When she reached her building, she pulled into the underground garage. "Tomorrow might be a long one," she told him. "Does it matter what time I get to your place?"

"No." He got out of the car, came around to her side, then held out his hand for her keys.

"So what, did you take like a charm-school course or something?"

"Top of my class. I have a plaque." He pressed the button for the elevator. "Now some women are insecure and find the simple courtesy of a man opening doors for them or pulling out their chair, whatever, troubling. Naturally you're secure enough in your own power and femininity not to be troubled."

"Naturally," she agreed, and rolled her eyes as he gestured her into the elevator. Then he took her hand and made her smile.

"I like your style, Blackhawk. I haven't been able to pin it down, not exactly, but I like it." She angled her head to study him. "You used to play baseball, right?"

"That and your father kept me in high school."

"Basketball was my game. You ever shoot hoops?"

"Now and then."

"Want to shoot some with me, on Sunday?"

"I might." He walked out of the elevator with her. "What time?"

"Oh, let's say two. I'll pick you up. We can go—" She broke off, shifting in front of him fast and pulling her weapon. "Keep back. Don't touch anything."

He saw it now. The fresh scrape and pry marks on the door. She used two fingers on the knob, turned it, then booted the door open with her foot. She went in low, slapping the lights on, starting her sweep even as Jonah stepped in front of her.

"Get back. What are you crazy?"

"One of the things I learned in charm school was not to use a woman as a shield."

"This woman happens to be the one with the badge, and the gun."

"I noticed. Besides." He'd already scanned the debris of the room. "He's long gone."

She knew it, felt it, but there were rules and procedure. "Well, pardon the hell out of me while I play cop and make sure. Don't touch anything," she said again, and stepping over a broken lamp, checked the rest of the apartment.

She was swearing in a low, steady voice as she headed for the phone.

"Your old friend Dennis?" Jonah asked.

"Maybe, but I don't think so. Lyle was heading south out of Denver." She jabbed her fingers into the keypad on the phone. "I think I just found out what he was doing here. This is Detective Fletcher. I've had a break-in."

Even before the crime scene unit arrived, Ally snapped on protective gloves and began to do inventory. Her stereo components, good ones, hadn't been stolen. But they had been smashed. Her laptop computer and the small TV that stood above the stereo had received the same treatment.

Every table lamp in the place—including the antique bookkeeper's light she'd bought for her desk—was broken. Her sofa had a long gash from end to end, and the guts of it spilled out in nasty puffs.

He'd poured the half gallon of paint she'd bought then had never gotten around to using, in the middle of her bed.

Over the bed, he'd slopped a message in the same paint.

Try To Sleep At Night

"He blames me for his sister's death. He knows I was the one. How does he know?"

"Jan," Jonah said from behind her. "She has to be the one who warned them something was wrong that night," he continued when Ally turned. "You got the Barneses back to their table, but they were still both gone for an unusual amount of time. They were nervous, upset. She picked up on it."

"Maybe." She nodded as she walked back out of the bedroom. "It was enough to make her start thinking. Worrying. She didn't notice when I left. She was busy, but Frannie did. She might have mentioned it to Jan in passing."

She picked her way through the living room, into the kitchen. "So she called it off, but just a little too late. Too late to save his sister. Doesn't look like he bothered much in here. Nothing worth smashing. I guess—" She broke off, walked slowly to the counter. "Oh, God."

When she turned her eyes were wide and horrified. "My bread knife." She laid her fingertips on the knife block, with one empty slot. "Long blade with serrated edge. God, Jonah. He killed her with my own knife."

Chapter 9

She wasn't going to let it shake her. She couldn't. For a cop, she reminded herself, nerves were as costly as rage and just as dangerous. The break-in at her apartment was a direct, and personal, attack. Her only choice was to stand up to it, maintain her objectivity, and do the job she'd sworn to do.

When the crime scene unit had left, adding their wreckage to what Lyle had left behind him, she hadn't argued with Jonah. He'd told her to pack what she thought she needed.

She was moving in with him until it was over.

Neither of them talked about the giant step they were taking; they told themselves it was simply a logical and convenient arrangement.

Then they had slept, tangled together, for what was left of the night.

"We've doubled the guards on Fricks," Kiniki told her at the morning briefing. "Lyle can't get to him."

"He's too smart to try." Ally stood in her lieutenant's office, hands in pockets. The horror had dulled, and the thin edge of fear was over. "He can wait, and he will. He's not in any hurry to pay Fricks back for what he might see as his part in his sister's death."

Behind the glass wall of Kiniki's office, the phones in the bull pen rang, and detectives went about the business of the day. Ally put herself into the mind of a dead woman she'd known for a matter of days.

"Jan Norton was easy. It was all an adventure to her, romantic, exciting. She was with him, and thought she was safe with him. The canvass of my building turned up two neighbors who saw a couple fitting Lyle's and Jan's description enter the building at around eight o'clock. Holding hands," she added. "She helped him trash my place, then once they were on the road again, he killed her. She stopped having a purpose."

She'd had plenty of time to think it through, lying awake through the darkest hours of the night in Jonah's bed. "He doesn't do anything without a purpose. There's a lot of anger in him for what he sees as the privileged class. There's a pattern in his background, in his previous arrests. All of them involve crimes against wealth—the hacking, the burglaries. Even the assaults were against wealthy superiors at his job when he held a computer programming position."

She pulled her hands out of her pockets, ticked off her fingers. "Wealth, authority, authority, wealth. They're synonymous to him, and both need to be taken down a peg. He's smarter than they are. Why should they have the easy life?"

In her mind she flipped through the steadily growing file of data on Matthew Lyle. "He grew up on the bottom rung of lower middle class. Not quite poor, but never really comfortable. His father had a history of unemployment. Always moving from one job to another. His stepfather was arrogant and domineering. Lyle followed the same patterns. The supervisors and coworkers I've been able to contact all said the same basic thing. He's brilliant with tech stuff, but not great socially. He's arrogant, belligerent and a loner. He came from a broken home, and both of his parents are dead. The only person he was ever close to was his sister."

Ally walked to the glass wall, looked out. "His sister played into his weaknesses, fed his monumental ego. One enabled the other. Now she's gone, and he's got no one but himself."

"Where would he go?"

"Not far," Ally calculated. "He's not finished yet. He has me to deal with, the Barneses, Blackhawk."

"I think your instincts are on target. We've put Mr. and Mrs. Barnes in a safe house. That leaves you, and Blackhawk."

She turned back. "I don't intend to take any unnecessary chances. But I have to keep visible, maintain a routine or he'll just go under and wait me out. He has my name, my address. He's probably got a reasonable description. He wants me to know it. To sweat it."

"We'll stake out your building."

"He may come back there. He doesn't want to just pick me off. It's not personal enough. And I don't think I'll be his first target."

"Blackhawk?"

"Yeah, in order of importance, Jonah's next. And as for Blackhawk, he's not cooperating."

And it still irked that he'd dismissed her idea of arranging protection.

"We can keep a couple of men on him, at a distance."

"You could keep them two miles away, and he'd spot them. Then he'd lose them on principle. Lieutenant, I'm...close to him. He trusts me. I can take care of it."

"You have an investigation to run, Detective, and your own butt to cover."

"I can do a considerable amount of all three at his club. And the fact is, I believe we might lure Lyle out, push him into making a move if he sees me with Blackhawk routinely."

"It's doubtful he knows you killed his sister. We've had a lid on that since the incident."

"But he knows I was part of the operation, the part inside the club. That Blackhawk and I worked together and started the steps that caused his sister's death."

"Agreed. I'm putting two men on Blackhawk, for the next seventy-two hours. Then we'll reevaluate."

"Yes, sir."

"On a different matter, you're aware that Dennis Overton's fingerprints were found on your hubcaps, your wheel wells. A search of his car turned up a recently purchased hunting knife. The lab work isn't back, but there were bits of tire rubber on the blade. He's been fired from the district attorney's office. They'd like to file formal charges."

"Sir—"

"Toughen your spine, Fletcher. If you don't file charges, he can walk. If you do, the D.A. will recommend psych evaluation. He needs it. Or do you want to wait until he shifts his obsession from you to somebody else?"

"No. No, I don't. I'll take care of it."

"Do it now. One lunatic out there after one of my detectives is enough."

The fact that he was right didn't make it any easier. Ally walked out to the squad room, plopped down at her desk and decided she deserved at least thirty seconds to brood.

She'd made mistakes with Dennis, right from the beginning. Hadn't paid enough attention, hadn't picked up on the cues. None of that was any excuse for his behavior, but it did weigh into her part in triggering it.

"What's the problem, Fletcher? The boss ream you?"

She glanced up at Hickman who made himself at home with his butt on the edge of her desk. "No. I'm about to ream somebody."

He bit into his midmorning Danish. "That usually puts me in a pretty chipper mood."

"That's because you're a heartless jerk."

"I love it when you flatter me."

"If I tell you you're a brainless moron, would you do me a favor?"

He took another bite, sprinkled crumbs on her desk. "My life for you, baby."

"I have to file on Dennis Overton. When the warrant comes through, would you pick him up? He knows you. It might be a little easier on him."

"Sure. Ally, he's not worth the regrets."

"I know it." She got to her feet, pulled her jacket from the back of her chair. Then she smiled, broke off a corner of his Danish and popped it into her mouth. "You're ugly, too."

"Girl of my dreams. Marry me."

Grateful Hickman knew how to lighten her mood, Ally headed out.

Two hours later she was walking into her father's office.

He met her at the door this time, ran his hands up and down her arms while he studied her face. Then he simply pulled her into his embrace.

"Good to see you," he murmured.

She burrowed in, let herself absorb his strength, his stability. "You're always there, you and Mom. No matter what, you're right there. I just wanted to say that first."

"She's worried about you."

"I know. I'm sorry for it. Listen." She gave him an extra squeeze, then drew back. "I know you're up-to-date, but I wanted you to know I'm okay. And I'm handling it. Lyle can't wait long to make a move. He's got nobody now. Everything we've got on him indicates he needs somebody, a woman, to admire him, feed his ego, play his games with him. Alone, he'll break."

"I agree. And it's my assessment that it's a woman he'll want most to punish. You're elected."

"Agreed. He's already made his first big mistake by breaking into my place. He exposed himself. He left prints everywhere. His grief, his anger, pushed him to show me what he is and what he wants. Using my knife to kill Jan, that was his way of saying it could have been me."

"So far we have no argument. Why are you alone?"

"He won't move on me during the day. He works at night. I'm not going to take stupid chances, Dad. That's a promise. I wanted you to know I've filed charges against Dennis."

"Good. I don't want you hassled, and I don't want you distracted. I went by your apartment this morning."

"I've got some serious redecorating to do."

"You can't stay there. Come home for a few days. Until this is closed."

"I've, ah, already made arrangements." She tucked her hands into her pockets, rocked back on her heels. This part, she thought, would be tricky. "I'm staying at Blackhawk's."

"You can't bunk in a club," he began. Then it hit him, a sneaky jab to the solar plexus. "Oh." Boyd ran a hand through his hair, walked to his desk. Shook his head, walked to the coffeepot. "You, ah… Hell."

"I'm sleeping with Jonah."

His back still to her, Boyd lifted a hand, waved it from side to side. Acknowledging the signal, Ally closed her mouth and waited.

"You're a grown woman." He got that much out, then set the coffeepot back down. "Damn it."

"Is that a comment on my age, or my relationship with Blackhawk?"

"Both." He turned back. She was so lovely, he thought, this woman who'd come from him.

"Do you have anything against him?"

"You're my daughter. He's a man. There you go. Don't grin at me when I'm having a paternal crisis."

Obediently she folded her lips. "Sorry."

"If you don't mind, I think I'll imagine you and Jonah are spending your time together discussing great works of literature and playing gin rummy."

"Whatever gets you through, Dad. I'd like to bring him to the Sunday barbecue."

"He won't come."

"Oh, yes." Ally smiled thinly. "He will."

She spent the rest of her shift doing follow-ups on the case and dealing with the threads of two others assigned to her. She closed one on sexual assault, opened another on armed robbery.

She parked her car in a secured lot and backtracked the block and a half to Blackhawk's.

She spotted the stakeout car from the end of the block, and had no doubt Jonah had tagged it, as well.

The first person she saw when she walked into the club was Hickman sitting hunched at the bar. She figured she could have spotted his black eye from a block away, as well.

She went to him, tapped a finger under his chin and studied his face while he sulked. "Who popped you?"

"Your good friend and general jerk-face Dennis Overton."

"You're kidding. He resisted?"

"Ran like a jackrabbit." He glanced toward Frannie, tapped his glass for a refill. "Had to chase him down. Before I could cuff him, he caught me." He picked up his dwindling beer, sipped morosely. "Now I'm wearing this, and I've taken about all the razzing I'm going to."

"Sorry, Hickman." To prove it, she leaned over and touched her lips to the swollen bruise. When she leaned back, she noticed Jonah had turned the corner into the bar. He merely lifted a brow at seeing her with her arm around Hickman's shoulders, then signaled to Will.

"I never figured him for a rabbit." With a heavy sigh, Hickman scooped up a handful of bar nuts. "Then I take him down and got this." He shifted on the stool to show her the hole in the knee of his trousers. "And he's flopping around like a landed trout, and crying like a baby."

"Oh, God."

"One ounce, one ounce of sympathy in his direction, Fletcher, and I'll pop you myself." Instead Hickman began popping the nuts into his mouth. "He swings back and his elbow catches me, right here, right on the cheekbone. I saw whole planets erupt. Stupid son of a bitch can do his crying in a cage tonight. What the hell'd you ever see in him?"

"Beats me. Frannie, put my pal's drinks on my tab, will you?"

"I'm switching to the imported stuff then."

She laughed, then glanced over her shoulder when Will came up behind her.

"Never used to have cops in here." But he said it with an easy smile, and winked at Frannie. "You want some ice on that eye, Officer?"

Hickman shook his head. "Nah." He used his good one to give Will the once-over. "You got a problem with cops?"

"Not in about five years. Say, is Sergeant Maloney still down at the sixty-third? He busted me twice. Was always straight about it."

Amused, Hickman turned around on the stool. "Yeah, he's still there. Still working vice, too."

"You see him, you tell him, Will Sloan said hi. He was always square with me."

"I'll be sure to do that."

"Anyway, the man says I should have some dinner sent out to your friends in the Ford across the street. Figures they'll get hungry sitting out there all night twiddling their thumbs."

"I'm sure they'll appreciate that," Ally said dryly.

"Least we can do." Giving Hickman a friendly slap on the back, Will headed toward the kitchen.

"I've got a couple of things to do." Ally gave Hickman's black eye another look. "Put some ice on that," she advised, then made her way into the club area to track down Beth.

"Got a minute?"

Beth continued to key in codes on the register. "It's Friday night, we're booked solid. And we're a couple of waitresses short."

Ally acknowledged the sting of the cool tone, but didn't back down. "I can wait until your break."

"I don't know when I'll be able to take one. We're busy."

"I'll wait. I won't take up much of your time."

"Suit yourself." Without a glance at her, Beth strode away.

"She's feeling pretty raw," Will commented.

Ally turned around. "Are you everywhere?"

"Mostly." He lifted his shoulders. "That's my job. She trained Jan like, you know, she trained you. I guess we're all pretty shaken up about what happened."

"And blaming me?"

"I don't. You were doing your job. That's how it works. Beth, she'll come around. She thinks too much of the man not to. You want me to get you a table? Band's going to start in about an hour, and it's a hot one so there won't be a square inch of free space if you wait."

"No, I don't need a table."

"Give a yell if you change your mind."

"Will." She touched his arm before he could walk away. "Thanks."

He gave her a wide, easy smile. "No problem. I got nothing but respect for cops. In the last five years."

Beth made her wait an hour, and Ally was having her eardrums rattled by the band's second number, when the head waitress quickly strode up to her.

"I've got ten minutes. You can have five of them. That'll have to be enough."

"Fine." She had to lift her voice to a shout. "Can we go back in the employee lounge, or would you rather yell at each other right here?"

Saying nothing, Beth spun around and marched out of the club area. She unlocked the door to the lounge, walked to the sofa and, sitting, took off her shoes.

"More questions, Detective Fletcher?"

Ally closed the door and shut off the worst of the racket behind it. "I'll keep it brief and to the point. You're aware of what happened to Jan?"

"Yes. I'm very aware of it."

"Her next of kin have been notified," Ally said in the same flat tone. "Her parents will be in Denver tomorrow, and would like her things. I'd like to box up whatever she might have in her locker, and have it available for them. It would be easier on them that way."

Beth's lips trembled, and she looked away. "I don't have the combination to her lock."

"I do. She had it written down in her address book."

"Then do what you have to do. You don't need me."

"I need a witness. I'd appreciate it if you'd verify that I list any and all items in her work locker, that I put nothing in from the outside, or misappropriate any of her property."

"That's all it is to you? All what happened to her is to you? Another bit of business?"

"The sooner I cover every bit of business, the sooner we find the man who did this to her."

"She was nothing to you. None of us were. You lied to us."

"Yes, I lied. And since under the same circumstances I'd lie again, I can't apologize for it."

Ally walked to the locker, spun the combination lock. "To your knowledge did anyone have the combination to this except Janet Norton?"

"No."

Ally removed the lock, opened the door. As she scanned the contents, she took a large evidence bag from her purse.

"It smells like her." Beth's voice trembled, then broke. "You can smell her perfume. Whatever she did, she didn't deserve to be killed, to be thrown out on the side of the road like trash."

"No, she didn't. I want the man who did it to her to pay as much as you do. More."

"Why?"

"Because there has to be justice, or there's nothing. Because her parents loved her, and their hearts are broken. Because I can smell her perfume. Cosmetic bag," Ally snapped out, grabbing the hot-pink case, yanking the zipper. "Two lipsticks, powder compact, three eyeliner pencils—"

She broke off when Beth touched her arm. "Let me help you. I'll write it down."

She took a tissue out of her pocket, wiped her eyes, then stuffed it away again to take out her pad. "I liked you, you see. I liked who I thought you were. It was a kind of an insult to find out you were someone else."

"Now you know. Maybe we can start from here."

"Maybe." Beth pulled out her pencil and began to write.

Ally ordered a light meal at the bar and kept her eye on Jonah. His Friday night crowd was thick and they were rowdy. The longer she sat, watching, listening, the more she began to see the myriad problems of keeping him safe.

She saw just as many problems convincing him he needed to make adjustments in his lifestyle until Matthew Lyle was in custody.

Because she considered herself on duty, she stuck with coffee. And when the caffeine started to jiggle her system, switched to bottled water.

When the inactivity threatened to drive her mad, she informed Frannie she was going to help out with the bar tables and grabbed a tray.

"I believe I fired you," Jonah said as she hauled a tray of empties to the bar.

"No, you didn't. I quit. House draft and a bump, Pete, campari and soda, Merlot with ice on the side and the complimentary ginger ale for the designated driver."

"You got it, Blondie."

"Go upstairs, get off your feet. You're tired."

Ally merely narrowed her eyes at Jonah's orders. "Pete, this guy's making insulting remarks about my looks. And he just put his hand on my butt."

"I'll break his face for you, honey, just as soon as I have a free hand."

"My new boyfriend here has biceps like oil tankers," Ally warned Jonah, and executed a stylish hair flip. "So you better watch your step, pretty boy."

He grabbed her chin, lifted her to her toes by it, then kissed her until her eyes threatened to roll back in her head. "I'm not paying you," he said mildly and strolled away.

"I'd work for that kind of tip," the woman on the stool beside her commented. "Anytime, anywhere."

"Yeah." Ally let out a long breath. "Who wouldn't?"

She worked through last call, then grabbed a table in the club and put her feet up while the band broke down and the staff prepared for closing.

And sitting, fell asleep.

Jonah sat across from her while the club went quiet.

"Anything I can do for you before I head out?"

He glanced up at Will. "No. Thanks."

"Guess she's worn-out."

"She'll bounce back."

"Well..." Will jiggled the change in his pockets. "I'm just going to have my nightcap, then head home. I'll see Frannie off and lock up. See you tomorrow."

The man was sunk, was all Will could think as he walked back to the bar. Who could've figured it? The man was sunk, and over a cop.

"A cop." Will slid onto a stool. On cue, Frannie set down his nightly brandy. "The man's hooked on the cop."

"You just clued into that?"

"I guess." He tugged on his beard. "You think it'll work out?"

"I'm no judge of romantic relationships. They look good together, though, and they won't be able to run over each other since both of them have heads like bricks."

"She conked out in there." Will jerked his head toward the club, then sipped his brandy. "He's just sitting, watching her sleep. I think you can mostly tell what's going on in a man by the way he watches a woman."

And because he caught himself watching Frannie as she mopped up the bar, he flushed and stared down at his drink as if the brandy suddenly contained the solution to a very complex problem.

But she caught it, this time she caught it because she was looking for it. She continued to wipe the bar dry as she inventoried her reaction. A nice little tug, she realized, and just a little heat to go with it.

She hadn't felt—or hadn't let herself—feel either for a man in a very, very long time.

"I guess you're heading home," she said casually.

"I guess. You?"

"I was thinking about ordering a pizza and watching this horror movie marathon on cable."

He smiled over at her. "You always had a thing for monster movies."

"Yeah. Nothing like giant tarantulas or blood-sucking vampires to chase away your troubles. Still… It's not a lot of fun by myself. You up for it?"

"Up for—" Brandy sloshed over the rim of his snifter and onto her clean bar. "Sorry. Damn. I'm clumsy."

"No, you're not." She slid the cloth over the spilled brandy, then looked him dead in the eye. "Do you want to split a pizza with me, Will, and watch old black-and-white monster movies, and neck on my sofa?"

"I— You—" He'd have gotten to his feet if he could have felt them. "Are you talking to me?"

She smiled, spread her cloth over the rim of the bar sink. "I'll get my jacket."

"I'll get it." He pushed to his feet, relieved when they held him upright. "Frannie?"

"Yes, Will?"

"I think you're beautiful. I just wanted to say that right out in case I'm too nervous later and forget."

"If you forget later, I'll remind you."

"Yeah. Okay. Good. I'll get your jacket," he said, and leaving her grinning, dashed off.

Jonah waited until the club was empty, until he heard Will and Frannie call out their good-nights. He rose, leaving Ally sleeping as he checked the locks and alarms himself. His heels clicked on the silver floor as he crossed it to go backstage. He chose the light pattern and music loop that suited his mood and set them.

Satisfied, he went back to Ally and bending down, kissed her awake.

She floated to the surface on the taste of him. Warm, a little rough, and very ready. When she opened her eyes, it was as though a thousand stars were twinkling against the night.

"Jonah."

"Dance with me." His mouth continued to nibble on hers as he lifted her to her feet.

She already was. Before the clouds cleared from her brain, she was moving with him, body molded to body as music rippled around them.

"The Platters." She stroked her cheek against his. "That's so weird."

"You don't like it? I can put on something else."

"No, I love it." She angled her head to give his lips freer access to her neck. "This number, it's my parents' song. 'Only You.' You know my mother was a night shift DJ at KHIP before she was station manager there. This is the song she played over the radio for my father the night she agreed to marry him. It's a nice story."

"I've heard pieces of it."

"You should see the way they look at each other when they dance to this. It's beautiful."

She dipped her fingers into his hair as they glided over the stars in the floor. "Very smooth," she whispered. "You're very smooth, Blackhawk. I should've figured it." She turned her head on his shoulder, watched the lights gleam. "Is everyone gone?"

"Yes." There's only you, he thought, brushing his lips over her hair. Only you.

Chapter 10

For the first time in weeks Ally woke without the need to jump out of bed and rush into the day.

Glorious Sunday.

Since Saturday night at Blackhawk's had been more crowded than the night before, she'd spent most of the time on her feet, and all of it mentally on duty.

Jonah might have shrugged off the guards outside the club, but she didn't think he'd take having her standing as his shield quite so casually.

Some things were best left undisclosed and undiscussed.

Besides, they were doing each other a favor. She couldn't stay in her apartment until it was cleaned out and refurnished. He was giving her a comfortable place to stay, and she was giving him a bodyguard. To her, it was a fair and rational deal.

And the deal had a distinctively superior side benefit. Intent on indulging in it, she ran her hand over his chest and began to nibble on the body she was more than happy to shield and protect.

He shot awake, fully aroused, with her mouth hot and greedy on his.

"Let me. Let me." Exhilarated, she chanted it, already straddling him, already riding. She hadn't known her blood could leap so fast, that her own needs could bolt from lazy to desperate in one hammer beat of the heart.

She took him in, surrounded him, her own body shuddering and bowing back as the sharp claws of pleasure raked her.

He kept the bedroom dark. It was all shadows and movement as he reared up to wrap his arms around her. Possession. It drove them both. He found her mouth, her throat, her breast, fed the hunger she'd unleashed in him before he could think, before he could do anything but feel.

Her release came like a whiplash, snapping and slicing the system. And when she melted against him, he laid her back. Began to love her.

A kiss, soft as the shadows. A touch, tender as the night. When she reached for him, he took her hands, cupping them together and bringing them to his lips in a gesture that had something rich, something sumptuous sliding through her to tangle with needs still raw.

"Now let me."

This was different. This was patient and sweet and slow. A fire banked and left to simmer with light.

She yielded herself, a surrender as powerful as seduction. He was murmuring to her, quiet words that stirred the soul even as he stirred her blood. As her breathing thickened she floated on the thin and delicate layers of silky sensations.

The brush of his fingertips, of his hair, the warmth of his lips, the glide of his tongue urged her higher, gradually higher. As the rise of desire became a deep and liquid yearning that spread to an aching need, she moaned his name.

He slid her over the first satin edge.

He needed to touch her this way, to take her this way. He needed, at least in the shadows, to have the right to. Here, she could belong to him.

Her arms came around him as he sank into a kiss, took it deep, fathoms deeper, until he was lost in it. And lost, he slipped inside her, held there linked, and desperately, helplessly in love.

When at last they lay quiet, she turned her face into his throat, wanting the taste of him to linger just a little longer. "No, don't move," she whispered. "Not yet."

Her body was gold, pulsing gold. She would have sworn even the dark had gilt edges.

"It's still night." She stroked her hands down his back, up again. "As long as we're like this, it's still night."

"It can be night for as long as you want."

Her lips curved against him. "Just a little longer." She sighed again, content to hold and be held. "I was going to get up and use your equipment, but then...well, there you were, and it just seemed like a much better idea to use you."

"Good thinking." He closed his eyes and kept her close.

* * *

She let the morning slide away, enjoyed a fast, hard workout with him in his gym while they argued over sports highlights that flashed by on the portable TV.

They shared a breakfast of bagels and coffee, along with the Sunday paper, while spread out lazily in bed. Natural, normal, almost domestic habits, Ally thought as they dressed for the day.

Not that a man like Blackhawk could or should be domesticated. But a slow, uncomplicated Sunday morning was a nice change of pace.

She sat on the side of the bed and laced up her ancient high-tops. Jonah tugged on a T-shirt, studied the endless line of her legs.

"Is your plan to wear those little shorts to distract me from whipping your excellent ass on the court?"

She lifted both eyebrows. "Please. With my innate skill I don't need such pitiful ploys."

"Good, because once I start a game, nothing distracts me until my opponent is crushed."

She stood, rolled strong shoulders shown to advantage in the sleeveless jersey. "We'll see who's crushed, Blackhawk, when the buzzer sounds. Now are you going to stand around here bragging, or are you ready to rock and roll?"

"More than ready, Detective Honey."

She waited until they were in his car. She thought the timing best. Besides, the longer she waited to bring it up, the shorter amount of time he'd have to argue with her.

Casually, she stretched out her legs and prepared to enjoy the ride. And smirked, just a little, when she saw his gaze shift, and slide down the length of her legs.

"So, are you ever going to let me drive this machine?"

Jonah switched on the engine. "No."

"I can handle it."

"Then buy your own Jag. Where's the court where you want to go down in inglorious defeat?"

"You mean where's the court where I plan to beat you into a whimpering pulp of humiliation? I'll give you directions. Of course, if I were driving, I could just take us there."

He merely flicked her a pitying glance, then slipped on his sunglasses. "Where's the court, Fletcher?"

"Out near Cherry Lake."

"Why the hell do you want to shoot hoops way out there? There are a half-dozen gyms around here."

"It's too nice a day to play indoors. Of course if you're afraid of a little fresh air…"

He reversed, and drove out of the parking lot.

"What do you do besides use that gorgeous equipment in your apartment over the club when you have a free day?" she asked him.

"Catch a game, check out a gallery." He sent her a slow smile. "Pick up women."

She tipped down her own sunglasses, peered at him over the tops. "What kind of game?"

"Depends on the season. If it's got a ball or a puck, I'll probably watch it."

"Me, too. I've got no resistance. What kind of gallery?"

"Whatever appeals at the time."

"You've got some great art. In the club and in your apartment."

"I like it."

"So… What kind of women?"

"The easy kind."

She laughed and tucked her glasses back in place. "You calling me easy, ace?"

"No, you're work. I like a change of pace now and again."

"Lucky me. You've got a lot of books," she commented. She studied his profile, the sexy, angular lines of it, the way the dark glasses concealed the fascinating contrast of those eyes of pure, light green. "It's hard to picture you curling up with a good book."

"Stretching out," he said, correcting her. "Women curl up with books, guys stretch out."

"Oh, I see. That's entirely different. This is your exit coming up. You'll take the two-two-five. And watch your speed. The traffic cops just love to nail pretty boys like you in their hot cars."

"I have pull in the police department."

"You think I'm going to fix a ticket for you when you won't even let me drive this thing?"

"It so happens I know the police commissioner."

As soon as he said it, it clicked.

"You said out in Cherry Lake?"

"That's right."

He got off the first exit and pulled into a convenience store parking lot.

"Problem?"

"Your family lives in Cherry Lake."

"That's right. And they have a basketball court—well half court. It was all we could push my parents into, even though my brothers and I campaigned pretty hard. They also have a barbecue pit, which my father puts to very good use. We try to get together a couple Sundays a month."

"Why didn't you tell me we were going to your parents'?"

She recognized the tone: anger, ruthlessly tethered. "What difference does it make?"

"I'm not intruding on your family." He shoved the car in Reverse again. "I'll drop you off. You can get a ride back when you're done."

"Hold on." She reached over, switched off the ignition. If he was angry, fine, they'd fight. But she'd be damned if he'd freeze her out. "What do you mean intruding? We're going to shoot some baskets, eat some steak. You don't need an engraved invitation."

"I'm not spending Sunday afternoon with your family."

"With a cop's family."

He pulled his sunglasses off, tossed them aside. "That has nothing to do with it."

"Then what does? I'm good enough to sleep with, but I'm not good enough for this?"

"That's ridiculous." He shoved out of the car, stalked to the end of the lot and stared out on a narrow grassy area.

"Then tell me something that isn't ridiculous." She marched up to him, jabbed his shoulder. "Why are you so angry that I want you to spend a few hours with my family?"

"You conned me into this, Allison. That's first."

"Why should I have to con you into it? Why is it, Jonah, that you've known my father for more than half your life but you've never accepted a single invitation to our home?"

"Because it's his home, and I have no place there.

Because I owe him. I'm sleeping with his daughter, for God's sake."

"I'm aware of that. So is he. What? Do you think he's going to dig out his police issue and shoot you between the eyes when you walk in the door?"

"This isn't a joke. It's so easy for you, isn't it?"

Here's the heat, she thought, pumping.

"Everything was always just right in your world. Solid, balanced and steady. You have no idea what mine was before he came into it, and what it would be now if he hadn't. This is not the way I intend to pay him back."

"No, you pay him back by insulting him. By refusing to acknowledge your relationship with me, as if it was something to be ashamed of. You think I don't know what your life was like? You think my world was so rarefied, Blackhawk. I'm the daughter of a cop. There's nothing you've seen I haven't, through his eyes. And now my own."

She drilled a finger in his chest. "Don't you talk up to me, and don't you talk down. Wherever, however each of us started, we're on level ground now. And you'd better remember it."

He grabbed her hand. "Stop poking at me."

"I'd like to flatten you."

"Same goes."

He walked away, waiting until he was sure he had some level of control again. Her mention of shame had gotten through. He could be angry with himself for falling in love with her. But he wouldn't be ashamed of it.

"I'll make you a deal. You get rid of the tail." He gestured to the shadow car that had pulled in a minute behind them. "And we'll take a couple of hours at your parents'."

"Give me a second."

She walked to the dark sedan, leaned in and had a short conversation with the driver. She had her hands in her pockets as she strode back over to Jonah.

"I cut them loose for the rest of the afternoon. It's the best I can do." She circled her shoulders. Apologies always tensed her up. "Look, I'm sorry I played it this way. I should have done it straight and we could have argued about it back at your place."

"You didn't play it straight because you knew I wouldn't be here to argue with."

"Okay, you're right." She threw up her hands in defeat. "Sorry again. My family's important to me. I'm involved with you. It just follows that I want you to feel comfortable with them."

"Comfort might be asking a little too much. But I'm not ashamed of my relationship with you. I don't want you to think I am."

"Fair enough. Jonah, it would mean a lot to me if you'd give it a try this afternoon."

"It's easier to argue with you when you're being obnoxious."

"Now see, that's what my brother Bryant always says. You'll get along fine." Hoping to soften things, she hooked her arm with his. "There's one thing, though," she began as they walked back to the car.

"What thing?"

"This deal at the house today? It's a little…more than I might have indicated. Sort of a kind of reunion. It's just that there'll be more people, that's all," she said quickly. "Aunts and uncles and cousins from back East, and my father's old partner and her family. It's really better for you this way," she insisted when he balled a fist and tapped it against her chin. "It's more a horde than a group, so nobody'll even notice you. Hey, why don't you let me drive the rest of the way?"

"Why don't I knock you unconscious and you can ride in the trunk the rest of the way?"

"Never mind. It was just a thought." She strolled around the car, reached for the door handle. But he beat her to it. It made her laugh and turn and take his face in her hands.

"You're a real case, Blackhawk." She gave him a noisy kiss, then climbed in. When he joined her, she leaned over, rubbed her knuckles over his cheek. "They're just people. Really nice people."

"I don't doubt it."

"Jonah. An hour. If you're uncomfortable being there after an hour, just tell me. I'll make an excuse and we'll go. No questions. Deal?"

"If I'm uncomfortable in an hour, I'll go. You stay with your family. That's the way it should be, so that's the deal."

"All right." She settled back, secured her belt. "Why don't I give you a quick rundown so you know the players? There's Aunt Natalie and her husband—Ryan Piasecki. She runs some of the interests of Fletcher Industries, but her real baby is Lady's Choice."

"Underwear?"

"Lingerie. Don't be a peasant."

"Terrific catalogues."

"Which you peruse for fashion's sake."

"Hell no. There are half-naked women in there."

She laughed, relieved they'd passed the crisis point. "Moving right along. Uncle Ry's an arson inspector in Urbana. They have three kids, fourteen, twelve and eight, if my math's right. Then there's my mother's sister, Aunt Deborah—Urbana's district attorney—her husband, Gage Guthrie."

"The Guthrie who has more money than the national treasury?"

"So rumor has it. Four kids for them. Sixteen, fourteen, twelve and ten. Like steps." She made upward motions with her hand. "Then there's Captain Althea Grayson, Dad's former partner, and her husband Colt Nightshade. Private Investigator. More of a troubleshooter really. Sort of a loose cannon. You'll like him. They have two kids, one of each, fifteen and twelve. No, thirteen now."

"So basically, I'm spending the afternoon with a teenage baseball team."

"They're fun," she promised him. "You don't like kids?"

"I have no idea. My exposure to their species has been limited."

"This exit," she told him. "Well, it won't be limited after today. I think you might have met my brothers somewhere along the line. Bryant's in Fletcher Industries. I guess he's a kind of troubleshooter, too. Does a lot of traveling and nailing butts to the wall. He loves it. And Keenan's a firefighter. We visited my aunt Natalie right after she hooked up with Uncle Ry, and Keen, he fell for the big red truck. That was it for him. Left at the next light. That wraps it up."

"I have a headache."

"No, you don't. Right at the corner, left two blocks down."

He'd already gotten a solid impression of the neighborhood. Stable, rich and exclusive with its big, beautiful houses on big, beautiful grounds. It gave him an itch between the shoulder blades he'd never be able to explain.

He was comfortable in the city, where the streets reminded him he'd overcome something, and the faces that crowded him were anonymous. But here, with the majestic trees, the sloped lawns, green and lush with approaching summer, the explosion of flowers and rambling old homes, he wasn't just a stranger.

He was an intruder.

"That one there, on the left, the cedar and river rock, with the zigzagging decks. I guess everyone's here already. Looks like a parking lot."

The double driveway was packed. The house itself was a huge and unique study of rooflines, jutting decks, wide expanses of glass, all accented by trees and flowering bushes with a meandering slate path ribboning up the gentle hill.

"I've reassessed the deal," Jonah told her. "I'm adding exotic sexual favors. I think this deserves them."

"Fine. I'll take 'em."

She reached for the door, but his arm shot out, pinned her back against the seat. She only laughed and rolled her eyes. "Okay, okay, we'll discuss exotic sexual favors later. Unless you're demanding a down payment on them here and now."

"Yeah, that'll put a cap on it." He jerked open his door, but before he could walk around the car, there was a war whoop, and a pretty young girl with a pixie cap of dark hair raced down the hill.

She grabbed Ally in a bear hug the minute she was out of the car. "There you are! Everyone's here. Sam already pushed Mick into the pool and Bing chased your neighbor's cat up a tree. Keenan got him down and my mom's inside putting something on the scratches. Hi."

She beamed a hundred-watt smile at Jonah. "I'm Addy Guthrie. You must be Jonah. Aunt Cilla said you were coming with Ally. You own a nightclub? What kind of music do you have?"

"She does shut up twice a year, for five minutes. We time it." Ally wrapped an arm around her cousin's neck and squeezed. "Sam is in the Piasecki branch, Mick is Addy's brother. And Bing is our family dog who has no manners whatsoever, so he fits in very well. Don't worry about remembering any of that, or you really will have a headache."

She reached out to take his hand, but Addy beat her to it. "Can I come to your club? We're not going home until Wednesday. Thursday if nagging works. I mean what's one more day? Gosh, you're really tall, aren't you? He looks great, too," she added peering around him to her cousin. "Nice job, Allison."

"Shut up, Addy."

"Somebody's always saying that to me."

Charmed despite himself, Jonah smiled at her. "Do you listen?"

"Absolutely not."

The noise level rose—screams, shouts. A couple of gangly teenagers of indeterminate sex raced by armed with enormous water guns. He saw a woman with a sunny sweep of hair in deep conversation with a striking redhead. A group of men—some stripped to the waist—battled it out brutally on a blacktopped basketball court. Another group of young people, dripping wet, raided a table loaded with food.

"Pool's around the other side of the house," Ally explained. "It's glassed in so we can use it all year."

One of the men on court pivoted, drove through the line of defense and dunked the ball. Then he caught sight of Ally, and deserted the field.

She met him halfway, shouting with laughter when he plucked her off her feet. "Put me down, moron. You're sweaty."

"So would you be if you were leading your team to a second consecutive victory." But he dropped her on her feet, wiped his hand on his jeans, then held it out to Jonah. "I'm Bryant, Ally's far superior brother. Glad you could make it. Want a beer?"

"Yes, actually."

Bryant eyed Jonah, measuring size and build. "You play any round ball?"

"Occasionally."

"Great, we're going to need fresh meat. Shirts and skins. Ally, get the man a beer while I finish trouncing these pansies."

"Come on inside." In a show of sympathy, Ally rubbed a hand up and down Jonah's arm. "Get your bearings. It's too confusing to try to meet everyone at once."

She drew him up onto a deck, where yet another table was spread with food and an enormous metal trough was filled with ice and cold drinks. She plucked out two beers and went in through the atrium doors.

The kitchen was spacious, broken up into family areas with counters and a banquette. In one corner a dark-haired man was trying to tug away from a dark-haired woman. "I'll live, Aunt Deb. Mom, get her off me."

"Don't be a baby." With her head stuck in the refrigerator, Cilla swore. "We're going to run out of ice. I knew it. Didn't I tell him we'd run out of ice?"

"Hold still, Keenan." Deborah covered the scratches with a gauze pad, taped it neatly. "There, now you can have a lollipop."

"I'm surrounded by smart alecks. Hey, speaking of which, here's Ally."

"Aunt Deb." Ally hurried over to hug her aunt, then reached over and grazed her knuckles over Keenan's cheek. "Hi, hero. This is Jonah Blackhawk. Jonah, my aunt, Deborah, my brother, Keenan. You've met my mother."

"Yes. Nice to see you again, Mrs. Fletcher."

A small army chose that moment to pour in through the door, full of shouted complaints and chased by an unbelievably large and ugly dog.

Ally was immediately absorbed into them. And before he could defend himself, so was Jonah.

Jonah intended to leave at the end of the hour. A deal was a deal. His plan was to make some polite conversation, keep as far out of the way as humanly possible, then fade back into his car and back into the city where he knew the rules.

And somehow, he was stripped out of his shirt and going elbow to gut in a vicious game of basketball with Ally's uncles, cousins, brothers. In the heat of competition, he lost track of intentions.

But he damn well knew it was Ally herself who stomped on his instep and cost him game point.

She was fast and sneaky, he conceded that as he ripped the ball away from an opponent and gave her one deadly glare. But she hadn't grown up on the streets where a single basket could mean a buck for a burger against a painfully empty stomach.

That made him faster. And sneakier.

"I like him." Natalie ignored her son's bloodcurdling scream of revenge and tucked an arm through Althea's.

"He was a hard-ass, but Boyd always liked him. Ouch, he plays dirty."

"What other way is there? Whoa, Ryan's going to be limping tomorrow. Serves him right," Natalie said with a laugh. "Taking on a guy half his age. Nice butt."

"Ry's? I've always thought so."

"Keep your eye off my husband, Captain. I was referring to our Ally's young man."

"Does Ryan know you ogle young men?"

"Naturally. We have a system."

"Well, I am forced to agree. Ally's young man has a very nice butt. Oh, ouch, that had to hurt."

"I think I could take him," Natalie murmured, then laughed at Althea's arch look. "In basketball. Get your mind out of the gutter." She swung an arm over her old friend's shoulder. "Let's go get some wine and pump Cilla for info on this new and very interesting situation."

"You read my mind."

"I know nothing, I say nothing," Cilla claimed as she poured another bag of ice into the trough. "Go away."

"It's the first guy she's brought to one of the family deals," Natalie pointed out.

Cilla merely straightened and mimed zipping her own lips.

"Give it up," Deborah advised. "I've been interrogating her for a half hour, and I got zero."

"You lawyers are too soft." Althea moved forward,

grabbing Cilla by the collar. "Now a good cop knows how to get to the truth. Spill it, O'Roarke."

"Do your worst, copper, I ain't no stool pigeon. Besides, I don't know anything yet. But I will," she murmured as she saw Ally dragging Jonah toward the deck. "Clear out, give me five minutes."

"It's nothing," Jonah insisted.

"It's blood. Rules of the house. If it bleeds, it gets mopped up."

"Ah, another victim." Cilla rubbed her hands together as her friends and relations conveniently scattered. "Bring him on."

"His face ran into something."

"Your fist," Jonah said with some bitterness. "Guarding the goal doesn't include left jabs."

"Around here it does."

"Let's see." Wisely Cilla kept her expression sober as she studied Jonah's bleeding lip. "Not so bad. Ally, go help your father."

"But I—"

"Go help your father," Cilla repeated, and snagging Jonah's hand dragged him up to the deck and into the kitchen. "Now let's see, where did I put my instruments of torture?"

"Mrs. Fletcher."

"Cilla. Sit down, and button it up. Whining is severely punished around here." She gathered up a damp cloth, ice and antiseptic. "Punched you, did she?"

"Yes, she did."

"Takes after her father. Sit," she ordered again and jabbed a finger into his bare stomach until he obeyed. "I appreciate your restraint in not hitting her back."

"I don't hit women." He winced when she dabbed at the cut.

"Good to know. She's a handful. Are you up to that?"

"I beg your pardon?"

"Is it just sex, or are you up for the whole package?"

He wasn't sure which shocked him more, the question or the sudden sting of antiseptic. He swore, ripely, then clenched his teeth. "Sorry."

"I've heard the word before. Was that your answer?"

"Mrs. Fletcher."

"Cilla." She leaned in close, then smiled into his eyes. Good eyes, she thought. Steady, clear. "I've embarrassed you. I didn't expect to. Almost done here. Hold this ice on it a minute."

She slid onto the bench across from him, crossed her arms on the table. By her calculations, she had two minutes tops before someone burst in the door and interrupted. "Boyd didn't think you would come today. I did. Allison is relentless when she's set her mind on something."

"Tell me about it."

"I don't know your mind, Jonah. But I know something about you, and I know what I see. So I want to tell you something."

"I didn't intend to stay this long—"

"Hush," she said mildly. "A lifetime ago. Nearly your lifetime ago, I met this cop. This irritating, fascinating, hardheaded cop. I didn't want to be interested. I certainly didn't want to be involved. My mother was a cop, and she died in the line of duty. I've never gotten over it. Not really."

She had to take a breath to steady herself, because it was perfectly true. "The last thing I wanted, the last thing I figured was good for me, was to find myself tangled up with a cop. I know how they think, what they are, what they risk. God, I didn't want that in my life. And here I am, a lifetime later. The wife of one, the mother of one."

She glanced out the window, caught sight of her husband, then her daughter. "Strange, isn't it, the way things turn out? It isn't easy, but I wouldn't give up a moment of it. Not one moment."

She patted the hand he'd laid on the table, then rose. "I'm glad you came today."

"Why?"

"Because it gave me a chance to see you and Ally together. It gave me a chance to look at you, close. An opportunity you haven't given me more than twice in, what is it, Jonah, seventeen years? And I like what I see."

Leaving him speechless, she turned to the fridge and pulled out a platter of burger patties. "Would you mind taking these to Boyd? If we don't feed the kids every couple of hours, it gets ugly."

"All right." He took the platter, struggled with himself while she just smiled at him out of the eyes Ally had inherited. "She's a lot like you, too."

"She inherited all of my and Boyd's most annoying qualities. Funny how that works." She rose on her toes, gently touched her lips to the wound at the corner of his mouth. "That comes with the treatment."

"Thanks." He shifted the tray, searched for something to say. No one in his life had ever kissed him where it hurt. "I have to get back to the city. Thank you for everything."

"You're welcome. You're welcome anytime, Jonah."

She smiled to herself as he went out. "Your turn at the plate, Boyd," she murmured. "Make it count."

Chapter 11

"It's all in the wrist," Boyd claimed, flipping a burger.

"I thought you said it was all in the timing." Ally stood, thumbs tucked into her pockets while her brother Bryant looked on, his elbow comfortably hooked on her shoulder.

"Timing is, of course, essential. There are many, many subtle aspects to the art of the barbecue."

"But when do we eat?" Bryant demanded.

"Two minutes if you're going for a burger. Another ten if you're holding out for steak." He peered through the billowing smoke as Jonah cut across the yard with a platter. "Looks like we have more supplies on the way."

"How about a burger, then steak?"

"You're tenth in line, I believe, for burger requests, son. Take a number." Boyd flipped another, sent it sizzling, then furrowed his brow as he caught sight of his wife on the side deck.

Dancing in place, she waved her arms, pointed at Jonah, pointed at Boyd, circled her fingers. He got the drift, and though he winced inwardly, gave a subtle shrug of acknowledgment.

Okay, okay, I'll talk to him. Damn it.

Cilla only smiled, then wagged her finger back and forth.

And I won't hurt him. Sheesh.

"Just set down the fresh rations, Jonah." Boyd jerked a thumb toward the high table beside the pit. "How's the lip?"

"I'll live." Jonah sent Ally a steely stare. "Especially since despite unsportsmanlike conduct by the opposing guard, I made the basket. And won."

"Lucky shot. We'll have a rematch after we eat."

"She loses," Bryant commented, "she demands a rematch. She wins, she rubs it in your face for days."

"And your point would be?" Ally fluttered her lashes at him.

"Mom would never let me hit her, because she was a girl." Bryant gave Ally's ear one hard tug. "I've always found that grossly unfair."

"Big deal. You just beat up on Keenan."

"Yeah." Instantly Bryant's face brightened. "Those were the days. I'm planning on punching on him later, for old times' sake."

"Can I watch? Like I used to."

"Naturally."

"Please. Your mother and I like to maintain the illusion we raised three well-balanced, competent adults. Don't shatter our dreams. Jonah, you haven't seen my workshop, have you?" At his daughter's answering snort, Boyd winged an eyebrow at her. "No comments. Bryant, this is a moment."

"Is it?"

"A monumental moment. I am passing the sacred tongs and spatula to you."

"Wait a minute, wait a minute." Ally elbowed her brother aside. "Why can't I do it?"

"Ah." Boyd held a hand to his heart. "How many times have I heard you say those very words in our long and exciting life together?"

Amused and fascinated by the family dynamics, Jonah watched mutiny settle over Ally's face. "Well, why can't I?"

"Allison, my treasure, there are some things a man must pass to his son. Son." Boyd laid a hand on Bryant's shoulder. "I'm trusting you with the Fletcher reputation. Don't let me down."

"Dad." Bryant wiped an imaginary tear from his eye. "I'm overwhelmed. Honored. I swear to uphold the family name, no matter what the cost."

"Take these." Boyd held out the barbecue tools. "Today, you are a man."

"That bites," Ally muttered as Boyd swung an arm around Jonah's shoulder.

"You're just a girl." Bryant leered and rubbed the tools together. "Live with it."

"She'll make him pay for that," Boyd murmured. "So, how are things?"

"Well enough." How the hell was Jonah supposed to make a quiet escape when someone or other was always dragging him somewhere? "I appreciate the hospitality today. I'm going to have to get back to the club."

"A business like that doesn't give you a lot of free

time, especially in the early years." Still he steered Jonah toward a wooden structure in the far corner of the yard. "Know anything about power tools?"

"They make a great deal of noise."

Boyd gave a hoot of laughter and opened the door of the workshop. "What do you think?"

The garage-size room was full of tables, machines, shelves, tools, stacks of wood. There appeared to be a number of projects in progress, but Jonah couldn't tell what they were, or what they were intended to be.

"Impressive," he decided, diplomatically. "What do you do here?"

"I make a great deal of noise. Other than that, I haven't figured it out. I helped Keenan build a birdhouse about ten years ago. Came out pretty good. Cilla started buying me tools. Boy toys, she calls them."

He ran his hand over the guard of a skill saw. "Then I needed a place to keep them. Before I knew it, I had a fully equipped workshop. I think it was all a ploy to get me out of her hair."

"Pretty clever."

"That she is." They stood for a moment, hands in pockets, soberly studying the tools. "Okay, let's get this over with so we can both relax and get something to eat. What's going on with you and my daughter?"

Jonah couldn't say it was unexpected, but it still made his stomach clench. "We're seeing each other."

With a nod, Boyd walked over to a small square refrigerator and took out two beers. He twisted off the tops, held one out to Jonah. "And?"

Jonah tipped back the beer, then gave Boyd a level look. "What do you want me to say?"

"The truth. Though I realize what you'd like to say is that it's none of my business."

"Of course it's your business. She's your daughter."

"There we have no argument." Deciding to get comfortable, Boyd boosted himself up on a worktable. "There's a matter of intent, Jonah. I'm asking what you intend in regard to my daughter."

"I don't have any intentions. I should never have touched her. I know that."

"Really." Intrigued, Boyd cocked his head. "Mind explaining that?"

"What do you want from me? Damn it." Giving into frustration, Jonah dragged a hand through his hair.

"The first time you asked me that, in almost that same tone, you were thirteen. Your lip was bleeding then, too."

Jonah steadied himself. "I remember."

"I've never known you to forget anything, which means you'll remember what I said to you then, but I'll say it again. What do you want from *you,* Jonah?"

"I've got what I want. A decent life run in a way I can respect and enjoy. And I know why I have it. I know what I owe you, Fletch. Everything. Everything I've got, everything I am started with you. You opened doors for me, you took me on when you had no reason to."

"Whoa." Genuinely shocked, Boyd held up a hand. "Hold on."

"You changed my life. You gave me a life. I know where I'd be if it wasn't for you. I had no right to take advantage of that."

"You're sure putting a lot on me here," Boyd said quietly. "What I did, Jonah, was see a street kid with potential. And I hassled him."

Emotion swirled into Jonah's eyes. "You made me."

"Oh, Jonah, no, I didn't. You made yourself. Though God knows I'm proud to have played a part in it."

Boyd slid off the table, wandered the shop. Whatever he'd expected from this talk, it hadn't been to have his emotions stirred. To feel very much like a father being given a precious gift by a son.

"If you feel there's a debt, then pay it off now by being straight with me." He turned back. "Are you involved with Ally because she's mine?"

"In spite of it," Jonah corrected. "I stopped thinking about her being yours. If I hadn't, I wouldn't be involved with her."

It was the answer he wanted, so Boyd nodded. The boy's suffering, he thought, and couldn't find it in himself to be overly sorry about it. "Define involved."

"For God's sake, Fletch." Jonah took a long gulp of beer.

"I don't mean that area." Boyd spoke quickly, took a deep drink himself. "Let's just leave that particular area behind a firmly locked door so we don't have to punch each other."

"Fine. Good."

"I meant, what are your feelings for her?"

"I care about her."

Boyd waited a beat, nodded again. "Okay."

Jonah swore. Boyd had asked him to play straight, and he was circling. "I'm in love with her. Damn it." He closed his eyes, imagined flinging the bottle against the wall, shattering glass. It didn't help. "I'm sorry." Jonah opened his eyes again, got a slippery grip on control. "But that's as straight as it gets."

"Yeah, I'd say so."

"You know what I'm built on. You can't think I'm good enough for her."

"Of course you're not," Boyd said simply, and noticed those clear green eyes didn't so much as flicker. "She's my little girl, Jonah. No one's good enough for her. But knowing what you're built on, I'd say you're pretty close. I wonder why that surprises you. The one area I don't recall you ever being low in is esteem."

"I'm over my head here," Jonah murmured. "It's been a long time since I've been over my head in anything."

"Women do that to you. The right woman, you never really surface again. She's beautiful, isn't she?"

"Yes. She blinds me."

"She's also smart, and she's strong, and she knows how to deal with what's dished out."

Absently, Jonah rubbed his thumb over his sore lip. "No argument."

"Then my advice to you is to play it straight with her, too. She won't let you get away with less, not for long."

"She isn't looking for anything else from me."

"You keep thinking that, son." At ease again, Boyd crossed to Jonah, laid a hand on his shoulder. "There's just one thing," he said as they started toward the door. "If you hurt her, I'll take you out. They'll never find your body."

"Well, I feel better now."

"Good. So, how do you like your steak?"

Ally saw them come out of the workshop and relaxed for the first time since the moment she'd watched them go in. Her father had his arm swung companionably around Jonah's shoulder. It looked as if they'd done no more than share a friendly beer and grunt over the power tools.

If her father had done any poking or prying into her relationship with Jonah, at least he hadn't drilled any embarrassing holes.

She liked seeing them together, liked very much witnessing the very real bond of affection and mutual respect. Her family was paramount in her life, and though she would have given her heart where her heart yearned, it would never have settled with full happiness on a man her family couldn't love.

She bobbled the bowl of potato salad, would have dropped it if Cilla hadn't made the grab.

"Butter fingers," Cilla said and set the bowl on the deck table.

"Mom."

"Hmm? We're going to run out of ice again."

"I'm in love with Jonah."

"I know, baby. Who's not blocked in? I need somebody to get some ice."

"How can you know?" Ally grabbed her mother's wrist before Cilla could go to the deck rail and shout for an ice run. "I just figured it out this second."

"Because I know you, and I see the way you are with him." Gently, she smoothed a hand over Ally's hair. "Scared or happy?"

"Both."

"Good." Cilla turned, sighed once, then kissed Ally on each cheek. "That's perfect." She slipped an arm around Ally's waist, turned to the rail. "I like him."

"Me, too. I really like who he is."

Cilla tipped her head toward her daughter's. "It's nice, isn't it, having the family together like this."

"It's wonderful. Jonah and I had a fight about coming here today."

"Looks like you won."

"Yeah. We're going to have another fight when I tell him we're getting married."

"You're your father's daughter. My money's on you."

"Place your bets," Ally suggested, and walked down the steps, crossed the lawn. It was a calculated move. She didn't mind being calculating, not when she had a point to make.

She strolled up to her father and Jonah, cupped Jonah's face in her hands and pressed her lips hard to his. He hissed, reminding her about his sore mouth. But she just laughed, shook back her hair.

"Suck it in, tough guy," she suggested and kissed him again.

His hands came to her waist, fused there, drawing her up on her toes that intimate inch.

"Dad?" She eased back down. "Mom needs more ice."

"She's just saying that to make me look bad." Boyd scanned the yard, homed in on his target. "Keenan! Go get your mother more ice."

"So..." As her father chased down her brother, Ally linked her hands at the back of Jonah's neck. "What were you talking about with my father?"

"Man stuff. What are you doing?" he demanded as she brushed her lips over his again.

"If you have to ask, I must not be doing it right."

"I'm outnumbered here, Allison. Are you trying to coax your family into stomping me into dust?"

"Don't worry. We're very big on kissing in my family."

"I noticed. Still." He drew her back.

"You've got this quietly proper streak. It's really cute. Are you having a good time?"

"Except for a couple of minor incidents," he said, deliberately tapping his finger on the corner of his mouth. "You have a nice family."

"They're great. You forget sometimes how steadying, how comforting it is to have them. How much you depend on them for a hundred little things. My cousins will remember coming out here when they were kids, or all of us piling into that gorgeous gothic fortress of Uncle Gage's, or trooping up to the mountains to..."

"What?"

"Wait. Give me a minute." She had his hand and squeezed it as she shut her eyes and let the pieces of the puzzle tumble together. "You're drawn back," she murmured. "You're always drawn back to memories, and places where you were happy with the people who mean the most. That's why people are always going back to visit their hometown, or driving by the house where they grew up." She paused and opened her eyes as a new thought hit her. "Where did he grow up?"

She tapped a fist against Jonah's chest. "Where did he and his sister grow up? Where did they live together? Where was he happy? He has to go somewhere, has to find a place to hide, to plan. He's gone home."

She spun around and raced for the house.

She was already dialing the kitchen phone when Jonah caught up with her. "What are you doing?"

"My job. Stupid, stupid, not to think of it before! Carmichael? It's Fletcher. I need you to do a check for me. I need an address—Matthew Lyle's old address, addresses maybe. Going back to when he was a kid. There's, ah..."

She paused, forced it into focus. "He was born in Iowa, and they moved around some. I can't remember when he came to Denver. The parents are dead. Yeah, you can reach me at this number." She recited it. "Or my cell phone. Thanks."

"You think he's gone back home?"

"He needs to feel close to his sister to feel safe, to feel powerful." Allison paced the kitchen as she tried to remember details of the file. "The psych profile tags him as dependent on her, even as he sees himself as her protector. She's his only real consistency, the only constant in his life. Parents divorced, kids got bounced around. Mother remarried, bounced around some more. Stepfather was…damn."

She pressed her fingers to her temple as if to push out the memory. "Ex-Marine. Very gung ho, and apparently very tough on the pudgy nerd and his devoted sister. Part of the whole authority complex comes from this instability of family life, ineffective father, the passive mother, the stern stepfather. Rocky foundations," she said as she paced.

"Lyle was bright, high IQ, but he was emotionally and socially inept. Except with his sister. His biggest trouble with the law was right after she got married. He got sloppy, careless. He was angry."

She checked her watch, urging Carmichael to hurry. "She stood by him, and it appears whatever rift there might have been between them was healed."

She leaped on the phone when it rang. "Fletcher. Yeah, what have you got?" She snatched up a pencil, began to scribble on the pad by the phone. "No, nothing out of state. He needs to stay close. Hold on." She covered the mouthpiece with her hand. "Do me a favor,

Blackhawk. Would you tell my father I need to talk to him for a minute?"

It took more than a minute. She moved into her father's office, booted up his computer. With him beside her, and Carmichael on the phone, they worked through the files, picked through Matthew Lyle's history.

"See, ten years ago he was listing a P.O. Box as his address. He kept that listing for six years, even though he had a house on the lake. Bought that house nine years ago, the same year his sister married Fricks. But he held on to the P.O. Box."

"And his sister lists the same P.O. Box as her address through the same period."

"But where did they live? I'm going to go in and pin Fricks down on this one." Then she pursed her lips, considered. "Carmichael, you up for another run? See what you can find me on property in the Denver metro area listed under the names Madeline Lyle or Madeline Matthews. Run Matthew and Lyle Madeline, too."

"Good move," Boyd approved. "Good thinking."

"He likes to own things," Ally noted. "Possessions are very important to him. If he stuck in the same spot for six years, more or less, he'd want his own place—or one for his sister."

She straightened in the chair. "Did you just say bingo? Carmichael, I think I love you. Yeah, yeah. All right. I've got it. I'll let you know. Really. Thanks."

She hung up, jumped out of the chair. "Lyle Madeline owns a condo in the center of downtown."

"Good work, Detective. Contact your lieutenant and assemble your team. And, Ally," Boyd added, "I want in."

"Commissioner, I'm sure we can make room for you."

* * *

It ran like clockwork. Within two hours the building was surrounded, the stairways and exits blocked. Using hand signals a dozen cops wearing Kevlar vests ranged the hallway outside of Matthew Lyle's two-level condo.

Ally had the floor plan in her head, every inch of the blueprint she'd studied. She gave the nod, and the two officers beside her hit the door with the battering ram.

She went in first, went in low.

A stream of men rushed by her and up the stairs to her right. Others fanned out to the rooms at her left. It took less than ten minutes to determine the condo was empty.

"He's been staying here." Ally gestured to the dishes in the sink. She dipped a finger into the dirt of an ornamental lemon tree potted by the kitchen window. "Damp. He's tending house. He'll be back."

In a bedroom upstairs they found three handguns, an assault rifle and a case of ammunition. "Be prepared," Ally murmured. "I see extra clips for a nine millimeter, but I don't see the nine millimeter, so he's armed."

"Detective Fletcher?" One of her team backed out of the closet, holding a long bladed knife with gloved fingers. "Looks like our murder weapon."

"Bag it." She picked up a black-and-silver matchbook from the dresser. "Blackhawk's." She shifted her eyes to her father. "That's his target. The only question is when."

Night had fallen when Ally confronted Jonah in his office. The man was mule stubborn, she thought. And more, he was just plain wrong.

"You close down for twenty-four hours. Forty-eight tops."

"No."

"I can close you down."

"No, you can't. And if you wrangle it, it'll take you longer than the forty-eight hours, which makes the entire process moot."

She dropped into a chair. It was important to stay calm, she reminded herself. Vital to stay in control. She hissed out a breath, then a stream of violent and inventive oaths.

"I don't believe your last suggestion is possible, regardless of my strength and flexibility."

She bolted forward. "Listen to me."

"No, you listen to me." His voice was quiet, cool, inflexible. "I could do what you're asking. What's to stop him from waiting me out? I close down, he goes under. I open, he surfaces. We could play that game indefinitely. I prefer running my own game, on my own turf."

"I'm not going to say you don't have a point, because you do. But we'll nail him within two days. I promise you. All you have to do is shut the place down, take a little vacation. My parents have a great place in the mountains."

"Would you be coming with me?"

"Of course not. I have to stay here and close this thing."

"You stay. I stay."

"You're a civilian."

"Exactly, and until this is a police state, I have a right to run my business and come and go as I please."

She wanted to tear at her hair, but knew that would

just amuse him. "It's my job to keep you alive to run your business."

He got to his feet. "Is that what you think? Are you my shield, Ally? Is that why you've been wearing your gun until we're up here behind locked doors? Is that why you keep it within reach even when we are here?"

He came around the desk, even as she cursed herself for the slip. "I don't like the implications of that."

She met him toe to toe. "You're a target."

"So are you."

"This is a waste of time."

He spun her around before she could stalk to the elevator. "You will not stand in front of me." He said it slowly, distinctly, with that rare glint of ready temper in his eyes. "Understand that."

"Don't tell me how to do my job."

"Don't tell me how to live my life."

She threw her head back, released a muffled scream. "All right. Okay. Forget it. We do it the hard way. Here's the deal. Twenty-four-hour guards outside. Cops in soft clothes in the bar and club areas at all times. You take on undercover officers as kitchen and wait help."

"I don't like that deal."

"Tough. Take it or leave it. Leave it and I pull strings and have you slapped into protective custody so fast even a slick customer like you won't be able to slide through the knots. I can do it, Blackhawk, and I will. My father will help me do it, because he cares about you. Please." She grabbed him by the lapels. "Do it for me."

"Forty-eight hours," he agreed. "And in the meantime, I put out word on the street I'm looking for him."

"Don't—"

"That's the deal. It's fair."

"All right. That's the deal."

"Now, what would you like to bet that I can go downstairs right now and pick out every cop you've already planted?"

She puffed out her cheeks, then showed her teeth in a smile. "No bet. I don't suppose I can convince you to stay up here tonight?"

He traced a fingertip down the center of her body. "I will if you will."

"That's what I figured." Sometimes compromise, however annoying, was the only out. "Hold that thought until closing."

"That I have no problem with." He walked over to call for the elevator. "Tonight, or tomorrow night."

"Yeah. It's just as likely, more really, that they'll take him at the condo. But if he slips through the net, or senses anything, it'll be here. And it'll be soon."

"Will's got good eyes. He'll know what to look for."

"I don't want you, or any of your people, taking chances. If he's spotted, you tell me." She glanced over, caught him studying her. "What?"

"Nothing." But he traced his fingers over her cheek. "When you've closed this down, can you take any time?"

"What do you mean time?"

"A few days. Away. Somewhere away."

"I might be talked into that. Do you have anywhere in mind?"

"No. Pick it."

"Well, aren't you open-minded and daring? I'll start thinking." She took a step out of the elevator, already shifting her focus, but he took her arm.

"Ally?"

"Yeah."

There was too much to say. Entirely too much to feel. And it wasn't the time, not the time to play it straight or any other way. "Later. We'll get into it later."

Chapter 12

Traditionally business at Blackhawk's was light on Sunday nights. There was no live music as a lure, and the first day of the work week loomed heavily.

Ally decided a great many people in Denver were taking advantage of the gorgeous weather and mild evening, and most who strolled in out of the night lingered an hour or more over their drinks or bowls of guacamole and chips.

She watched the entrance, checked the exits, studied faces and counted heads. Throughout the evening she slipped into the lounge at regular intervals to check in with the stakeout at Lyle's condo.

An hour before closing, and still he hadn't been spotted.

Itchy, she roamed the floor, checking faces, watching doors. The crowd was thinning out, and she imagined there'd be no more than a scatter of customers left by last call.

Where was he? she asked herself. Where the hell was he? He'd run out of places to hide.

"Detective." Jonah danced his fingers over her shoulder. "I thought you'd be interested to know one of my sources reports a man fitting Lyle's description has been asking questions about me."

"When?" She gripped his arm and pulled him toward the alcove. "Where?"

"Tonight, actually. At my other place."

"Fast Break?" She swore, whipped out her phone. "We didn't put anyone there. They never hit there. It's not his style."

"I'd say that holds true." He laid a hand over hers before she could dial the phone. "The bartender there just got in touch. Apparently Lyle—I assume it was Lyle though he was wearing glasses and sporting a beard—dropped into Fast Break a few hours ago, loitered at the bar, started asking if I ever came in."

"Hold on." Ally tapped his hand away and put her call through. "Balou? Cut a pair of uniforms loose from the condo. Tell them to see the bartender at Fast Break. The address is…"

She looked at Jonah, repeated the address he gave her. "Lyle was in there tonight. He's reported to be wearing a beard and glasses. Make sure that gets out."

She disconnected, looked back at Jonah.

"As I was saying," he continued, "my man didn't think anything of it initially, then it started to bother him. He says Lyle was jumpy. Hung around about a half hour then said to tell me he'd see me around."

"His center's crumbling. He's psyching himself up to

move." She wanted Jonah out of the way. "Look, why don't you go up, give your man another call. Let him know a couple of cops are on their way."

"Do I look like I'd fall for that lame a con?"

He strolled away from her to check on a table of customers who were preparing to leave.

The shouts came from the kitchen, followed by an explosive crash of dishes. Ally had her gun out, bolting for the door when it burst open.

He'd ditched the glasses, and the beard was a thin and scraggly dusting over his chin. But she saw she'd been right. He'd psyched himself up. His eyes were wide and wild.

And he had the barrel of the nine millimeter pressed to the soft underside of Beth's jaw.

"Don't move! Don't anybody move!" he shouted over the screams, the rush of running feet as customers scattered.

"Stay calm. Everybody stay calm." She sidestepped, kept her gun trained on him, her eyes trained on him. Forced herself to block out Beth's terrified face. "Lyle, take it easy. You want to let her go."

"I'll kill her. I'll blow her head off."

"You do that, I kill you. Think, you need to think. Where does that get you?"

"Put your gun down. Drop it, kick it over here, or she's dead."

"I'm not going to do that. And neither are any of the other cops in here. You know how many weapons you have aimed at you right now, Lyle? Look around. Do a count. It's over. Save yourself."

"I'll kill her." His gaze jittered around the room, bounced off guns. "Then I'll kill you. That'll be enough."

Someone was sobbing. Out of the corner of her eye she could see the bar area where civilians were being rushed outside to safety.

"You want to live, don't you? Madeline would want you to live."

"Don't you say her name! Don't you say my sister's name!" He shoved the gun harder against Beth's throat and made her cry out.

No place to run, Ally thought. His sister had had no place to run, and still she'd turned and fired.

"She loved you." Ally edged closer, keeping his focus on her. If she could get him to lower the gun, a few inches, get him to shift it toward her. Away from Beth. "She died for you."

"She was all I had! I got nothing to lose now. I want the cop who killed her, and I want Blackhawk. Now! Right now or she dies!"

Out of the corner of her eye, Ally saw Jonah move forward. "Look at me!" She shouted the words. "I'm the one who killed your sister."

He screamed, one long howl as he jerked the gun away from Beth, swung it toward Ally. There was a burst of gunfire, a blur of movement, wails of terror.

With fear locked in her throat, Ally rushed forward to where Jonah lay tangled with Lyle. Blood coated them both.

"Damn you! Damn, are you crazy?" With urgent hands she began to pat him down, looking for wounds. He'd thrown himself at the gun. In front of the gun.

He was breathing. She held on to that. He was breathing, and she would make sure he kept on breathing. "Jonah. Oh, God."

"I'm all right. Stop poking at me."

"All right? You jumped into cross fire. You nearly got yourself killed."

"You, too." He looked past her to where the starry floor was cracked an inch from where she'd stood.

"I'm wearing a vest."

"And that takes care of your hard head, too?" He sat back as a cop turned Lyle over.

"He's gone."

Jonah spared Lyle's face one glance, then looked into Ally's eyes. "I'd like to calm my customers down."

"You're not calming anyone down." Ally rose with him. "You've got blood all over you. Is all of it his?"

"Mostly."

"What do you mean mostly?"

"I'm going to deal with my customers and my people." He held her at arm's length before she could snatch at him again. "Do your job, and let me do mine."

He turned away to take Beth from the female officer who was holding her. "Come on, Beth, come on with me. Everything's all right now."

Ally pressed her fingers to her eyes then looked down at what was left of Matthew Lyle. "Yeah, everything's dandy."

"Slipped in the back," Hickman told her while they sat in the nearly empty club. The civilians were gone, the body had been removed and the crime scene unit was packing up.

She wondered idly what time it was, and how soon she could fall on her face and tune the world out. "He stopped being smart," she said. "He stopped thinking."

"You got that right," Hickman agreed. "Got himself one of those white kitchen uniforms, slapped on a wig and glasses. Before the cop who spotted him could call in or move, all hell broke loose."

"He didn't think we were smart enough to close him in. I saw his face when he spotted all the cops. Pure shock. My guess? He figured on breaking in here, taking Jonah down, me if I was around, then he's got hostages. He'd demand we turn over the cop who killed his sister. He really figured we'd do it, and he'd get out."

"Arrogant. Speaking of which, it was pretty cocky, telling him you were the one he wanted."

"I don't know why he didn't spot me in the first place."

"You look different." Hickman scanned a look up, then down. "Very un-Fletcherlike."

"Give me a break, Hickman. I look how I look. I'll tell you how it was. He came in here for Jonah. When he looked at me, all he saw was cop—no face, no form, just another cop. He didn't put me together with the one who'd worked here."

"Maybe." He got to his feet. "I guess we'll never know."

He glanced over at the starburst crack in the floor. "Too bad about that—classy floor. Bet it'll cost an arm and two legs to fix it."

"Maybe he'll leave it like that. Conversation piece. Draw a crowd."

"Yeah." The idea tickled Hickman. "We'd've taken him out right away, you know, but he would've gotten that shot off anyway. At that range, the vest would've stopped the bullet. Probably. But one way or the other, if the shot hadn't been deflected, you'd have been seriously hurt."

Absently she rubbed a hand between her breasts,

imagined the breathless pain. "You ever taken one in the vest?"

"Nope, but Deloy did. Had himself a softball-size bruise." Hickman held up his hands, made a circle. "Knocked him clean off his feet, too, and tossed him back like a rag doll. Ended up with a concussion where his head hit the pavement. That has to hurt."

"I'll take it over a bullet."

"Any day of the week. I'm going home." He got to his feet. "See you tomorrow."

"Yeah. Nice work."

"Back at you. Oh, your guy's in the kitchen, getting patched up."

"What do you mean patched up?"

"Caught a little friendly fire. Just a nick."

"He's shot? *Shot?* Why didn't anyone tell me?"

Hickman didn't bother to answer. She was already gone.

Ally slammed into the kitchen, her eyes dark and furious when she saw Jonah at one of the worktables, stripped to the waist, calmly drinking a brandy while Will rolled gauze over his upper arm.

"Hold it. Just hold it. Let me see that." She slapped Will away, unwound the gauze and poked at the long shallow cut until Jonah pushed her face up with the heel of his hand on her chin.

"Ouch," he said.

"Put that drink down, you're going to the hospital."

He kept his eyes on hers, lifted the brandy. Sipped. "No."

"No, my butt. What is this? Some idiot, male, macho deal? You've been shot."

"Not really. Grazed is more the accepted term. Now

if you don't mind, Will's got a kinder touch with this than you. I'd like him to finish so he can go home."

"It could get infected."

"I could get hit by a truck, but I don't intend for either to happen."

"It's okay, Ally, really." Playing peacemaker, Will patted her shoulder before picking up the gauze again. "I cleaned it real good. We got some worse in the old days, didn't we, Jonah?"

"Sure did. Looks like I'm another scar up on you now."

"Well, isn't that nice?" Ally grabbed the brandy, glugged.

"I thought you hated brandy."

"I do."

"Why don't you get a glass of wine," Will suggested. "I'm nearly done here."

"I'm fine. I'm okay." Ally blew out a breath. Now, she thought, after everything, her hands wanted to shake. "Damn it, Blackhawk. I was probably the one who shot you."

"Probably. I've decided to weigh in the circumstances and not hold it against you."

"That's real big of you. Now listen to me—"

"Frannie went home with Beth," he added, wanting to distract her. "She's okay. Shaky yet, but okay. She wanted to thank you, but you were busy."

"There we go." Will stepped back. "Your arm's in a lot better shape than your shirt. I'd say that's a loss." He held up the bloodstained linen and made Ally's stomach turn over. "Want me to go up and get you a fresh one before I go?"

"No. Thanks." Jonah lifted his arm, flexed. "Nice job. Haven't lost your touch."

"All in a day's work." Will picked up his discarded jacket. "You sure stand up, Ally. Could've been an awful mess out there tonight. But you sure stand up."

"All in a day's work."

"I'll lock up. 'Night."

Ally sat at the table, waited until she heard silence. "Okay, smart guy, what the hell were you thinking? You interfered with a police operation."

"Oh, I don't know. Maybe I was thinking that lunatic was going to kill you. It bothered me." He held out the brandy snifter. "How about a refill, since you drank mine."

"Fine. Sit here and swill brandy and look stoic." She shoved back, grabbed the glass, then gave in and wrapped her arms around his neck. "Don't *ever* scare me like that again."

"I won't if you won't. No, just stay right there a minute." He turned his face into her hair, breathed deep. "I'm going to see you stepping in front of that gun for a long time. That's hard."

"I know. I know it is."

"I'll deal with that, Ally, because that's the way it is." He drew her back, his eyes intense on hers. "There are some things you need to figure out if you can deal with. If you want to deal with."

"What are they?"

He rose to get the brandy himself, poured, set the bottle on the table. "Are there still cops in my place?"

"Other than me?"

"Yeah, other than you."

"No. We're clear."

"Then sit down."

"Sounds very serious." She pulled up her chair. "I'm sitting."

"My mother left when I was sixteen." He didn't know why he started there. It just seemed to be the spot. "I couldn't blame her, still don't. My father was a hard man, and she was tired of it."

"She left you with him?"

"I was self-sufficient."

"You were sixteen."

"Ally. I was never sixteen the way you were. And I had your father."

Everything inside her softened. "That's a lovely thing to say."

"It's just fact. He made me go to school. He came down on me when I needed it, which was most of the time. And he was the first person in my life to ever tell me I was worth anything. To ever see I might be. He's... I don't know anyone who comes up to him."

She reached across the table, took his hand. "I love him, too."

"Let me get through some of this." He squeezed her hand, then drew his away. "I didn't go to college, even Fletch couldn't browbeat me into that. I took some business courses because it suited me. When I was twenty, my father died. Three packs of cigarettes a day and a general meanness catches up with you. It was long and ugly, and when it was over, the only thing I felt was relief."

"Is that supposed to make me think less of you?"

"There's a contrast here, and you see it as well as I do."

"Yeah, you had a lousy childhood. I had a great one.

As fate would have it, we both got lucky and ended up with Boyd Fletcher as a father. Don't look at me like that. That's exactly what he is to you."

"I'm going to make something clear to you before this goes any farther. I wasn't a victim, Allison. I was a survivor, and used whatever methods worked. I stole and cheated and conned, and I don't apologize for it. Things would've turned out differently if I hadn't had your father hounding me. But they didn't."

"I think that was my point."

"Don't interrupt. I'm a businessman. I don't steal or cheat because I don't have to. That doesn't mean I don't play the game my way."

"A real tough guy, aren't you? Blackhawk, you're a fraud. Cool customer, slick hands, icy stare. And this big, soft heart. Soft, hell, it's gooey."

Amused at the speechless shock on his face, she got up, sauntered to the fridge and hunted up an open bottle of white wine.

She wasn't tired anymore, she realized. She was revved.

"Do you think I didn't run you, pal? Run your friends, get the stories? You gather up your sick and wounded like a mama chick."

Enjoying herself now, Ally drew out the stopper, found a glass. "Frannie—got her off the streets, got her clean, gave her work. Will—straightened him up, paid off his debts before he got his knees capped, gave him a suit and some dignity."

"None of that's relevant."

"I'm not finished." She poured the wine. "The iceman got Beth into a women's shelter, bought her kids presents from Santa Claus when she didn't have the money or the energy to deal with it. Jonah Blackhawk was buying Barbie dolls."

"I did not buy dolls." That was going just a little too far. "Frannie did. And it has nothing to do with this."

"Yeah, right. Then there's Maury, one of your line chefs." She sat down, wiggled into the chair and propped her feet up. "And the dough you lent him—and I use the word *lent* advisedly—to help his mother through a bad patch."

"Shut up."

She merely smiled, dipped a finger into her wine, licked it. "Sherry, the little busgirl, who's working her way through college. Who paid her tuition last semester when she couldn't scrape it together? Why, I believe it was you. And what about Pete the bartender's little problem last year when an uninsured driver totaled his car?"

"Investing in people is good business."

"That's your story, you stick to it."

Irritation and embarrassment warred for top gun inside him. He tossed his weight to the side of irritation. "You're ticking me off, Allison."

"*Ooooh*, really?" She leaned forward, leading with her chin. "Go ahead, hard case, slap me around and shut me up. Dare you."

"Be careful." He said it, meant it, then pushed to his feet. "This is irrelevant, and isn't getting us anywhere."

She crossed her ankles and made clucking noises.

"You're really asking for it."

"Yeah, yeah. I'm shaking. Sucker."

He cracked and lifted her right off the chair. "One more word. I swear, it's only going to take one more word."

She bit him, one quick nip on his already tender mouth. "Softy."

He pushed her aside and spun toward the door.

"Where you going?"

"To put on a damn shirt. I can't talk to you."

"Then I'll just have to rip it off you again. I've got a soft spot for wounded tough guys with gooey centers." And laughing, she launched herself at him, landed piggyback. "I'm crazy about you, Blackhawk."

"Go away. Go arrest somebody. I've had enough of cops for one day."

"You'll never get enough of me." She bit his earlobe, his shoulder. "Come on, shake me off."

He would have. He told himself he could have. It was just his bad luck he looked down and saw the scar in the floor. From a bullet meant for her.

He dragged her around, yanked her against him so hard, so fast, she swore her ribs knocked together. His mouth was on hers, fused there with a heat borne of desperation.

"Better. Much better. Here, Jonah. Now. We both need to make it right again. I need you to love me. Like our lives depended on it."

He was on the floor with her, without any thought but to prove to himself that she was whole and safe and alive beneath him.

The cool, hard surface of the floor might have been a feather bed, or clouds, or the jagged, unforgiving peaks of a mountain. Nothing mattered but that she was wrapped around him, that her breath was fast and hot against his skin, that her heart beat like wild wings against his.

All the fear, the tension, the ugliness poured out of

her when he touched her. Her hands tangled with his, fighting to strip away boundaries. Until they were free to drive together.

When he filled her—temper, passion, desperation—it was like coming home.

His breath was in rags, his system spent, and still he rocked against her.

"Just hold me a minute more." She pressed her face against his shoulder. "Just hold me." But she felt the warm wetness on her fingers, and pulled away. "Damn it. You're bleeding again. Let me fix it."

"It's fine. It's all right."

"It'll only take a minute."

"Ally, leave it be."

The snap of his voice had her eyes narrowing. "Don't think you can step back from me now. Don't think you'll get away with it this time."

"Just get dressed." He pushed back his hair and began to follow his own orders.

"Fine." She snatched at clothes, dragged them on. "You want to go another round, we'll go another round. You stupid son of a bitch."

He heard the tremor in her voice, cursed her. Cursed himself. "Don't cry. That's playing dirty."

"I'm not crying. You think I'd cry over you?"

He could feel his heart start to shatter as he brushed a tear off her cheek with his thumb. "Don't."

She sniffled, flicked her hands over her face to dry it and sneered. "Sucker."

Fury whipped into his eyes and scalded her. She couldn't have been more delighted. She got to her feet before he did, but it was close.

"You're in love with me." She punched her fist

against his chest. "And you won't admit it. That doesn't make you tough, it makes you hardheaded."

"You weren't listening to me before."

"You weren't listening to me, either, so we're even."

"Listen now." He grabbed her face with both hands. "You have connections."

"Why, you insulting…" She wondered why the top of her head didn't fly off. "How dare you talk about my family's money at a time like this."

"I don't mean money." He jerked her up to her toes, then dropped her back on the flat of her feet again. "Now who's stupid? Money's nothing. I don't give a damn about your portfolio. I have my own. I'm talking about emotional connections. Foundations, roots, for God's sake."

"You have your own there, too. Frannie. Will. Beth. My father." She waved a hand, settling down again. "But I get you. You're saying, basically, that someone like me, who comes from the kind of place I come from, should hook herself up with a man who say, comes from a good, upstanding family. Probably upper-middle-class. He should have a good education, and hold a straight job. A profession. Like say a lawyer or a doctor. Is that the theme here?"

"More or less."

"Interesting. Yes, that's interesting," she said with a considering nod. "I can see the logic in that. Hey, you know who fits that bill to a tee? Dennis Overton. Remember him? Stalker, tire slasher, general pain in the ass?"

She'd turned it around and boxed him into his own corner. All he could do was steam.

"Don't cop to excuses, Blackhawk, if you haven't

got the guts to tell me how you feel about me, and what you want for us."

She flipped her hair back, tucked in her shirt. "My work is done here. See you around, pal."

He got to the door before she did. He was good at that. But this time he slapped a hand on it, held it closed while she glared at him. "You don't walk until we're finished."

"I said I was finished." She jerked on the door.

"I'm not. Shut up and listen."

"You tell me to shut up one more time, and—"

He shut her up. One hard, exasperated kiss. "I've never loved another woman. Never even came close. So cut me a damn break here."

Her heart did a lovely bounding leap. But she nodded, stepped back. "Okay. Spill it."

"You hit me between the eyes the first minute you walked in the room. I still can't see straight."

"Well." She backed up, slid onto a stool. "I'm liking this so far. Keep going."

"You see that? That right there." He stabbed a finger at her. "Anyone else would want to deck you."

"But not you. You love that about me."

"Apparently." He crossed to her, laid his hands on the bar on either side of her. "I love you, so that's it."

"Oh, I don't think so. Make me a deal."

"You want a deal? Here it is. You ditch the apartment and move in, officially, upstairs."

"Full gym and sauna privileges?"

Half the knots in his stomach loosened when he laughed. "Yeah."

"So far, I can live with it. What else are you offering me?"

"Nobody's ever going to love you like I do. I guarantee it. And nobody's ever going to put up with you. But I will."

"Same goes. But that's not enough."

Those wonderful eyes narrowed on her face. "What do you want?"

She rested her back against the bar. "Marriage."

Now those narrowed eyes darkened. "Do you mean that?"

"I say what I mean. Now I could ask you, but I have to figure that a guy who makes a habit of opening doors for women, and buying Christmas presents for little children—"

"Leave that part alone."

"Okay." But she sat up, brushed her knuckles over his cheek. "We'll just say I figure you've got enough of a traditional-guy streak to want to propose on your own. So, I'll let you." She linked her hands at the back of his neck. "I'm waiting."

"I'm just thinking. It's the middle of the night. We're in a bar and my arm's bleeding."

"So's your mouth."

"Yeah." He swiped at it with the back of his hand. "I guess that makes it close to perfect for you and me."

"Works for me. Jonah. You work for me."

He pulled the clip out of her hair, tossed it aside. "First tell me you love me. Use my name."

"I love you, Jonah."

"Then marry me, and let's see where it takes us."

"That's a deal."

Epilogue

With a howl of outrage, Ally bolted up from the sofa. "Off side! Off side! What, are those refs blind? Did you see that?" Instead of kicking in the TV, which occurred to her, she settled for leaning down and pounding on Jonah's shoulder.

"You're just mad because your team's losing, and you're going to owe me."

"I don't know what you're talking about." She sniffed, pushing back her hair. "My team is *not* going to lose, despite corrupt and myopic officials." But it looked very dim for her side. She planted her hands on her hips. "Besides, must I remind you there is no bet because you don't have a license for gambling."

He skimmed his eyes down her long black robe. "You're not wearing your badge."

"Metaphorically, Blackhawk." She leaned over to

kiss him. "I'm always wearing my badge." Then she narrowed her eyes. "You swear you didn't hear who won this game? You have no information?"

"Absolutely not."

But she didn't like the way he smiled at her. They'd missed the regular Monday night broadcast and were watching the hotly contested football game on video-tape. "I don't know about you. You're slippery."

"We made a deal." He skimmed his hand up the sleeve of her robe, trailing his fingers over flesh. "I never go back on a deal." He reached for the remote, paused the screen. "Since you're up…" He held up his empty glass. "How about a refill?"

"I got it last time."

"You were up last time, too. If you'd sit down and stay down, you wouldn't get tagged."

Conceding his point, she took the glass. "Don't start the game until I get back."

"Wouldn't think of it."

She headed back to the kitchen. There were times she missed the apartment on top of the club. But even a couple of die-hard urbanites needed a little elbow room, she thought. And the house suited them. So did marriage, she thought with a contented sigh as she poured Jonah's habitual bottled water over ice.

There'd been a lot of changes in the eighteen months since they, well, closed the deal, she supposed. Good changes. The kind lives were built on. They were building strong, and they were building solid.

Sipping his water, she walked back to the great room and frowned when she found it empty. Then with a shake of her head, she set the glass down. She knew just where to find him.

She wound her way quietly through the house, and stopped at the door to the bedroom.

The winter moonlight streamed through the windows, glowing over him, and the infant he held in his arms. Love burst through her, a nova of feeling, then settled again to a steady warmth.

"You woke her up."

"She was awake."

"You woke her up," Ally repeated, crossing to him. "Because you can't keep your hands off her."

"Why should I?" He pressed his lips to his daughter's head. "She's mine."

"No question of that." Ally traced a finger over the baby's soft black hair. "She's going to have your eyes."

The idea of it was a staggering thrill. He looked down at that perfect little face, with those dark and mysterious eyes of the newborn. He could see his whole life in those eyes. Sarah's eyes.

"You can't tell at two weeks. The books say it takes longer."

"She's going to have your eyes," Ally repeated. She draped an arm around his waist and together they studied their miracle. "Is she hungry?"

"No. She's just a night person." And his, like the woman beside him was his. Two years before they hadn't existed for him. Now they were the world.

He turned his head, leaning down as Ally lifted her mouth. As the kiss sweetened, the baby stirred in his arms. He shifted, tucking Sarah's head on his shoulder with a natural grace that never failed to make Ally smile.

He'd taken to fatherhood as if he'd only been waiting

for the moment. Then again, she thought, thinking of her own father, he'd had a wonderful teacher.

She angled her head, studied the two of them. "I guess she wants to watch the game now."

Jonah rubbed his cheek over his daughter's hair. "She mentioned it."

"She'll just fall asleep."

"So will you."

With a laugh, Ally took the blanket from the bassinet. "Give her up," she said, holding out her arms.

"No."

Ally rolled her eyes. "Okay, you get her till halftime, then it's my turn."

"Deal."

With the baby on his shoulder and his hand linked with the woman's he loved, he went out to enjoy the night.

* * * * *

SECRET STAR

To generous hearts

Chapter 1

The woman in the portrait had a face created to steal a man's breath and haunt his dreams. It was, perhaps, as close to perfection as nature would allow. Eyes of laser blue whispered of sex and smiled knowingly from beneath thick black lashes. The brows were perfectly arched, with a flirty little mole dotting the downward point of the left one. The skin was porcelain-pure, with a hint of warm rose beneath—just warm enough that a man could fantasize that heat was kindling only for him. The nose was straight and finely sculpted.

The mouth—and, oh, the mouth was hard to ignore—was curved invitingly, appeared pillow-soft, yet strong in shape. A bold red temptation that beckoned as clearly as a siren's call.

Framing that staggering face was a rich, wild tumble of ebony hair that streamed over creamy bare shoulders.

Glossy, gorgeous, generous. The kind of hair even a strong man would lose himself in—fisting his hands in all that black silk, while his mouth sank deep, and deeper, into those soft, smiling lips.

Grace Fontaine, Seth thought, a study in the perfection of feminine beauty.

It was too damn bad she was dead.

He turned away from the portrait, annoyed that his gaze and his mind kept drifting back to it. He'd wanted some time alone at the crime scene, after the forensic team finished, after the M.E. took possession of the body. The outline remained, an ugly human-shaped silhouette marring the glossy chestnut floor.

It was simple enough to determine how she'd died. A nasty tumble from the floor above, right through the circling railing, now splintered and sharp-edged, and down, beautiful face first, into the lake-size glass table.

She'd lost her beauty in death, he thought, and that was a damn shame, too.

It was also simple to determine that she'd been given some help with that last dive.

It was, he mused, looking around, a terrific house. The high ceilings offered space and half a dozen generous skylights gave light, rosy, hopeful beams from the dying sun. Everything curved—the stairs, the doorways, the windows. Female again, he supposed. The wood was glossy, the glass sparkling, the furniture all obviously carefully selected antiques.

Someone was going to have a tough time getting the bloodstains out of the dove-gray upholstery of the sofa.

He tried to imagine how it had all looked before whoever helped Grace Fontaine off the balcony stormed through the rooms.

There wouldn't have been broken statuary or ripped cushions. Flowers would have been meticulously arranged in vases, rather than crushed into the intricate pattern of the Oriental rugs.

There certainly wouldn't have been blood, broken glass, or layers of fingerprint dust.

She'd lived well, he thought. But then, she had been able to afford to live well. She'd become an heiress when she turned twenty-one, the privileged, pampered orphan and the wild child of the Fontaine empire. An excellent education, a country-club darling, and the headache, he imagined, of the conservative and staunch Fontaines, of Fontaine Department Stores fame.

Rarely had a week gone by that Grace Fontaine didn't warrant a mention in the society pages of the *Washington Post*, or a paparazzi shot in one of the glossies. And it usually hadn't been due to a good deed.

The press would be screaming with this latest, and last, adventure in the life and times of Grace Fontaine, Seth knew, the moment the news leaked. And they would be certain to mention all of her escapades. Posing nude at nineteen for a centerfold spread, the steamy and very public affair with a very married English lord, the dalliance with a hot heartthrob from Hollywood.

There'd been other notches in her designer belt, Seth remembered. A United States senator, a bestselling author, the artist who had painted her portrait, the rock star who, rumor had it, had attempted to take his own life when she dumped him.

She'd packed a lot of men into a short life.

Grace Fontaine was dead at twenty-six.

It was his job to find out not only the how, but the who. And the why.

He had a line on the why already. The Three Stars of Mithra—a fortune in blue diamonds, the impulsive and desperate act of a friend, and greed.

Seth frowned as he walked through the empty house, cataloging the events that had brought him to this place, to this point. Since he had a personal interest in mythology, had since childhood, he knew something about the Three Stars. They were the stuff of legends, and had once been grouped in a gold triangle that had been held in the hands of a statue of the god Mithra.

One stone for love, he remembered, skimming through details as he climbed the curved stairs to the second level. One for knowledge, and the last for generosity. Mythologically speaking, whoever possessed the Stars gained the god's power. And immortality.

Which was, logically, a crock, of course. Wasn't it odd, though, he mused, that he'd been dreaming lately of flashing blue stones, a dark castle shrouded in mist, a room of glinting gold? And there was a man with eyes as pale as death, he thought, trying to clear the hazy details. And a woman with the face of a goddess.

And his own violent death.

Seth shook off the uneasy sensation that accompanied his recalling the snippets of dreams. What he required now were facts, basic, logical facts. And the fact was that three blue diamonds weighing something over a hundred carats apiece were worth six kings' ransoms. And someone wanted them, and didn't mind killing to gain possession.

He had bodies piling up like cordwood, he thought, dragging a hand through his dark hair. In order of death, the first had been Thomas Salvini, part owner of Salvini, gem experts who had been contracted by the

Smithsonian Institution to verify and assess the three stones. Evidence pointed to the fact that verifying and assessing hadn't been quite enough for Thomas Salvini, or his twin, Timothy.

Over a million in cash indicated that they'd had other plans—and a client who wanted the Stars for himself.

Added to that was the statement from one Bailey James, the Salvinis' stepsister, and eyewitness to fratricide. A gemologist with an impeccable reputation, she claimed to have discovered her stepbrothers' plans to copy the stones, sell the originals and leave the country with the profits.

She'd gone in to see her brothers alone, he thought with a shake of his head. Without contacting the police. And she'd decided to face them down after she shipped two of the stones to her two closest friends, separating them to protect them. He gave a short sigh at the mysterious minds of civilians.

Well, she'd paid for her impulse, he thought. Walking in on a vicious murder, barely escaping with her life—and with her memory of the incident and everything before it blocked for days.

He stepped into Grace's bedroom, his heavy-lidded gold-toned eyes cooly scanning the brutally searched room.

And had Bailey James gone to the police even then? No, she'd chosen a P.I., right out of the phone book. Seth's mouth thinned in annoyance. He had very little respect and no admiration for private investigators. Through blind luck, she'd stumbled across a fairly decent one, he acknowledged. Cade Parris wasn't as bad as most, and he'd managed—through more blind luck, Seth was certain—to sniff out a trail.

And nearly gotten himself killed in the process. Which brought Seth to death number two. Timothy Salvini was now as dead as his brother. He couldn't blame Parris overmuch for defending himself from a man with a knife, but taking the second Salvini out left a dead end.

And through the eventful Fourth of July weekend, Bailey James's other friend had been on the run with a bounty hunter. In a rare show of outward emotion, Seth rubbed his eyes and leaned against the door jamb.

M. J. O'Leary. He'd be interviewing her soon, personally. And he'd be the one telling her, and Bailey James, that their friend Grace was dead. Both tasks fell under his concept of duty.

O'Leary had the second Star and had been underground with the skip tracer, Jack Dakota, since Saturday afternoon. Though it was only Monday evening now, M.J. and her companion had managed to rack up a number of points—including three more bodies.

Seth reflected on the foolish and unsavory bail bondsman who'd not only set Dakota up with the false job of bringing in M.J., but also moonlighted with blackmail. The hired muscle who'd been after M.J. had likely been part of some scam of his and had killed him. Then they'd had some very bad luck on a rain-slicked road.

And that left him with yet another dead end.

Grace Fontaine was likely to be third. He wasn't certain what her empty house, her mangled possessions, would tell him. He would, however, go through it all, inch by inch and step by step. That was his style.

He would be thorough, he would be careful, and he would find the answers. He believed in order, he believed in laws. He believed, unstintingly, in justice.

Seth Buchanan was a third-generation cop, and had worked his way up the rank to lieutenant due to an inherent skill for police work, an almost terrifying patience, and a hard-edged objectivity. The men under him respected him—some secretly feared him. He was well aware he was often referred to as the Machine, and took no offense. Emotion, temperament, the grief and the guilt civilians could indulge in, had no place in the job.

If he was considered aloof, even cold and controlled, he saw it as a compliment.

He stood a moment longer in the doorway, the mahogany-framed mirror across the wide room reflecting him. He was a tall, well-built man, muscles toned to iron under a dark suit jacket. He'd loosened his tie because he was alone, and his nightwing hair was slightly disordered by the rake of his fingers. It was full and thick, with a slight wave. He pushed it back from an unsmiling face that boasted a square jaw and tawny skin.

His nose had been broken years before, when he was in uniform, and it edged his face toward the rugged. His mouth was hard, firm, and rare to smile. His eyes, the dark gold of an old painting, remained cool under straight black brows.

On one wide-palmed hand he wore the ring that had been his father's. On either side of the heavy gold were the words *Serve* and *Protect.*

He took both duties seriously.

Bending, he picked up a pool of red silk that had been tossed on the mountain of scattered clothing heaped on the Aubusson carpet. The callused tips of his fingers skimmed over it. The red silk gown matched the short robe the victim had been wearing, he thought.

He wanted to think of her only as the victim, not as

the woman in the portrait, certainly not as the woman in those new and disturbing dreams that disrupted his sleep. And he was irritated that his mind kept swimming back to that stunning face—the woman behind it. That quality was—had been, he corrected—part of her power. That skill in drilling into a man's mind until he was obsessed with her.

She would have been irresistible, he mused, still holding the wisp of silk. Unforgettable. Dangerous.

Had she slipped into that little swirl of silk for a man? he wondered. Had she been expecting company—a private evening of passion?

And where was the third Star? Had her unexpected visitor found it, taken it? The safe in the library downstairs had been broken open, cleaned out. It seemed logical that she would have locked something that valuable away. Yet she'd taken the fall from up here.

Had she run? Had he chased her? Why had she let him in the house? The sturdy locks on the doors hadn't been tampered with. Had she been careless, reckless enough to open the door to a stranger while she wore nothing but a thin silk robe?

Or had she known him?

Perhaps she'd bragged about the diamond, even shown it off to him. Had greed taken the place of passion? An argument, then a fight. A struggle, a fall. Then the destruction of the house as cover.

It was an avenue, he decided. He had her thick address book downstairs, and would go through it name by name. Just as he, and the team he assigned, would go through the empty house in Potomac, Maryland, inch by inch.

But he had people to see now. Tragedy to spread and

details to tie up. He would have to ask one of Grace Fontaine's friends, or a member of her family, to come in and officially identify the body.

He regretted, more than he wanted to, that anyone who had cared for her would have to look at that ruined face.

He let the silk gown drop, took one last look at the room, with its huge bed and trampled flowers, the scatter of lovely old antique bottles that gleamed like precious gems. He already knew that the scent here would haunt him, just as that perfect face painted beautifully in oils in the room downstairs would.

It was full dark when he returned. It wasn't unusual for him to put long, late hours into a case. Seth had no life to speak of outside of the job, had never sought to make one. The women he saw socially, or romantically, were carefully, even calculatingly, selected. Most tolerated the demands of his work poorly, and they rarely cemented a relationship. Because he knew how difficult and frustrating those demands of time, energy and heart were on those who waited, he expected complaints, sulking, even accusations, from the women who felt neglected.

So he never made promises. And he lived alone.

He knew there was little he could do here at the scene. He should have been at his desk—or at least, he thought, have gone home just to let his mind clear. But he'd been pulled back to this house. No, to this woman, he admitted. It wasn't the two stories of wood and glass, however lovely, that dragged at him.

It was the face in the portrait.

He'd left his car at the top of the sweep of the drive,

and walked to the house sheltered by grand old trees and well-trimmed shrubs green with summer. He'd let himself in, turned the switch that had the foyer chandelier blazing light.

His men had already started the tedious door-to-door of the neighborhood, hoping that someone, in another of the big, exquisite homes, would have heard something, seen anything.

The medical examiner was slow—understandably, Seth reminded himself. It was a holiday, and the staff was down to bare minimum. Official reports would take a bit longer.

But it wasn't the reports or lack of them that nagged at his mind as he wandered back, inevitably, to the portrait over the glazed-tile hearth.

Grace Fontaine had been loved. He'd underestimated the depth friendship could reach. But he'd seen that depth, and that shocked and racking grief in the faces of the two women he'd just left.

There had been a bond between Bailey James, M. J. O'Leary and Grace that was as strong as he'd ever seen. He regretted—and he rarely had regrets—that he'd had to tell them so bluntly.

I'm sorry for your loss.

Words cops said to euphemize the death they lived with—often violent, always unexpected. He had said the words, as he had too often in the past, and watched the fragile blonde and the cat-eyed redhead simply crumble. Clutching each other, they had simply crumbled.

He hadn't needed the two men who had ranged themselves as the women's champions to tell him to leave them alone with their grief. There would be no questions, no statements, no answers, that night. Nothing he could say or do would penetrate that thick curtain of grief.

Grace Fontaine had been loved, he thought again, looking into those spectacular blue eyes. Not simply desired by men, but loved by two women. What was behind those eyes, what was behind that face, that had deserved that kind of unquestioning emotion?

"Who the hell were you?" he murmured, and was answered by that bold, inviting smile. "Too beautiful to be real. Too aware of your own beauty to be soft." His deep voice, rough with fatigue, echoed in the empty house. He slipped his hands in his pockets, rocked back on his heels. "Too dead to care."

And though he turned from the portrait, he had the uneasy feeling that it was watching him. Measuring him.

He had yet to reach her next of kin, the aunt and uncle in Virginia who had raised her after the death of her parents. The aunt was summering in a villa in Italy and was, for tonight, out of touch.

Villas in Italy, he mused, blue diamonds, oil portraits over fireplaces of sapphire-blue tile. It was a world far removed from his firmly middle-class upbringing, and from the life he'd embraced through his career.

But he knew violence didn't play favorites.

He would eventually go home to his tiny little house on its postage-stamp lot, crowded together with dozens of other tiny little houses. It would be empty, as he'd never found a woman who moved him to want to share even that small private space. But his home would be there for him.

And this house, for all its gleaming wood and acres

of gleaming glass, its sloping lawn, sparkling pool and trimmed bushes, hadn't protected its mistress.

He walked around the stark outline on the floor and started up the stairs again. His mood was edgy—he could admit that. And the best thing to smooth it out again was work.

He thought perhaps a woman with as eventful a life as Grace Fontaine would have noted those events—and her personal feelings about them—in a diary.

He worked in silence, going through her bedroom carefully, knowing very well that he was trapped in that sultry scent she'd left behind.

He'd taken his tie off, tucked it in his pocket. The weight from his weapon, snug in his shoulder harness, was so much a part of him it went unnoticed.

He went through her drawers without a qualm, though they were largely empty now, as their contents were strewn around the room. He searched beneath them, behind them and under the mattress.

He thought, irrelevantly, that she'd owned enough clothing to outfit a good-size modeling troupe, and that she'd leaned toward soft materials. Silks, cashmeres, satins, thin brushed wools. Bold colors. Jewel colors, with a bent toward blues.

With those eyes, he thought as they crept back into his mind, why not?

He caught himself wondering how her voice had sounded. Would it have fit that sultry face, been husky and low, another purr of temptation for a man? He imagined it that way, a voice as dark and sensual as the scent that hung on the air.

Her body had fit the face, fit the scent, he mused, stepping into her enormous walk-in closet. Of course, she'd helped nature along there. And he wondered why a woman would feel impelled to add silicone to her body to lure a man. And what kind of pea-brained man would prefer it to an honest shape.

He preferred honesty in women. Insisted on it. Which, he supposed, was one of the reasons he lived alone.

He scanned the clothes still hanging with a shake of his head. Even the killer had run out of patience here, it seemed. The hangers were swept back so that garments were crowded together, but he hadn't bothered to pull them all out.

Seth judged that the number of shoes totaled well over two hundred, and one wall of shelves had obviously been fashioned to hold handbags. These, in every imaginable shape and size and color, had been pulled out of their slots, ripped open and searched.

A cupboard had held more—sweaters, scarves. Costume jewelry. He imagined she'd had plenty of the real sparkles, as well. Some would have been in the now empty safe downstairs, he was sure. And she might have a lockbox at a bank.

That he would check on first thing in the morning.

She'd enjoyed music, he mused, scanning the wireless speakers. He'd seen speakers in every room of the house, and there had been CDs, tapes, even old albums, tossed around the living area downstairs. She'd had eclectic taste there. Everything from Bach to the B-52s.

Had she spent many evenings alone? he wondered. With music playing through the house? Had she ever curled up in front of that classy fireplace with one of the hundreds of books that lined the walls of her library?

Snuggled up on the couch, he thought, wearing that

little red robe, with her million-dollar legs tucked up. A glass of brandy, the music on low, the starlight streaming through the roof windows.

He could see it too well. He could see her look up, skim that fall of hair back from that staggering face, curve those tempting lips as she caught him watching her. Set the book aside, reach out a hand in invitation, give that low, husky purr of a laugh as she drew him down beside her.

He could almost taste it.

Because he could, he swore under his breath, gave himself a moment to control the sudden upbeat of his heart rate.

Dead or alive, he decided, the woman was a witch. And the damn stones, preposterous or not, only seemed to add to her power.

And he was wasting his time. Completely wasting it, he told himself as he rose. He was covering ground best covered through rules and routine. He needed to go back, light a fire under the M.E., push for an estimated time of death. He needed to start calling the numbers in the victim's address book.

He needed to get out of this house that smelled of this woman. All but breathed of her. And stay out of it, he determined, until he was certain he could rein in his uncharacteristic imaginings.

Annoyed with himself, irked by his own deviation from strict routine, he walked back through the bedroom. He'd just started down the curve of the stairs when a movement caught his eye. His hand reached for his weapon. But it was already too late for that.

Very slowly, he dropped his hand, stood where he was and stared down. It wasn't the automatic pointed at his heart that stunned him motionless. It was the fact that it was held, steady as a rock, in the hand of a dead woman.

"Well," the dead woman said, stepping forward into the halo of light from the foyer chandelier. "You're certainly a messy thief, and a stupid one." Those shockingly blue eyes stared up at him. "Why don't you give me one good reason why I shouldn't put a hole in your head before I call the police?"

For a ghost, she met his earlier fantasy perfectly. The voice was a purr, hot and husky and stunningly alive. And for the recently departed, she had a very warm flush of temper in her cheeks. It wasn't often that Seth's mind clicked off. But it had. He saw a woman, runway-fresh in white silk, the glint of jewels at her ears and a shiny silver gun in her hand.

He pulled himself back roughly, though none of the shock or the effort showed as he met her demand with an unsmiling response. "I *am* the police."

Her lips curved, a generous bow of sarcasm. "Of course you are, handsome. Who else would be creeping around a locked house when no one's at home but an overworked cop on his beat?"

"I haven't been a beat cop for quite some time. I'm Buchanan. Lieutenant Seth Buchanan. If you'd aim your weapon just a little to the left of my heart, I'll show you my badge."

"I'd just love to see it." Watching him, she slowly shifted the barrel of the gun. Her heart was thudding like a jackhammer with a combination of fear and anger, but she took another casual step forward as he reached two fingers into his pocket. The badge looked real enough, she mused. What she could see of the identification with the gold shield on the flap that he held up.

And she began to get a very bad feeling. A worse sinking in the stomach sensation than she'd experienced when she pulled up to the drive, saw the strange car and the lights blazing inside her empty house.

She flicked her eyes from the badge up to his again. Damned if he didn't look more like a cop than a crook, she decided. Very attractive, in a straight-edged, buttoned-down sort of fashion. The solid body, broad of shoulder and narrow of hip, appeared ruthlessly disciplined.

Eyes like that, cool and clear and golden brown, that seemed to see everything at once, belonged to either a cop or a criminal. Either way, she imagined, they belonged to a dangerous sort of man.

Dangerous men usually appealed to her. But at the moment, as she took in the oddity of the situation, her mood wasn't receptive.

"All right, Buchanan, Lieutenant Seth, why don't you tell me what you're doing in my house." She thought of what she carried in her purse—what Bailey had sent her only days before—and felt that unsettling sensation in her stomach deepen.

What kind of trouble are we in? she wondered. And just how do I slide out of it with a cop staring me down?

"Have you got a search warrant to go along with that badge?" she demanded.

"No, I don't." He'd have felt better, considerably better, if she'd put the gun down altogether. But she seemed content to hold it, aiming it lower now, no less steadily, but lower. Still, his composure had snapped back. Keeping his eyes on hers, he came down the rest of the stairs and stood in the lofty foyer, facing her. "You're Grace Fontaine."

She watched him tuck his badge back into his pocket, while those unreadable cop's eyes skimmed over her face. Memorizing features, she thought, irritated. Making mental note of any distinguishing marks. Just what the hell was going on?

"Yes, I'm Grace Fontaine. This is my property, my home. And as you're in it, without a proper warrant, you're trespassing. As calling a cop seems superfluous, maybe I'll just call my lawyer."

He angled his head, and unwillingly caught a whiff of that siren's scent of hers. Perhaps it was that, and feeling its instant and unwelcome effect on his system, that had him speaking without thought.

"Well, Ms. Fontaine, you look damn good for a dead woman."

Chapter 2

Her response was to narrow her eyes, arch a brow. "If that's some sort of cop humor, I'm afraid you'll have to translate."

It annoyed him that she'd jarred the remark out of him. It wasn't professional. Cautious, he brought a hand up slowly, tipped the barrel of the gun farther to the left. "Do you mind?" he said, then, quickly, before she could agree, he twisted it neatly out of her hand, pulled out the clip. It wasn't the time to ask if she had a license to carry, so he merely handed her back the empty gun and pocketed the clip.

"It's best to keep both hands on your weapon," he said easily, and with such sobriety that she suspected amusement lurked beneath. "And, if you want to keep it, not to get within reach."

"Thanks so much for the lesson in self-defense." Obviously irritated, she opened her bag and dumped the gun inside. "But you still haven't answered my initial question, Lieutenant. Why are you in my house?"

"You've had an incident, Ms. Fontaine."

"An incident? More copspeak?" She blew out a breath. "Was there a break-in?" she asked, and for the first time took her attention off the man and glanced past him into the foyer. "A robbery?" she added, then caught sight of an overturned chair and some smashed crockery through the archway in the living area.

Swearing, she started to push past him. He curled a hand over her arm to stop her. "Ms. Fontaine—"

"Get your hand off me," she snapped, interrupting him. "This is my home."

He kept his grip firm. "I'm aware of that. Exactly when was the last time you were in it?"

"I'll give you a damn statement after I've seen what's missing." She managed another two steps and saw from the disorder in the living area that it hadn't been a neat or organized robbery. "Well, they did quite a job, didn't they? My cleaning service is going to be very unhappy."

She glanced down to where Seth's fingers were still curled around her arm. "Are you testing my biceps, Lieutenant? I do like to think they're firm."

"Your muscle tone's fine." From what he could see of her in the filmy ivory slacks, it appeared more than fine. "I'd like you to answer my question, Ms. Fontaine. When were you home last?"

"Here?" She sighed, shrugged one elegant shoulder. Her mind was flitting around the annoying details that were the backwash of a robbery. Calling her insurance agent, filing a claim, giving statements. "Wednesday afternoon. I went out of town for a few days." She was more shaken than she cared to admit that her house had been robbed and ransacked in her absence. Her things touched and taken by strangers. But she slid him a smiling glance from under her lashes. "Aren't you going to take notes?"

"As a matter of fact, I am. Shortly. Who was staying in the house in your absence?"

"No one. I don't care to have people in my home when I'm away. Now if you'll excuse me..." She gave her arm a quick, hard jerk and strode through the foyer and under the arch. "Good God." The anger came first, quick and intense. She wanted to kick something, no matter that it was broken and ruined already. "Did they have to break what they didn't cart out?" she muttered. She glanced up, saw the splintered railing and swore again. "And what the devil did they do up there? A lot of good an alarm system does if anyone can just..."

She stopped her forward motion, her voice trailing off, as she saw the outline on the gleaming chestnut wood of the floor. As she stared at it, unable to tear her eyes away, the blood drained out of her face, leaving it painfully cold and stiff.

Placing one hand on the back of the stained sofa for balance, she stared down at the outline, the diamond glitter of broken glass that had been her coffee table, and the blood that had dried to a dark pool.

"Why don't we go into the dining room?" he said quietly.

She jerked her shoulders back, though he hadn't touched her. The pit of her stomach was cased in ice, and the flashes of heat that lanced through her did nothing to melt it. "Who was killed?" she demanded. "Who died here?"

"Up until a few minutes ago, it was assumed you did."

She closed her eyes, vaguely concerned that her vision was dimming at the edges. "Excuse me," she said, quite clearly, and walked across the room on numb legs. She picked up a bottle of brandy that lay on its side on the floor, fumbled open a display cabinet for a glass. And poured generously.

She took the first drink as medicine. He could see that in the way she tossed it back, shuddered twice, hard. It didn't bring the color back to her face, but he imagined it had shocked her system into functioning again.

"Ms. Fontaine, I think it would be better if we talked about this in another room."

"I'm all right." But her voice was raw. She drank again before turning to him. "Why did you think it was me?"

"The victim was in your house, dressed in a robe. She met your general description. Her face had been… damaged by the fall. She was your approximate height and weight, your age, your coloring."

Her coloring, Grace thought on a wave of staggering relief. Not Bailey or M.J., then. "I had no houseguest while I was gone." She took a deep breath, knowing the calm was there, if only she could reach it. "I have no idea who the woman was, unless it was one of the burglars. How did she—" Grace looked up again at the broken railing, the viciously sharp edges of wood. "She must have been pushed."

"That has yet to be determined."

"I'm sure it has. I can't help you as to who she was, Lieutenant. As I don't have a twin, I can only—" She broke off, her color draining a second time. Now her free hand fisted and pressed hard to her stomach. "Oh, no. Oh, God."

He understood, didn't hesitate. "Who was she?"

"I— It could have been… She's stayed here before while I was away. That's why I stopped leaving a spare key outside. She might have had it copied, though. She'd think nothing of that."

Turning her gaze away from the outline, she walked back through the debris, sat on the arm of the sofa. "A cousin." Grace sipped brandy again, slowly, letting it ease warmth back into her system. "Melissa Bennington— No, I think she took the Fontaine back a few months ago, after the divorce. I'm not sure." She pushed a hand through her hair. "I wasn't interested enough to be sure of a detail like that."

"She resembles you?"

She offered a weak, humorless smile. "It's Melissa's mission to *be* me. I went from finding it mildly flattering to mildly annoying. In the last few years I found it pathetic. There's a surface resemblance, I suppose. She's augmented it. She let her hair grow, dyed it my color. There was some difference in build, but she… augmented that, as well. She shops the same stores, uses the same salons. Chooses the same men. We grew up together, more or less. She always felt I got the better deal on all manner of levels."

She made herself look back, look down, and felt a wash of grief and pity. "Apparently I did, this time around."

"If someone didn't know you well, could they mistake you?"

"A passing glance, I suppose. Maybe a casual acquaintance. No one who—" She broke off again, got to her feet. "You think someone killed her believing her to be me? Mistaking her for me, as you did? That's absurd. It was a break-in, a burglary. A terrible accident."

"It's possible." He had indeed taken out his book to note down her cousin's name. Now he glanced up, met her eyes. "It's also more than possible that someone came here, mistook her for you, and assumed she had the third Star."

She was good, he decided. There was barely a flicker in her eyes before she lied. "I have no idea what you're talking about."

"Yes, you do. And if you haven't been home since Wednesday, you still have it." He glanced down at the bag she continued to hold.

"I don't generally carry stars in my purse." She sent him a smile that was shaky around the edges. "But it's a lovely, almost poetic, thought. Now, I'm very tired—"

"Ms. Fontaine." His voice was clipped and cool. "This victim is the sixth body I've dealt with today that traces back to those three blue diamonds."

Her hand shot out, gripped his arm. "M.J. and Bailey?"

"Your friends are fine." He felt her grip go limp. "They've had an eventful holiday weekend, all of which could have been avoided if they'd contacted and cooperated with the police. And it's cooperation I'll have from you now, one way or the other."

She tossed her hair back. "Where are they? What did you do, toss them in a cell? My lawyer will have them out and your butt in a sling before you can finish reciting the Miranda." She started toward the phone, saw it wasn't on the Queen Anne table.

"No, they're not in a cell." It goaded him, the way she

snapped into gear, ready to buck the rules. "I imagine they're planning your funeral right about now."

"Planning my—" Her fabulous eyes went huge with distress. "Oh, my God, you told them I was dead? They think I'm dead? Where are they? Where's the damn phone? I have to call them."

She crouched to push through the rubble, shoving at him when he took her arm again. "They're not home, either of them."

"You said they weren't in jail."

"And they're not." He could see he'd get nothing out of her until she'd satisfied herself. "I'll take you to them. Then we're going to sort this out, Ms. Fontaine—I promise you."

Grace didn't speak as he drove her toward the tidy suburbs edging D.C. He'd assured her that Bailey and M.J. were fine, and her instincts told her that Lieutenant Seth Buchanan was saying nothing but the truth. Facts were his business, after all, she thought. But she still gripped her hands together until her knuckles ached.

She had to see them, touch them.

Guilt was already weighing on her, guilt that they should be grieving for her, when she'd spent the past few days indulging her need to be alone, to be away. To be somewhere else.

What had happened to them over the long weekend? Had they tried to contact her while she was out of reach? It was painfully obvious that the three blue diamonds Bailey had been assessing for the museum were at the bottom of it all.

As the afterimage of that stark outline on the chestnut floor flashed into her head, Grace shuddered once again.

Melissa. Poor, pathetic Melissa. But she couldn't think of that now. She couldn't think of anything but her friends.

"They're not hurt?" she managed to ask.

"No." Seth left it at that, drove through the wash of streetlights and headlights. Her scent was sliding silkily through his car, teasing his senses. Deliberately he opened his window and let the light, damp breeze chase it away. "Where have you been the last few days, Ms. Fontaine?"

"Away." Weary, she laid her head back, shut her eyes. "It's one of my favorite spots."

She jerked upright again when he turned down a tree-lined street, then swung into the drive of a brick house. She saw a shiny Jaguar, then an impossibly decrepit boat of a car. But no spiffy MG, no practical little compact.

"Their cars aren't here," she began, tossing him a look of distrust and accusation.

"But they are."

She climbed out and, ignoring him, hurried toward the front door. Her knock was brisk, businesslike, but her fist trembled. The door opened, and a man she'd never seen before stared down at her. His cool green eyes flickered with shock, then slowly warmed. His flash of a smile was blinding. Then he reached out, laid a hand gently on her cheek.

"You're Grace."

"Yes, I—"

"It's absolutely wonderful to see you." He gathered her into his arms, one of which was freshly bandaged, with such easy affection that she didn't have time to register surprise. "I'm Cade," he murmured, his gaze meeting Seth's over Grace's head. "Cade Parris. Come on in."

"Bailey. M.J."

"Just in here. They'll be fine as soon as they see you." He took her arm, felt the quick, hard tremors in it. But in the doorway of the living room, she stopped, laid a hand over his arm.

Inside, Bailey and M.J. stood, facing away, hands linked. Their voices were low, with tears wrenching through them. A man stood a short distance away, his hands thrust in his pockets and a look of helplessness on his bruised and battered face. When he saw her, his eyes, the gray of storm clouds, narrowed, flashed. Then smiled.

Grace took one shuddering breath, exhaled it slowly. "Well," she said in a clear, steady voice, "it's gratifying to know someone would weep copiously over me."

Both women whirled. For a moment, all three stared, three pair of eyes brimming over. To Seth's mind, they all moved as one, as a unit, so that their leaping rush across the room to each other held an uncanny and undeniably feminine grace. Then they were fused together, voices and tears mixing.

A triangle, he thought, frowning. With three points that made a whole. Like the golden triangle that held three priceless and powerful stones.

"I think they could use a little time," Cade said quietly, and gestured to the other man. "Lieutenant?" He motioned down the hall, lifting his brows when Seth hesitated. "I don't think they're going anywhere just now."

With a barely perceptible shrug, Seth stepped back. He could give them twenty minutes. "I need your phone."

"There's one in the kitchen. Want a beer, Jack?"

The third man grinned. "You're playing my song."

"Amnesia," Grace said a little time later. She and Bailey were huddled together on the sofa, with M.J. sitting on the floor at their feet. "Everything just blanked?"

"Everything." Bailey kept her hold on Grace's hand tight, afraid to break the link. "I woke up in this horrible little hotel room with no memory, over a million in cash, and the diamond. I picked Cade's name out of the phone book. Parris." She smiled a little. "Funny, isn't it?"

"I'm going to get you to France yet," Grace promised.

"He helped me through everything." The warmth in her tone had Grace sharing a quick look with M.J. This was something to be discussed in detail later. "I started to remember, piece by piece. You and M.J., just flashes. I could see your faces, even hear your voices, but nothing fit. He's the one who narrowed it down to Salvini, and when he took me there… He broke in."

"Shortly before we did," M.J. added. "Jack could tell the rear locks had been picked."

"We got inside," Bailey continued, and her tear-ravaged eyes went glassy. "And I remembered, I remembered it all then, how Thomas and Timothy were planning to steal the stones, copy them. How I'd shipped one off to each of you to keep it from happening. Stupid, so stupid."

"No, it wasn't." Grace slid an arm around Bailey's shoulders. "It makes perfect sense to me. You didn't have time for anything else."

"I should have called the police, but I was so sure I could turn things around. I was going into Thomas's office to have a showdown, tell them it was over. And I saw…" She trembled again. "The fight. Horrible. The lightning flashing through the windows, their faces. Then Timothy grabbed the letter opener, the knife. The power went out, but the lightning kept flashing, and I could see what he was doing…to Thomas. All the blood."

"Don't," M.J. murmured, rubbing a comforting hand on Bailey's knee. "Don't go back there."

"No." Bailey shook her head. "I have to. He saw me, Grace. He would have killed me. He came after me. I had grabbed the bag with their deposit money, and I ran through the dark. And I hid down under the stairs. In this little cave under the stairs. But I could see him hunting for me, blood all over his hands. I still don't remember how I got out, got to that room."

Grace couldn't bear to imagine it—her quiet, serious-minded friend, pursued by a murderer. "The important thing is that you did get away, and you're safe." Grace looked down at M.J. "We all are." She tried a bolstering grin. "And how did you spend your holiday?"

"On the run with a bounty hunter, handcuffed to a bed in a cheap motel, being shot at by a couple of creeps—with a little detour up to your place in the mountains."

Bounty hunter, Grace thought, trying to keep pace. The man named Jack, she supposed, with the bronze-tipped ponytail and the stormy gray eyes. And the killer grin. Handcuffs, cheap motels, and shootings. Pressing fingertips to her eyes, she latched on to the least disturbing detail.

"You were at my place? When?"

"It's a long story." M.J. gave a quick version of a handful of days from her first encounter with Jack, when he'd tried to take her in, believing her to be a bail jumper, to the two of them escaping that setup and working their way back to the core of the puzzle.

"We know someone's pulling the strings," M.J. concluded. "But we haven't gotten very far on figuring that out yet. The bail bondsman-cum-blackmailer who gave Jack the fake paperwork on me is dead, the two guys who came after us are dead, the Salvinis are dead."

"And Melissa," Grace murmured.

"It was Melissa?" Bailey turned to Grace. "In your house?"

"It must have been. When I got home, the cop was there. The place was torn up, and they'd assumed it was me." It took a moment, a carefully indrawn breath, a steady exhale, before she could finish. "She'd fallen off the balcony—or been pushed. I was miles away when it happened."

"Where did you go?" M.J. asked her. "When Jack and I got to your country place, it was locked up tight. I thought… I was sure you'd just been there. I could smell you."

"I left late yesterday morning. Got an itch to be near the water, so I drove down the Eastern Shore, found a little B-and-B. I did some antiquing, rubbed elbows with tourists, watched a fireworks display. I didn't leave until late today. I nearly stayed over another night. But I called both of you from the B-and-B and got your machines. I started feeling uncomfortable about being out of contact, so I headed home."

She shut her eyes a moment. "Bailey, I hadn't been

really thinking. Just before I left for the country, we lost one of the children."

"Oh, Grace, I'm sorry."

"It happens all the time. They're born with AIDS or a crack addiction or a hole in the heart. Some of them die. But I can't get used to it, and it was on my mind. So I wasn't really thinking. When I started back, I started to think. And I started to worry. Then the cop was there in my house. He asked about the stone. I didn't know what you wanted me to tell him."

"We've told the police everything now." Bailey sighed. "Neither Cade nor Jack seem to like this Buchanan very much, but they respect his abilities. The two stones are safe now, as we are."

"I'm sorry for what you went through, both of you. I'm sorry I wasn't here."

"It wouldn't have made any difference," M.J. declared. "We were scattered all over—one stone apiece. Maybe we were meant to be."

"Now we're together." Grace took each of their hands in hers. "What happens next?"

"Ladies." Seth stepped into the room, skimmed his cool gaze over them, then focused on Grace. "Ms. Fontaine. The diamond?"

She rose, picked up the purse she'd tossed carelessly on the end of the couch. Opening it, she took out a velvet pouch, slid the stone out into her palm. "Magnificent, isn't it?" she murmured, studying the flash of bold blue light. "Diamonds are supposed to be cold to the touch, aren't they, Bailey? Yet this has…heat." She lifted her eyes to Seth's as she crossed to him. "Still, how many lives is it worth?"

She held her open palm out. When his fingers closed

around the stone, she felt the jolt—his fingers on her skin, the shimmering blue diamond between their hands.

Something clicked, almost audibly.

She wondered if he'd felt it, heard it. Why else did those enigmatic eyes narrow, or his hand linger? The breath caught in her throat.

"Impressive, isn't it?" she managed, then felt the odd wave of emotion and recognition ebb when he took the stone from her hand.

He didn't care for the shock that had run up his arm, and he spoke bitingly. "I imagine this one's out of even your price range, Ms. Fontaine."

She merely smiled. No, she told herself, he couldn't have felt anything—and neither had she. Just imagination and stress. "I prefer to decorate my body in something less…obvious."

Bailey rose. "The Stars are my responsibility, unless and until the Smithsonian indicates otherwise." She looked over at Cade, who remained in the doorway. "We'll put them in the safe. All of them. And I'll speak with Dr. Linstrum in the morning."

Seth turned the stone over in his hand. He imagined he could confiscate it, and its mates. They were, after all, evidence in several homicides. But he didn't relish driving back to the station with a large fortune in his car.

Parris was an irritant, he reflected. But he was an honest one. And, technically, the stones were in Bailey James's keeping until the Smithsonian relieved her of them. He wondered just what the powers at the museum would have to say about the recent travels of the Three Stars.

But that wasn't his problem.

"Lock it up," he said, passing the stone off to Cade. "And I'll be talking with Dr. Linstrum in the morning, as well, Ms. James."

Cade took one quick, threatening step forward. "Look, Buchanan—"

"No." Quietly, Bailey stepped between them, a cool breeze between two building storms. "Lieutenant Buchanan's right, Cade. It's his business now."

"That doesn't stop it from being mine." He gave Seth one last, warning look. "Watch your step," he said, then walked away with the stone.

"Thank you for bringing Grace by so quickly, Lieutenant."

Seth looked down at the extended, and obviously dismissing, hand Bailey offered him. Here's your hat, he thought, what's your hurry. "I'm sorry you were disturbed, Ms. James." His gaze flicked over to M.J. "Ms. O'Leary. You'll keep available."

"We're not going anywhere." M.J.'s chin angled, a cocky gesture as Jack crossed to her. "Drive carefully, Lieutenant."

He acknowledged the second dismissal with a slight nod. "Ms. Fontaine? I'll drive you back."

"She's not leaving." M.J. jumped in front of Grace like a tiger defending her cub. "She's not going back to that house tonight. She's staying here, with us."

"You may not care to go back home, Ms. Fontaine," Seth said coolly. "You may find it more comfortable to answer questions in my office."

"You can't be serious—"

He cut Bailey's protest off with a look. "I have a body in the morgue. I take it very seriously."

"You're a class act, Buchanan," Jack drawled, but the

sound was low and threatening. "Why don't you and I go in the other room and…talk about our options?"

"It's all right." Grace stepped forward, working up a believable smile. "It's Jack, isn't it?"

"That's right." He took his attention from Buchanan long enough to smile at her. "Jack Dakota. Pleased to meet you… Miss April."

"Oh, my misspent youth survives." With a little laugh, she kissed his bruised cheek. "I appreciate the offer to beat up the lieutenant for me, Jack, but you look like you've already gone several rounds."

Grinning now, he stroked a thumb over his bruised jaw. "I've got a few more rounds in me."

"I don't doubt it. But, sad to say, the cop's right." She pushed her hair to her back and turned that smile, several degrees cooler now, on Seth. "Tactless, but right. He needs some answers. I need to go back."

"You're not going back to your house alone," Bailey insisted. "Not tonight, Grace."

"I'll be fine. But if it's all right with your Cade, I'll deal with this, pick up a few things and come back." She glanced over at Cade as he came back into the room. "Got a spare bed, darling?"

"You bet. Why don't I go with you, help you pick up your things and bring you back?"

"You stay here with Bailey." She kissed him, as well—a casual and already affectionate brush of lips. "I'm sure Lieutenant Buchanan and I will manage." She picked up her purse, turned and embraced both M.J. and Bailey again. "Don't worry about me. After all, I'm in the arms of the law."

She eased back, shot Seth one of those full candlepower smiles. "Isn't that right, Lieutenant?"

"In a manner of speaking." He stepped back and waited for her to walk to the door ahead of him.

She waited until they were in his car and pulling out of the drive. "I need to see the body." She didn't look at him, but lifted a hand to the four people crowded at the front door, watching them drive away. "You need— She'll have to be identified, won't she?"

It surprised him that she'd take the duty on. "Yes."

"Then let's get it over with. After—afterwards, I'll answer your questions. I'd prefer we handle that in your office," she added, using that smile again. "My house isn't ready for company."

"Fine."

She'd known it would be hard. She'd known it would be horrible. Grace had prepared herself for it—or she'd thought she had. Nothing, she realized as she stared down at what remained of the woman in the morgue, could have prepared her.

It was hardly surprising that they'd mistaken Melissa for her. The face Melissa had been so proud of was utterly ruined. Death had been cruel here, and, through her involvement with the hospital, Grace had reason to know it often was.

"It's Melissa." Her voice echoed flatly in the chilly white room. "My cousin, Melissa Fontaine."

"You're sure?"

"Yes. We shared the same health club, among other things. I know her body as well as I know mine. She has a sickle-shaped birthmark at the small of her back, just left of center. And there's a scar on the bottom of her left foot, small, crescent-shaped, in the ball of her foot, where she stepped on a broken shell in the Hamptons when we were twelve."

Seth shifted, found the scar, then nodded to the M.E.'s assistant. "I'm sorry for your loss."

"Yes, I'm sure you are." With muscles that felt like glass, she turned, her dimming vision passing over him. "Excuse me."

She made it nearly to the door before she swayed. Swearing under his breath, Seth caught her, pulled her out into the corridor and put her in a chair. With one hand, he shoved her head between her knees.

"I'm not going to faint." She squeezed her eyes tightly shut, battling fiercely against the twin foes of dizziness and nausea.

"Could have fooled me."

"I'm much too sophisticated for something as maudlin as a swoon." But her voice broke, her shoulders sagged, and for a moment she kept her head down. "Oh, God, she's dead. And all because she hated me."

"What?"

"Doesn't matter. She's dead." Bracing herself, she sat up again, let her head rest against the cold white wall. Her cheeks were just as colorless. "I have to call my aunt. Her mother. I have to tell her what happened."

He gauged this woman, studying the face that was no less staggeringly lovely for being bone-white. "Give me the name. I'll take care of it."

"It's Helen Wilson Fontaine. I'll do it."

He didn't realize until her hand moved that he'd placed his own over it. He pulled back on every level, and rose. "I haven't been able to reach Helen Fontaine or her husband. She's in Europe."

"I know where she is." Grace shook back her hair, but

didn't try to stand. Not yet. "I can find her." The thought of making that call, saying what had to be said, squeezed her throat. "Could I have some water, Lieutenant?"

His heels echoed on tile as he strode off. Then there was silence—a full, damning silence that whispered of what kind of business was done in such places. There were scents here that slid slyly under the potent odors of antiseptics and industrial cleaning solutions.

She was pitifully grateful when she heard his footsteps on the return journey.

She took the paper cup from him with both hands, drinking slowly, concentrating on the simple act of swallowing liquid.

"Why did she hate you?"

"What?"

"Your cousin. You said she hated you. Why?"

"Family trait," she said briefly. She handed him back the empty cup as she rose. "I'd like to go now."

He took her measure a second time. Her color had yet to return, her pupils were dilated, the electric-blue irises were glassy. He doubted she'd last another hour.

"I'll take you back to Parris's," he decided. "You can get your things in the morning, come in to my office to make your statement."

"I said I'd do it tonight."

"And I say you'll do it in the morning. You're no good to me now."

She tried a weak laugh. "Why, Lieutenant, I believe you're the first man who's ever said that to me. I'm crushed."

"Don't waste the routine on me." He took her arm, led her to the outside doors. "You haven't got the energy for it."

He was exactly right. She pulled her arm free as they stepped back into the thick night air. "I don't like you."

"You don't have to." He opened the car door, waited. "Any more than I have to like you."

She stepped to the door, and with it between them met his eyes. "But the difference is, if I had the energy—or the inclination—I could make you sit up and beg."

She got in, sliding those long, silky legs in.

Not likely, Seth told himself as he shut the door with a snap. But he wasn't entirely sure he believed it.

Chapter 3

She felt like a weakling, but she didn't go home. She'd needed friends, not that empty house, with the shadow of a body drawn on the floor.

Jack had gone over, fetched her bags out of her car and brought them to her. For a day, at least, she was content to make do with that.

Since she was driving in to meet with Seth, Grace had made do carefully. She'd dressed in a summer suit she'd just picked up on the Shore. The little short skirt and waist-length jacket in buttercup yellow weren't precisely professional—but she wasn't aiming for professional. She'd taken the time to catch her waterfall of hair back in a complicated French braid and made up her face with the concentration and determination of a general plotting a decisive battle.

Meeting with Seth again felt like a battle.

Her stomach was still raw from the call she'd made to her aunt, and the sickness that had overwhelmed her after it. She'd slept poorly, but she had slept, tucked into one of Cade's guest rooms, secure that those who meant most to her were close by.

She would deal with the relatives later, she thought, easing her convertible into the lot at the station house. It would be hard, but she would deal with them. For now, she had to deal with herself. And Seth Buchanan.

If anyone had been watching as she stepped from her car and started across the lot, he would have seen a transformation. Subtly, gradually, her eyes went from weary to sultry. Her gait loosened, eased into a lazy, hip-swinging walk designed to cross a man's eyes. Her mouth turned up slightly at the corners, into a secret, knowing female smile.

It wasn't really a mask, but another part of her. Innate and habitual, it was an image she could draw on at will. She willed it now, flashing a slow under-the-lashes smile at the uniform who stepped to the door as she did. He flushed, moved back and nearly bobbled the door in his hurry to open it for her.

"Why, thank you, Officer."

Heat rose up his neck, into his face, and made her smile widen. She was right on target. Seth Buchanan wouldn't see a pale, trembling woman this morning. He'd see Grace Fontaine, just hitting her stride.

She sauntered up to the sergeant on duty at the desk, skimmed a fingertip along the edge. "Excuse me?"

"Yes, ma'am." His Adam's apple bobbed three times as he swallowed.

"I wonder if you could help me? I'm looking for a

Lieutenant Buchanan. Are you in charge?" She skimmed her gaze over him. "You must be in charge, Commander."

"Ah, yes. No. It's sergeant." He fumbled for the sign-in book, the passes. "I— He's— You'll find the lieutenant upstairs, detective division. To the left of the stairs."

"Oh." She took the pen he offered and signed her name boldly. "Thank you, Commander. I mean, Sergeant."

She heard his little expulsion of breath as she turned, and felt his gaze on her legs as she climbed the stairs.

She found the detective division easily enough. One sweeping glance took in the front-to-front desks, some manned, some not. The cops were in shirtsleeves in an oppressive heat that was barely touched by what had to be a faulty air-conditioning unit. A lot of guns, she thought, a lot of half-eaten meals and empty cups of coffee. Phones shrilling.

She picked her mark—a man with a loosened tie, feet on the desk, a report of some kind in one hand and a Danish in the other. As she started through the crowded room, several conversations stopped. Someone whistled softly—it was like a sigh. The man at the desk swept his feet to the floor, swallowed the Danish.

"Ma'am."

About thirty, she judged, though his hairline was receding rapidly. He wiped his crumb-dusted fingers on his shirt, rolled his eyes slightly to the left, where one of his associates was grinning and pounding a fist to his heart.

"I hope you can help me." She kept her eyes on his, and only his, until a muscle began to twitch in his jaw. "Detective?"

"Yeah, ah, Carter, Detective Carter. What can I do for you?"

"I hope I'm in the right place." For effect, she turned her head, swept her gaze over the room and its occupants. Several stomachs were ruthlessly sucked in. "I'm looking for Lieutenant Buchanan. I think he's expecting me." Gracefully she brushed a loose flutter of hair away from her face. "I'm afraid I just don't know the proper procedure."

"He's in his office. Back in his office." Without taking his eyes from her he jerked a thumb. "Belinski, tell the lieutenant he has a visitor. A Miss..."

"It's Grace." She slid a hip onto the corner of the desk, letting her skirt hike up a dangerous inch. "Grace Fontaine. Is it all right if I wait here, Detective Carter? Am I interrupting your work?"

"Yes— No. Sure."

"It's so exciting." She brought the temperature of the overheated room up ten more degrees with a dazzling smile. "Detective work. You must have so many interesting stories."

By the time Seth had finished the phone call he was on when he was notified of Grace's arrival, shrugged back into the jacket he'd removed as a concession to the heat and made his way into the bull pen, Carter's desk was completely surrounded. He heard a low, throaty female laugh rise out of the center of the crowd.

And saw a half a dozen of his best men panting like puppies over a meaty bone.

The woman, he decided, was going to be an enormous headache.

"I see all cases have been closed this morning, and miraculously crime has come to a halt."

His voice had the desired effect. Several men jerked straight. Those less easily intimidated grinned as they skulked back to their desks. Deserted, Carter flushed from his neck to his receding sandy hairline. "Ah, Grace—that is, Miss Fontaine to see you, Lieutenant. Sir."

"So I see. You finish that report, Detective?"

"Working on it." Carter grabbed the papers he'd tossed aside and buried his nose in them.

"Ms. Fontaine." Seth arched a brow, gestured toward his office.

"It was nice meeting you, Michael." Grace trailed a finger over Carter's shoulder as she passed.

He'd feel the heat of that skimming touch for hours.

"You can cut the power back now," Seth said dryly as he opened the door to his office. "You won't need it."

"You never know, do you?" She sauntered in, moving past him, close enough for them to brush bodies. She thought she felt him stiffen, just a little, but his eyes remained level, cool, and apparently unimpressed. Miffed, she studied his office.

The institutional beige of the walls blended depressingly into the dingy beige of the aging linoleum floor. An overburdened department-issue desk, gray file cabinets, computer, phone and one small window didn't add any spark to the no-nonsense room.

"So this is where the mighty rule," she murmured. It disappointed her that she found no personal touches. No photos, no sports trophies. Nothing she could hold on to, no sign of the man behind the badge.

As she had in the bull pen, she eased a hip onto the

corner of his desk. To say she resembled a sunbeam would have been a cliché. And it would have been incorrect, Seth decided. Sunbeams were tame—warm, welcoming. She was an explosive bolt of heat lightning— Hot. Fatal.

A blind man would have noticed those satiny legs in the snug yellow skirt. Seth merely walked around, sat, looked at her face.

"You'd be more comfortable in a chair."

"I'm fine here." Idly she picked up a pen, twirled it. "I don't suppose this is where you interrogate suspects."

"No, we have a dungeon downstairs for that."

Under other circumstances, she would have appreciated his dust-dry tone. "Am I a suspect?"

"I'll let you know." He angled his head. "You recover quickly, Ms. Fontaine."

"Yes, I do. You had questions, Lieutenant?"

"Yes, I do. Sit down. In a chair."

Her lips moved in what was nearly a pout. A luscious come-on-and-kiss-me pout. He felt the quick, helpless pull of lust, and damned her for it. She moved, sliding off the desk, settling into a chair, taking her time crossing those killer legs.

"Better?"

"Where were you Saturday, between the hours of midnight and 3:00 a.m.?"

So that was when it had happened, she thought, and ignored the ache in her stomach. "Aren't you going to read me my rights?"

"You're not charged, you don't need a lawyer. It's a simple question."

"I was in the country. I have a house in western

Maryland. I was alone. I don't have an alibi. Do I need a lawyer now?"

"Do you want to complicate this, Ms. Fontaine?"

"There's no way to simplify it, is there?" But she flicked a hand in dismissal. The thin diamond bracelet that circled her wrist shot fire. "All right, Lieutenant, as uncomplicated as possible. I don't want my lawyer—for the moment. Why don't I just give you a basic rundown? I left for the country on Wednesday. I wasn't expecting my cousin, or anyone, for that matter. I did have contact with a few people over the weekend. I bought a few supplies in the town nearby, shopped at the gardening stand. That would have been Friday afternoon. I picked up some mail on Saturday. It's a small town, the postmistress would remember. That was before noon, however, which would give me plenty of time to drive back. And, of course, there was the courier who delivered Bailey's package on Friday."

"And you didn't find that odd? Your friend sends you a blue diamond, and you just shrug it off and go shopping?"

"I called her. She wasn't in." She arched a brow. "But you probably know that. I did find it odd, but I had things on my mind."

"Such as?"

Her lips curved, but the smile wasn't reflected in her eyes. "I'm not required to tell you my thoughts. I did wonder about it and worried a little. I thought perhaps it was a copy, but I didn't really believe that. A copy couldn't have what that stone has. Bailey's instructions in the package were to keep it with me until she contacted me. So that's what I did."

"No questions?"

"I rarely question people I trust."

He tapped a pencil on the edge of the desk. "You stayed alone in the country until Monday, when you drove back to the city."

"No. I drove down to the Eastern Shore on Sunday. I had a whim." She smiled again. "I often do. I stayed at a bed-and-breakfast."

"You didn't like your cousin?"

"No, I didn't." She imagined that quick shift of topic was an interrogation technique. "She was difficult to like, and I rarely make the effort with difficult people. We were raised together after my parents were killed, but we weren't close. I intruded into her life, into her space. She compensated for it by being disagreeable. I was often disagreeable in return. As we got older, she had a less…successful talent with men than I. Apparently she thought by enhancing the similarities in our appearance, she'd have better success."

"And did she?"

"I suppose it depends on your point of view. Melissa enjoyed men." To combat the guilt coating her heart, Grace leaned back negligently in the chair. "She certainly enjoyed men—which is one of the reasons she was recently divorced. She preferred the species in quantity."

"And how did her husband feel about that?"

"Bobbie's a…" She trailed off, then relieved a great deal of her own tension with a quick, delighted and very appealing laugh. "If you're suggesting that Bobbie—her ex—tracked her down to my house, murdered her, trashed the place and walked off whistling, you couldn't be more wrong. He's a cream puff. And he is, I believe, in England, even as we speak. He enjoys tennis and never misses Wimbledon. You can check easily enough."

Which he would, Seth thought, noting it down. "Some people find murder distasteful on a personal level, but not at a distance. They just pay for a service."

This time she sighed. "We both know Melissa wasn't the target, Lieutenant. I was. She was in my house." Restless, she rose, a graceful and feline movement. Walking to the tiny window, she looked out on his dismal view. "She's made herself at home in my Potomac house twice before when I was away. The first time, I tolerated it. The second, she enjoyed the facilities a bit too enthusiastically for my taste. We had a spat about it. She left in a huff, and I removed the spare key. I should have thought to change the locks, but it never occurred to me she'd go to the trouble of having copies made."

"When was the last time you saw her or spoke with her?"

Grace sighed. Dates ran through her head, people, events, meaningless social forays. "About six weeks ago, maybe eight. At the health club. We ran into each other in the steam room, didn't have much conversation. We never had much to say to each other."

She was regretting that now, Seth realized. Going over in her head opportunities lost or wasted. And it would do no good. "Would she have opened the door to someone she didn't know?"

"If the someone was male and was marginally attractive, yes." Weary of the interview, she turned back. "Look, I don't know what else I can tell you, what help I can possibly be. She was a careless, often arrogant woman. She picked up strange men in bars when she felt the urge. She let someone in that night, and she died for it. Whatever she was, she didn't deserve to die for that."

She brushed at her hair absently, tried to clear her mind as Seth simply sat, waiting. "Maybe he demanded she give him the stone. She wouldn't have understood. She paid for her trespassing, for her carelessness and her ignorance. And the stone is back with Bailey, where it belongs. If you haven't spoken to Dr. Linstrum yet this morning, I can tell you that Bailey should be meeting with him right now. I don't know anything else to tell you."

He kicked back for a moment, his eyes cool and steady on her face. If he discounted the connection with the diamonds, it could play another way. Two women, at odds all their lives. One of them returns home unexpectedly to find the other in her home. An argument. Escalating into a fight. And one of them ends up taking a dive off a second-floor balcony into a pool of glass.

The first woman doesn't panic. She trashes her own home to cover herself, then drives away. Puts distance between herself and the scene.

Was she a skilled enough actress to fake that stark shock, the raw emotion he'd seen on her face the night before?

He thought she was.

But despite that, the scene just didn't click. There was the undeniable connection of the diamonds. And he was dead sure that if Grace Fontaine had caused her cousin's fall, she would have been just as capable of picking up the phone and coolly reporting an accident.

"All right, that's all for now."

"Well." Her breath was a huff of relief. "That wasn't so bad, all in all."

He stood up. "I'll have to ask you to stay available."

She switched on the charm again, a hot, rose-colored light. "I'm always available, handsome. Ask anyone." She picked up her purse, moved with him to the door. "How long before I can have my house dealt with? I'd like to put things back to order as quickly as possible."

"I'll let you know." He glanced at his watch. "When you're up to going through things and doing an inventory to see what's missing, I'd like you to contact me."

"I'm on my way over now to do just that."

His brow furrowed a moment as he juggled responsibilities. He could assign a man to go with her, but he preferred dealing with it himself. "I'll follow you over."

"Police protection?"

"If necessary."

"I'm touched. Why don't I give you a lift, handsome?"

"I'll follow you over," he repeated.

"Suit yourself," she began, and grazed a hand over his cheek. Her eyes widened slightly as his fingers clamped on her wrist. "Don't like to be petted?" She purred the words, surprised at how her heart had jumped and started to race. "Most animals do."

His face was very close to hers, their bodies were just touching, with the heat from the room and something even more sweltering between them. Something old, and almost familiar.

He drew her hand down slowly, kept his fingers on her wrist.

"Be careful what buttons you push."

Excitement, she realized with surprise. It was pure, primal excitement that zipped through her. "Wasted advice," she said silkily, daring him. "I enjoy pushing new ones. And apparently you have a few interesting buttons just begging for attention." She skimmed her gaze deliberately down to his mouth. "Just begging."

He could imagine himself shoving her back against the door, moving fast into that heat, feeling her go molten. Because he was certain she was aware of just how perfectly a man would imagine it, he stepped back, released her and opened the door to the din of the bull pen.

"Be sure to turn in your visitor's badge at the desk," he said.

He was a cool one, Grace thought as she drove. An attractive, successful, unmarried—she'd slipped that bit of data out of an unsuspecting Detective Carter—and self-contained man.

A challenge.

And, she decided as she passed through the quiet, well-designed neighborhood, toward her home, a challenge was exactly what she needed to get through the emotional upheaval.

She'd have to face her aunt in a few hours, and the rest of the relatives soon after. There would be questions, demands, and, she knew, blame. She would be the recipient of all of it. That was the way her family worked, and that was what she'd come to expect from them.

Ask Grace, take from Grace, point the finger at Grace. She wondered how much of that she deserved, and how much had simply been inherited along with the money her parents left her.

It hardly mattered, she thought, since both were hers, like it or not.

She swung into her drive, her gaze sweeping over and up. The house was something she'd wanted. The clever and unique design of wood and glass, the gables, the cornices, the decks and the ruthlessly groomed grounds. She'd wanted the space, the elegance that lent itself to entertaining, the convenience to the city. The proximity to Bailey and M.J.

But the little house in the mountains was something she'd needed. And that was hers, and hers alone. The relatives didn't know it existed. No one could find her there unless she wanted to be found.

But here, she thought as she set the brakes, was the neat, expensive home of one Grace Fontaine. Heiress, socialite and party girl. The former centerfold, the Radcliffe graduate, the Washington hostess.

Could she continue to live here, she wondered, with death haunting the rooms? Time would tell.

For now, she was going to concentrate on solving the puzzle of Seth Buchanan, and finding a way under that seemingly impenetrable armor of his.

Just for the fun of it.

She heard him pull in and, in a deliberately provocative move, turned, tipped down her shaded glasses and studied him over the tops.

Oh, yes, she thought. He was very, very attractive. The way he controlled that lean and muscled body. Very economical. No wasted movements. He wouldn't waste them in bed, either. And she wondered just how long it would be before she could lure him there. She had a hunch—and she rarely doubted her hunches where men were concerned—that there was a volcano bubbling under that calm and somewhat austere surface.

She was going to enjoy poking at it until it erupted.

As he crossed to her, she handed him her keys. "Oh, but you have your own now, don't you?" She tipped her glasses back into place. "Well, use mine…this time."

"Who else has a set?"

She skimmed the tip of her tongue over her top lip, darkly pleased when she saw his gaze jerk down. Just for an instant, but it was progress. "Bailey and M.J. I don't give my keys to men. I'd rather open the door for them myself. Or close it."

"Fine." He dumped the keys back in her hand, looking amused when her brows drew together. "Open the door."

One step forward, two steps back, she mused, then stepped up on the flagstone portico and unlocked her home.

She'd braced for it, but it was still difficult. The foyer was as it had been, largely undisturbed. But her gaze was drawn up now, helplessly, to the shattered railing.

"It's a long way to fall," she murmured. "I wonder if you have time to think, to understand, on the way down."

"She wouldn't have."

"No." And that was better, somehow. "I suppose not." She stepped into the living area, forced herself to look at the chalk outline. "Well, where to begin?"

"He got to your safe down here. Emptied it. You'll want to list what was taken out."

"The library safe." She moved through, under an arch and into a wide room filled with light and books. A great many of those books littered the floor now, and an art deco lamp in the shape of an elongated woman's body—a small thing she'd loved—was cracked in two. "He wasn't subtle, was he?"

"I say he was rushed. And pissed off."

"You'd know best." She walked to the safe, noting the open door and the empty interior. "I had some jewelry—quite a bit, actually. A few thousand in cash."

"Bonds, stock certificates?"

"No, they're in my safe-deposit box at the bank. One doesn't need to take out stock certificates and enjoy the way they sparkle. I bought a terrific pair of diamond earrings just last month." She sighed, shrugged. "Gone now. I have a complete list of my jewelry, and photographs of each piece, along with the insurance papers, in my safety box. Replacing them's just a matter of—"

She broke off, made a small, distressed sound and rushed from the room.

The woman could move when she wanted, Seth thought as he headed upstairs after her. And she didn't lose any of that feline grace with speed. He turned into her bedroom, then into her walk-in closet behind her.

"He wouldn't have found it. He couldn't have found it." She repeated the words like a prayer as she twisted a knob on the built-in cabinet. It swung out, revealing a safe in the wall behind.

Quickly, her fingers not quite steady, she spun the combination, wrenched open the door. Her breath expelled in a whoosh as she knelt and took out velvet boxes and bags.

More jewelry, he thought with a shake of his head. How many earrings could one woman wear? But she was opening each box carefully, examining the contents.

"These were my mother's," she murmured, with a catch of undiluted emotion in the words. "They matter. The sapphire pin my father gave her for their fifth anniversary, the necklace he gave her when I was born. The pearls. She wore these the day they married." She stroked the creamy white strand over her cheek as if it were a loved one's hand. "I had this built for them, didn't keep them with the others. Just in case."

She sat back on her heels, her lap filled with jewelry that meant so much more than gold and pretty stones. "Well," she managed as her throat closed. "Well, they're here. They're still here."

"Ms. Fontaine."

"Oh, call me Grace," she snapped. "You're as stuffy as my Uncle Niles." Then she pressed a hand to her forehead, trying to work away the beginnings of a tension headache. "I don't suppose you can make coffee."

"Yes, I can make coffee."

"Then why don't you go down and do that little thing, handsome, and give me a minute here?"

He surprised her, and himself, by crouching down first, laying a hand on her shoulder. "You could have lost the pearls, lost all of it. You still wouldn't have lost your memories."

Uneasy that he'd felt compelled to say it, he straightened and left her alone. He went directly to the kitchen, pushing through the mess to fill the coffeepot. He set it up to brew and switched the machine on. Stuck his hands in his pockets, then pulled them out.

What the hell was going on? he asked himself. He should be focused on the case, and the case alone. Instead, he felt himself being pulled, tugged at, by the woman upstairs—by the various faces of that woman. Bold, fragile, sexy, sensitive.

Just which was she? And why had he spent most of the night with her face lodged in his dreams?

He shouldn't even be here, he admitted. He had no official reason to be spending this time with her. It was true he felt the case warranted his personal attention. It was serious enough. But she was only one small part of the whole.

And he'd be lying to himself if he said he was here strictly on an investigation.

He found two undamaged cups. There were several broken ones lying around. Good Meissen china, he noted. His mother had a set she prized dearly. He was just pouring the coffee when he sensed her behind him.

"Black?"

"That's fine." She stepped in, and winced as she took a visual inventory of the kitchen. "He didn't miss much, did he? I suppose he thought I might stick a big blue diamond in my coffee canister or cookie jar."

"People put their valuables in a lot of odd places. I was involved in a burglary case once where the victim saved her in-house cash because she'd kept it in a sealed plastic bag in the bottom of the diaper pail. What self-respecting B-and-E man is going to paw through diapers?"

She chuckled, sipped her coffee. Whether or not it had been his purpose, his telling of the story had made her feel better. "It makes keeping things in a safe seem foolish. This one didn't take the silver, or any of the electronics. I suppose, as you said, he was in too much of a hurry, and just took what he could stuff in his pockets."

She walked to the kitchen window and looked out. "Melissa's clothes are upstairs. I didn't see her purse. He might have taken that, too, or it could just be buried under the mess."

"We'd have found it if it had been here."

She nodded. "I'd forgotten. You've already searched through my things." She turned back, leaned on the counter and eyed him over the rim of her cup. "Did you go through them personally, Lieutenant?"

He thought of the red silk gown. "Some of it. You have your own department store here."

"I'd come by that naturally, wouldn't I? I have a weakness for things. All manner of things. You make excellent coffee, Lieutenant. Isn't there anyone who brews it for you in the morning?"

"No. Not at the moment." He set his coffee aside. "That wasn't very subtle."

"It wasn't intended to be. It's not that I mind competition. I just like to know if I have any. I still don't think I like you, but that could change." She lifted a hand to finger the tail of her braid. "Why not be prepared?"

"I'm interested in closing a case, not in playing games with you… Grace."

It was such a cool delivery, so utterly dispassionate it kindled her spirit of competition. "I suppose you don't like aggressive women."

"Not particularly."

"Well, then." She smiled as she stepped closer to him. "You're just going to hate this."

In a slick and practiced move, she slid a hand up into his hair and brought his mouth to hers.

Chapter 4

The jolt, lightning wrapped in black velvet, stabbed through him in one powerful strike. His head spun with it, his blood churned, his belly ached. No part of his system was spared the rapid onslaught of that lush and knowing mouth.

Her taste, unexpected yet familiar, plunged into him like hot spiced wine that rushed immediately to his head, leaving him dazed and drunk and desperate.

His muscles bunched, as if poised to leap. And in leaping, he would possess what was somehow already his. It took a vicious twist of will to keep his arms locked at his sides, when they strained to reach out, take, relish. Her scent was as dark, as drugging, as her flavor. Even the low, persuasive hum that sounded in her throat as she moved that glorious fantasy of a body against his was a tantalizing hint of what could be.

For a slow count of five, he fisted his hands, then relaxed them and let the internal war rage while his lips remained passive, his body rigid in denial.

He wouldn't give her the satisfaction of response…

She knew it was a mistake. Even as she moved toward him, reached for him, she'd known it. She'd made mistakes before, and she tried never to regret what was done and couldn't be undone.

But she regretted this.

She deeply regretted that his taste was utterly unique and perfect for her palate. That the texture of his hair, the shape of his shoulders, the strong wall of his chest, all taunted her, when she'd only meant to taunt him, to show him what she could offer. If she chose.

Instead, swept into need, rushed into it by that mating of lips, she offered more than she'd intended. And he gave nothing back.

She caught his bottom lip between her teeth, one quick, sharp nip, then masked an outrageous rush of disappointment by stepping casually back and aiming an amused smile at him.

"My, my, you're a cool one, aren't you, Lieutenant?"

His blood burned with every heartbeat, but he merely inclined his head. "You're not used to being resistible, are you, Grace?"

"No." She rubbed a fingertip lightly over her lip in a movement that was both absent and provocative. The essence of him clung stubbornly there, insisting it belonged. "But then, most of the men I've kissed haven't had ice water in their veins. It's a shame." She took her finger from her own lip, tapped it on his. "Such a nice mouth. Such potential. Still, maybe you just don't care for…women."

The grin he flashed stunned her. His eyes glowed with it, in fascinating tones of gold. His mouth softened with a charm that had a wicked and unpredictable appeal. Suddenly he was approachable, nearly boyish, and it made her heart yearn.

"Maybe," he said, "you're just not my type."

She gave one short, humorless laugh. "Darling, I'm every man's type. Well, we'll just chalk it up to a failed experiment and move on." Telling herself it was foolish to be hurt, she stepped to him again, reached up to straighten the tie she'd loosened.

He didn't want her to touch him, not then, not when he was so precariously perched on the edge. "You've got a hell of an ego there."

"I suppose I do." With her hands still on his tie, she looked up, into his eyes. The hell with it, she thought, if they couldn't be lovers, maybe they could be cautious friends. The man who had looked at her and grinned would be a good, solid friend.

So she smiled at him with a sweetness that was without art or guile, lancing his heart with one clean blow. "But then, men are generally predictable. You're just the exception to the rule, Seth, the one that proves it."

She brushed her hands down, smoothing his jacket and said something more, but he didn't hear it over the roaring in his ears. His control broke; he felt the snap, like the twang of a sword violently broken over an armored knee. In a movement he was hardly aware of, he spun her around, pressed her back against the wall, and was ravaging her mouth.

Her heart kicked in her chest, drove the breath out of her body. She gripped his shoulders as much for balance as in response to the sudden, violent need that shot from him to her and fused them together.

She yielded, utterly, then locked her arms around his neck and poured herself back.

Here, was all her dazzled mind could think. Oh, here, at last.

His hands raced over her, molded and somehow recognized each curve. And the recognition seared through him, as hot and real as the surge of desire. He wanted that taste, had to have it inside him, to swallow it whole. He assaulted her mouth like a man feeding after a lifelong fast, filled himself with the flavors of her, all of them dark, ripe, succulent.

She was there for him, had always been there—impossibly there. And he knew that if he didn't pull back, he'd never be able to survive without her.

He slapped his hands on the wall on either side of her head to stop himself from touching, to stop himself from taking. Fighting to regain both his breath and his sanity, he eased out of the kiss, stepped away.

She continued to lean back against the wall, her eyes closed, her skin luminous with passion. By the time her lashes fluttered up and those slumberous blue eyes focused, he had his control snapped back ruthlessly in place.

"Unpredictable," she managed, barely resisting the urge to press both hands to her galloping heart. "Very."

"I warned you about pushing the wrong buttons." His voice was cool, edging toward cold, and had the effect of a backhand slap.

She flinched from it, might have reeled, if she hadn't been braced by the wall. His eyes narrowed fractionally at the reaction. Hurt? he wondered. No, that was ridiculous. She was a veteran game player and knew all the angles.

"Yes, you did." She straightened, pride stiffening her spine and forcing her lips to curve in a casual smile. "I'm just so resistant to warnings."

He thought she should be required by law to carry one—Danger! Woman!

"I've got work to do. I can give you another five minutes, if you want me to wait while you pack some things."

Oh, you bastard, she thought. How can you be so cool, so unaffected? "You toddle right along, handsome. I'll be fine."

"I'd prefer you weren't in the house alone for the moment. Go pack some things."

"It's my home."

"Right now, it's a crime scene. You're down to four and a half minutes."

Fury vibrated through her in hot, pulsing beats. "I don't need anything here." She turned, started out, whirling back when he took her arm. "What?"

"You need clothes," he said, patient now. "For a day or two."

"Do you really think I'd wear anything that bastard might have touched?"

"That's a foolish and a predictable reaction." His tone didn't soften in the least. "You're not a foolish or a predictable woman. Don't be a victim, Grace. Go pack your things."

He was right. She could have despised him for that alone. But the frustrated need still fisted inside her was a much better reason. She said nothing at all, simply turned again and walked away.

When he didn't hear the front door slam, he was satisfied that she'd gone upstairs to pack, as he'd told her to. Seth turned off the coffeemaker, rinsed the cups and set them in the sink, then went out to wait for her.

She was a fascinating woman, he thought. Full of temperament, energy and ego. And she was undoing him, knot by carefully tied knot. How she knew exactly what strings to pull to do so was just one more mystery.

He'd taken this case on, he reminded himself. Riding a desk and delegating were only part of the job. He needed to be involved, and he'd involved himself with this—and therefore with her. Grace's part of the whole was small, but he needed to treat her with the same objectivity that he treated every other piece of the case with.

He looked up, his gaze drawn to the portrait that smiled down so invitingly.

He'd have to be more machine than man to stay objective when it came to Grace Fontaine.

It was midafternoon before he could clear his desk enough to handle a follow-up interview. The diamonds were the key, and he wanted another look at them. He hadn't been surprised when his phone conversation with Dr. Linstrum at the Smithsonian resulted in a testimonial to Bailey James's integrity and skill. The diamonds she'd gone to such lengths to protect remained at Salvini, and in her care.

When Seth pulled into the parking lot of the elegant corner building just outside D.C. that housed Salvini, he nodded to the uniformed cop guarding the main door. And felt a faint tug of sympathy. The heat was brutal.

"Lieutenant." Despite a soggy uniform, the officer snapped to attention.

"Ms. James inside?"

"Yes, sir. The store's closed to the public for the next week." He indicated the darkened showroom through the thick glass doors with a jerk of the head. "We have a guard posted at every entrance, and Ms. James is on the lower level. It's easier access through the rear, Lieutenant."

"Fine. When's your relief, Officer?"

"I've got another hour." The cop didn't wipe his brow, but he wanted to. Seth Buchanan had a reputation for being a stickler. "Four-hour rotations, as per your orders, sir."

"Bring a bottle of water with you next time." Well aware that the uniform sagged the minute his back was turned, Seth rounded the building. After a brief conversation with the duty guard at the rear, he pressed the buzzer beside the reinforced steel door. "Lieutenant Buchanan," he said when Bailey answered through the intercom. "I'd like a few minutes."

It took her some time to get to the door. Seth visualized her coming out of the workroom on the lower level, winding down the short corridor, passing the stairs where she'd hidden from a killer only days before.

He'd been through the building himself twice, top to bottom. He knew that not everyone could have survived what she'd been through in there.

The locks clicked, the door opened. "Lieutenant." She smiled at the guard, silently apologizing for his miserable duty. "Please come in."

She looked neat and tidy, Seth thought, with her trim blouse and slacks, her blond hair scooped back. Only the faint shadows under her eyes spoke of the strain she'd been under.

"I spoke with Dr. Linstrum," Seth began.

"Yes, I expect you did. I'm very grateful for his understanding."

"The stones are back where they started."

She smiled a little. "Well, they're back where they were a few days ago. Who knows if they'll ever see Rome again. Can I get you something cold to drink?" She gestured toward a soft-drink machine standing brightly against a dark wall.

"I'll buy." He plugged in coins. "I'd like to see the diamonds, and have a few words with you."

"All right." She pressed the button for her choice, and retrieved the can that clunked down the shoot. "They're in the vault." She continued to speak as she led the way. "I've arranged to have the security and alarm system beefed up. We've had cameras in the showroom for a number of years, but I'll have them installed at the doors, as well, and for the upper and lower levels. All areas."

"That's wise." He concluded that there was a practical streak of common sense beneath the fragile exterior. "You'll run the business now?"

She opened a door, hesitated. "Yes. My stepfather left it to the three of us, with my stepbrothers sharing eighty percent between them. In the event any of us died without heirs, the shares go to the survivors." She drew in a breath. "I survived."

"That's something to be grateful for, Bailey, not guilty about."

"Yes, that's what Cade says. But you see, I once had the illusion, at least, that they were family. Have a seat, I'll get the Stars."

He moved into the work area, glanced at the equipment, the long worktable. Intrigued, he stepped closer, examining the glitter of colored stones, the twists of gold. It was going to be a necklace, he realized, running a fingertip over the silky length of a closely linked chain. Something bold, almost pagan.

"I needed to get back to work," she said from behind him. "To do something...different, my own, I suppose, before I faced dealing with these again."

She set down a padded box that held the trio of diamonds.

"Your design?" he asked, gesturing to the piece on the worktable.

"Yes. I see the piece in my head. I can't draw worth a lick, but I can visualize. I wanted to make something for M.J. and for Grace to..." She sighed, sat on the high stool. "Well, let's say to celebrate survival."

"And this is the one for Grace."

"Yes." She smiled, pleased that he'd sensed it. "I see something more streamlined for M.J. But this is Grace." Carefully she set the unfinished work in a tray, slid the padded box containing the Three Stars between them. "They never lose their impact. Each time I see them, it stuns."

"How long before you're finished with them?"

"I'd just begun when—when I had to stop." She cleared her throat. "I've verified their authenticity. They are blue diamonds. Still, both the museum and the insurance carrier prefer more in-depth verification. I'll be running a number of other tests beyond what I've already started or completed. A metallurgist is testing the triangle, but that will be given to me for further study in a day or two. It shouldn't take more than a week altogether before the museum can take possession."

He lifted a stone from the bed, knew as soon as it was in his hand that it was the one Grace had carried with her. He told himself that was impossible. His untrained eye couldn't tell one stone from either of its mates.

Yet he felt her on it. In it.

"Will it be hard to part with them?"

"I should say no, after the past few days. But yes, it will."

Grace's eyes were this color, Seth realized. Not sapphire, but the blue of the rare, powerful diamond.

"Worth killing for," he said quietly, looking at the stone in his hand. "Dying for." Then, annoyed with himself, he set the stone down again. "Your stepbrothers had a client."

"Yes, they spoke of a client, argued about him. Thomas wanted to take the money, the initial deposit, and run."

The money was being checked now, but there wasn't much hope of tracing its source.

"Timothy told Thomas he was a fool, that he'd never be able to run far or fast enough. That he—the client—would find him. He's not even human. Timothy said that, or something like it. They were both afraid, terribly afraid, and terribly desperate."

"Over their heads."

"Yes, I think very much over their heads."

"It would have to be a collector. No one could move these stones for resale." He glanced at the gems sparkling in their trays like pretty stars. "You acquire, buy and sell to collectors of gems."

"Yes—certainly not on a scale like the Three Stars, but yes." She skimmed her fingers absently through her hair. "A client might come to us with a stone, or a request for one. We'd also acquire certain gems on spec, with a particular client in mind."

"You have a client list, then? Names, preferences?"

"Yes, and we have records of what a client had purchased, or sold." She gripped her hands together. "Thomas would have kept it, in his office. Timothy would have copies in his. I'll find them for you."

He touched her shoulder lightly before she could slide from the stool. "I'll get them."

She let out a breath of relief. She had yet to be able to face going upstairs, into the room where she'd seen murder. "Thank you."

He took out his notebook. "If I asked you to name the top gem collectors, your top clients, what names come to mind? Off the top of your head?"

"Oh." Concentrating, she gnawed on her lip. "Peter Morrison in London, Sylvia Smythe-Simmons of New York, Henry and Laura Muller here in D.C., Matthew Wolinski in California. And I suppose Charles Van Horn here in D.C., too, though he's new to it. We sold him three lovely stones over the last two years. One was a spectacular opal I coveted. I'm still hoping he'll let me set it for him. I have this design in my head…"

She shook herself, trailed off when she realized why he was asking. "Lieutenant, I know these people. I've dealt with them personally. The Mullers were friends of my stepfather's. Mrs. Smythe-Simmons is over eighty. None of them are thieves."

He didn't bother to glance up, but continued to write. "Then we'll be able to check them off the list. Taking anything or anyone at face value is a mistake in an investigation, Ms. James. We've had enough mistakes already."

"With mine standing out." Accepting that fact, she nudged her untouched soft drink over the table. "I should have gone to the police right away. I should have turned the information—at the very least, my suspicions—over to the authorities. Several people would still be alive if I had."

"It's possible, but it's not a given." Now he did glance up, noted the haunted look in those soft brown eyes. Compassion stirred. "Did you know your stepbrother was being blackmailed by a second-rate bail bondsman?"

"No," she murmured.

"Did you know that someone was pulling the strings, pulling them hard enough to turn your stepbrother into a killer?"

She shook her head, bit down hard on her lip. "The things I didn't know were the problem, weren't they? I put the two people I love most in terrible danger, then I forgot about them."

"Amnesia isn't a choice, it's a condition. And your friends handled themselves. They still are—in fact, I saw Ms. Fontaine just this morning. She doesn't look any the worse for wear to me."

Bailey caught the disdainful note and turned to face him. "You don't understand her. I would have thought a man who does what you do for a living would be able to see more clearly than that."

He thought he caught a faint hint of pity in her voice, and resented it. "I've always thought of myself as clear-sighted."

"People are rarely clear-sighted when it comes to Grace. They only see what she lets them see—unless they care enough to look deeper. She has the most generous heart of any person I've ever known."

Bailey caught the quick flicker of amused disbelief in his eyes and felt her anger rising against it. Furious, she pushed off the stool. "You don't know anything about her, but you've already dismissed her. Can you conceive of what she's going through right now? Her cousin was murdered—and in her stead."

"She's hardly to blame for that."

"Easy to say. But she'll blame herself, and so will her family. It's easy to blame Grace."

"You don't."

"No, because I know her. And I know she's dealt with perceptions and opinions just like yours most of her life. And her way of dealing with it is to do as she chooses, because whatever she does, those perceptions and opinions rarely change. Right now, she's with her aunt, I imagine, and taking the usual emotional beating."

Her voice heated, became rushed, as emotions swarmed. "Tonight, there'll be a memorial service for Melissa, and the relatives will hammer at her, the way they always do."

"Why should they?"

"Because that's what they do best." Running out of steam she turned her head, looked down at the Three Stars. Love, knowledge, generosity, she thought. Why did it seem there was so little of it in the world? "Maybe you should take another look, Lieutenant Buchanan."

He'd already taken too many, he decided. And he was wasting time. "She certainly inspires loyalty in her friends," he commented. "I'm going to look for those lists."

"You know the way." Dismissing him, Bailey picked up the stones to carry them back to the vault.

* * *

Grace was dressed in black, and had never felt less like grieving. It was six in the evening, and a light rain was beginning to fall. It promised to turn the city into a massive steam room instead of cooling it off. The headache that had been slyly brewing for hours snarled at the aspirin she'd already taken and leaped into full, vicious life.

She had an hour before the wake, one she had arranged quickly and alone, because her aunt demanded it. Helen Fontaine was handling grief in her own way—as she did everything else. In this case, it was by meeting Grace with a cold, damning and dry eye. Cutting off any offer of support or sympathy. And demanding that services take place immediately, and at Grace's expense and instigation.

They would be coming from all points, Grace thought as she wandered the large, empty room, with its banks of flowers, thick red drapes, deep pile carpeting. Because such things were expected, such things were reported in the press. And the Fontaines would never give the public media a bone to pick.

Except, of course, for Grace herself.

It hadn't been difficult to arrange for the funeral home, the music, the flowers, the tasteful canapés. Only phone calls and the invocation of the Fontaine name were required. Helen had brought the photograph herself, the large color print in a shining silver frame that now decorated a polished mahogany table and was flanked with red roses in heavy silver vases that Melissa had favored.

There would be no body to view.

Grace had arranged for Melissa's body to be released

from the morgue, had already written the check for the cremation and the urn her aunt had chosen.

There had been no thanks, no acknowledgment. None had been expected.

It had been the same from the moment Helen became her legal guardian. She'd been given the necessities of life—Fontaine-style. Gorgeous homes in several countries to live in, perfectly prepared food, tasteful clothing, an excellent education.

And she'd been told, endlessly, how to eat, how to dress, how to behave, who could be selected as a friend and who could not. Reminded, incessantly, of her good fortune—unearned—in having such a family behind her. Tormented, ruthlessly, by the cousin she was there tonight to mourn, for being orphaned, dependent.

For being Grace.

She'd rebelled against all of it, every aspect, every expectation and demand. She'd refused to be malleable, biddable, predictable. The ache for her parents had eventually dimmed, and with it the child's desperate need for love and acceptance.

She'd given the press plenty to report. Wild parties, unwise affairs, unrestricted spending.

When that didn't ease the hurt, she'd found something else. Something that made her feel decent and whole.

And she'd found Grace.

For tonight, she would be just what her family had come to expect. And she would get through the next endless hours without letting them touch her.

She sat heavily on a sofa with overstuffed velvet seats. Her head pounded, her stomach clutched. Closing her eyes, she willed herself to relax. She would spend this last hour alone, and prepare herself for the rest.

But she'd barely taken the second calming breath when she heard footsteps muffled on the thick patterned carpet. Her shoulders turned to rock, her spine snapped straight. She opened her eyes. And saw Bailey and M.J.

She let her eyes close again, on a pathetic rush of gratitude. "I told you not to come."

"Yeah, like we were going to listen to that." M.J. sat beside her, took her hand.

"Cade and Jack are parking the car." Bailey flanked her other side, took her other hand. "How are you holding up?"

"Better." Tears stung her eyes as she squeezed the hands clasped in hers. "A lot better now."

On a sprawling estate not so many miles from where Grace sat with those who loved her, a man stared out at the hissing rain.

Everyone had failed, he thought. Many had paid for their failures. But retribution was a poor substitute for the Three Stars.

A delay only, he comforted himself. The Stars were his, they were meant to be his. He had dreamed of them, had held them in his hands in those dreams. Sometimes the hands were human, sometimes not, but they were always his hands.

He sipped wine, watched the rain, and considered his options.

His plans had been delayed by three women. That was humiliating, and they would have to be made to pay for that humiliation.

The Salvinis were dead—Bailey James.

The fools he'd hired to retrieve the second Star were dead—M. J. O'Leary.

The man he'd sent with instructions to acquire the third Star at any cost was dead—Grace Fontaine.

And he smiled. That had been indiscreet, as he'd disposed of the lying fool himself. Telling him there'd been an accident, that the woman had fought him, run from him, and fallen to her death. Telling him he'd searched every corner of the house without finding the stone.

That failure had been irritating enough, but then to discover that the wrong woman had died and that the fool had stolen money and jewels without reporting them. Well, such disloyalty in a business associate could hardly be tolerated.

Smiling dreamily, he took a sparkling diamond earring out of his pocket. Grace Fontaine had worn this on her delectable lobe, he mused. He kept it now as a good-luck charm while he considered what steps to take next.

There were only days left before the Stars would be in the museum. Extracting them from those hallowed halls would take months, if not years, of planning. He didn't intend to wait.

Perhaps he had failed because he had been overcautious, had kept his distance from events. Perhaps the gods required a more personal risk. A more intimate involvement.

It was time, he decided, to step out of the shadows, to meet the women who had kept his property from him, face-to-face. He smiled again, excited by the thought, delighted with the possibilities.

When the knock sounded on the door, he answered with great cheer and good humor. "Enter."

The butler, in stern formal black, ventured no farther

than the threshold. His voice held no inflection. “I beg your pardon, Ambassador. Your guests are arriving.”

“Very well.” He sipped the last of his wine, set the empty crystal flute on a table. “I’ll be right down.”

When the door closed, he moved to the mirror, examined his flawless tuxedo, the wink of diamond studs, the gleam of the thin gold watch at his wrist. Then he examined his face—the smooth contours, the pampered, pale gold skin, the aristocratic nose, the firm, if somewhat thin, mouth. He brushed a hand over the perfectly groomed mane of silver-threaded black hair.

Then, slowly, smilingly, met his own eyes. Pale, almost translucent blue smiled back. His guests would see what he did, a perfectly groomed man of fifty-two, erudite and educated, well mannered and suave. They wouldn’t know what plans and plots he held in his heart. They would see no blood on his hands, though it had been only twenty-four short hours since he used them to kill.

He felt only pleasure in the memory, only delight in the knowledge that he would soon dine with the elite and the influential. And he could kill any one of them with a twist of his hands, with perfect immunity.

He chuckled to himself—a low, seductive sound with shuddering undertones. Tucking the earring back in his pocket, he walked from the room.

The ambassador was mad.

Chapter 5

Seth's first thought when he walked into the funeral parlor was that it seemed more like a tedious cocktail party than like a memorial service. People stood or sat in little cliques and groups, many of them nibbling on canapés or sipping wine. Beneath the strains of a muted Chopin étude, voices murmured. There was an occasional roll or tinkle of laughter.

He heard no tears.

Lights were respectfully dimmed, and set off the glitter and gleam of gems and gold. The fragrance of flowers mixed and merged with the scents worn by both men and women. He saw faces, both elegant and bored.

He saw no grief.

But he did see Grace. She stood looking up into the face of a tall, slim man whose golden tan set off his golden hair and bright blue eyes. He held one of her hands in his and smiled winningly. He appeared to be speaking quickly, persuasively. She shook her head once, laid a hand on his chest, then allowed herself to be drawn into an anteroom.

Seth's lip curled in automatic disdain. A funeral was a hell of a place for a flirtation.

"Buchanan." Jack Dakota wandered over. He scanned the room, stuck his hands in the pockets of the suit coat he wished fervently was still in his closet, instead of on his back. "Some party."

Seth watched two women air kiss. "Apparently."

"Doesn't seem like one a sane man would want to crash."

"I have business," he said briefly. Which could have waited until morning, he reminded himself. He should have let it wait. It annoyed him that he'd made the detour, that he'd been thinking of Grace—more, that he'd been unable to lock her out of his head.

He pulled a copy of a mug shot out of his pocket, handed it to Jack. "Recognize him?"

Jack scanned the picture, considered. Slick-looking dude, he thought. Vaguely European in looks, with the sleek black hair, dark eyes and refined features. "Nope. Looks like a poster boy for some wussy cologne."

"You didn't see him during your amazing weekend adventures?"

Jack took one last, harder look, handed the shot back. "Nope. What's his connection?"

"His prints were all over the house in Potomac."

Jack's interest rose. "He the one who killed the cousin?"

Seth met Jack's eyes coolly. "That has yet to be determined."

"Don't give me the cop stand, Buchanan. What'd the guy say? He stopped by to sell vacuum cleaners?"

"He didn't say anything. He was too busy floating facedown in the river."

With an oath, Jack's gaze whipped around the room again. He relaxed fractionally when he spotted M.J. huddled with Cade. "The morgue must be getting crowded. You got a name?"

Seth started to dismiss the question. He didn't care for professions that stood a step back from the police. But there was no denying that the bounty hunter and the private investigator were involved. And there was no avoiding the connection, he told himself.

"Carlo Monturri."

"Doesn't ring a bell either."

Seth hadn't expected it would, but the police—on several continents—knew the name. "He's out of your league, Dakota. His type keeps a fancy lawyer on retainer and doesn't use the local bail bondsman to get sprung."

As he spoke, Seth's eyes moved around the room as a cop's did, sweeping corner to corner, taking in details, body language, atmosphere. "Before he took his last swim, he was expensive hired muscle. He worked alone because he didn't like to share the fun."

"Connections in the area?"

"We're working on it."

Seth saw Grace come out of the anteroom. The man who was with her had his arm draped over her shoulders, pulled her close in an intimate embrace, kissed her. The flare of fury kindled in Seth's gut and bolted up to his heart.

"Excuse me."

Grace saw him the moment he started across the room. She murmured something to the man beside her, dislodged him, then dismissed him. Straightening her spine, she fixed on an easy smile.

"Lieutenant, we didn't expect you."

"I apologize for intruding in your—" he flicked a glance toward the golden boy, who was helping himself to a glass a wine "—grief."

The sarcasm slapped, but she didn't flinch. "I assume you have a reason for coming by."

"I'd like a moment of your time—in private."

"Of course." She turned to lead him out and came face-to-face with her aunt. "Aunt Helen."

"If you could tear yourself away from entertaining your suitors," Helen said coldly, "I want to speak to you."

"Excuse me," Grace said to Seth, and stepped into the anteroom again.

Seth debated moving off, giving them privacy. But he stayed where he was, two paces from the doorway. He told himself murder investigations didn't allow for sensitivity. Though they kept their voices low, he heard both women clearly enough.

"I assume you have Melissa's things at your home," Helen began.

"I don't know. I haven't been able to go through the house thoroughly yet."

Helen said nothing for a moment, simply studied her niece through cold blue eyes. Her face was smooth and showed no ravages of grief in the carefully applied makeup. Her hair was sleek, lightened to a tasteful ash blond. Her hands were freshly manicured and glittered with the diamond wedding band she continued to wear, though she'd shared little but her husband's name in over a decade, and a square-cut sapphire given to her by her latest lover.

"I sincerely doubt Melissa came to your home without a bag. I want her things, Grace. All of her things. You'll have nothing of hers."

"I never wanted anything of hers, Aunt Helen."

"Didn't you?" There was a crackle in the voice—a whip flicking. "Did you think she wouldn't tell me of your affair with her husband?"

Grace merely sighed. It was new ground, but sickeningly familiar. Melissa's marriage had failed, publicly. Therefore, it had to be someone else's fault. It had to be Grace's fault.

"I didn't have an affair with Bobbie. Before, during or after their marriage."

"And whom do you think I would believe? You, or my own daughter?"

Grace tilted her head, twisted a smile on her face. "Why, your own daughter, of course. As always."

"You've always been a liar and a sneak. You've always been ungrateful, a burden I took on out of family duty who never once gave anything back. You were spoiled and willful when I opened my door to you, and you never changed."

Grace's stomach roiled viciously. In defense, she smiled, shrugged. Deliberately careless, she smoothed a hand over the hair sleeked into a coiled twist at the nape of her neck. "No, I suppose I didn't. I'll just have to remain a disappointment to you, Aunt Helen."

"My daughter would be alive if not for you."

Grace willed her heart to go numb. But it ached, and it burned. "Yes, you're right."

"I warned her about you, told her time and again what you were. But you continually lured her back, playing on her affection."

"Affection, Aunt Helen?" With a half laugh, Grace pressed her fingers to the throb in her left temple. "Surely even you don't believe she ever had an ounce of affection for me. She took her cue from you, after all. And she took it well."

"How dare you speak of her in that tone, after you've killed her!" In the pampered face, Helen's eyes burned with loathing. "All of your life you've envied her, used your wiles to influence her. Now your unconscionable life-style has killed her. You've brought scandal and disgrace down on the family name once again."

Grace went stiff. This wasn't grief, she thought. Perhaps grief was there, buried deep, but what was on the surface was venom. And she was weary of being struck by it. "That's the bottom line, isn't it, Aunt Helen? The Fontaine name, the Fontaine reputation. And, of course, the Fontaine stock. Your child is dead, but it's the scandal that infuriates you."

She absorbed the slap without a wince, though the blow printed heat on her cheek, brought blood stinging to the surface. She took one long, deep breath. "That should end things appropriately between the two of us," she said evenly. "I'll have Melissa's things sent to you as soon as possible."

"I want you out of here." Helen's voice shook for the first time—whether in grief or in fury, Grace couldn't have said. "You have no place here."

"You're right again. I don't. I never did."

Grace stepped out of the alcove. The color that had drained out of her face rose slightly when she met Seth's eyes. She couldn't read them in that brief glance, and didn't want to. Without breaking stride, she continued past him and kept walking.

The drizzle that misted the air was a relief. She welcomed the heat after the overchilled, artificial air inside, and the heavy, stifling scent of funeral flowers. Her heels clicked on the wet pavement as she crossed the lot to her car. She was fumbling in her bag for her keys when Seth clamped a hand on her shoulder.

He said nothing at first, just turned her around, studied her face. It was white again—but for the red burn from the slap—the eyes a dark contrast and swimming with emotion. He could feel the tremors of that emotion under the palm of his hand.

"She was wrong."

Humiliation was one more blow to her overwrought system. She jerked her shoulder, but his hand remained in place. "Is that part of your investigative technique, Lieutenant? Eavesdropping on private conversations?"

Did she realize, he wondered, that her voice was raw, her eyes were devastated? He wanted badly to lift a hand to that mark on her face, cool it. Erase it. "She was wrong," he said again. "And she was cruel. You aren't responsible."

"Of course I am." She spun away, jabbing her key at the door lock. After three shaky attempts, she gave up, and they dropped with a jingling splash to the wet pavement as she turned into his arms. "Oh, God." Shuddering, she pressed her face into his chest. "Oh, God."

He didn't want to hold her, wanted to refuse the role of comforter. But his arms came around her before he could stop them, and one hand reached up to brush the smooth twist of her hair. "You didn't deserve that, Grace. You did nothing to deserve that."

"It doesn't matter."

"Yes, it does." He found himself weakening, drawing her closer, trying to will her trembling away. "It always does."

"I'm just tired." She burrowed into him while the rain misted her hair. There was strength here, was all she could think. A haven here. An answer here. "I'm just tired."

Her head lifted, their mouths met, before either of them realized the need was there. The quiet sound in her throat was of relief and gratitude. She opened her battered heart to the kiss, locking her arms around him, urging him to take it.

She had been waiting for him, and, too dazed to question why, she offered herself to him. Surely comfort and pleasure and this all-consuming need were reason enough. His mouth was firm—the one she'd always wanted on hers. His body was hard and solid—a perfect match for hers.

Here he is, she thought with a ragged sigh of joy.

She trembled still, and he could feel his own muscles quiver in response. He wanted to gather her up, carry her out of the rain to someplace quiet and dark where it was only the two of them. To spend years where it would only be the two of them.

His heart pounded in his head, masking the slick sound of traffic over the rain-wet street beyond the lot. Its fast, demanding beat muffled the warning struggling to sound in the corner of his brain, telling him to step back, to break away.

He'd never wanted anything more in his life than to bury himself in her and forget the consequences.

Swamped with emotions and needs, she held him close. "Take me home," she murmured against his mouth. "Seth, take me home, make love with me. I need you to touch me. I want to be with you." Her mouth met his again, in a desperate plea she hadn't known herself capable of.

Every cell in his body burned for her. Every need he'd ever had coalesced into one, and it was only for her. The almost vicious focus of it left him vulnerable and shaky. And furious.

He put his hands on her shoulders, drew her away. "Sex isn't the answer for everyone."

His voice wasn't as cool as he'd wanted, but it was rigid enough to stop her from reaching for him again. Sex? she thought as she struggled to clear her dazzled mind. Did he really believe she'd been speaking about something as simple as sex? Then she focused on his face, the hard set of his mouth, the faint annoyance in his eyes, and realized he did.

Her pride might have been tattered, but she managed to hold on to a few threads. "Well, apparently it's not for you." Reaching up, she smoothed her hair, brushed away rain. "Or if it is, you're the type who insists on being the initiator."

She made her lips curve, though they felt cold now and stiff. "It would have been just fine and dandy if you'd made the move. But when I do, it makes me—what would the term be? Loose?"

"I don't believe it's a term I used."

"No, you're much too controlled for insults." She bent down, scooped up her wet keys, then stood jin-

her rake her fingers through it again as she hung up the phone and pushed a pile of invoices aside. If that was her idea of filing, he thought, it suited the rest of the room.

It was barely big enough to turn around in, crowded with boxes, files, papers, and one ratty chair, on which sat an enormous and overflowing purse.

"Ms. O'Leary?"

She looked up, her brow still creased in annoyance. It didn't clear when she recognized her visitor. "Just what I needed to make my day perfect. A cop. Listen, Buchanan, I'm behind here. As you know, I lost a few days recently."

"Then I'll try to be quick." He stepped inside, pulled the picture out of his pocket and tossed it onto the desk under her nose. "Look familiar?"

She pursed her lips, gave the slickly handsome face a slow, careful study. "Is this the guy Jack told me about? The one who killed Melissa?"

"The Melissa Fontaine case is still open. This man is a possible suspect. Do you recognize him?"

She rolled her eyes, pushed the photo back in Seth's direction. "No. Looks like a creep. Did Grace recognize him?"

He angled his head slightly, his only outward sign of interest. "Does she know many men who look like creeps?"

"Too many," M.J. muttered. "Jack said you came by the memorial service last night to show Grace this picture."

"She was…occupied."

"Yeah, it was a rough night for her." M.J. rubbed her eyes.

"Apparently, though she seemed to have been handling it well enough initially." He glanced down at the photo again, thought of the man he'd seen her kiss. "This looks like her type."

M.J.'s hand dropped, her eyes narrowed. "Meaning?"

"Just that." Seth tucked the photo away. "If one's going by type, this one doesn't appear, on the surface, too far a step from the one she was cozy with at the service."

"Cozy with?" The narrowed eyes went hot, angry green flares. "Grace wasn't cozy with anyone."

"About six-one, a hundred and seventy, blond hair, blue eyes, five-thousand-dollar Italian suit, lots of teeth."

It only took her a moment. At any other time, she would have laughed. But the cool disdain on Seth's face had her snarling. "You stupid son of a bitch, that was her cousin Julian, and he was hitting her up for money, just like he always does."

Seth frowned, backtracked, played the scene through his mind again. "Her cousin...and that would be the victim's...?"

"Stepbrother. Melissa's stepbrother—her father's son from a previous."

"And the deceased's stepbrother was asking Grace for money at his stepsister's memorial?"

This time she appreciated the coating of disgust over his words. "Yeah. He's slime—why should the ambience stop him from shaking her down? Most of them squeeze her for a few bucks now and then." She rose, geared up. "And you've got a hell of a nerve coming in here with your attitude and your superior morals, ace. She wrote that pansy-faced jerk a check for a few thousand to get him off her back, just like she used to pass bucks to Melissa, and some of the others."

"I was under the impression the Fontaines were wealthy."

"Wealth's relative—especially if you live the high life and your allowance from your trust fund is overdrawn, or if you've played too deep in Monte Carlo. And Grace has more of the green stuff than most of them, because her parents didn't blow the bucks. That just burns the relatives," she muttered. "Who do you think paid for that wake last night? It wasn't the dearly departed's mama or papa. Grace's witch of an aunt put the arm on her, then put the blame on her. And she took it, because she thinks it's easier to take it and go her own way. You don't know anything about her."

He thought he did, but the details he was collecting bit by bit weren't adding up very neatly. "I know that she's not to blame for what happened to her cousin."

"Yeah, try telling her that. I know that when we realized she'd left and we got back to Cade's, she was in her room crying, and there was nothing any of us could do to help her. And all because those bastards she has the misfortune to be related to go out of their way to make her feel rotten."

Not just her relatives, he thought with a quick twinge of guilt. He'd had a part in that.

"It seems she's more fortunate in her friends than in her family."

"That's because we're not interested in her money, or her name. Because we don't judge her. We just love her. Now, if that's all, I've got work to do."

"I need to speak with Ms. Fontaine." Seth's voice was as stiff as M.J.'s had been passionate. "Would you know where I might find her?"

Her lips curled. She hesitated a moment, knowing Grace wouldn't appreciate the information being passed along. But the urge to see the cop's preconceptions slapped down was just too tempting. "Sure. Try Saint Agnes's Hospital. Pediatrics or maternity." Her phone rang, so she snatched it up. "You'll find her," she said. "Yeah, O'Leary," she barked into the phone, and turned her back on Seth.

He assumed she was visiting the child of a friend, but when he asked at the nurses' station for Grace Fontaine, faces lit up.

"I think she's in the intensive-care nursery." The nurse on duty checked her watch. "It's her usual time there. Do you know the way?"

Baffled, Seth shook his head. "No." He listened to the directions, while his mind turned over a dozen reasons why Grace Fontaine should have a usual time in a nursery. Since none of them slipped comfortably into a slot, he headed down corridors.

He could hear the high sound of babies crying behind a barrier of glass. And perhaps he stopped for just a moment outside the window of the regular nursery, and his eyes might have softened, just a little, as he scanned the infants in their clear-sided beds. Tiny faces, some slack in sleep, others screwed up into wrinkled balls of fury.

A couple stood beside him, the man with his arm over the woman's robed shoulders. "Ours is third from the left. Joshua Michael Delvecchio. Eight pounds, five ounces. He's one day old."

"He's a beaut," Seth said.

"Which one is yours?" the woman asked.

Seth shook his head, shot one more glance through

the glass. "I'm just passing through. Congratulations on your son."

He continued on, resisting the urge to look back at the new parents lost in their own private miracle.

Two turns down the corridor away from the celebration was a smaller nursery. Here machines hummed, and nurses walked quietly. And behind the glass were six empty cribs.

Grace sat beside one, cuddling a tiny, crying baby. She brushed away tears from the pale little cheek, rested her own against the smooth head as she rocked.

It struck him to the core, the picture she made. Her hair was braided back from her face and she wore a shapeless green smock over her suit. Her face was soft as she soothed the restless infant. Her attention was totally focused on the eyes that stared tearfully into hers.

"Excuse me, sir." A nurse hurried up. "This is a restricted area."

Absently, his eyes still on Grace, Seth reached for his badge. "I'm here to speak with Ms. Fontaine."

"I see. I'll tell her you're here, Lieutenant."

"No, don't disturb her." He didn't want anything to spoil that picture. "I can wait. What's wrong with the baby she's holding?"

"Peter's an AIDS baby. Ms. Fontaine arranged for him to have care here."

"Ms. Fontaine?" He felt a fist lodge in his gut. "It's her child?"

"Biologically? No." The nurse's face softened slightly. "I think she considers them all hers. I honestly don't know what we'd do without her help. Not just the foundation, but her."

"The foundation?"

"The Falling Star Foundation. Ms. Fontaine set it up a few years ago to assist critically ill and terminal children and their families. But it's the hands-on that really matters." She gestured back toward the glass with a nod of her head. "No amount of financial generosity can buy a loving touch or sing a lullaby."

He watched the baby calm, drift slowly to sleep in Grace's arms. "She comes here often?"

"As often as she can. She's our angel. You'll have to excuse me, Lieutenant."

"Thank you." As she walked away, he stepped closer to the isolation glass. Grace started toward the crib. It was then that her eyes met his.

He saw the shock come into them first. Even she wasn't skilled enough to disguise the range of emotions that raced over her face. Surprise, embarrassment, annoyance. Then she smoothed the expressions out. Gently, she laid the baby back into the crib, brushed a hand over his cheek. She walked through a side door and disappeared.

It was several minutes before she came out into the corridor. The smock was gone. Now she was a confident woman in a flame-red suit, her mouth carefully tinted to match. "Well, Lieutenant, we meet in the oddest places."

Before she could complete the casual greeting she'd practiced while she tidied her makeup, he took her chin firmly in his hand. His eyes locked intently on hers, probed.

"You're a fake." He said it quietly, stepping closer. "You're a fraud. Who the hell are you?"

"Whatever I like." He unnerved her, that long, intense and all-too-personal study with those golden-brown eyes. "And I don't believe this is the place for an interrogation. I'd like you to let me go now," she said steadily. "I don't want any scenes here."

"I'm not going to cause a scene."

She lifted her brows. "I might." Deliberately she pushed his hand away and started down the corridor. "If you want to discuss the case with me, or have any questions regarding it, we'll do it outside. I won't have it brought in here."

"It was breaking your heart," he murmured. "Holding that baby was breaking your heart."

"It's my heart." Almost viciously, she punched a finger at the button for the elevator. "And it's a tough one, Seth. Ask anyone."

"Your lashes are still wet."

"This is none of your business." Her voice was low and vibrating with fury. "Absolutely none of your business."

She stepped into the crowded elevator, faced front. She wouldn't speak to him about this part of her life, she promised herself. Just the night before, she'd opened herself to him, only to be pushed away, refused. She wouldn't share her feelings again, and certainly not her feelings about something as vital to her as the children.

He was a cop, just a cop. Hadn't she spent several miserable hours the night before convincing herself that was all he was or could be to her? Whatever he stirred in her would have to be stopped—or, if not stopped, at least suppressed.

She would not share with him, she would not trust him, she would not give to him.

By the time she reached the lobby doors, she was steadier. Hoping to shake him quickly, she started toward the lot. Seth merely took her arm, steered her away.

"Over here," he said, and headed toward a grassy area with a pair of benches.

"I don't have time."

"Make time. You're too upset to drive, in any case."

"Don't tell me what I am."

"Apparently that's just what I've been doing. And apparently I've missed several steps. That's not usual for me, and I don't care for it. Sit down."

"I don't want—"

"Sit down, Grace," he repeated. "I apologize."

Annoyed, she sat on the bench, found her sunglasses in her bag and slipped them on. "For?"

He sat beside her, removed the shielding glasses and looked into her eyes. "For not letting myself look beneath the surface. For not wanting to look. And for blaming you because I don't seem able to stop wanting to do this."

He took her face in his hands and captured her mouth with his.

Chapter 6

She didn't move into him. Not this time. Her emotions were simply too raw to risk. Though her mouth yielded beneath his, she lifted a hand and laid it on his chest, as if to keep him at a safe distance.

And still her heart stumbled.

This time she was holding back. He sensed it, felt it in the press of her hand against him. Not refusing, but resisting. And with a knowledge that came from somewhere too deep to measure, he gentled the kiss, seeking not only to seduce, but also to soothe.

And still his heart staggered.

"Don't." It made her throat ache, her mind haze, her body yearn. And it was all too much. She pulled away from him and stood staring out across the little patch of grass until she thought she could breathe again.

"What is it with timing?" Seth wondered aloud. "That makes it so hard to get right?"

"I don't know." She turned then to look at him. He was an attractive man, she decided. The dark hair and hard face, the odd tint of gold in his eyes. But she'd known many attractive men. What was it about this one that changed everything and made her world tilt? "You bother me, Lieutenant Buchanan."

He gave her one of his rare smiles—slow and full and rich. "That's a mutual problem, Ms. Fontaine. You keep me up at night. Like a puzzle where the pieces are all there, but they change shape right before your eyes. And even when you put it all together—or think you have—it doesn't stay the same."

"I'm not a mystery, Seth."

"You are the most fascinating woman I've ever met." His lips curved again when she lifted her brows. "That isn't entirely a compliment. Along with fascination comes frustration." He stood, but didn't step toward her. "Why were you so upset that I found you here, saw you here?"

"It's private." Her tone was stiff again, dismissive. "I go to considerable trouble to keep it private."

"Why?"

"Because I prefer it that way."

"Your family doesn't know about your involvement here?"

The fury that seared through her eyes was burning-cold. "My family has *nothing* to do with this. Nothing. This isn't a Fontaine project, one of their charitable sops for good press and a tax deduction. It's mine."

"Yes, I can see that," he said calmly. Her family had hurt her even more than he'd guessed. And more, he thought, than she had acknowledged. "Why children, Grace?"

"Because they're the innocents." It was out before she realized she meant to say it. Then she closed her eyes and sighed. "Innocence is a precious and perishable commodity."

"Yes, it is. Falling Star? Your foundation. Is that how you see them, stars that burn out and fall too quickly?"

It was her heart he was touching simply by understanding, by seeing what was inside. "It has nothing to do with the case. Why are you pushing me on this?"

"Because I'm interested in you."

She sent him a smile—half inviting, half sarcastic. "Are you? You didn't seem to be when I asked you to bed. But you see me holding a sick baby and you change your tune." She walked toward him slowly, trailed a fingertip down his shirt. "Well, if it's the maternal type that turns you on, Lieutenant—"

"Don't do that to yourself." Again his voice was quiet, controlled. He took her hand, stopped her from backtracking the trail of her finger. "It's foolish. And it's irritating. You weren't playing games in there. You care."

"Yes, I do. I care enormously. And that doesn't make me a hero, and it doesn't make me any different than I was last night." She drew her hand away and stood her ground. "I want you. I want to go to bed with you. That irritates you, Seth. Not the sentiment, but the bluntness of the statement. Isn't it games you'd prefer? That I'd pretend reluctance and let you conquer?"

He only wished it was something just that ordinary. "Maybe I want to know who you are before we end up in bed. I spent a long time looking at your face—that portrait of you in your house. And, looking, I wondered about you. Now, I want you. But I also want all those pieces to fit."

"You might not like the finished product."

"No," he agreed. "I might not."

Then again, she thought… Considering, she angled her head. "I have a thing tonight. A cocktail party hosted by a major contributor to the hospital. I can't afford to skip it. Why don't you take me, then we'll see what happens next?"

He weighed the pros and cons, knew it was a step that would have ramifications he might not be able to handle smoothly. She wasn't simply a woman, and he wasn't simply a man. Whatever was between them had a long reach and a hard grip.

"Do you always think everything through so carefully?" she asked as she watched him.

"Yes." But in her case it didn't seem to matter, he realized. "I can't guarantee my evenings will be free until this case is closed." He shifted times and meetings and paperwork in his head. "But if I can manage it, I'll pick you up."

"Eight's soon enough. If you're not there by quarter after, I'll assume you were tied up."

No complaints, he thought, no demands. Most of the women he'd known shifted to automatic sulk mode when his work took priority. "I'll call if I can't make it."

"Whatever." She sat again, relaxed now. "I don't imagine you came by to see my secret life, or to make a tentative date for a cocktail party." She slipped her sunglasses back on, sat back. "Why are you here?"

He reached inside his jacket for the photo. Grace caught a brief glimpse of his shoulder holster, and the weapon snug inside it. And wondered if he'd ever had occasion to use it.

"I imagine your time is taken up mainly with administration duties." She took the picture from him, but continued to look at Seth's face. "You wouldn't participate in many, what—busts?"

She thought she caught a faint glint of humor in his eyes, but his mouth remained sober. "I like to keep my hand in."

"Yes," she murmured, easily able to imagine him whipping the weapon out. "I suppose you would."

She shifted her gaze, scanned the face in the photo. This time the humor was in her eyes. "Ah, Joe Cool. Or more likely Juan or Jean-Paul Cool."

"You know him?"

"Not personally, but certainly as a type. He likely speaks the right words in three languages, plays a steely game of baccarat, enjoys his brandy and wears black silk underwear. His Rolex, along with his monogrammed gold cufflinks and diamond pinkie ring, would have been gifts from admirers."

Intrigued, Seth sat beside her again. "And what are the right words?"

"You're the most beautiful woman in the room. I adore you. My heart sings when I look into your eyes. Your husband is a fool, and darling, you must stop buying me gifts."

"Been there?"

"With some variations. Only I've never been married and I don't buy trinkets for users. His eyes are cold," she added, "but a lot of women, lonely women, would only see the polish. That's all they want to see." She took a quick, short breath. "This is the man who killed Melissa, isn't it?"

He started to give her the standard response, but she looked up then, and he was close enough to read her eyes through the amber tint of her glasses. "I think it is. His prints were all over the house. Some of the surfaces were wiped, but he missed a lot, which leads me to think he panicked. Either because she fell or because he wasn't able to find what he'd come for."

"And you're leaning toward the second choice, because this isn't the type of man to panic because he'd killed a woman."

"No, he isn't."

"She couldn't have given him what he'd come for. She wouldn't have known what he was talking about."

"No. That doesn't make you responsible. If you indulge yourself by thinking it does, you'd have to blame Bailey, too."

Grace opened her mouth, closed it again, breathed deep. "That's clever logic, Lieutenant," she said after a moment. "So I shed my sackcloth and ashes and blame this man. Have you found him?"

"He's dead." He took the photo back, tucked it away. "And my clever logic leads me to believe that whoever hired him decided to fire him, permanently."

"I see." She felt nothing, no satisfaction, no relief. "So, we're nowhere."

"The Three Stars are under twenty-four-hour guard. You, M.J. and Bailey are safe, and the museum will have its property in a matter of days."

"And a lot of people have died. Sacrifices to the god?"

"From what I've read about Mithra, it isn't blood he wants."

"Love, knowledge and generosity," she said quietly. "Powerful elements. The diamond I held, it has vitality. Maybe that's the same as power. Does he want them because they're beautiful, priceless, ancient, or because he truly believes in the legend? Does he believe that if he has all of them in their triangle, he'll possess the power of the god, and immortality?"

"People believe what they choose to believe. Whatever reason he wants them, he's killed for them." Staring out across the grass, he stepped over one of his own rules and shared his thoughts with her. "Money isn't the driving force. He's laid out more than a million already. He wants to own them, to hold them in his hands, whatever the cost. It's more than coveting," he said quietly, as a murky scene swam into his mind.

A marble altar, a golden triangle with three brilliantly blue points. A dark man with pale eyes and a bloody sword.

"And you don't think he'll stop now. You think he'll try again."

Baffled and uneasy with the image, he shook it off, turned back to logic and instinct. "Oh, yeah." Seth's eyes narrowed, went flat. "He'll try again."

Seth made it to Cade's at 8:14. His final meeting of the day, with the chief of police, had gone past seven, and that had barely given him time to get home, change and drive out again. He'd told himself half a dozen times that he'd be better off staying at home, putting the reports and files away and having a quiet evening to relax his mind.

The press conference set for nine sharp the next morning would be a trial by fire, and he needed to be sharp. Yet here he was, sitting in his car feeling ridiculously nervous and unsettled.

He'd tracked a homicidal junkie through a condemned tenement without breaking a sweat, with a steady pulse he'd interrogated cold, vicious killers—but now, as the white ball of the sun dipped low in the sky, he was as jittery as a schoolboy.

He hated cocktail parties. The inane conversations, the silly food, the buffed faces, all feigning enthusiasm or ennui, depending on their style.

But it wasn't the prospect of a few hours socializing with strangers that unnerved him. It was spending time with Grace without the buffer of the job between them.

He'd never had a woman affect him as she did. And he couldn't deny—at least to himself—that he had been deeply, uniquely affected, from the moment he saw her portrait.

It didn't help to tell himself she was shallow, spoiled, a woman used to men falling at her feet. It hadn't helped before he discovered she was much more than that, and it was certainly no good now.

He couldn't claim to understand her, but he was beginning to uncover all those layers and contrasts that made her who and what she was.

And he knew they would be lovers before the night was over.

He saw her step out of the house, a charge of electric blue from the short strapless dress molded to her body, the long, luxurious fall of ebony hair, the endless and perfect legs.

Did she shock every man's system, Seth wondered, just the look of her? Or was he particularly, specifically vulnerable? He decided either answer would be hard to live with, and got out of his car.

Her head turned at the sound of his door, and that heart-stopping face bloomed with a smile. "I didn't think you were going to make it." She crossed to him, unhurried, and touched her mouth to his. "I'm glad you did."

"I'd said I'd call if I wouldn't be here."

"So you did." But she hadn't counted on it. She'd left the address of the party inside, just in case, but she'd resigned herself to spending the evening without him. She smiled again, smoothed a hand down the lapel of his suit. "I never wait by the phone. We're going to Georgetown. Shall we take my car, or yours?"

"I'll drive." Knowing she expected him to make some comment on her looks, he deliberately kept silent as he walked around the car to open her door.

She slipped in, her legs sliding silkily inside. He wanted his hands there, right there where the abbreviated hem of her dress kissed her thighs. Where the skin would be tender as a ripened peach and smooth as white satin.

He closed the door, walked back around the car and got behind the wheel. "Where in Georgetown?" was all he said.

It was a beautiful old house, with soaring ceilings, heavy antiques and deep, warm colors. The lights blazed down on important people, people of influence and wealth, who carried the scent of power under their perfumes and colognes.

She belonged, Seth thought. She'd melded with the

whole from the moment she stepped through the door to exchange sophisticated cheek brushes with the hostess.

Yet she stood apart. In the midst of all the sleek black, the fussy pastels, she was a bright blue flame daring anyone to touch and be burned.

Like the diamonds, he thought. Unique, potent… irresistible.

"Lieutenant Buchanan, isn't it?"

Seth shifted his gaze from Grace and looked at the short, balding man who was built like a boxer and dressed in Savile Row. "Yes. Mr. Rossi, counsel for the defense. If the defense has deep enough pockets."

Unoffended, Rossi chuckled. "I thought I recognized you. I've crossed you on the stand a few times. You're a tough nut. I've always believed I'd have gotten Tremaine off, or at least hung the jury, if I'd have been able to shake your testimony."

"He was guilty."

"As sin," Rossi agreed readily, "but I'd have hung that jury."

As Rossi started to rehash the trial, Seth resigned himself to talking shop.

Across the room, Grace took a glass from a passing waiter and listened to her hostess's gossip with half an ear. She knew when to chuckle, when to lift a brow, purse her lips, make some interesting comment. It was all routine.

She wanted to leave immediately. She wanted to get Seth out of that dark suit. She wanted her hands on him, all over him. Lust was creeping along her skin like a hot rash. Sips of champagne did nothing to cool her throat, and only added to the bubbling in her blood.

"My dear Sarah."

"Gregor, how lovely to see you."

Grace shifted, sipped, smiled at the sleek, dark man with the creamy voice who bent gallantly over their hostess's hand. Mediterranean, she judged, by the charm of the accent. Fiftyish, but fit.

"You're looking particularly wonderful tonight," he said, lingering over her hand. "And your hospitality, as always, is incomparable. And your guests." He turned smiling pale silvery-blue eyes on Grace. "Perfect."

"Gregor." Sarah simpered, fluttered, then turned to Grace. "I don't believe you've met Gregor, Grace. He's fatally charming, so be very careful. Ambassador DeVane, I'd like to present Grace Fontaine, a dear friend."

"I am honored." He lifted Grace's hand, and his lips were warm and soft. "And enchanted."

"Ambassador?" Grace slipped easily into the role. "I thought ambassadors were old and stodgy. All the ones I've met have been. That is, up until now."

"I'll just leave you with Grace, Gregor. I see we have some late arrivals."

"I'm sure I'm in delightful hands." With obvious reluctance, he released Grace's fingers. "Are you perhaps a connection of Niles Fontaine?"

"He's an uncle, yes."

"Ah. I had the pleasure of meeting your uncle and his charming wife in Capri a few years ago. We have a mutual hobby, coins."

"Yes, Uncle Niles has quite a collection. He's mad for coins." Grace brushed her hair back, lifted it off her bare shoulder. "And where are you from, Ambassador DeVane?"

"Gregor, please, in such friendly surroundings. Then I might be permitted to call you Grace."

"Of course." Her smile warmed to suit the new intimacy.

"I doubt you would have heard of my tiny country. We are only a small dot in the sea, known chiefly for our olive oil and wine."

"Terresa?"

"Now I am flattered again that such a beautiful woman would know my humble country."

"It's a beautiful island. I was there briefly, two years ago, and very much enjoyed it. Terresa is a small jewel in the sea, dramatic cliffs to the west, lush vineyards in the east, and sandy beaches as fine as sugar."

He smiled at her, took her hand again. The connection was as unexpected as the woman, and he found himself compelled to touch. And to keep. "You must promise to return, to allow me to show you the country as it should be seen. I have a small villa in the west, and the view would almost be worthy of you."

"I'd love to see it. How difficult it must be to spend the summer in muggy Washington, when you could be enjoying the sea breezes of Terresa."

"Not at all difficult. Now." He skimmed a thumb over her knuckles. "I find the treasures of your country more and more appealing. Perhaps you would consider joining me one evening. Do you enjoy the opera?"

"Very much."

"Then you must allow me to escort you. Perhaps—" He broke off, a flicker of annoyance marring his smooth features as Seth stepped up to them.

"Ambassador Gregor DeVane of Terresa, allow me to introduce Lieutenant Seth Buchanan."

"You are military," DeVane said, offering a hand.

"Cop," Seth said shortly. He didn't like the ambassador's looks. Not one bit. When he saw DeVane with Grace, he'd had a fast, turbulent impulse to reach for his weapon. But, strangely, his instinctive movement hadn't been up, to his gun, but lower on the side. Where a man would carry a sword.

"Ah, the police." DeVane blinked in surprise, though he already had a full dossier on Seth Buchanan. "How fascinating. I hope you'll forgive me for saying it's my fondest wish never to require your services." Smoothly DeVane slipped a glass from a passing tray, handed it to Seth, then took one for himself. "But perhaps we should drink to crime. Without it, you'd be obsolete."

Seth eyed him levelly. There was recognition, inexplicable, and utterly adversarial, when their eyes locked, pale silver to dark gold. "I prefer drinking to justice."

"Of course. To the scales, shall we say, and their constant need for balancing?" Gregor drank, then inclined his head. "You'll excuse me, Lieutenant Buchanan, I've yet to greet my host. I was—" he turned to Grace and kissed her hand again "—beautifully distracted from my duty."

"It was a pleasure to meet you, Gregor."

"I hope to see you again." He looked deeply into her eyes, held the moment. "Very soon."

The moment he turned away, Grace shivered. There had been something almost possessive in that last, long stare. "What an odd and charming man," she murmured.

Energy was shooting through Seth, the need to do battle. His system sparked with it. "Do you usually let odd and charming men drool over you in public?"

It was small of her, Grace supposed, but she enjoyed a kick of satisfaction at the annoyance in Seth's tone. "Of course. Since I so dislike them drooling over me in private." She turned into him, so that their bodies brushed lightly. Then slanted a look up from under that thick curtain of lashes. "You don't plan to drool, do you?"

He could have damned her for shooting his system from slow burn up to sizzle. "Finish your drink," he said abruptly, "and say your goodbyes. We're going."

Grace gave an exaggerated sigh. "Oh, I do love being dominated by a strong man."

"We're about to put that to the test." He took her half-finished drink, set it aside. "Let's go."

DeVane watched them leave, studied the way Seth pressed a hand to the small of Grace's back to steer her through the crowd. He would have to punish the cop for touching her.

Grace was his property now, DeVane thought as he gritted his teeth painfully tight to suppress the rage. She was meant for him. He'd known it from the moment he took her hand and looked into her eyes. She was perfect, flawless. It wasn't just the Three Stars that were fated for him, but the woman who had held one, perhaps caressed it, as well.

She would understand their power. She would add to it.

Along with the Three Stars of Mithra, DeVane vowed, Grace Fontaine would be the treasure of his collection.

She would bring the Stars to him. And then she would belong to him. Forever.

As she stepped outside, Grace felt another shudder sprint down her spine. She hunched her shoulder blades against it, looked back. Through the tall windows filled with light she could see the guests mingling.

And she saw DeVane, quite clearly. For a moment, she would have sworn their eyes met—but this time there was no charm. An irrational sense of fear lodged in her stomach, had her turning quickly away again.

When Seth pulled open the car door, she got in without complaint or comment. She wanted to go, to get away from those brilliantly lit windows and the man who seemed to watch her from beyond them. Briskly she rubbed the chill from her arms.

"You wouldn't be cold if you'd worn clothes." Seth stuck the key in the ignition.

The single remark, issued with cold and savage control, made her chuckle and chased the chill away. "Why, Lieutenant, and here I was wondering how long you would let me keep on what I am wearing."

"Not a hell of a lot longer," he promised, and pulled out into the street.

"Good." Determined to see that he kept that promise, she squirmed over and began to nibble his ear. "Let's break some laws," she whispered.

"I could already charge myself with intent."

She laughed again, quick, breathless, and had him hard as iron.

He wasn't sure how he managed to handle the car, much less drive it through traffic out of D.C. and back into Maryland. She worked his tie off, undid half the buttons of his shirt. Her hands were everywhere, and her mouth teased his ear, his neck, his jaw, while she murmured husky promises, suggestions.

The fantasies she wove with unerring skill had the blood beating painfully in his loins.

He pulled to a jerky stop in his driveway, then dragged her across the seat. She lost one shoe in the car and the other halfway up the walk as he half carried her. Her laughter, dark, wild, damning, roared in his head. He all but broke his own door down to get her inside. The instant they were, he pushed her back against the wall and savaged her mouth.

He wasn't thinking. Couldn't think. It was all primal, violent need. In the darkened hallway, he hiked up her skirt with impatient hands, found the thin, lacy barrier beneath and ripped it aside. He freed himself, then, gripping her hips, plunged into her where they stood.

She cried out, not in protest, not in shock at the almost brutal treatment. But in pure, overwhelming pleasure. She locked herself around him, let him drive her ruthlessly, crest after torrential crest. And met him thrust for greedy, desperate thrust.

It was mindless and hot and vicious. And it was all that mattered. Sheer animal need. Violent animal release.

Her body shattered, went limp, as she felt him pour into her.

He slapped his hand against the wall to keep his balance, struggled to slow his breathing, clear his fevered brain. They were no more than a step inside his door, he realized, and he'd mounted her like a rutting bull.

There was no point in apologies, he thought. They'd both wanted fast and urgent. No, *wanted* was too tame a word, he decided. They'd craved it, the way starving animals craved meat.

But he'd never treated a woman with less care, or so completely ignored the consequences.

"I meant to get you out of that dress," he managed, and was pleased when she laughed.

"We'll get around to it."

"There's something else I didn't get around to." He eased back, studied her face in the dim light. "Is that going to be a problem?"

She understood. "No." And though it was rash and foolish, she felt a twinge of regret that there would be no quickening of life inside her as a result of their carelessness. "I take care of myself."

"I didn't want this to happen." He took her chin in his hand. "I should have been able to keep my hands off you."

Her eyes glimmered in the dark—confident and amused. "I hope you don't expect me to be sorry you didn't. I want them on me again. I want mine on you."

"While they are." He lifted her chin a little higher. "No one else's are. I don't share."

Her lips curved slowly as she kept his gaze. "Neither do I."

He nodded, accepting. "Let's go upstairs," he said, and swept her into his arms.

Chapter 7

He switched on the light as he carried her into his room. This time he needed to see her, to know when her eyes clouded or darkened, to witness those flickers of pleasure or shock.

This time he would remember man's advantage over the animal, and that the mind and heart could play a part.

She got a sense of a room of average size, simple buff-colored curtains at the windows, clean-lined furniture without color, a large bed with a navy spread tucked in with precise, military tidiness.

There were paintings on the walls that she told herself she would study later, when her heart wasn't skipping. Scenes both urban and rural were depicted in misty, dreamy watercolors that made a personal contrast to the practical room.

But all thoughts of art and decor fled when he set

her on her feet beside the bed. She reached out, undid the final buttons of his shirt, while he shrugged out of his jacket. Her brows lifted when she noted he wore his shoulder holster.

"Even to a cocktail party?"

"Habit," he said simply, and took it off, hung it over a chair. He caught the look in her eye. "Is it a problem?"

"No. I was just thinking how it suits you. And wondering if you look as sexy putting it on as you do taking it off." Then she turned, scooped her hair over her shoulder. "I could use some help."

He let his gaze wander over her back. Instead of reaching for the zipper, he drew her against him and lowered his mouth to her bare shoulder. She sighed, tipped her head back.

"That's even better."

"Round one took the edge off," he murmured, then slid his hands around her waist, and up, until they cupped her breasts. "I want you whimpering, wanting, weak."

His thumbs brushed the curves just above the bold blue silk. Focused on the sensation, she reached back, linked her arms around his neck. Her body began to move, timed to his strokes, but when she tried to turn, he held her in place.

She moaned, shifted restlessly, when his fingers curved under her bodice, the backs teasing her nipples, making them heat and ache. "I want to touch you."

"Whimpering," he repeated, and ran his hands down her dress to the hem, then beneath. "Wanting." And cupped her. "Weak." Pierced her.

The orgasm flooded her, one long, slow wave that

swamped the senses. The whimper he'd waited for shuddered through her lips.

He toed off his shoes, then lowered her zipper inch by inch. His fingers barely brushed her skin as he spread the parted material, eased it down her body until it pooled at her feet. He turned her, stepped back.

She wore only a garter, in the same hot blue as the dress, with stockings so sheer they appeared to be little more than mist. Her body was a fantasy of generous curves, and satin skin. Her hair fell like wild black rain over her shoulders.

"Too many men have told you you're beautiful for it to matter that I say it."

"Just tell me you want me. That matters."

"I want you, Grace." He stepped to her again, took her into his arms, but instead of the greedy kiss she'd expected, he gave her one to slowly drown in. Her arms clutched around him, then went limp, at this new assault to the senses.

"Kiss me again," she murmured when his lips wandered to her throat. "Just like that. Again."

So his mouth met hers, let her sink a second time. With a dreamy hum of pleasure, she slipped his shirt away, let her hands explore. It was lovely to be savored, to be given the gift of a slow kindling flame, to feel the control slip out of her hands into his. And to trust.

He let himself learn her body inch by generous inch. Pleasured them both by possessing those full firm breasts, first with hands, then with mouth. He lowered his hands, flicked the hooks of her stockings free one by one—hearing her quick catch of breath each time. Then slid his hands under the filmy fabric to flesh.

Warm, smooth. He lowered her to the bed, felt her

body yield beneath his. Soft, willing. Her lips answered his. Eager, generous.

They watched each other in the light. Moved together. First a sigh, then a groan. She found muscle, the rough skin of an old scar, and the taste of man. Shifting, she drew his slacks down, feasted on his chest as she undressed him. When he took her breasts again, pulled her closer to suckle, her arms quivered and her hair drifted forward to curtain them both.

She felt the heat rising, sliding through her blood like a fever, until her breath was short and shallow. She could hear herself saying his name, over and over, as he patiently built her toward the edge.

Her eyes went cobalt, fascinating him. Her pillowsoft lips trembled, her glorious body quaked. Even as the need for release clawed at him, he continued to savor. Until he finally shifted her to her back and, with his eyes locked on hers, buried himself inside her.

She arched upward, her hands fisting in the sheets, her body stunned with pleasure. "Seth." Her breath expelled in a rush, burned her lungs. "It's never… Not like this. Seth—"

Before she could speak again, he closed her mouth with his and took her.

When sleep came, Grace dreamed she was in her garden in the mountains, with the woods, thick and green and cool, surrounding her. The hollyhocks loomed taller than her head and bloomed in deep, rich reds and clear, shimmering whites. A hummingbird, shimmering sapphire and emerald, drank from a trumpet flower. Cosmos and coneflowers, dahlias and zinnias made a cheerful wave of mixed colors.

Pansies turned their exotic little faces toward the sun and smiled.

Here she was happy, at peace with herself. Alone, but never lonely. Here there was no sound but the song of the breeze through the leaves, the hum of bees, the faint music of the creek bubbling over rocks.

She watched deer walk quietly out of the woods to drink from the slow-moving creek, their hooves lost in the low-lying mist that hugged the ground. The dawn light shimmered like silver, sparkled off the soft dew, caught rainbows in the mist.

Content, she walked through her flowers, fingers brushing blooms, scents rising up to please her senses. She saw the glint among the blossoms, the bright, beckoning blue, and, stooping, plucked the stone from the ground.

Power shimmered in her hand. It was a clean, flowing sensation, pure as water, potent as wine. For a moment, she stood very still, her hand open. The stone resting in her palm danced with the morning light.

Hers to guard, she thought. To protect. And to give.

When she heard the rustle in the woods, she turned, smiling. It would be him, she was certain. She'd waited for him all her life, wanted so desperately to welcome him, to walk into his arms and know they would wrap around her.

She stepped forward, the stone warming her palm, the faint vibrations from it traveling like music up her arm and toward her heart. She would give it to him, she thought. She would give him everything she had, everything she was. For love had no boundaries.

All at once, the light changed, hazed over. The air went cold and whipped with the wind. By the creek, the deer lifted their heads, alert, alarmed, then turned as one and fled into the sheltering trees. The hum of bees died into a rumble of thunder, and lightning snaked over the dingy sky.

There in the darkened wood, close, too close to where her flowers bloomed, something moved stealthily. Her fingers clutched reflexively, closing fast over the stone. And through the leaves she saw eyes, bright, greedy. And watching.

The shadows parted and opened the path to her.

"No." Frantic, Grace pushed at the hands that held her. "I won't give it to you. It's not for you."

"Easy." Seth pulled her up, stroked her hair. "Just a nightmare. Shake it off now."

"Watching me..." She moaned it, pressed her face into his strong, bare shoulder, drew in his scent and was soothed. "He's watching me. In the woods, watching me."

"No, you're here with me." Her heart was pounding hard enough to bring real concern. Seth tightened his grip, as if to slow it and block the tremors that shook her. "It's a dream. There's no one here but me. I've got you."

"Don't let him touch me. I'll die if he touches me."

"I won't." He tipped her face back. "I've got you," he repeated, and warmed her trembling lips with his.

"Seth." Relief shuddered through her as she clutched at him. "I was waiting for you. In the garden, waiting for you."

"Okay. I'm here now." To protect, he thought. And then to cherish. Shaken by the depth of that, he eased her backward, brushed the tumbled hair away from her face. "Must have been a bad one. Do you have a lot of nightmares?"

"What?" Disoriented, trapped between the dream and the present, she only stared at him.

"Do you want the light?" He didn't wait for an answer, but reached around her to switch on the bedside lamp. Grace turned her face away from the glare, pressed her fisted hand against her heart. "Relax now. Come on." He took her hand, started to open her fingers.

"No." She jerked it back. "He wants it."

"Wants what?"

"The Star. He's coming for it, and for me. He's coming."

"Who?"

"I don't… I don't know." Baffled now, she looked down at her hand, slowly opened it. "I was holding the stone." She could still feel the heat, the weight. "I had it. I found it."

"It was a dream. The diamonds are locked in a vault. They're safe." He tipped a finger under her chin until her eyes met his. "You're safe."

"It was a dream." Saying it aloud brought both relief and embarrassment. "I'm sorry."

"It's all right." He studied her, saw that her face was white, her eyes were fragile. Something moved inside him, shifted, urged his hand to reach out, stroke that pale cheek. "You've had a rough few days, haven't you?"

It was just that, the quiet understanding in his voice, that had her eyes filling. She closed them to will back the tears and took careful breaths. The pressure in her chest was unbearable. "I'm going to get some water."

He simply reached out and drew her in. She'd hidden all that fear and grief and weariness inside her very well, he realized. Until now. "Why don't you let it go?"

Her breath hitched, tore. "I just need to—"

"Let it go," he repeated, and settled her head on his shoulder.

She shuddered once, then clung. Then wept.

He offered no words. He just held her.

At eight the next morning, Seth dropped her off at Cade's. She'd protested the hour at which he shook her out of sleep, tried to curl herself into the mattress. He'd dealt with that by simply picking her up, carrying her into the shower and turning it on. Cold.

He'd given her exactly thirty minutes to pull herself together, then packed her into the car.

"The gestapo could have taken lessons from you," she commented as he pulled up behind M.J.'s car. "My hair's still wet."

"I didn't have the hour to spare it must take to dry all that."

"I didn't even have time to put my makeup on."

"You don't need it."

"I suppose that's your idea of a compliment."

"No, it's just a fact."

She turned to him, looking arousing, rumpled and erotic in the strapless dress. "You, on the other hand, look all pressed and tidy."

"I didn't take twenty minutes in the shower." She'd sung in the shower, he remembered. Unbelievably off-key. Thinking of it made him smile. "Go away. I've got work to do."

She pouted, then reached for her purse. "Well, thanks for the lift, Lieutenant." Then laughed when he pushed her back against the seat and gave her the long, thorough kiss she'd been hoping for.

"That almost makes up for the one miserly cup of

coffee you allowed me this morning." She caught his bottom lip between her teeth, and her eyes sparkled into his. "I want to see you tonight."

"I'll come by. If I can."

"I'll be here." She opened the door, shot him a look over her shoulder. "If I can."

Unable to resist, he watched her every sauntering step toward the house. The minute she closed the front door behind her, he shut his eyes.

My God, he thought, he was in love with her. And it was totally impossible.

Inside, Grace all but danced down the hall. She was in love. And it was glorious. It was new and fresh and the first. It was what she'd been waiting for her entire life. Her face glowed as she stepped into the kitchen and found Bailey and Cade at the table, sharing coffee.

"Good morning, troops." She all but sang it as she headed to the coffeepot.

"Good morning to you." Cade tucked his tongue in his cheek. "I like your pajamas."

Laughing, she carried her cup to the table, then leaned down and kissed him full on the mouth. "I just adore you. Bailey, I just adore this man. You'd better snap him up quick, before I get ideas."

Bailey smiled dreamily into her coffee, then looked up, eyes shining and damp. "We're getting married in two weeks."

"What?" Grace bobbled her mug, sloshed coffee dangerously close to the rim. "What?" she repeated, and sat heavily.

"He won't wait."

"Why should I?" Reaching over the table, Cade took Bailey's hand. "I love you."

"Married." Grace looked down at their joined hands. A perfect match, she thought, and let out a shaky sigh. "That's wonderful. That's incredibly wonderful." Laying a hand over theirs, she stared into Cade's eyes. And saw exactly what she needed to see. "You'll be good to her." It wasn't a question, it was acceptance.

After giving his hand a quick squeeze, she sat back. "Well, a wedding to plan, and a whole two weeks to do it. That ought to make us all insane."

"It's just going to be a small ceremony," Bailey began. "Here at the house."

"I'm going to say one word." Cade put a plea in his voice. *"Elopement."*

"No." With a shake of her head, Bailey drew back, picked up her mug. "I'm not going to start our life together by insulting your family."

"They're not human. You can't insult the inhuman. Muffy will bring the beasts with her."

"Don't call your niece and nephew beasts."

"Wait a minute." Grace held up a hand. Her brows knit. "Muffy? Is that Muffy Parris Westlake? She's your sister?"

"Guilty."

Grace managed to suppress most of the snort of laughter. "That would make Doro Parris Lawrence your other sister." She rolled her eyes, picturing the two annoying and self-important Washington hostesses. "Bailey, run for your life. Go to Vegas. You and Cade can get married by a nice Elvis-impersonator judge and have a delightful, quiet life in the desert. Change your names. Never come back."

"See?" Pleased, Cade slapped a hand on the table. "She knows them."

"Stop it, both of you." Bailey refused to laugh, though her voice trembled with it. "We'll have a small, dignified ceremony—with Cade's family." She smiled at Grace. "And mine."

"Keep working on her." Cade rose. "I've got a couple things to do before I go into the office."

Grace picked up her coffee again. "I don't know his family well," she told Bailey. "I've managed to avoid that little pleasure, but I can tell you from what I do know, you've got the cream of the crop."

"I love him so much, Grace. I know it's all happened quickly, but—"

"What does time have to do with it?" Because she knew they were both about to get teary, she leaned forward. "We have to discuss the important, the vital, aspects of this situation, Bailey." She took a deep breath. "When do we go shopping?"

M.J. staggered in to the sound of laughter, and scowled at both of them. "I hate cheerful people in the morning." She poured coffee, tried to inhale it, then turned to study Grace. "Well, well," she said dryly. "Apparently you and the cop got to know each other last night."

"Well enough that I know he's more than a badge and an attitude." Irritated, she pushed her mug aside. "What have you got against him?"

"Other than the fact he's cold and arrogant, superior and stiff, nothing at all. Jack says they call him the Machine. Small wonder."

"I always find it interesting," Grace said coolly, "when people only skim the surface, then judge another human being. All those traits you just listed describe a man you don't know."

"M.J., drink your coffee." Bailey rose to get the cream.

"You know you're not fit to be around until you've had a half a gallon."

M.J. shook her head, fisted a hand on a hip covered with a tattered T-shirt and equally tattered shorts. "Just because you slept with him, doesn't mean you know him, either. You're usually a hell of a lot more careful than that, Grace. You might let other people assume you pop into bed with a new guy every other night, but we know better. What the hell were you thinking of?"

"I was thinking of *me*," she shot back. "I wanted him. I needed him. He's the first man who's ever really touched me. And I'm not going to let you stand there and make something beautiful into something cheap."

No one spoke for a moment. Bailey stood near the table, the creamer in one hand. M.J. slowly straightened from the counter, whistled out a breath. "You're falling for him." Staggered, she raked a hand through her hair. "You're really falling for him."

"I've already hit the ground with a splat. So what?"

"I'm sorry." M.J. struggled to adjust. She didn't have to like the man, she told herself. She just had to love Grace. "There must be something to him, if he got to you. Are you sure you're okay with it?"

"No, I'm not sure I'm okay with it." Temper drained, and doubt snuck in. "I don't know why it's happened or what to do about it. I just know it is. It wasn't just sex." She remembered how he had held her while she cried. How he'd left the light on for her without her having to ask. "I've been waiting for him all my life."

"I know what that means." Bailey set the creamer down, took Grace's hand. "Exactly."

"So do I." With a sigh, M.J. stepped forward. "What's happening to us? We're three sensible women, and suddenly we're guarding ancient mythical stones, running from bad guys and falling headlong into love with men we've just met. It's crazy."

"It's right," Bailey said quietly. "You know it feels right."

"Yeah." M.J. laid her hand over theirs. "I guess it does."

It wasn't easy for Grace to go back into her house. This time, though, she wasn't alone. M.J. and Jack flanked her like bookends.

"Man." Scanning the wreck of the living area, M.J. hissed out a breath. "I thought they did a number on my place. Of course, you've got a lot more toys to play with."

Then her gaze focused on the splintered railing. And the outline below. "You don't want to do this now, Grace."

"The police cleared the scene. I have to get started on it sometime."

M.J. shook her head. "Where?"

"I'll start in the bedroom." Grace managed a smile. "I'm about to make my dry cleaner a millionaire."

"I'll see what I can do with the railing," Jack told her. "Jury-rig something so it's safe until you have it rebuilt."

"I'd appreciate it."

"Go on up," M.J. suggested. "I'll get a broom. And a bulldozer." She waited until Grace was upstairs before she turned to Jack. "I'm going to do this down here. Get rid of...things." Her gaze wandered to the outline. "She shouldn't have to handle that."

He leaned down to kiss her forehead. "You're a stand-up pal, M.J."

"Yeah, that's me." She inhaled sharply. "Let's see if

we can dig up the stereo or the TV out of this mess. I could use some racket in here."

It took most of the afternoon before Grace was satisfied that the house was cleared out enough to call in her cleaning service. She wanted every room scrubbed before she lived there again.

And she was determined to do just that. To live, to be at home, to face whatever ghosts remained. To prove to herself that she could, she separated from M.J. and Jack and went shopping for the first replacements. Then, because the entire day had left her feeling raw, she stopped by Salvini.

She needed to see Bailey.

And she needed to see the Stars.

Once she was buzzed in, she found Bailey up in her office on the phone. With a smile, Bailey gestured her in. "Yes, Dr. Linstrum, I'm faxing the report to you now, and I'll bring you the original personally before five. I can complete the final tests you've ordered tomorrow."

She listened a moment, ran a finger down the soapstone elephant on her desk. "No, I'm fine. I appreciate your concern, and your understanding. The Stars are my priority. I'll have full copies of all the reports for your insurance carrier by end of business day Friday. Yes, thank you. Goodbye."

"You're working very quickly," Grace commented.

"Despite all that happened, hardly any time was lost. And everyone will feel more comfortable when the stones are in the museum."

"I want to see them again, Bailey." She let out a little laugh. "It's silly, but I really need to. I had this dream last night—nightmare, really."

"What kind of dream?"

Grace sat on the edge of the desk and told her. Though her voice was steady, her fingers tapped with nerves.

"I had dreams, too," Bailey murmured. "I'm still having them. So is M.J."

Uneasy, Grace shifted. "Like mine?"

"Similar enough to be more than coincidence." She rose, held out a hand for Grace's. "Let's go take a look."

"You're not breaking any laws, are you?"

As they walked downstairs together, Bailey sent her an amused look. "I think after what I've already done, this is a minor infraction." She tried to block it, but a shudder escaped as they descended the last flight of steps, under which she'd once hidden from a killer.

"Are you going to be all right here?" Instinctively Grace hooked an arm around Bailey's shoulder. "I hate thinking of what happened, and now thinking of you working here, remembering it."

"It's getting better. Grace, I've had my stepbrothers cremated. Or rather, Cade took care of the arrangements. He wouldn't let me handle any of it."

"Good for him. You don't owe them anything, Bailey. You never did. We're your family. We always will be."

"I know."

She passed into the vault room and approached the massive reinforced-steel doors. The security system was complex and intricate, and even with the ease of long practice, it took Bailey three full minutes to disengage.

"Maybe I ought to have one of these installed in my house," Grace said lightly. "That bastard popped my library safe like it was a gumball machine. He must have fenced the jewelry fast. I hate losing the pieces you made for me."

"I'll make you more. In fact—" Bailey picked up a square velvet box "—let's start now."

Curious, Grace opened the box to a pair of heavy gold earrings. The smooth crescent-shaped gold was studded with stones in deep, dark hues of emerald, ruby and sapphire.

"Bailey, they're beautiful."

"I'd just finished them before...well, before. As soon as I had, I knew they were yours."

"It's not my birthday."

"I thought you were dead." Bailey's voice shook, then strengthened when Grace looked up. "I thought I would never see you again. So let's consider these a celebration of the rest of our lives."

Grace removed the simple studs in her ears, began to replace them with Bailey's gift. "When I'm not wearing them, I'll keep them with my mother's jewelry. The things that matter most."

"They look perfect on you. I knew they would." Bailey turned, took the heavy padded box from its shelf in the vault. Holding it between them, she opened it.

Grace let out a long, uneven sigh. "I honestly thought one would be gone. I would drive up to the mountains and find it in my garden, sitting on the ground beneath the flowers. It was so real, Bailey."

Reaching out, Grace took a stone. Her stone. "I felt it in my hand, just as I do now. It pulsed in my hand like a heart." She laughed a little, but the sound was hollow. "My heart. That's what it seemed like. I didn't realize that until now. It was like holding my own heart."

"There's a link." A little pale, Bailey took another stone from the box. "I don't understand it, but I know it. This is the Star I had. If M.J. was here, she'd have picked hers."

"I never thought I believed in this sort of thing." Grace turned the stone in her hand. "I was wrong. It's incredibly easy to believe it. To know it. Are we protecting them, Bailey, or are they protecting us?"

"I like to think it's both. They brought me Cade." Gently, she replaced her stone, touched a fingertip to the second Star in its hollow. "Brought M.J. Jack." Her face softened. "I opened up the showroom for them a little while ago," she told Grace. "Jack dragged her in and bought her a ring."

"A ring?" Grace lifted a hand to her heart as it swelled. "An engagement ring?"

"An engagement ring. She argued the whole time, kept telling him not to be a jerk. She didn't need any ring. He just ignored her and pointed to this lovely green tourmaline—square-cut, with diamond baguettes. I designed it a few months ago, thinking that it would make a wonderful, nontraditional engagement ring for the right woman. He knew she was the right woman."

"He's perfect for her." Grace brushed a tear from her lashes and beamed. "I knew it as soon as I saw them together."

"I wish you'd seen them today. There she is, grumbling, rolling her eyes, insisting all this fuss is a waste of time and effort. Then he put that ring on her finger. She got this big, sloppy grin on her face. You know the one."

"Yeah." And she could see it, perfectly. "I'm so happy for her, for you. It's like all that love was there, waiting, and the stones…" She looked down at them again. "They opened the door for it."

"And you, Grace? Have they opened the door for you?"

"I don't know if I'm ready for that." Nerves suddenly sprang to her fingertips. She laid the stone back in its bed. "Seth certainly wouldn't be. I don't think he'd believe in magic of any sort. And as for love…even if that door is wide open and the opportunity is there, he's not a man to fall easily."

"Easy or not—" Bailey closed the lid, replaced the box "—when you're meant to fall, you fall. He's yours, Grace. I saw that in your eyes this morning."

"Well." Grace swallowed the nerves. "I think I may wait awhile to let him in on that."

Chapter 8

There were flowers waiting for her when Grace returned to Cade's. A gorgeous crystal vase was filled with long spears of paper-white long-stemmed roses. Her heart thudded foolishly into her throat as she snatched up the card, tore open the envelope.

Then it deflated and sank.

Not from Seth, she noted. Of course, it had been silly of her to think that he'd have indulged in such a romantic and extravagant gesture. The card read simply:

Until we meet again,
Gregor

The ambassador with the oddly compelling eyes, she mused, and leaned forward to sniff at the tender, just-opening blooms. It had been sweet of him, she told herself. A bit over-the-top, as there were easily three dozen roses in the vase, but sweet.

And she was irritated to realize that if they had been from Seth, she would have mooned over them like a starstruck teenager, would likely have pressed one between the pages of a book, even shed a few tears. She berated herself for being six times a fool.

If these appalling highs and lows were side effects of being in love, Grace thought she could have waited quite a bit longer to experience the sensation. She was just about to toss the card on the table when the phone rang.

She hesitated, as both Cade's and Jack's cars were in the drive, but when the phone rang the third time, she picked it up. "Parris residence."

"Is Grace Fontaine available?" The crisp tones of a well-trained secretary sounded in her ear. "Ambassador DeVane calling."

"Yes, this is she."

"One moment, please, Ms. Fontaine."

Lips pursed thoughtfully, Grace flipped the edge of the card against her palm. The man certainly had had no trouble tracking her down, Grace mused. And just how was she going to handle him?

"Grace." His voice flowed through the phone. "How delightful to speak with you again."

"Gregor." She flipped her hair behind her shoulder, edged a hip onto the table. "How extravagant of you. I've just walked in to your roses." She tipped one down, sniffed again. "They're glorious."

"Merely a token. I was disappointed not to have more time with you last evening. You left so early."

She thought of the wild ride to Seth's, the wilder sex. "I had…a previous engagement."

"Perhaps we can make up for it tomorrow evening. I have a box at the theater. *Tosca.* It's such a beautiful tragedy. There's nothing I would enjoy more than sharing it with you, then a late supper, perhaps."

"It sounds lovely." She rolled her eyes toward the flowers. Oh, dear, she thought. This would never do. "I'm so terribly sorry, Gregor, but I'm not free." With no regret whatsoever, she set the card aside. "Actually, I'm involved with someone, quite seriously."

For me, in any case, she thought. Then she looked through the glass panels of the front door, and her face lit up with surprise and pleasure when she saw Seth's car pull in.

"I see." She was too busy trying to steady her abruptly dancing pulse to notice how his voice had chilled. "Your escort of last evening."

"Yes. I'm terribly flattered, Gregor, and if I were any less involved, I'd leap at the invitation. I hope you'll forgive me, and understand."

Struggling not to squirm with delight, she crooked her finger in invitation as Seth stepped up to the door.

"Of course. If your circumstances change, I hope you'll reconsider."

"I certainly will." With a sultry smile, she walked her fingers up Seth's chest. "And thank you again, Gregor, so much, for the flowers. They're divine."

"It was my pleasure," he said, and his hands balled into bone-white fists as he hung up the receiver.

Humiliated, he thought, snapping his teeth together, grinding them viciously. Rejected for a suitful of muscles and a badge.

She would pay, he promised himself, taking her photo

from his file and gently tapping a well-manicured finger against it. She would pay dearly. And soon.

With the ambassador completely forgotten the moment the connection was broken, Grace tipped her face up to Seth's. "Hello, handsome."

He didn't kiss her, but looked at the flowers, then at the card she'd tossed carelessly beside them. "Another conquest?"

"Apparently." She heard the cold distance in his tone and wasn't certain whether to be flattered or annoyed. She opted for a different tack altogether, and purred. "The ambassador was interested in an evening at the opera and…whatever."

The spurt of jealousy infuriated him. It was a new experience, and one he detested. It left him helpless, made him want to drag her out to his car by the hair, cart her off, lock her up where only he could see and touch and taste.

But more, there was fear, for her. A bone-deep sense of danger.

"It seems the ambassador—and you—move quickly."

No, she realized, the temper was going to come. There was no stopping it. She eased off the table, her smile an icy dare. "I move however it suits me. You should know."

"Yes." He dipped his hands into his pockets to keep them off her. "I should. I do."

Crushed, she angled her chin, aimed those laser blue eyes. "Which am I now, Lieutenant? The whore or the goddess? The ivory princess atop the pedestal, or the tramp? I've been them all—it just depends on the man and how he chooses to look."

"I'm looking at you," he said calmly. "And I don't know what I see."

"Let me know when you make up your mind." She started to move around him, came up short when he took her arm. "Don't push me." She tossed her head so that her hair flew out, settled.

"I could say the same, Grace."

She drew in one hot, deep breath, shoved his hand aside. "If you're interested, I gave the ambassador my regrets and told him I was involved with someone." She flashed a frigid smile and swung toward the stairs. "That, apparently, was my mistake."

He scowled after her, considered striding up the stairs of a house that wasn't his own and finishing the confrontation—one way or the other. Appalled, he pinched the bridge of his nose between his thumb and forefinger and tried to squeeze off the bitter headache plaguing him.

His day had been grueling, and had ended ten long hours after it began, with him staring at the group of photos on his board. Photos of the dead who were waiting for him to find the connection.

And he was already furious with himself because he'd already begun to run a search for data on Gregor DeVane. He couldn't be sure if he had done so due to a basic cop's hunch, or a man's territorial instinct. Or the dreams. It was a question, and a conflict, he'd never had to face before.

But one answer was clear as glass. He'd been out of line with Grace. He was still standing by the foyer table, frowning at the steps and weighing his options, when Cade strolled in from the rear of the house.

"Buchanan." More than a little surprised to see the

homicide lieutenant standing in his foyer scowling, Cade stopped, scratched his jaw. "Ah, I didn't know you were here."

He had no business being there, Seth reminded himself. "Sorry. Grace let me in."

"Oh." After one beat, Cade pinpointed the source of the heat still flashing in the air. "Oh," he said again, and wisely controlled a grin. "Fine. Something I can do for you?"

"No. I'm just leaving."

"Have a spat?"

Seth turned his head, met Cade's obviously amused eyes blandly. "Excuse me?"

"Just a wild stab in the dark. What did you do to tick her off?" Though Seth didn't answer, Cade noted that his gaze shifted briefly to the roses. "Oh, yeah. Guess you didn't send them, huh? If some guy sent Bailey three dozen white roses, I'd probably have to stuff them down his throat, one at a time."

It was the gleam of appreciation that flashed briefly in Seth's eyes that made Cade decide to revise his stance. Maybe he could like Lieutenant Seth Buchanan after all.

"Want a beer?"

The casual and friendly invitation threw Seth off balance. "I— No, I was leaving."

"Come on out back. Jack and I already popped a couple of tops. We're going to fire up the grill and show the women how real men cook." Cade's grin spread charmingly. "Besides, oiling yourself with a couple of brews will make it easier for you to crawl. You're going to crawl anyway, so you might as well be comfortable."

Seth hissed out a breath. "Why the hell not?"

* * *

Grace stayed stubbornly in her room for an hour. She could hear laughter, music, and the silly whack of mallets striking balls as people played an enthusiastic game of croquet. She knew Seth's car was still in the drive, and had promised herself she wouldn't go back down until it was gone.

But she was feeling deprived, and hungry.

Since she'd already changed into shorts and a thin cotton shirt, she paused at the mirror only long enough to freshen her lipstick, spritz on some perfume. Just to make him suffer, she told herself, then sauntered downstairs and out onto the patio.

Steaks were smoking on the grill with Cade at the helm wielding an enormous barbecue fork. Bailey and Jack were arguing over the croquet match, and M.J. was sulking at a picnic table while she nibbled on potato chips.

"Jack knocked me out of the game," she complained, and gestured with her beer. "I still say he cheated."

"Any time you lose," Grace pointed out as she picked up a chip, "it's because someone cheated." Then she slid her gaze to Seth.

He'd taken off his tie, she noted, and his jacket. He still wore his holster. She imagined that was because he didn't feel comfortable hanging his gun over a tree branch. He, too, had a beer in his hand, and was watching the game with apparent interest.

"You still here?"

"Yeah." He'd had two beers, but didn't think crawling was going to be any more comfortable with the lubricant. "I've been invited to dinner."

"Isn't that cozy?" Grace spied what she recognized

as a pitcher of M.J.'s special margaritas and poured herself a glass. The taste was tart, icy, and perfect. In dismissal, she wandered over to the grill to kibitz.

"I know what I'm doing," Cade was saying, and shifted to guard his territory as Seth joined them. "I marinated these vegetable kabobs personally. Go away and leave this to a man."

"I was merely asking if you preferred your mushrooms blackened."

Cade sent her a withering look. "Get her off my back, Seth. An artist can't work with critics breathing down his neck and picking on his mushrooms."

"Let's go over here." Seth took her elbow, and was braced for her jerk. He kept his grip firm and hauled her away into the rose garden.

"I don't want to talk to you," Grace said furiously.

"You don't have to talk. I'll talk." But it took him a minute. Apologies didn't come easily to a man who made it a habit not to make mistakes. "I'm sorry. I overreacted."

She said nothing, simply folded her arms and waited.

"You want more?" He nodded, didn't bother to sigh. "I was jealous, an atypical reaction for me, and I handled it poorly. I apologize."

Grace shook her head. "That's the weakest excuse for an apology I've ever heard. Not the words, Seth, the delivery. But fine, I'll accept it in the same spirit it was offered."

"What do you want from me?" he demanded, frustrated enough to raise his voice and grab her arms. "What the hell do you want?"

"That." She tossed back her head. "Just that. A little emotion, a little passion. You can take your cardboard-stiff apology and stuff it, just like you can stuff the cold, deliberate and dispassionate routine you gave me over the flowers. That icy control doesn't cut it with me. If you feel something—whatever the hell it is—then let me know."

She sucked in her breath, stunned, when he yanked her against him, savaged her mouth with heat and anger and need. She twisted once and was hauled roughly back. Then was left weak and singed and shaken by the time he drew away.

"Is that enough for you?" He hauled her to her toes, his fingers digging in. His eyes weren't dispassionate now, weren't cool, but turbulent. Human. "Enough emotion, enough passion? I don't like to lose control. You can't afford to lose control on the job."

Her breath was heaving. And her heart was flying. "This isn't the job."

"No, but it was supposed to be." He willed his grip to loosen. "You were supposed to be. I can't get you out of my head. Damn it, Grace. I can't get you out."

She laid a hand on his cheek, felt the muscle twitch. "It's the same for me. Maybe the only difference right now is that I want it to be that way."

For how long? he wondered, but he didn't say it. "Come home with me."

"I'd love to." She smiled, stroked her fingers back, into his hair. "But I think we'd better stay for dinner, at least. Otherwise, we'd break Cade's heart."

"After dinner, then." It wasn't difficult at all, he discovered, to bring her hands to his lips, linger over them, then look into her eyes. "I am sorry. But, Grace—?"

"Yes?"

"If DeVane calls you again, or sends flowers?"

Her lips twitched. "Yes?"

"I'll have to kill him."

With a delighted laugh, she threw her arms around Seth's neck. "Now we're talking."

"That was nice." With a satisfied sigh, Grace sank down in the seat of Seth's car and watched the moon shimmer in the sky. "I like seeing the four of them together. But it's funny. It's as if I blinked, and everyone took this huge, giant step forward."

"Red light, green light."

Confused, Grace turned her head to look at him. "What?"

"The game—the kid's game? You know, the person who's it has to say, 'Green light,' turn his back. Everybody can go forward, but then he says, 'Red light' and spins around. If he sees anybody move, they have to go back to the start."

When she gave a baffled laugh, it was his turn to look. "Didn't you ever play games like that when you were a kid?"

"No. I was given the proper lessons, lectured on etiquette and was instructed to take brisk daily walks for exercise. Sometimes I ran," she said softly, remembering. "Fast, and hard, until my heart was bumping in my chest. But I guess I always had to go back to the start."

Annoyed with herself, she shook her shoulders. "My, doesn't that sound pathetic? It wasn't, really. It was just structured." She scooped back her hair, smiled at him. "So what other games did young Seth Buchanan play?"

"The usual." Didn't she know how heartbreaking it was to hear that wistfulness in her voice, then see that quick, careless shrug as she pushed it all aside? "Didn't you have friends?"

"Of course." Then she looked away. "No. It doesn't matter. I have them now. The best of friends."

"Do you know any one of the three of you can start a sentence and either of the other two can finish it?"

"We don't do that."

"Yes, you do. A dozen times tonight, at least. You don't even realize it. And you have this code," he continued. "Little quirks and gestures. M.J.'s half smirk or eye roll, Bailey's downsweep of the lashes or hair-around-the-finger twist. And you lift your left brow, just a fraction, or catch your tongue between your teeth. When you do, you let each other know the joke's your little secret."

She hummed in her throat, not at all sure she liked being deciphered so easily. "Aren't you observant…"

"That's my job." He pulled into his driveway, turned to her. "It shouldn't bother you."

"I haven't decided if it does or not. Did you become a cop because you're observant, or are you observant because you're a cop?"

"Hard to say. I was never really anything else."

"Not even when you were young Seth Buchanan?"

"It was always part of my life. My grandfather was a cop. And my father. My father's brother. Our house was filled with them."

"So it was expected of you?"

"It was understood," he corrected. "If I'd wanted to be a plumber or a mechanic, that would have been fine. But it was what I wanted."

"Why?"

"There's right and there's wrong."

"Just that simple?"

"It should be." He looked at the ring on his finger. "My father was a good cop. Straight. Fair. Solid. You can't ask for more than that."

She laid a hand over his. "You lost him."

"Line of duty. A long time ago." The hurt had passed a long time before, as well, and left room for pride. "He was a good cop, a good father, a good man. He always said there was a choice between doing the right thing or the wrong thing. Either one had a price. But you could pay up on the first and still look yourself in the eye every morning."

Grace leaned over, kissed him lightly. "He did the right thing by you."

"Always. My mother was a cop's wife, steady as a rock. Now she's a cop's mother, and she's still steady. Still there. When I got my gold shield, it meant as much to her as it did to me."

There was a bond, she realized. Deep and true and unquestioned. "But she worries about you."

"Some. But she accepts it. Has to," he added, with the ghost of a smile. "I've got a younger brother and sister. We're all cops."

"It runs through the blood," she murmured. "Are you close?"

"We're family," he said simply, then thought of hers and remembered that such things weren't simple. They were precious. "Yes, we're close."

He was the oldest, she mused. He would have taken his generational placement seriously, and, when his father died, his responsibilities as man of the house with equal weight.

It was hardly a wonder, then, that authority, responsibility, duty, sat so naturally on him. She thought of the weapon he wore, touched a fingertip to the leather strap.

"Have you ever..." She lifted her gaze to his. "Have you ever had to?"

"Yes. But I can still look myself in the eye in the morning."

She accepted that without question. But the next subject was more difficult. "You have a scar, just here." Her memory of it was perfect as she touched her finger just under his right shoulder now. "You were shot?"

"Five years ago. One of those things." There was no point in relaying the details. The bust gone wrong, the shouts and the electric buzz of terror. The insult of the bullet and the bright, stupefying pain. "Most police work is routine—paperwork, tedium, repetition."

"But not all."

"No, not all." He wanted to see her smile again, wanted to prolong what had evolved into a sweet and intimate interlude in a darkened car. Just conversation, without the sizzle of sex. "You've got a tattoo on your incredibly perfect bottom."

She laughed then, and tossed her hair back. "I didn't think you'd noticed."

"I noticed. Why do you have a tattoo of a winged horse on your butt, Grace?"

"It was an impulse, one of those wild-girl things I dragged M.J. and Bailey into."

"They have winged horses on their—"

"No, and what they do have is their little secret. I wanted the winged horse because it was free. You couldn't catch it unless it wanted to be caught." She lifted a hand to his face, changed the mood subtly. "I never wanted to be caught. Before."

He nearly believed her. Lowering his head, he met her lips with his, let the kiss spin out. It was quiet, without urgency. The slow meeting of tongues, the lazy change of angles and depths. Easy sips. Testing nibbles.

Her body shifted fluidly, her hands sliding up his chest to link at the nape of his neck. A purr sounded in her throat. "It's been a long time since I necked in the front seat of a car."

He nudged her hair aside so that his mouth could find that sweet, sensitive curve between neck and shoulder. "Want to try the back seat?"

Her laugh was low and delighted. "Absolutely."

The need had snuck up on him, crept into his bloodstream to stagger his heart. "We'll go inside."

Her breath was a bit unsteady as she leaned back, grinned at him in the shimmer of moonlight. "Chicken."

His eyes narrowed fractionally, making her grin widen. "There's a perfectly good bed in the house."

She made a soft clucking noise, then, chuckling, rubbed her lips over his. "Let's pretend," she whispered, pressing her body to his, sliding it against his. "We're on a dark, deserted road and you've told me the car's broken down."

He said her name, an exasperated sound against her tempting lips. It was only another challenge to her.

"I pretend I believe you, because I want to stay, I want you to...persuade me. You'll say you just want to touch me, and I'll pretend I believe that, too." She took his hand, laid it on her breast and felt the quick thrill when his fingers flexed. "Even though I know that's not all you want. It's not all you want, is it, Seth?"

What he wanted was that dark, slippery slide into her.

His hands moved under her shirt, found flesh. "We're not going to make it into the back seat," he warned her.

She only laughed.

He wasn't sure if he felt smug or stunned by his own behavior when he finally unlocked his front door. Had he been this randy as a teenager? he wondered. That ridiculously reckless? Or was it only Grace who made such things as making desperate love in his own driveway one more adventure?

She stepped inside, lifted the hair off her neck, then let it fall in a gesture that simply stopped his heart. "My place should be ready by tomorrow, the next day at the latest. We'll have to go there. We can skinny-dip in my pool. It's so hot out now."

"You're so beautiful."

She turned, surprised at the mix of resentment and desire in his voice. He stood just inside the door, as if he might turn at any moment and leave her.

"It's a dangerous weapon. Lethal."

She tried to smile. "Arrest me."

"You don't like to be told." He let out a half laugh. "You don't like to be told you're beautiful."

"I didn't do anything to earn how I look."

She said it, he realized, as if beauty were more of a curse than a gift. And in that moment he felt a new level of understanding. He stepped forward, took her face gently in his hands, looked deep and long.

"Well, maybe your eyes are a little too close together."

Her hitch of laughter was pure surprise. "They are not."

"And your mouth, I think it might be just a hair off center. Let me check." He measured it with his own, lingering over the kiss when her lips curved. "Yeah. Just a hair, but it does throw things off, now that I really look. And let's see…" He turned her head to each side, paused to consider. "Yep. The left profile's weak. Are you getting a double chin there?"

She slapped his hand away, torn between insult and laughter. "I certainly am not."

"I really should check that, too. I don't know if I want to take this whole thing any further if you're getting a double chin."

He grabbed her, tugging her head back gently by the hair so that he could nibble freely under her jaw. She giggled—a young, foolish sound—and squirmed. "Stop that, you idiot." She let out a shriek when he hauled her up into his arms.

"You're no lightweight, either, by the way."

Her eyes went to slits. "Okay, buster, that's all. I'm leaving."

It was a delight to watch him grin—that quick, boyish flash of humor. "I forgot to tell you," he said as he headed for the stairs. "My car's broken down. I'm out of gas. The cat ate my homework. I'm just going to touch you."

He'd made it up two steps when the phone rang. "Damn." He brushed his lips absently over her brow. "I have to get that."

"It's all right. I'll remember where you were." Though he set her down, she didn't think her feet hit the floor. Love was a cushy buffer.

But her smile faded as she saw his eyes change. Suddenly they were flat again, unreadable. She knew as she walked across the room toward him that he'd shifted seamlessly from man to cop.

"Where?" His voice was cool again, controlled. "Is the scene secured?" He swore lightly, barely a whisper under the breath. "Get it secured. I'm on my way." As he hung up, his eyes skimmed over her, focused. "I'm sorry, Grace, I have to go."

She moistened her lips. "Is it bad?"

"I have to go," was all he'd say. "I'll call for a black-and-white to take you back to Cade's."

"Can't I wait here for you?"

"I don't know how long I'll be."

"It doesn't matter." She offered a hand, but wasn't sure she could reach him. "I'd like to wait. I want to wait for you."

No woman ever had. That thought passed quickly through his mind, distracting him. "If you get tired of waiting, call the precinct. I'll leave word there for a uniform to drive you home if you call in."

"All right." But she wouldn't call in. She would wait. "Seth." She moved into him, brushed her lips against his. "I'll see you when you get back."

Chapter 9

Alone, Grace switched on the television, settled on the sofa. Five minutes later, she was up and wandering the house.

He didn't go in for knickknacks, she mused. Probably thought of them as dustcatchers. No plants, no pets. The living room furniture was simple, masculine, and good quality. The sofa was comfortable, of generous size and a deep hunter green. She would have spruced it up with pillows. Burgundy, navy, copper. The coffee table was a square of heavy oak, highly polished and dust-free.

She decided he had a weekly housekeeper. She just couldn't picture Seth wielding a polishing rag. There was a bookcase under the side window and, crouching, she scanned the titles. It pleased her that they had read many of the same books. There was even a gardening book she'd studied herself.

That she could see, she decided. Yes, she could see Seth working out in the yard, turning the earth, planting something that would last.

There was art in this room, as well. She moved closer, certain the watercolor portraits grouped on the wall were the work of the same artist who had done the cityscape and rural scene in his bedroom. She searched for the signature first, and found Marilyn Buchanan looped in the lower corner.

Sister, mother, cousin? she wondered. Someone he loved, and who loved him. She shifted her gaze and studied the first painting.

Seth's father, Grace realized with a jolt. It had to be. The resemblance was there, in the eyes, clear, intense, tawny. The jaw, squared off, almost chiseled. The artist had seen strength, a touch of sadness, and honor. A whisper of humor around the mouth and an innate pride in the set of the head. All were evident in the three-quarter profile view that had the subject staring off at something only he could see.

The next portrait was a woman, perhaps in her forties. It was a pretty face, but the artist hadn't hidden the faint and telltale lines of age, the touches of gray in the dark, curling hair. The hazel eyes looked straight ahead, with humor and with patience. And there was Seth's mouth, Grace thought, smiling easily.

His mother, she concluded. How much strength was contained inside those quiet hazel eyes? Grace wondered. How much was required to stand and accept when everyone you loved faced danger daily?

Whatever the amount, this woman possessed it.

There was another man, young, twenty-something, with a cocky grin and daredevil eyes shades darker than Seth's. Attractive, sexy, with a dark shock of hair falling carelessly over his brow. His brother, certainly.

The last was of a young woman with a shoulder-length sweep of dark hair, the tawny eyes alert, the sculpted mouth just curved in the beginnings of a smile. Lovely, with more of Seth's seriousness about her than the young man. His sister.

She wondered if she would ever meet them, or if she would know them only through their portraits. Seth would take the woman he loved to them, she thought, and let the little slice of hurt pass through her. He would want to—need to—bring her into his mother's home, watch how she melded and mixed with his family.

It was a door he'd have to open on both sides in welcome. Not just because it was traditional, she realized, but because it would matter to him.

But a lover? No, she decided. It wasn't necessary to share a lover with family. He'd never take a woman with whom he shared only sex home to meet his mother.

Grace closed her eyes a moment. Stop feeling sorry for yourself, she ordered briskly. You can't have everything you want or need, so you make the best of what there is.

She opened her eyes again, once more scanned the portraits. Good faces, she thought. A good family.

But where, Grace wondered, was Seth's portrait? There had to be one. What had the artist seen? Had she painted him with that cool cop's stare, that surprisingly beautiful smile, the all-too-rare flash of that grin?

Determined to find out, she left the television blaring and went on the hunt. In the next twenty minutes, she discovered that Seth lived tidily, kept a phone and notepad in every room, used the second bedroom as a combination guest room and office, had turned the tiny third bedroom into a minigym and liked deep colors and comfortable chairs.

She found more watercolors, but no portrait of the man.

She circled the guest room, curious that here, and only here, he'd indulged in some whimsy. Recessed shelves held a collection of figures, some carved in wood, others in stone. Dragons, griffins, sorcerers, unicorns, centaurs. And a single winged horse of alabaster caught soaring in midflight.

Here the paintings reflected the magical—a misty landscape where a turreted castle rose silver into a pale rose-colored sky, a shadow-dappled lake where a single white deer drank.

There were books on Arthur, on Irish legends, the gods of Olympus, and those who had ruled Rome. And there, on the small cherrywood desk, was a globe of blue crystal and a book on Mithra, the god of light.

It made her tremble, clutch her arms. Had he picked up the book because of the case? Or had it already been here? She touched a hand to the slim volume and was certain it was the latter.

One more link between them, she realized, forged before they'd even met. It was so easy for her to accept that, even to be grateful. But she wondered if he felt the same.

She went downstairs, oddly at home after her self-guided tour. It made her smile to see their coffee cups from that morning still in the sink, a little touch of intimacy. She found a bottle of wine in the refrigerator, poured herself a glass and took it with her into the living room.

She went back to the bookcase, thinking of curling up on the couch with the TV for company and a book to pass the time. Then a chill washed over her, so quick, so intense, the wine shook in her hand. She found herself staring out the window, her breath coming short, her other hand clutched on the edge of the bookcase.

Someone watching. It pounded in her brain, a frightened, whispering voice that might have been her own.

Someone watching.

But she saw nothing but the dark, the shimmer of moonlight, the quiet house across the street.

Stop it, she ordered herself. There's no one there. There's nothing there. But she straightened and quickly twitched the curtains closed. Her hands were shaking.

She sipped wine, tried to laugh at herself. The late-breaking bulletin on the television had her turning slowly. A family of four in nearby Bethesda. Murdered.

She knew where Seth had gone now. And could only imagine what he was dealing with.

She was alone. DeVane sat in his treasure room, stroking an ivory statue of the goddess Venus. He'd come to think of it as Grace. As his obsession festered and grew, he imagined Grace and himself together, immortal through time. She would be his most prized possession. His goddess. And the Three Stars would complete his collection of the priceless.

Of course, she would have to be punished first. He knew what had to be done, what would matter most to her. And the other two women were not blameless—they had complicated his plans, caused him to fail. They would have to die, of course.

After he had the Stars, after he had Grace, they would die. And their deaths would be her punishment.

Now she was alone. It would be so easy to take her now. To bring her here. She'd be afraid, at first. He wanted her to be afraid. It was part of her punishment. Eventually he would woo her, win her. Own her. They would have, after all, several lifetimes to be together.

In one of them he would take her back to Terresa. He would make her a queen. A god could settle for no less than a queen.

Take her tonight. The voice that spoke louder and louder in his head every day taunted him. He couldn't trust it. DeVane steadied his breathing, shut his eyes. He would not be rushed. Every detail had to be in place.

Grace would come to him when he was prepared. And she would bring him the Stars.

Seth downed one last cup of sludgy coffee and rubbed at the ache at the back of his neck. His stomach was still raw from what he'd seen in that neat suburban home. He knew civilians and rookie cops believed the vets became immune to the results of violent death—the sights, the smells, the meaningless waste.

It was a lie.

No one could become used to seeing what he'd seen. If they could, they shouldn't wear a badge. The law needed to retain its sense of disgust, of horror, for murder.

What drove a man to take the lives of his own children, of the woman he'd made them with, and then his own? There'd been no one left in that neat suburban home to answer that question. He knew it would haunt him.

Seth scrubbed his hands over his face, felt the knots of tension and fatigue. He rolled his shoulders once, twice, then squared them before cutting through the bull pen, toward the locker room.

Mick Marshall was there, rubbing his sore feet. His wiry red hair stood up like a bush that needed trimming from a face lined with weariness. His eyes were shadowed, his mouth was grim.

"Lieutenant." He pulled his socks back on.

"You didn't have to come in on this, Detective."

"Hell, I heard the gunshots from my own living room." He picked up one of his shoes, but just rested his elbows on his knees. "Two blocks over. Jesus, my kids played with those kids. How the hell am I going to explain this?"

"How well did you know the father?"

"Didn't, really. It's just like they always say, Lieutenant. He was a quiet guy, polite, kept to himself." He gave a short, humorless laugh. "They always do."

"Mulrooney's taking the case. You can assist if you want. Now go home, get some sleep. Go in and kiss your kids."

"Yeah." Mick scraped his fingers through his hair. "Listen, Lieutenant, I got some data on that DeVane guy."

Seth's spine tingled. "Anything interesting?"

"Depends on what floats your boat. He's fifty-two, never married, inherited a big fat pile from his old man, including this big vineyard on that island, that Terresa. Grows olives, too, runs some cattle."

"The gentleman farmer?"

"Oh, he's got more going than that. Lots of interests, spread out all over hell and back. Shipping, communications, import-export. Lots of fingers in lots of pies generating lots of dough. He was made ambassador to the U.S. three years ago. Seems to like it here. He bought some nifty place on Foxhall Road, big mansion, likes to entertain. People don't like to talk about him, though. They get real nervous."

"Money and power make some people nervous."

"Yeah. I haven't gotten a lot of information yet. But there was a woman about five years ago. Opera singer. Pretty big deal, if you're into that sort of thing. Italian lady. Seems like they were pretty tight. Then she disappeared."

"Disappeared." Seth's waning interest snapped back. "How?"

"That's the thing. She just went poof. Italian police can't figure it. She had a place in Milan, left all her things—clothes, jewelry, the works. She was singing at that opera house there, in the middle of a run, you know? Didn't show for the evening performance. She went shopping on that afternoon, had a bunch of things sent back to her place. But she never went back."

"They figure kidnapping?"

"They did. But then there was no ransom call, no body, no sign of her in nearly five years. She was…" Mick screwed up his face in thought. "Thirty, supposed to be at the top of her form, and a hell of a looker. She left a big pile of lire in her accounts. It's still there."

"DeVane was questioned?"

"Yeah. Seems he was on his yacht in the Ionian Sea, soaking up rays and drinking ouzo, when it all went down. A half-dozen guests on board with him. The Italian cop I talked to—big opera fan, by the way—he didn't think DeVane seemed shocked enough, or upset enough. He smelled something, but couldn't make anything stick. Still, the guy offered a reward, five million lire, for her safe return. No one ever collected."

"I'd say that was fairly interesting. Keep digging." And, Seth thought, he'd start doing some digging himself.

"One more thing." Mick cracked his neck from side to side. "And I thought this was interesting too—the guy's a collector. He has a little of everything—coins, stamps, jewelry, art, antiques, statuary. He does it all. But he's also reputed to have a unique and extensive gem collection—rivals the Smithsonian's."

"DeVane likes rocks."

"Oh, yeah. And get this. Two years ago, more or less, he paid three mil for an emerald. Big rock, sure, but its price spiked because it was supposed to be a magic rock." The very idea made Mick's lips curl. "Merlin was supposed to have, you know, conjured it up for Arthur. Seems to me a guy who'd buy into that would be pretty interested in three big blue rocks and all that god and immortality stuff that goes with them."

"I just bet he would." And wasn't it odd, Seth mused, that DeVane's name hadn't been on Bailey's list? A collector whose U.S. residence was only miles from Salvini, yet he'd never done business with them?

No, the lack was too odd to believe.

"Get me what you've got when you go on shift, Mick. I'd like to talk to that Italian cop personally. I appreciate the extra time you put into this."

Mick blinked. Seth never failed to thank his men for good work, but it was generally mechanical. There had been genuine warmth this time, on a personal level. "Sure, no sweat. But you know, Lieutenant, even if you can tie this guy to the case, he'll bounce. Diplomatic immunity. We can't touch him."

"Let's tie him first, then we'll see." Seth glanced over, distracted, when a locker slammed open nearby as a cop was coming on shift. "Get some sleep," he began, then broke off. There, taped to the back of the locker, was Grace, young, laughing and naked.

Her head was tossed back, and that teasing smile, that feminine confidence, that silky power, sparkled in her eyes. Her skin was like polished marble, her curves were generous, with only that rainfall of hair, artfully draped to drive a man insane, covering her.

Mick turned his head, saw the centerfold and winced. Cade had filled him in on the lieutenant's relationship with Grace, and all Mick could think was that someone—very likely the cop currently standing at his locker whistling moronically—was about to die.

"Ah, Lieutenant…" Mick began, with some brave thought of saving his associate's life.

Seth merely held up a hand, cut Mick off and walked to the locker. The cop changing his shirt glanced over. "Lieutenant."

"Bradley," Seth said, and continued to study the glossy photo.

"She's something else, isn't she? One of the guys on day shift said she'd been in and looked just as good in person."

"Did he?"

"You bet. I dug this out of a pile of magazines in my garage. None the worse for wear."

"Bradley." Mick whispered the name and buried his head in his hands. The guy was dead meat.

Seth took a long breath, resisted the urge to rip the

photo down. "Female officers share this locker room, Bradley. This is inappropriate." Where was the tattoo? Seth thought hazily. What had she been when she posed for this? Nineteen, twenty? "Find somewhere else to hang your art."

"Yes, sir."

Seth turned away, then shot one last look over his shoulder. "And she's better in person. Much better."

"Bradley," Mick said as Seth strode out, "you just dodged one major bullet."

Dawn was breaking when Seth let himself into the house. He'd gone by the book on the case in Bethesda. It would close when the forensic and autopsy reports confirmed what he already knew. A man of thirty-six who made a comfortable living as a computer programmer had gotten up from his sofa, where he was watching television, loaded his revolver and ended four lives in the approximate space of ten minutes.

For this crime, Seth could offer no justice.

He could have headed home two hours earlier. But he'd made use of the time difference in Europe to make calls, ask questions, gather data. He was slowly putting together a picture of Gregor DeVane.

A man of wealth he had never sweated for. One who enjoyed prestige and power, who traveled in exalted circles, and had no family.

There was no crime in any of that, Seth thought as he closed his front door behind him.

There was no crime in sending white roses to a beautiful woman.

Or in once being involved with one who'd disappeared. But wasn't it interesting that DeVane had been involved with another woman? A Frenchwoman, a prima ballerina of great beauty who'd been considered the finest dancer of the decade. And who had been found dead of a drug overdose in her Paris home.

The verdict had been suicide, though those closest to her insisted she had never used drugs. She had been fiercely disciplined about her body. DeVane had been questioned in that matter, as well, but only as a matter of form. He had been dining at the White House at the very hour the young dancer slipped into a coma, and then into death.

Still, Seth and the Italian detective agreed it was quite a fascinating coincidence.

A collector, Seth mused, switching off lights automatically. An acquirer of beautiful things, and beautiful women. A man who would pay double the value of an emerald to possess a legend, as well.

He would see how many more threads he could tie, and he would, he decided, have an official chat with the ambassador.

He stepped into the living room, started to hit the next switch, and saw Grace curled upon the couch.

He'd assumed she'd gone home. But there she was, curled into a tight, protective ball on his couch, sleeping. What the hell was she doing here? he wondered.

Waiting for you. Just as she said she would. As no woman had waited before. As he'd wanted no woman to wait.

Emotion thudded into his chest, flooded into his heart. It undid him, he realized, this irrational love. His heart wasn't safe here, wasn't even his own any longer. He wanted it back, wanted desperately to be able to turn away, leave her and go back to his life.

It terrified him that he wouldn't. Couldn't.

She was bound to get bored before too much longer, to lose interest in a relationship he imagined was fueled by impulse and sex on her part. Would she just drift away, he wondered, or end it cleanly? It would be clean, he decided. That would be her way. She wasn't, as he'd once wanted to believe, callous or cold or calculating. She had a very giving heart, but he thought it was also a restless one.

Moving over, he crouched in front of her, studied her face. There was a faint line between her brows. She didn't sleep easily, he realized. What dreams chased her? he asked himself. What worries nagged her?

Poor little rich girl, he thought. Still running until you're out of breath and there's nothing to do but go back to the start.

He stroked a thumb over her brow to smooth it; then slid his arms under her. "Come on, baby," he murmured, "time for bed."

"No." She pushed at him, struggled. "Don't."

More nightmares? Concerned, he gathered her close. "It's Seth. It's all right. I've got you."

"Watching me." She turned her face into his shoulder. "Outside. Everywhere. Watching me."

"Shhh... No one's here." He carried her toward the steps, realizing now why every light in the house had been blazing. She'd been afraid to be alone in the dark. Yet she'd stayed. "No one's going to hurt you, Grace. I promise."

"Seth." She surfaced to the sound of his voice, and her heavy eyes opened and focused on his face. "Seth," she said again. She touched a hand to his cheek, then her lips. "You look so tired."

"We can switch. You can carry me."

She slid her arms around him, pressed her cheek, warm to his. "I heard, on the news. The family in Bethesda."

"You didn't have to wait."

"Seth." She eased back, met his eyes.

"I won't talk about it," he said flatly. "Don't ask."

"You won't talk about it because it troubles you to talk about it, or because you won't share those troubles with me?"

He set her down beside the bed, turned away and peeled off his shirt. "I'm tired, Grace. I have to be back in a few hours. I need to sleep."

"All right." She rubbed the heel of her hand over her heart, where it hurt the most. "I've already had some sleep. I'll go downstairs and call a cab."

He hung his shirt over the back of a chair, sat to take off his shoes. "If that's what you want."

"It's not what I want, but it seems it's what you want." She barely lifted a brow when he heaved his shoe across the room. Then he stared at it as if it had leaped there on its own.

"I don't do things like that," he said between his teeth. "I never do things like that."

"Why not? It always makes me feel better." And because he looked so exhausted, and so baffled by himself, she relented. Walking to him, she stepped in close to where he sat and began to knead the stiff muscles of his shoulders. "You know what you need around here, Lieutenant?" She dipped her head to kiss the top of his. "Besides me, of course. You need to get yourself a bubble tub, something you can sink down into that'll beat all these knots out of you. But for now we'll see what I can do about them."

Her hands felt like glory, smoothing out the knotted muscles in his shoulders. "Why?"

"That's one of your favorite questions, isn't it? Come on, lie down, let me work on this rock you call a back."

"I just need to sleep."

"Um-hmm." Taking charge, she nudged him back, climbed onto the bed to kneel beside him. "Roll over, handsome."

"I like this view better." He managed a half smile, toyed with the ends of her hair. "Why don't you come here? I'm too tired to fight you off."

"I'll keep that in mind." She gave him a push. "Roll over, big boy."

With a grunt, he rolled over on his stomach, then let out a second grunt when she straddled him and those wonderful hands began to press and stroke and knead.

"You, being you, would consider a regular massage an indulgence. But that's where you're wrong." She pressed down with the heels of her hands, worked forward to knead with her fingertips. "You give your body relief, it works better for you. I get one every week at the club. Stefan could do wonders for you."

"Stefan." He closed his eyes and tried not to think about another man with his hands all over her. "Figures."

"He's a professional," she said dryly. "And his wife is a pediatric therapist. She's wonderful with the children at the hospital."

He thought of the children, and that was what weakened him. That, and her soothing hands, her quiet voice.

Sunlight filtered, a warm red, through his closed lids, but he could still see.

"The kids were in bed."

Her hands froze for a moment. Then, with a long, quiet breath, she moved them again, up and down his spine, over his shoulder blades, up to the tight length of his neck. And she waited.

"The youngest girl had a doll—one of those Raggedy Anns. An old one. She was still holding it. There were Disney posters all over the walls. All those fairy tales and happy endings. The way it's supposed to be when you're a kid. The older girl had one of those teen magazines beside the bed—the kind ten-year-olds read because they can't wait to be sixteen. They never woke up. Never knew neither one of them would get to be sixteen."

She said nothing. There was nothing that could be said. But, leaning down, she touched her lips to the back of his shoulder and felt him let loose a long, ragged breath.

"It twists you when it's kids. I don't know a cop who can deal with it without having it twist his guts. The mother was on the stairs. Looks like she heard the shots, starting running up to her kids. After, he went back to the living room, sat down on the sofa and finished it."

She curled herself into him, hugged herself to his back and just held on. "Try to sleep," she murmured.

"Stay. Please."

"I will." She closed her eyes, listened to his breathing deepen. "I'll stay."

But he woke alone. As sleep was clearing, he wondered if he'd dreamed the meeting at dawn. Yet he could smell her—on the air, on his own skin where she'd curled close. He was still stretched crosswise over the bed, and he tilted his wrist to check the watch he'd neglected to take off.

Whatever else was going on inside him, his internal clock was still in working order.

He gave himself an extra two minutes under the shower to beat back fatigue, and when shaving promised himself to do nothing more than vegetate on his next personal day. He pretended it wasn't going to be another hot, humid, hazy day while he knotted his tie.

Then he swore, scooped fingers though his just-combed hair, remembering he'd neglected to set the timer on his coffeemaker. The minutes it would take to brew it would not only set his teeth on edge, they would eat into his schedule.

But the one thing he categorically refused to do was start the day with the poison that simmered at the cop shop.

His mind was so focused on coffee that when the scent of it wafted like a siren's call as he came down the stairs, he thought it was an illusion.

Not only was the pot full of gloriously rich black liquid, Grace was sitting at his kitchen table, reading the morning paper and nibbling on a bagel. Her hair was scooped back from her face, and she appeared to be wearing nothing more than one of his shirts.

"Good morning." She smiled up at him, then shook her head. "Are you human? How can you look so official and intimidating on less than three hours' sleep?"

"Practice. I thought you'd gone."

"I told you I'd stay. Coffee's hot. I hope you don't mind that I helped myself."

"No." He stood exactly where he was. "I don't mind."

"If it's all right with you, I'll just loiter over coffee awhile before I get dressed. I'll get myself back to Cade's and change. I want to drop by the hospital later this morning, then I'm going home. It's time I did. The cleaning crew should be finished by this afternoon, so I thought…" She trailed off as he just continued to stare at her.

"What is it?" She gave an uncertain smile and rubbed at her nose.

Keeping his eyes on hers, he took the phone from the wall and punched in a number on memory. "This is Buchanan," he said. "I won't be in for a couple hours. I'm taking personal time." He hung up, held out a hand. "Come back to bed. Please."

She rose, and put her hand in his.

When clothes were scattered carelessly on the floor, the sheets turned back, the shades pulled to filter the beat of the sun, he covered her.

He needed to hold, to touch, to indulge himself for one hour with the flow of emotion she caused in him. Only an hour, yet he didn't hurry. Instead, he lingered over slow, deep, drugging kisses that lasted eons, loitered over long, smooth, soft caresses that stretched into forever.

She was there for him. Simply there. Open, giving, offering a seemingly endless supply of warmth.

She sighed, shakily, as he stroked her to helpless response, moving over her tenderly, his patience infinite. Each time their mouths met, with that slow slide of tongue, her heart shuddered in her breast.

There were the soft, slippery sounds of intimacy, the quiet murmurs of lovers, drifting into sighs and moans.

Both of them were lost, mired in thick layers of sensation, the air around them like syrup, causing movement to slow and pleasure to last.

Her breath sighed out as he trailed lazily down her body with hands and mouth, as her own hands stroked over his back, then his shoulders. She opened for him, arching up in welcome, then shuddering as his tongue brought on a long, rolling climax.

And because he needed it as much as she, she let her hands fall limply, let him take her wherever he chose. Her blood beat hot and the heat brought a dew of roused passion to her skin. His hands slicked over her skin like silk.

"Tell me you want me." He trailed slow, openmouthed kisses up her torso.

"Yes." She gripped his hips, urged him. "I want you."

"Tell me you need me." His tongue slid over her nipple.

"Yes." She moaned again when he suckled gently. "I need you."

Tell me you love me. But that he demanded only in his mind as he brought his mouth to hers again, sank into that wet, willing promise.

"Now." He kept his eyes open and on hers.

"Yes." She rose to meet him. "Now."

He glided inside her, filling her so slowly, so achingly, that they both trembled. He saw her eyes swim with tears and found the urge for tenderness stronger than any other. He kissed her again, softly, moved inside her one slow beat at a time.

The sweetness of it had a tear spilling over, trailing down her glowing cheek. Her lips trembled, and he felt her muscles contract and clutch him. "Don't close your eyes." He whispered it, sipped the tear from her cheek. "I want to see your eyes when I take you over."

She couldn't stop it. The tenderness stripped her. Her vision blurred with tears, and the blue of her eyes deepened to midnight. She said his name, then murmured it again against his lips. And her body quivered as the next long, undulating wave swamped her.

"I can't—"

"Let me have you." He was falling, falling, falling, and he buried his face in her hair. "Let me have all of you."

Chapter 10

In the nursery, Grace was rocking an infant. The baby girl was barely big enough to fill the crook of her arm from elbow to wrist, but the tiny infant watched her steadily with the deeply blue eyes of a newborn.

The hole in her heart had been repaired, and her prognosis was good.

"You're going to be fine, Carrie. Your mama and papa are so worried about you, but you're going to be just fine." She stroked the baby's cheek and thought—hoped—Carrie smiled a little.

Grace was tempted to sing her to sleep, but knew the nursing staff rolled their eyes and snickered whenever she tried a lullaby. Still, the babies were rarely critical of her admittedly poor singing voice, so she half sang, half murmured, until Carrie's baby owl's eyes grew heavy.

Even when she slept, Grace continued to rock. It

was self-serving now, she knew. Anyone who had ever rocked a baby understood that it soothed the adult, as well as the child. And here, with an infant dozing in her arms, and her own eyes heavy, she could admit her deepest secret.

She pined for children of her own. She longed to carry them inside her, to feel the weight, the movement within, to push them into life with that last sharp pang of childbirth, to hold them to her breast and feel them drink from her.

She wanted to walk the floor with them when they were fretful, to watch them sleep. To raise them and watch them grow, she thought, closing her eyes as she rocked. To care for them, to comfort them in the night, even to watch them take that first wrenching step away from her.

Motherhood was her greatest wish and her most secret desire.

When she first involved herself with the pediatric wing, she'd worried that she was doing so to assuage that gnawing ache inside her. But she knew it wasn't true. The first time she held a sick child in her arms and gave comfort, she'd understood that her commitment encompassed so much more.

She had so much to give, such an abundance of love that needed to be offered. And here it could be accepted without question, without judgment. Here, at least, she could do something worthwhile, something that mattered.

"Carrie matters," she murmured, kissing the top of the sleeping baby's head before she rose to settle her in her crib. "And one day soon you'll go home, strong and healthy. You won't remember that I once rocked you to sleep when your mama couldn't be here. But I will."

She smiled at the nurse who came in, stepped back. "She seems so much better."

"She's a tough little fighter. You've got a wonderful touch with the babies, Ms. Fontaine." The nurse picked up charts, began to make notes.

"I'll try to give you an hour or so in a couple of days. And you'll be able to reach me at home again, if you need to."

"Oh?" The nurse looked up, peered over the top of wire-framed glasses. The murder at Grace's home, and the ensuing investigation, were hot topics at the hospital. "Are you sure you'll be...comfortable at home?"

"I'm going to make sure I'm comfortable." Grace gave Carrie a final look, then stepped out into the hall.

She just had time, she decided, to stop by the pediatric ward and visit the older children. Then she could call Seth's office and see if he was interested in a little dinner for two at her place.

She turned and nearly walked into DeVane.

"Gregor?" She fixed a smile on her face to mask the sudden odd bumping of her heart. "What a surprise. Is someone ill?"

He stared at her, unblinking. "Ill?"

What was wrong with his eyes? she wondered, that they seemed so pale and unfocused. "We are in the hospital," she said, keeping the smile on her face, and, vaguely concerned, she laid a hand on his arm. "Are you all right?"

He snapped back, appalled. For a moment, his mind seemed to have switched off. He'd only been able to see her, to smell her. "Quite well," he assured her. "Momentarily distracted. I didn't expect to see you, either."

Of course, that was a lie, he'd planned the meeting meticulously. He took her hand, bowed over it, kissed her fingers.

"It is, of course, a pleasure to see you anywhere. I've come by here as our mutual friends interested me in the care children receive here. Children and their welfare are a particular interest of mine."

"Really?" Her smile warmed immediately. "Mine, too. Would you like a quick tour?"

"With you as my guide, how could I not?" He turned, signaled to two men who stood stiffly several paces back. "Bodyguards," he told Grace, tucking her hand into the crook of his arm and patting it. "Distressingly necessary in today's climate. Tell me, why am I so fortunate as to find you here today?"

As she usually did, she covered the truth and kept her privacy. "The Fontaines donated significantly to this particular wing. I like to stop in from time to time to see what the hospital's doing with it." She flashed a twinkling look. "And you just never know when you might run into a handsome doctor—or ambassador."

She strolled along, explaining various sections and wondering how much she might, with a little time and charm, wheedle out of him for the children. "General pediatrics is on the floor above. Since this section houses maternity, they wouldn't want kids zooming down the corridors while mothers are in labor or resting."

"Yes, children can be quite boisterous." He detested them. "It's one of my deepest regrets that I have none of my own. But having never found the right woman…"

He gestured with his free hand. "As I grow older, I'm resigned to having no one to carry on my name."

"Gregor, you're in your prime. A strong, vital man who can have as many children as he likes for years yet."

"Ah." He looked into her eyes again. "But there is still the right woman to be found."

She felt a shiver of discomfort at his pointed statement and intense gaze. "I'm sure you'll find her. We have some preemies here." She stepped closer to the glass. "So tiny," she said softly. "So defenseless."

"It's a pity when they're flawed."

She frowned at his choice of words. "Some of them need more time under controlled conditions and medical care to fully develop. But I wouldn't call them flawed."

Another error, he thought with an inner sense of irritation. He could not seem to keep his mind sharp with her scent invading his senses. "Ah, my English is sometimes awkward. You must forgive me."

She smiled again, wanting to ease his obvious discomfort. "Your English is wonderful."

"Is it clever enough to convince you to share a quiet lunch with me? As friends," he said, lacing his smile with regret. "With similar interests."

She glanced, as he did, at the babies. It was tempting, she admitted. He was a charming man—a wealthy and influential one. She might, with careful campaigning, persuade him to assist her in setting up an international branch of Falling Star, an ambition that had been growing in her lately.

"I would love to, Gregor, but right now I'm simply swamped. I was just on my way home when I ran into you. I have to check on some...repairs." That seemed the simplest way to explain it. "But I'd love to have a rain check. One I'd hope to cash in very soon. There's something concerning our similar interests that I'd love to have your advice on, and your input."

"I would love to be of any service whatsoever." He kissed her hand again. Tonight, he thought. He would have her tonight, and there would be no more need for this charade.

"That's so kind of you." Because she felt guilty for her disinterest and coolness in the face of his interest, she kissed his cheek. "I really must run. Do call me about that rain check. Next week, perhaps, for lunch." With a final, flashing smile, she dashed off.

As he watched her, his fisted fingers dug crescents into his palms. Fighting for control, he nodded to one of the silent men who waited for him. "Follow her only," he ordered. "And wait for instructions."

Cade didn't think of himself as a whiner—and, considering how well he tolerated his own family, he believed himself one of the most patient, most amiable, of men. But he was certain that if Grace had him shift one more piece of furniture from one end of her enormous living area to the other, he would break down and weep.

"It looks great."

"Hmm..." She stood, one hand on her hip, the fingers of the other tapping against her lip.

The gleam in her eye was enough to strike terror in Cade's heart and had his already aching muscles crying out in protest. "Really, fabulous. A hundred percent. Get the camera. I see a cover of *House and Garden* here."

"You're wheedling, Cade," she said absently. "Maybe the conversation pit did look better facing the other way." His moan was pitiful, and only made her lips twitch. "Of course, that would mean the coffee table and those two accent pieces would have to shift. And the palm tree—isn't it a beauty?—would have to go there."

The beauty weighed fifty pounds if it weighed an ounce. Cade abandoned pride and whined. "I still have stitches," he reminded her.

"Ah, what's a few stitches to a big, strong man like you?" She fluttered at him, patted his cheek and watched his ego war with his sore back. Giving in, she let loose a long, rolling laugh. "Gotcha. It's fine, darling, absolutely fine. You don't have to carry another cushion."

"You mean it?" His eyes went puppylike with hope. "It's done?"

"Not only is it done, but you're going to sit down, put up your feet, while I go get you an icy beer that I stocked in my fridge just for tall, handsome private investigators."

"You're a goddess."

"So I've been told. Make yourself at home. I'll be right back."

When Grace came back bearing a tray, she saw that Cade had taken her invitation to heart. He sat back on the thick cobalt-blue cushions of her new U-shaped sofa arrangement, his feet propped on the mirror-bright surface of the ebony coffee table, his eyes shut.

"I really did wear you out, didn't I?"

He grunted, opened one eye. Then both popped open in appreciation when she set the loaded tray on the table. "Food," he said, and sprang for it.

She had to laugh as he dived into her offer of glossy green grapes, Brie and crackers, the heap of caviar on ice with toast points. “It’s the least I can do for such an attractive moving man.” Settling beside him, she picked up the glass of wine she’d poured for herself. “I owe you, Cade.”

With his mouth half-full, he scanned the living room, nodded. “Damn straight.”

“I don’t just mean the manual labor. You gave me a safe haven when I needed one. And most of all, I owe you for Bailey.”

“You don’t owe me for Bailey. I love her.”

“I know. So do I. I’ve never seen her happier. She was just waiting for you.” Leaning over, Grace kissed his cheek. “I always wanted a brother. Now, with you and Jack, I have two. Instant family. They fit, too, don’t they?” she commented. “M.J. and Jack. As if they’ve always been a team.”

“They keep each other on their toes. It’s fun to watch.”

“It is. And speaking of Jack, I thought he was going to give you a hand with our little redecorating project.”

Cade scooped caviar onto a piece of toast. “He had a skip to trace.”

“A what?”

“A bail jumper to bring in. He didn’t think it was going to take him long.” Cade swallowed, sighed. “He doesn’t know what he’s missing.”

“I’ll give him the chance to find out.” She smiled. “I still have plans for a couple of the rooms upstairs.”

It gave Cade his opening. “You know, Grace, I wonder if you’re rushing this a little. It’s going to take some time to put a house this size back in shape. Bailey and I would like you to stay at our place for a while.”

Their place, Grace mused. Already it was their place. “It’s more than livable here, Cade. M.J. and I talked about it," she continued. "She and Jack are going to her apartment. It's time we all got back to our routines."

But M.J. wasn't going to be alone, Cade thought, and thoughtfully sipped his beer. "There's still somebody pulling the strings out there. Somebody who wants the Three Stars."

"I don't have them," Grace reminded him. "I can't get them. There's no reason to bother with me at this point."

"I don't know how much reason has to do with it, Grace. I don't like you being here alone."

"Just like a brother." Delighted with him, she gave his arm a squeeze. "Listen, Cade, I've got a new alarm system, and I'm considering buying a big, mean, ugly dog." She started to mention the pistol she had in her nightstand, and the fact that she knew how to use it, but thought that would only worry him more. "I'll be fine."

"What does Buchanan think?"

"I haven't asked him. He's going to come by later—so I won't really be alone."

Satisfied with that, Cade handed her a grape. "You've got him worried."

Her lips curved as she popped the grape into her mouth. "Do I?"

"I don't know him well—I don't think anyone does. He's… I guess *self-contained* would be the word. Doesn't let a lot show on the surface. But when I walked in yesterday, after you'd gone upstairs, he was just standing there, looking up after you." Now Cade grinned. "There was plenty on the surface then. It was pretty illuminating. Seth Buchanan, human being." Then he winced, tipped back his beer. "Sorry, I didn't mean to—"

"It's all right. I know exactly what you mean. He's

got an almost terrifying self control, and that impenetrable aura of authority."

"It seems to me that you've managed to dent the armor. In my opinion, that's just what he needed. You're just what he needed."

"I hope he thinks so. It turns out he's just what I needed. I'm in love with him." With a half laugh, she shook her head and sipped her wine. "I can't believe I told you that. I rarely tell men my secrets."

"Brothers are different."

She smiled at him. "Yes, they are."

"I hope Seth appreciates just how lucky he is."

"I don't think Seth believes in luck."

She suspected Seth didn't believe in the Three Stars of Mithra, either. And she had discovered that she did. In a very short time, she'd simply opened her mind, stretched her imagination and accepted. They had magic, and they had power. She had been touched by both—as had Bailey and M.J. and the men who were linked to them.

Grace had no doubt that whoever wanted that magic, that power, would stop at nothing to gain them. It wouldn't matter when they were in the museum. He would still crave them, still plot to possess them.

But he could no longer reach the stones through her. That part of her connection, she thought with relief, was over. She was safe in her own home, and would learn to live there again. Starting now.

She dressed carefully in a long white dress of thin watered silk that left her shoulders bare and flirted with her ankles. Beneath the flowing silk she wore only skin, creamed and scented.

She left her hair loose, scooped back at the sides with silver combs, her mother's sapphire drops at her ears, gleaming like twin stars. On impulse, she'd clasped a thick silver bracelet high on her forearm—a touch of pagan.

When she looked into the mirror after dressing, she'd felt an odd jolt—as if she could see herself in the glass, with the faint ghost of someone else merged with her.

But she'd laughed it off, chalked it up to nerves and anticipation, and busied herself completing her preparations.

She filled the rooms she'd redone with candles and flowers, pleased with the welcome they offered. On the table by the window facing her side garden she arranged the china and crystal for her meticulously plotted dinner for two.

The champagne was iced, the music was on low and the lights were romantically dimmed. All she needed was the man.

Seth saw the candles in the windows when he pulled up in the drive. Fatigue layered over frustration and had him, in the dim light of the car, rubbing gritty eyes.

And there were candles in the windows.

He was forced to admit that for the first time in his adult life he didn't have a handle on himself, or on the world around him. He certainly didn't have a handle on the woman who had lit those candles, and who was waiting in that soft, flickering light.

He'd moved on DeVane on pure instinct—and part of that instinct, he knew, was territorial. Nothing could have been more out of character for him. Perhaps that was why he was feeling slightly…out of himself. Out of control. Grace had become a center, a focal point.

Or was it an obsession?

Hadn't he come here because he couldn't keep away? Just as he had dug into DeVane's background because the man roused some primal defense mechanism.

Maybe that was how it started, Seth admitted, but his cop's instincts were still honed. DeVane was dirty. And with a little more time, a little more digging, he would link the man with the deaths surrounding the diamonds.

Without the diplomatic block, Seth thought, he had enough already to bring the man in for questioning. DeVane liked to collect—and he collected the rare, the precious, and frequently those items that held some whiff of magic.

And Gregor DeVane had financed an expedition the year before to search for the legendary Stars. A rival archaeologist had found them first, and the Washington museum had acquired them.

DeVane had lost more than two million dollars on the hunt and the Stars had slipped through his fingers.

And the rival archaeologist had met with a tragic and fatal accident three months after the find, in the jungles of Costa Rica.

Seth didn't believe in coincidence. The man who had kept DeVane from possessing the diamonds was dead. And so, Seth had discovered, was the head of the expedition DeVane had put together.

No, he didn't believe in coincidence.

DeVane had been a resident of D.C. for nearly two years, on and off, without ever meeting Grace. Now, directly after Grace's connection with the Stars, the man was not only at the same social function, but happened to make a play for her?

Life simply wasn't that tidy.

A little more time, Seth promised himself, rubbing his temples to clear the headache. He'd find the solid connection—link DeVane to the Salvinis, to the bail bondsman, to the men who had died in a crashed van, to Carlo Monturri. He needed only one link, and then the rest of the chain would fall into place.

But at the moment, he needed to get out of the stuffy car, go inside and face what was happening to his personal life.

With a short laugh, Seth climbed out of the car. A personal life. Wasn't that part of the problem? He'd never had one, hadn't allowed himself one. Now, a matter of days after he'd met Grace, it was threatening to swallow him.

He needed time there, too, he told himself. Time to step back, gain some distance for a more objective look. He'd allowed things to move too fast, to get out of control. That would have to be fixed. A man who fell in love overnight couldn't trust himself. It was time to reassert some logic.

They were dynamically different—in backgrounds, in life-styles and in goals. Physical attraction was bound to fade, or certainly stabilize. He could already foresee her easing back once the initial excitement peaked. She'd grow restless, certainly annoyed with the demands on his work. He would be neither willing nor able to spin her through the social whirl that was such an intricate part of her life.

She was bound to look toward someone else who would. A beautiful woman, vital, sought-after, flattered at every turn, wouldn't be content to light a candle in the window for many nights.

He'd be doing them both a favor by slowing down, stepping back. As he lifted a hand to the gleaming brass knocker, he refused to hear the mocking voice inside his head that called him a liar—and a coward.

She answered the knock quickly, as if she'd only been waiting for it. She stood in the doorway, soft light filtering through the long flow of white silk. The power of her, pure and pagan, stopped his breath.

Though he kept his arms at his sides, she moved into him, and ripped at his heart with a welcoming kiss.

"It's good to see you." Grace skimmed her fingers along his cheekbones, under his shadowed eyes. "You've had a long one, Lieutenant. Come in and relax."

"I haven't got a lot of time. I've got work." He waited, saw the flicker of disappointment in her eyes. It helped justify what he was determined to do. But then she smiled, took his hand.

"Well, let's not waste what time you've got standing in the foyer. You haven't eaten, have you?"

Why didn't she ask him why he couldn't stay? he wondered, irrationally irritated. Why wasn't she complaining? "No."

"Good. Sit down and have a drink. Can you have a drink, or are you officially on duty?" She walked into the living area as she spoke, then drew the chilling champagne from its silver bucket. "I don't suppose one glass would matter, in any case. And I won't tell." She released the cork with an expert's twist and a muffled, celebratory pop. "I've just put the canapés out, so help yourself."

She gestured toward the silver tray on the coffee

table before moving off with a quiet, slippery rustle of silk to pour two flutes.

"Tell me what you think. I worked poor Cade to death pushing things around in here, but I wanted to get at least the living space in order again quickly."

It looked as if it had been clipped from a glossy magazine on perfect living. Nothing was out of place, everything was gleaming and lovely. Bold colors mixed with whites and blacks, tasteful knickknacks, and artwork that appeared to have been selected with incredible care over a long period of time.

Yet she'd done it in days—or hours. That, Seth supposed, was the power of wealth and breeding.

Yet the room didn't look calculated or cold. It looked generous and welcoming. Soft surfaces, soft edges, with touches that were so Grace everywhere. Antique bottles in jewel tones, a china cat curled up for a nap, a lush, thriving fern in a copper pot.

And flowers, candlelight.

He looked up, noted the unbroken gleam of wood circling the balcony. "I see you've had it repaired."

Something's wrong, was all she could think as she stepped forward and handed him his glass. "Yes, I wanted that done as soon as possible. That, and the new security system. I think you'll approve."

"I'll take a look at it, if you like."

"I'd like it better if you'd relax while you can. Why don't I bring dinner in?"

"You cooked?"

Now she laughed. "I wouldn't do that to you, but I'm an expert at ordering in—and at presentation. Try to unwind. I'll be right back."

As she glided out, he looked down at the tray. A silver bowl of glossy black caviar, little fancy bites of elegant finger foods. He turned his back on them and, carrying his glass, walked over to study her portrait.

When she came back, wheeling an antique cart, he continued to look at her painted face. "He was in love with you, wasn't he? The artist?"

Grace drew a careful breath at that cool tone. "Yes, he was. He knew I didn't love him. I often wished I could have. Charles is one of the kindest, gentlest men I know."

"Did you sleep with him?"

A chill snaked up her spine, but she kept her hands steady as she set plates on the candle-and flower-decked table. "No. It wouldn't have been fair, and I care about him too much."

"You'd rather sleep with men you don't care about."

She hadn't seen it coming, Grace realized. How foolish of her not to have seen this coming. "No, but I won't sleep with men who I could hurt like that. I would have hurt Charles by being his lover, so I stayed his friend."

"And the wives?" He did turn now, eyes narrowed as he studied the woman instead of the portrait. "Like the woman who was married to that earl you were mixed up with? Didn't you worry about hurting her?"

Grace picked up her wine again, quite deliberately cocked her head. She had never slept with the earl he'd mentioned, or with any other married man. But she had never bothered to argue with public perception. Nor would she bother to deny it now.

"Why would I? I wasn't married to her."

"And the guy who tried to kill himself after you broke your engagement?"

She touched the glass to her lips, swallowed frothy

wine that burned like shards of glass in her throat. "Overly dramatic of him, wasn't it? I don't think you're in the mood for Caesar salad and steak Diane, are you, Lieutenant? Rich food doesn't set well during interrogations."

"No one's interrogating you, Grace."

"Oh, yes, you are. But you neglected to read me my rights."

Her frigid anger helped justify his own. It wasn't the men—he knew it wasn't the men he'd very deliberately tossed in her face that scraped at him. It was the fact that they didn't matter to him, that somehow nothing seemed to matter but her.

"It's odd you're so sensitive about answering questions about men, Grace. You hadn't troubled to hide your…track record."

"I expected better from you." She said it softly, so he barely heard, then shook her head, smiled coolly. "Foolish of me. No, I've never troubled to hide anything—unless it mattered. The men didn't matter, for the most part. Do you want me to tell you that you're different? Would you believe me if I did?"

He was afraid he would. Terrified he would. "It isn't necessary. We've moved too fast, Grace. I'm not comfortable with it."

"I see." She thought she did now, perfectly. "You'd like to slow things down." She set her glass aside, knowing her hand would start to shake. "It appears you've taken a couple of those giant steps while I've had my back turned. I really should have played that game as a child, so I'd be more alert for sudden moves."

"This isn't a game."

"No, I suppose it isn't." She had her pride, but she

also had her heart. And she had to know. "How could you have made love with me like that this morning, Seth, and do this tonight? How could you have touched me the way you have—the way no one ever has—and hurt me like this?"

It was because of what had swamped him that morning, he realized. The helplessness of his need. "I'm not trying to hurt you."

"No, that only makes it worse. You're doing both of us a favor, aren't you? Isn't that how you've worked it out? Break things off before they get too messy? Too late." Her voice broke, but she managed to shore it up again. "It's already messy."

"Damn it." He took a step toward her, then stopped dead when her head whipped up, and those hot blue eyes scorched him.

"Don't even think about touching me now, when those thoughts are still in your head. You go your tidy way, Lieutenant, and I'll go mine. I don't believe in slowing down. You either go forward, or you stop."

Furious with herself, she lifted a hand and flicked a tear off her cheek. "Apparently, we've stopped."

Chapter 11

He stood there wondering what in the hell he was doing. Here was the woman he loved, who—by some wild twist of fate—might actually love him. Here was a chance for that life he'd never allowed himself, the family, the home, the woman. He was pushing them all away, with both hands, and couldn't seem to stop.

"Grace… I want to give us both time to consider what we're doing, where this is going."

"No, you don't." She tossed back her hair with one angry jerk of her head. "Do you think because I've only known you a matter of days that I don't understand how your head works? I've been more intimate with you than I've been with anyone in my life. I *know* you." She managed a deep, ragged breath. "What you want is to get that wheel back under your hands, that control button back under your thumb. This whole thing has run away from you, and you just can't let that happen."

"That may be true." Was true, he realized. Was absolutely, mortifyingly true. "But it doesn't change the point. I'm in the middle of an investigation, and I'm not as objective as I need to be, because I'm involved with you. After it's done—"

"After it's done, what?" she demanded. "We pick up where you left off? I don't think so, Lieutenant. What happens when you're in the middle of the next investigation? And the next? Do I strike you as someone who's going to wait around until you have the time, and the room, to continue an on-again, off-again relationship with me?"

"No." His spine stiffened. "I'm a cop, and my work takes priority."

"I don't believe I've ever asked you to change that. In fact, I found your dedication to your work admirable, attractive. Even heroic." Her smile was thin and brief. "But that's irrelevant, and so is this conversation." She turned away, picked up her wine again. "You know the way out."

No, she'd never asked him to change anything. Never questioned his work. What the hell had he done? "This needs to be discussed."

"That's your style, not mine. Do you actually think you can stand here, in my home…" Her voice began to hitch and jerk. "In my home, and break my heart, dump me and expect a civilized conversation? I want you *out.*" She slammed her glass down, snapping the fragile stem of the glass, splattering wine. "Right now."

Where had the panic come from? he wondered. His beeper went off and was ignored. "We're not leaving it this way."

"Exactly this way," she corrected. "Do you think

I'm stupid? Do you think I don't see that you walked in here tonight looking to pick a fight so that it would end exactly this way? Do you think I don't know now that no matter how much I gave you, you'd hold back from me, question, analyze, dissect everything? Well, analyze this. I was willing to give more, whatever you wanted to take. Now you can spend the rest of your life wondering just what you lost here tonight."

As his beeper sounded again, she swept by him, wrenched open the front door. "You'll have to answer that call of duty elsewhere, Lieutenant."

He stepped to her, but, though his arms ached, he resisted the need to reach out. "When I'm done with this, I'm coming back."

"You won't be welcome."

He could feel himself step up to a line he'd never crossed. "That isn't going to matter. I'm coming back."

She said nothing at all, simply shut the door in his face and turned the lock with a hard, audible click.

She leaned back against the door, her breath shallow now, and hot, as pain swept through her. It was worse now that the door was closed, now that she had shut him out. And the candles still flickered, the flowers still bloomed.

She saw that every step she'd taken that day, and the day before, all they way back to the moment she'd walked into her own home and seen him coming down the stairs toward her, had been leading to this moment of blind grief and loss.

She'd been powerless to stop it, she thought, to change what she was, what had come before or what would come after. It was only fools who believed they controlled their own destiny as she'd once believed she controlled hers.

And she'd been a fool to indulge in those pathetic fantasies, dreams where they had belonged together, where they'd made a life together, a home and children together. Where she'd believed she was only waiting for him to finally make all those longings that had always, always, been one handspan out of her reach, come true.

The mythical power of the stones, she thought with a half laugh. Love, knowledge and generosity. Their magic had been cruel to her, giving her that tantalizing glimpse of her every desire, then wrenching it away again and leaving her alone.

The knock on the door had her closing her eyes. How dare he come back, she thought. How dare he, after he'd smashed all her dreams, her hopes, her needs. And how dare she still love him in spite of it.

Well, he wouldn't see her cry, she promised herself, and straightened to scrub her hands over her damp cheeks. He wouldn't see her crawl. He wouldn't see her at all, because she wouldn't let him in.

Resolutely she headed for the phone. He wouldn't be pleased when she called 911 and reported an intruder, she mused. But it would make her point. She picked up the receiver just as the sound of shattering glass had her whirling toward her terrace doors.

She had time to see the man burst through them, time to hear her alarm scream in warning. She even had time to struggle as thick arms grabbed her. Then the cloth was over her face, smelling sickeningly of chloroform.

And she had time only to think of Seth before her world spun and went black.

* * *

Seth was barely three miles away when the next call came through. He jerked up his phone, snarled into it. "Buchanan."

"Lieutenant, Detective Marshall again. I just heard an automatic come through on dispatch. Suspected break-in, 2918 East Lark Lane, Potomac."

"What?" For one stunning moment, his mind went blank. "Grace?"

"I recognized the address from the homicide. Her alarm system's been triggered, she didn't answer the check-in call."

"I'm five minutes from there." He was already swinging around in a fast, tire-squealing turn. "Get the two closest black-and-whites on the scene. Now."

"I'm already on it. Lieutenant—"

But Seth had already tossed the phone aside.

It was a new system, Seth told himself, fighting for calm and logic. New systems often had glitches.

She was upset, not answering her phone, ignoring the confusion. It would be just like her. She was even now defiantly pouring herself another glass of champagne, cursing him.

Maybe she'd even set off the alarm herself, just so he'd come streaking back with his stomach encased in ice and his heart paralyzed. It would be just like her.

And that was one more lie, he thought as he careened around a corner. It was nothing like her at all.

The candles were still burning in her windows. He tried to be relieved by that as he stood on the brakes in her driveway and bolted out of his car. Dinner would still be warm, the music would still be playing, and Grace would be there, standing under her portrait, furious with him.

He beat on the door foolishly, wildly, before he snapped himself back. She wouldn't answer. She was too angry to answer. When the first patrol car pulled up, he turned, flashed his badge.

"Check the east side," he ordered. "I'll take the west."

He turned on his heel, started around the side. He caught the glimmer of the blue water in her pool in the moonlight, and the thought slid in and out of his mind that they'd never used it together, never slipped into that cool water naked.

Then he saw the broken glass. His heart simply stopped. His weapon was in his hand and he was through the shattered door, with no thought to procedure. Someone was shouting her name, racing from room to room in blind panic. It couldn't be him, yet he found himself on the stairs, short of breath, ice cold, dizzy with fear and watching a uniformed cop bend to pick up a scrap of cloth.

"Smells like chloroform, Lieutenant." The officer hesitated, took a step toward the man clinging to the banister. "Lieutenant?"

He couldn't speak. His voice was gone, and every sweaty hour of training with it. Seth's dulled gaze shifted, focused on the face, the portrait. Slowly, and with great effort, he widened his vision again, pulled on the mask of control.

"Search the house. Every inch of it." His eyes locked on the second uniform. "Call in for backup. Now. Then make a sweep of the grounds. Move."

Grace came to slowly, with a roll of nausea and a blinding headache. A nightmare, still black at the edges, circled dully, like a vulture patiently waiting to drop.

She squeezed her eyes tighter, rolled her head on the pillow, then cautiously opened them.

Where? The thought was dull, foolish. Not my room, she realized, and struggled to fight off the clinging mists that clouded her brain.

It was satin beneath her cheek. She knew the cool, slippery feel of satin against the skin. White satin, like a bride's dress. Baffled, she skimmed her hand over the thick, luxurious spread of the huge canopied bed.

She could smell jasmine, and roses, and vanilla. All white scents, cool white scents. The walls of the room were ivory and had a sheen like silk. For a moment, she thought she was in a coffin, a huge, elaborate coffin, and her heart beat thick and fast.

She made herself sit up, almost afraid that her head would hit the lid and she would find herself screaming and clawing for freedom as she smothered. But there was nothing, only that fragrant air, and she took a long, unsteady breath of it.

She remembered now—the crash of glass, the big man in black with thick arms. She wanted to panic and forced herself to take another of those jerky breaths. Carefully, hampered by her spinning head, she slid her legs over the edge of the bed until her feet sank into thick, virginal white carpet. She swayed, nearly retched, then forced her feet over that sea of white to the door.

She went slippery with panic when the knob resisted her. Her breath came in ragged gulps as she fought and tugged on the knob of faceted crystal. Then she turned her back, leaned against it and made herself survey what she understood now was her prison.

White on white on white, blinding to the eye. A dainty Queen Anne chair brocaded in white, filmy lace curtains hung like ghosts, heaps of white pillows on a curved white chaise. There were edges of gold that only enhanced the avalanche of white, elegant furniture in pale wood smothered in that snowfall.

She went to the windows first, shuddered when she found them barred, the slices of night beyond them silvered by the moon. She saw nothing familiar—a long roll of lawn, meticulously planted flowers and shrubs, tall, shielding trees.

Wheeling, she saw another door, bolted for it, nearly wept when the knob turned easily. But beyond was a lustrous bath, white-tiled, the frosted-glass windows barred, the angled skylight a soaring ten feet above the floor.

And on the long gleaming counter were jars, bottles, creams, powders. All her own preferences, her scents, her lotions. Her stomach knotted greasily.

Ransom, she told herself. It was a kidnapping, someone who believed her family could be forced to pay for her safe return.

But she knew that was a lie.

The Stars. She leaned weakly against the jamb, pressed her lips together to keep the whimper silent. She'd been taken because of the Three Stars. They would be her ransom.

Her knees trembled as she turned away, ordered herself to calm down, to think clearly. There had to be a way out. There always was.

Her alarm had gone off, she remembered. Seth couldn't have been far away. Would he have gotten the report, come back? It didn't matter. He would have gotten it soon enough. Whatever had happened between them, he would do everything in his power to find her. From duty, if nothing else.

In the meantime, she was on her own. But that didn't mean she was defenseless.

She took two stumbling steps back when the lock on her door clicked, then forced herself to stop, straighten. The door opened, and two men stepped inside. One she recognized quickly enough as her abductor. The other was smaller, wiry, dressed in formal black, with a face as giving as rock.

"Ms. Fontaine," he said in a voice both British and cultured. "If you'd come with me, please."

A butler, she realized, and had to swallow a bubble of hysteria. She knew the type too well, and she assumed an amused and annoyed expression. "Why?"

"He's ready to see you now."

When she made no move to obey, the bigger man stepped in, towering over her, then jerked a thumb toward the doorway.

"Charming," she said dryly. She took a step forward, calculating how quickly she would have to move. The butler inclined his head impassively.

"You're on the third floor," he told her. "Even if you could somehow reach the main level on your own, there are guards. They are under order not to harm you, unless it's unavoidable. If you'll pardon me, I would advise against risking it."

She would risk it, she thought, and a great deal more. But not until she had at least an even chance of success. Without so much as a flick of a glance at the man beside her, she followed the butler out of the room and down a gently lit corridor.

The house was old, she calculated, but beautifully restored. At least three stories, so it was large. A glimpse at her watch told her it had been less than two hours since she was drugged. Time enough to drive some distance, she imagined.

But the view through the bars hadn't been countryside. She'd seen lights—city lights, houses through the trees. A neighborhood, she decided. Exclusive, wealthy, but a neighborhood.

Where there were houses, there were people. And where there were people, there was help.

She was led down a wide, curving staircase of gleaming oak. And saw the guard at the landing, his gun holstered but visible.

Down another hallway. Antiques, paintings, artwork. Her eye was expert enough to recognize the Monet on the wall, the porcelain vase from the Han dynasty on a pedestal, the Nok terra-cotta head from Nigeria.

Her host, she thought, had excellent and eclectic taste. The treasures she saw, small and large, spanned continents and centuries.

A collector, she realized with a chill. Now he had her, and was hoping to trade her for the Three Stars of Mithra.

With what Grace considered absurd formality, under the circumstances, the butler approached tall double doors, opened them, and with seamless expertise bowed slightly from the waist.

"Miss Grace Fontaine."

Seeing no immediate alternative, she stepped through the open doors into an enormous dining room with a frescoed ceiling and a dazzling trio of chandeliers. She scanned the long mahogany table, the Georgian candelabra gaily lit and spaced at precise intervals down its length, and focused on the man who rose and smiled charmingly.

Her worlds overlapped—reality and fear. "Gregor."

"Grace." Elegant in his tux, diamonds winking, he crossed to her, took her numb hand in his. "How delightful to see you." He tucked her arm through his, patted it affectionately. "I don't believe you've dined."

He knew where she was. Seth had no doubt of it, but his first fiery urge to rush to the elegant estate in D.C. and tear it apart single-handedly had to be suppressed.

He could get her killed.

He was certain Ambassador Gregor DeVane had killed before.

The call that interrupted his scene with Grace had been confirmation of yet another woman who had once been linked to the ambassador, a beautiful German scientist who had been found murdered in her home in Berlin, the apparent victim of a bungled burglary.

The dead woman had been an anthropologist who had a keen interest in Mithraism. For six months during the previous year, she had been romantically linked with Gregor DeVane. Then she was dead, and none of her research notes on the Three Stars of Mithra had been recovered.

He knew DeVane was responsible, just as he knew DeVane had Grace. But he couldn't prove it, and he didn't have probable cause to sway any judge to issue a search warrant into the home of a foreign ambassador.

Once more he stood in Grace's living room. Once more he stared up at her portrait and imagined her dead. But this time, he wasn't thinking like a cop.

He turned as Mick Marshall stepped beside him.

"We won't find anything here to link him. In twelve hours, the diamonds will be turned over to the museum. He's going to use her to see that doesn't happen. I'm going to stop him."

Mick looked up at the portrait. "What do you need?"

"No. No cops."

"Lieutenant… Seth, if you're right, and he's got her, you're not going to get her out alone. You need to put together a team. You need a hostage negotiator."

"There's no time. We both know that." His eyes weren't flat and cool now, weren't cop's eyes. They were full of storms and passions. "He'll kill her."

His heart was coated with a sheet of ice, but it beat with fiery heat inside the casing. "She's smart. She'll play whatever game she needs to in order to stay alive, but if she makes the wrong move he'll kill her. I don't need a psychiatric profile to see into his head. He's a sociopath with a god complex and an obsession. He wants those diamonds and what he believes they represent. Right now he wants Grace, but if she doesn't serve his purpose, she'll end up like the others. That's not going to happen, Mick."

He reached into his pocket, took out his badge and held it out. This time he wouldn't go by the book, couldn't afford to play by the rules. "You take this for me, hang on to it. I may want it back."

"You're going to need help," Mick insisted. "You're going to need men."

"No cops," Seth repeated, and pushed his badge into Mick's reluctant hand. "Not this time."

"You can't go in solo. It's suicide, professional and literal."

Seth cast one last glance at the portrait. "I won't be alone."

* * *

She wouldn't tremble, Grace promised herself. She wouldn't show him how frightened she was. Instead, she brushed her hair from her shoulder with a careless hand.

"Do you always have your dinner companions abducted from their homes and drugged, Ambassador?"

"You must forgive the clumsiness." Considerately he drew out a chair for her. "It was necessary to be quick. I trust you're suffering no ill effects."

"Other than great annoyance, no." She sat, skimmed her gaze over the dish of marinated mushrooms a silent servant placed before her. They reminded her, painfully, of the noise-filled cookout at Cade's. "And a loss of appetite."

"Oh, you must at least sample the food." He sat at the head of the table, picked up his fork. It was gold and heavy and had once slipped between the lips of an emperor. "I've gone to considerable trouble to have your favorites prepared." His smile remained genial, but his eyes went cold. "Eat, Grace. I detest waste."

"Since you've gone to such lengths." She forced down a bite, ordered her hand not to shake, her stomach not to revolt.

"I hope your room is comfortable. I had to have it prepared for you rather quickly. You'll find appropriate clothing in the armoire and bureau. You've only to ask if there's something else you wish."

"I prefer windows without bars, and doors without locks."

"Temporary precautions, I promise you. Once you're at home here..." his hand covered hers, the grip tightening cruelly when she attempted to pull away "...and

I do very much want you to be at home here, such measures won't be necessary."

She didn't wince as the bones in her hand ground together. When she stopped the resistance, his fingers relaxed, stroked once, then slid away.

"And just how long do you intend to keep me here?"

He smiled, picked up her wineglass, held it out to her. "Eternity. You and I, Grace, are destined to share eternity."

Under the table, her aching hand shook and went clammy. "That's quite some time." She started to set her wine down, untouched, then caught the hard glint in his eye and sipped. "I'm flattered, but confused."

"It's pointless to pretend you don't understand. You held the Star in your hand. You survived death, and you came to me. I've seen your face in my dreams."

"Yes." She could feel her blood drain slowly, as if leeched out of her veins. Looking into his eyes she remembered the nightmares—the shadow in the woods. Watching. "I've seen you in mine."

"You'll bring me the Stars, Grace, and the power. I understand why I failed now. Every step was simply another on the path that brought us here. Together we'll possess the Stars. And I will possess you. Don't worry," he said when she flinched. "You'll come to me a willing bride. But my patience has limits. Beauty is my weakness," he continued, and skimmed a fingertip down her bare arm, toyed idly with the thick silver bracelet she wore. "And perfection my greatest delight. You, my dear, have both. Understand, you'll have no choice should my patience run out. My household staff is…well trained."

Fear was a bright, icy flash, but her voice was steady

with disgust. "And would turn a deaf ear and blind eye to rape?"

"I don't enjoy that word during dinner." He gave a sulky little shrug and signaled for the next course. "A woman of your appetites will grow hungry soon enough. And one of your intelligence will undoubtedly see the wisdom of an amiable partnership."

"It's not sex you want, Gregor." She couldn't bear to look down at the tender pink salmon on her plate. "It's subjugation. I'm so poor at subjugation."

"You misunderstand me." He forked up fish and ate with enjoyment. "I intend to make you a goddess, and subject to no one. And I will have everything. No mortal man will come between us." He smiled again. "Certainly not Lieutenant Buchanan. The man is becoming a nuisance. He's probing into my affairs, where he has no business probing. I've seen him..."

DeVane's voice trailed off to a whisper, and there was a hint of fear in it. "In the night. In my dreams. He comes back. He always comes back. No matter how often I kill him." Then his eyes cleared, and he sipped wine the color of melted gold. "Now he's stirring up old business and looking for new."

She could feel the alarming beat of her pulse in her throat, at her wrists, in her temples. "He'll be looking for me, very soon now."

"Possibly. I'll deal with him, when and if the time comes. That could have been tonight, had he not left you so abruptly. Oh, I have considered just what will be done about the lieutenant. But I prefer to wait until I have the Stars. It's possible..." Thoughtfully DeVane picked up his napkin, dabbed at his lips. "I may spare him once I have what belongs to me. If you wish it. I can be magnanimous...under the right circumstances."

Her heart was in her throat now, filling it, blocking it. "If I do what you want, you'll leave him alone?"

"It's possible. We'll discuss it. But I'm afraid I developed an immediate dislike for the man. And I am still annoyed with you, dear Grace, for rejecting my own invitation for such an ordinary man."

She didn't hesitate, couldn't afford to, while her mind whirled with fear for Seth. She made her lips curve silkily. "Gregor, surely you forgive me for that. I was so... crushed when you didn't press your case. A woman, after all, enjoys a more determined pursuit."

"I don't pursue. I take."

"Obviously." She pouted. "It was horrid of you to have manhandled me that way, and frightened me half to death. I may not forgive you for it."

"Be careful how deep you play the game." His voice was low with warning and, she thought, with interest. "I'm not green."

"No." She skimmed a hand over his cheek before she rose. "But maturity has so many advantages."

Her legs were watery, but she roamed the cavernous room, her gaze traveling quickly toward windows, exits. Escape. "You have such a beautiful home. So many treasures." She angled her head, hoped the challenge she issued was worth the risk. "I do love...things. But I warn you, Gregor, I won't be any man's pretty toy."

She walked to him slowly, skimming a fingertip down her throat, between her breasts, while the silk she wore whispered around her. "And when I'm backed into a corner... I scratch."

Seductively she laid a hand on the table, leaned toward him. "You want me?" she breathed it, purred it, watching his eyes darken, sliding her fingers toward the knife beside his plate. "To touch me? To have me?" Her fingers closed over the handle, gripped hard.

"Not in a hundred lifetimes," she said as she struck.

She was fast, and she was desperate. But he'd shifted to draw her to him, and the knife struck his shoulder instead of his heart. As he cried out in shock and rage, she whirled. Grabbing one of the heavy chairs, she smashed the long window and sent glass raining out. But when she leaped forward, strong arms grabbed her from behind.

She fought viciously, her breath panting out. The fragile silk she wore ripped. Then she froze when the knife she had used was pressed against her throat. She didn't bother to struggle against the arms that held her as DeVane leaned his face close to hers. His eyes were mad with fury.

"I could kill you for that. But it would be too little and too quick. I would have made you my equal. I would have shared that with you. Now I'll just take what I choose from you. Until I tire of you."

"You'll never get the Stars," she said steadily. "And you'll never get Seth."

"I'll have exactly what I choose. And you'll help me."

She started to shake her head, flinched as the blade nicked. "I'll do nothing to help you."

"But you will. If you don't do exactly as I tell you, I will pick up the phone. With one single word from me, Bailey James and M. J. O'Leary will die tonight. It will only take a word."

He saw the wild fear come into her eyes, the helpless terror that hadn't been there for her own life. "I have men waiting for that word. If I give it, there will be a terrible and tragic explosion in the night at Cade Parris's home. Another at a small neighborhood pub, just before closing. And as one last twist, a third explosion will destroy the home, and the single occupant, of a certain Lieutenant Buchanan's residence. Their fate is in your hands, Grace. And the choice is yours."

She wanted to call his bluff, but, staring into his eyes, she understood that he wouldn't hesitate to do as he threatened. No, he longed to do it. Their lives meant nothing to him. And everything to her.

"What do you want me to do?"

Bailey was fighting against panic when the phone rang. She stared at it as if it were a snake that had rattled into life. With a silent prayer, she lifted the receiver. "Hello?"

"Bailey."

"Grace." Her fingers went white-knuckled as she whirled. Seth shook his head, held up a hand in caution. "Are you all right?"

"For the moment. Listen very carefully, Bailey, my life depends on it. Do you understand?"

"No. Yes." Stall, she knew she'd been ordered to stall. "Grace, I'm so frightened for you. What happened? Where are you?"

"I can't go into that now. You have to be calm, Bailey. You have to be strong. You were always the calm one. Like when we took that art history exam in college and I was so intimidated by Professor Greenbalm, and you were so cool. You have to be cool now, Bailey, and you have to follow my instructions."

"I will. I'll try." She looked helplessly at Seth as he signaled her to stretch it out. "Just tell me if you're hurt."

"Not yet. But he will hurt me. He'll kill me, Bailey, if you don't do what he wants. Get him what he wants. I know I'm asking a great deal. He wants the stones. You have to go get them. You can't take Cade. You can't call…the police."

String it out, Bailey reminded herself. Keep Grace talking. "You don't want me to call Seth?"

"No. He isn't important. He's just another cop. You know he doesn't matter. You're to wait until 1:30 exactly, then you're to leave the house. Go to Salvini, Bailey. You've got to go to Salvini. Leave M.J. out of it, just like we used to. Understand?"

Bailey nodded, kept her eyes on Seth's. "Yes, I understand."

"Once you get to Salvini, put the stones in a briefcase. Wait there. You'll get a call with the next set of instructions. You'll be all right. You know how you used to like to sneak out of the dorm at night and go out driving alone after curfew? Just think of it that way. Exactly that way, Bailey, and you'll be fine. If you don't, he'll take everything away from me. Do you understand?"

"Yes. Grace—"

"I love you," she managed before the phone went dead.

"Nothing," Cade said tightly as he stared down at the tracing equipment. "He's got it jammed. The signal's all over the board. It wouldn't home in."

"She wants me to go to Salvini," Bailey said quietly.

"You're not going anywhere," Cade said, interrupting her, but Bailey laid a hand on his arm, looked toward M.J.

"No, she meant that part. You understood?"

"Yeah." M.J. pressed her fingers to her eyes, tried to think past the terror. "She was pumping in as much as she could. Bailey and Grace never left me out of anything, so she wanted me along. She wants us out of here, but she was stringing him about the stones. Bailey never jumped curfew."

"She was giving you signals," Jack said. "Trying to punch in what she could manage."

"She knew we'd understand. He must have told her something would happen to us if she didn't cooperate." Bailey reached out for M.J.'s hand. "She wanted us to contact Seth. That's why she said you didn't matter—because we know you do."

Seth dragged a hand through his hair—a rare wasted motion. He had no choice but to trust their instincts. No choice but to trust Grace's sense of survival. "All right. She wants me to know what's happening, and wants you out of the house."

"Yes. She wants us out of the house, thinks we'll be safer at Salvini."

"You'll be safer at the precinct," Seth told her. "And that's where both of you are going."

"No." Bailey's voice remained calm. "She wants us at Salvini. She made a point of it."

Seth studied her, and gauged his options. He could have them taken into protective custody. That was the logical step. Or he could let the game play out. That was a risk. But it was the risk that fit.

"Salvini, then. But Detective Marshall will arrange for guards. You'll stay put until you hear differently."

M.J. bristled. "You expect us to just sit around and wait while Grace is in trouble?"

"That's exactly what you're going to do," Seth said coolly. "She's risking her life to see that you're safe. I'm not going to disappoint her."

"He's right, M.J." Jack lifted a brow as she snarled at him. "Go ahead and fume. But you're outnumbered here. You and Bailey follow instructions."

Seth noted with some surprise that M.J. closed her mouth, gave one brisk nod in assent. "What was the business about the art history exam, Bailey?"

Bailey sucked in air. "Professor Greenbalm's first name was Gregory."

"Gregory." *Gregor.* "Close enough." Seth looked at the two men he needed. "We don't have a lot of time."

Chapter 12

Grace doubted very much that she would live through the night. There were so many things she hadn't done. She had never shown Bailey and M.J. Paris, as they had always planned. She would never see the willow she'd planted on her country hillside grow tall and bend gracefully over her tiny pond. She had never had a child.

The unfairness clawed at her, along with the fear. She was only twenty-six years old, and she was going to die.

She'd seen her sentence in DeVane's eyes. And she knew he intended to kill those she loved, as well. He wouldn't be satisfied with anything less than erasing all the lives that had touched what his obsessed mind considered his.

All she could hang on to now was the hope that Bailey had understood her.

"I'm going to show you what you could have had."

His arm bandaged, a fresh tuxedo covering the damage, DeVane led her through a concealed panel, and down a well-lit set of stone stairs that were polished like ebony. He'd taken a painkiller. His eyes were glassy with it, and vicious.

They were the eyes that had stared out of the woods in her nightmares. And as he walked down the curve of those glossy black stairs, she felt the tug of some deep memory.

By torchlight then, she thought hazily. Down and down, with the torches flickering and the Stars glittering in their home of gold, on a white stone. And death waiting.

The harsh breathing of the man beside her. DeVane's? Someone else's? It was a hot, secret sound that chilled the skin. A room, she thought, struggling to grip the slippery chain of memories. A secret room of white and gold. And she had been locked in it for eternity.

She stopped at the last curve, not so much in fear as in shock. Not here, she thought frantically, but somewhere else. Not her, but part of her. Not him, but someone like him.

DeVane's fingers dug into her arm, but she barely felt the pain. Seth—the man with Seth's eyes, dressed as a warrior, coated with dust and the dents of battle. He'd come for her, and for the Stars.

And died for it.

"No." The stairway spun, and she gripped the cool wall for balance. "Not again. Not this time."

"There's little choice." DeVane jerked her forward, pulled her down the remaining steps. He stopped at a thick door, gestured impatiently for his guard to step back. Holding Grace's arm in a bruising grip, he drew out a heavy key, fit it in an old lock that for reasons Grace couldn't fathom made her think of Alice's rabbit hole.

"I want you to see what could have been yours. What I would have shared with you."

At his rough shove, she stumbled inside and stood blinking in shock.

No, not the rabbit hole, she realized, her dazzled eyes wide and stunned. Ali Baba's cave. Gold gleamed in mountains, jewels winked in rivers. Paintings she recognized as works of the masters crowded together on the walls. Statues and sculpture, some as small as the Fabergé eggs perched on gold stands, others soaring to the ceiling, were jammed inside.

Furs and sweeps of silk, ropes of pearls, carvings and crowns, were jammed into every available space. Mozart played brilliantly on hidden speakers.

It was, she realized, not a fairy-tale cave at all. It was merely a spoiled boy's elaborate and greedy clubhouse. Here he could hide his possessions from the world, keep them all to himself and chortle over them, she imagined.

And how many of these toys had he stolen? she wondered. How many had he killed for?

She wouldn't die here, she promised herself. And neither would Seth. If this was indeed history overlapping, she wouldn't allow it to repeat itself. She would fight with whatever weapons she had.

"You have quite a collection, Gregor, but your presentation could use some work." The first weapon was mild disdain, laced with amusement. "Even the precious loses impact when crammed together in such a disorganized manner."

"It's mine. All of it. A lifetime's work. Here." Like

that spoiled boy, he snatched up a goblet of gold, thrust it out to her for admiration. "Queen Guinevere sipped from this before she cuckolded Arthur. He should have cut out her heart for that."

Grace turned the cup in her hand and felt nothing. It was empty not only of wine, she mused, but of magic.

"And here." He grabbed a pair of ornate diamond earrings, thrust them into Grace's face. "Another queen—Marie Antoinette—wore these while her country plotted her death. You might have worn them."

"While you plotted mine." With deliberate scorn, she dismissed the offering and turned away. "No, thank you."

"I have an arrow the goddess Diana hunted with. The girdle worn by Juno."

Her heart thrummed like a harp, but she only chuckled. "Do you really believe that?"

"They're mine." Furious with her reaction, he pushed his way through his collection, laid a hand over the cold marble slab he'd had built. "I'll have the Stars soon. They will be the apex of my collection. I'll set them here, with my own hands. And I'll have everything."

"They won't help you. They won't change you." She didn't know where the words came from, or the knowledge behind them, but she saw his eyes flicker in surprise. "Your fate's already sealed. They'll never be yours. It's not meant, not this time. They're for the light, and for the good. You'll never see them here in the dark."

His stomach jittered. There was power in her words, in her eyes, when she should have been cowed and frightened. It unnerved him. "By sunrise I'll have them here. I'll show them to you." His breath was short and shallow as he approached her. "And I'll have you. I'll keep you as long as I wish. Do with you what I wish."

The hand against her cheek was cold, made her think wildly of a snake, but she didn't cringe away. "You'll never have the Stars, and you'll never have me. Even if you hold us, you'll never have us. That was true before, but it's only more true now. And that will eat away at you, day after day, until there's nothing left of you but madness."

He struck her, hard enough to knock her back against the wall, to have pain spinning in her head. "Your friends will die tonight." He smiled at her, as if he were discussing a small mutual interest. "You've already sent them to oblivion. I'm going to let you live a long time knowing that."

He took her by the arm and, pulling open the door, dragged her from the room.

"He'll have surveillance cameras," Seth said as they prepared to scale the wall at the rear of DeVane's D.C. estate. "He's bound to have guards patrolling the grounds."

"So we'll be careful." Jack checked the point of his knife, stuck it in his boot, then examined the pistol he'd tucked in his belt. "And we'll be quiet."

"We stick together until we reach the house." Cade went over the plan in his head. "I find security, disarm it."

"Failing that, set the whole damn business off. We could get lucky in the confusion. It'll bring the cops. If things don't go well, you could be dealing with a lot more than a bust for a B-and-E."

Jack issued a pithy one-word opinion on that. "Let's

go get her out." He shot Seth one quick grin as he boosted himself up. "Man, I hope he doesn't have dogs. I really hate when they have dogs."

They landed on the soft grass on the other side. It was possible their presence was detected from that moment. It was a risk they were willing to take. Like shadows, they moved through the starstruck night, slipping through the heavy dark amid the sheltering trees.

Before, on his quest for the Stars and the woman, he'd come alone, and perhaps that arrogance had been his defeat. Baffled by the sudden thought, the quick spurt of what some might have called vision, Seth pushed the feeling aside.

He could see the house through the trees, the glimmer of lights in windows. Which room was she in? How badly was she frightened? Was she hurt? Had he touched her?

Baring his teeth, he bit off the thoughts. He had to focus only on getting inside, finding her. For the first time in years, he felt the weight of his weapon at his side. Knew he intended to use it.

He gave no thought to rules, to his career, to the life he'd built step by deliberate step.

He saw the guard pass by, only a yard beyond the verge of the grove. When Jack tapped his shoulder and signaled, Seth met his eyes, nodded.

Seconds later, Jack sprang at the man from behind, and with a quick twist, rammed his head into the trunk of an oak and then dragged the unconscious body into the shadows.

"One down," he breathed and tucked his newly acquired weapon away.

"They'll have regular check-in," Cade murmured. "We can't know how soon they'll miss his contact."

"Then let's move." Seth signaled Jack to the north, Cade to the south. Staying low, they rushed those gleaming lights.

The guard who escorted Grace back to her room was silent. At least two hundred and fifty pounds of muscle, she calculated. But she'd seen his eyes flicker down over her bodice, scan the ripped silk that exposed flesh at her side.

She knew how to use her looks as a weapon. Deliberately she tipped her face up to his, let her eyes fill helplessly. "I'm so frightened. So alone." She risked touching a hand to his arm. "You won't hurt me, will you? Please don't hurt me. I'll do anything you want."

He said nothing, but his eyes were keen on her face when she moistened her lips with the tip of her tongue, keeping the movement slow and provocative. "Anything," she repeated, her voice husky, intimate. "You're so strong, so…in charge." Did he even speak English? she wondered. What did it matter? The communication was clear enough.

At the door to her prison, she turned, flashed a smoldering look, sighed deeply. "Don't leave me alone," she murmured. "I'm so afraid of being alone. I need… someone." Taking a chance, she lifted a fingertip, rubbed it over his lips. "He doesn't have to know," she whispered. "No one has to know. It's our secret."

Though it revolted her, she took his hand, placed it on her breast. The flex of his fingers chilled her skin, but she made herself smile invitingly as he lowered his head and crushed her mouth.

Don't think of it, don't think, she warned herself as his hands roamed her. It's not you. He's not touching you.

"Inside." She hoped he interpreted her quick shudder as desire. "Come inside with me. We'll be alone."

He opened the door, his eyes still hungry on her face, on her body. She would either win here, she thought, or lose everything. She let out a teasing laugh as he grabbed for her the moment the door was locked behind him.

"Oh, there's no hurry now, handsome." She tossed her hair back, glided out of his reach. "No need to rush such a lovely friendship. I want to freshen up for you."

Still he said nothing, but his eyes were narrowing with impatience, suspicion. Still smiling, she reached for the heavy cut-crystal atomizer on the bureau. A woman's weapon, she thought coldly as she gently spritzed her skin, the air. "I prefer using all of my senses." Her fingers tightened convulsively on the bottle as she swayed toward him.

She jerked the bottle up and sprayed perfume directly into his leering eyes. He hissed in shock, grabbed instinctively for his stinging eyes. Putting all her strength behind it, she smashed the crystal into his face, and her knee into his groin.

He staggered, but didn't go down. There was blood on his face, and beneath it, his skin had gone a pasty shade of white. He was fumbling for his gun and, frantic, she kicked out, aiming low again. This time he went to his knees, but his hands were still reaching for the gun snapped to his side.

Sobbing now, she heaved up a footstool, upholstered in white, tasseled in gold. She rammed it into his already bleeding face, then, lifting it high, crashed it onto his head. Desperately she scrabbled to unstrap his gun, her clammy hands slipping off leather and steel. When she held it in two shaking hands, prepared to do whatever was necessary, she saw that he was unconscious.

Her breath tore out of her lungs in a wild laugh. "I guess I'm just not that kind of girl." Too frightened for caution, she yanked the keys free of his clip, stabbed one after the other at the lock until it gave. And raced like a deer fleeing wolves, down the corridor, through the golden light.

A shadow moved at the head of the stairs, and with a low, keening moan, she lifted the gun.

"That's the second time you've pointed a weapon in my direction."

Her vision grayed at the sound of Seth's voice. Clamping down hard on her lip, she cleared it as he stepped out of the shadows and into the light. "You. You came."

It wasn't armor he wore, she thought dizzily. But black—shirt, slacks, shoes. It wasn't a sword he carried, but a gun.

It wasn't a memory. It was real.

Her dress was torn, bloody. Her face was bruised, her eyes were glassy with shock. He'd killed two men to get this far. And seeing her this way, he thought it hadn't been enough. Not nearly enough.

"It's all right now." He resisted the urge to rush to her, grab her close. She looked as though she might shatter at a touch. "We're going to get you out. No one's going to hurt you."

"He's going to kill them." She forced air in and out of her lungs. "He's going to kill them no matter what I do. He's insane. They're not safe from him. We're none of us safe from him. He killed you before," she ended on a whisper. "He'll try again."

He took her arm to steady her, gently slipped the gun from her hand. "Where is he, Grace?"

"There's a room, through a panel in the library, down the stairs. Just like before...lifetimes ago. Do you remember?" Spinning between images, she pressed a hand to her head. "He's there with his toys, all the glittering toys. I stabbed him with a dinner knife."

"Good girl." How much of the blood was hers? He could detect no wound other than the bruises on her face and arms. "Come on now, come with me."

He led her down the stairs. There was the guard she'd seen before. But he wasn't standing now. Averting her eyes, she stepped around him, gestured. She was steadier now. The past didn't always run in a loop, she knew. Sometimes it changed. People made it change.

"It's back there, the third door down on the left." She cringed when she caught a movement. But it was Jack, melting out of a doorway.

"It's clear," he said to Seth.

"Take her out." His eyes said everything as he nudged her into Jack's arms. *Take care of her. I'm trusting you.*

Jack hitched her against his side to keep his weapon hand free. "You're okay, honey."

"No." She shook her head. "He's going to kill them. He has explosives, something, at the house, at the pub. You have to stop him. The panel. I'll show you."

She wrenched away from Jack, staggered like a drunk toward the library. "Here." She turned a rosette in the carving of the chair rail. "I watched him." The panel slid smoothly open.

"Jack, get her out. Call in a 911. I'll deal with him."

She was floating, just under the surface of thick, warm water. "He'll have to kill him," she said faintly as Seth disappeared into the opening. "This time he can't fail."

"He knows what he has to do."

"Yes, he always does." And the room spun once, wildly. "Jack, I'm sorry," she managed before she spun with it.

He hadn't locked the door, Seth noted. Arrogant bastard, so sure no one would trespass on his sacred ground. With his weapon lifted, Seth eased the heavy door open, blinked once at the bright gleam of gold.

He stepped inside, focused on the man sitting in a thronelike chair in the center of all the glory. "It's done, DeVane."

DeVane wasn't surprised. He'd known the man would come. "You risk a great deal." His smile was cold as a snake's, his eyes mad as a hatter's. "You did before. You remember, don't you? Dreamed of it, didn't you? You came to steal from me before, to take the Stars and the woman. You had a sword then, heavy and unjeweled."

Something vague and quick passed through Seth's mind. A stone castle, a stormy sky, a room of great wealth. A woman beloved. On an altar, a triangle wrenched from the hands of the god, adorned with diamonds as blue as stars.

"I killed you." DeVane laughed softly. "Left your body for the crows."

"That was then." Seth stepped forward. "This is now."

DeVane's smile spread. "I am beyond you." He lifted his hand, and the gun he held in it.

Two shots were fired, so close together they sounded as one. The room shook, echoed, settled, and went back to gleaming. Slowly Seth stepped closer, looked down at the man who lay facedown on a hill of gold.

"Now you are," Seth murmured. "You're beyond me now."

She heard the shots. For one unspeakable moment everything inside her stopped. Heart, mind, breath, blood. Then it started again, a tidal wave of feeling that had her springing off the bench where Jack had put her, the air heaving in and out of her lungs.

And she knew, because she felt, because her heart could beat, that it hadn't been Seth who'd met the bullet. If he had died, she would have known. Some piece of her heart would have broken off from the whole and shattered.

Still, she waited, her eyes on the house, because she had to see.

The stars wheeled overhead, the moon shot light through the trees. Somewhere in the distance, a night bird began to call out, with hope and joy.

Then he walked out of the house. Whole. Tears clogged her throat and were swallowed. They stung her eyes and were willed away. She had to see him clearly, the man she had accepted that she loved, and couldn't have.

He walked to her, his eyes dark and cool, his gait steady.

He'd already regained control, she realized. Already tucked whatever he'd had to do away in some compartment where it wouldn't interfere with what had to be done next.

She wrapped her arms around herself, hands clamped

tight on her forearms. She'd never know that one gesture, that turning into herself and not him, was what stopped him from reaching for her.

So he stood, with an armspan of distance between them and looked at the woman he accepted that he loved, and had pushed away.

She was pale, and even now he could see the quick trembles that ripped through her. But he wouldn't have said she was fragile. Even now, with death shimmering between them, she wasn't fragile.

Her voice was strong and steady. "It's over?"

"Yeah, it's over."

"He was going to kill them."

"That's over, too." His need to touch her, to hold on, was overwhelming. He felt that his knees were about to give way. But she turned, shifted her body away, and looked out into the dark.

"I need to see them. Bailey and M.J."

"I know."

"You need my statement."

God. His control wavered enough for him to press his fingers against burning eyes. "It can wait."

"Why? I want it over. I need to put it behind me." She steadied herself again, then turned slowly. And when she faced him, his hands were at his sides and his eyes clear. "I need to put it all behind me."

Her meaning was clear enough, Seth thought. He was part of that all.

"Grace, you're hurt and you're in shock. An ambulance is on the way."

"I don't need an ambulance."

"Don't tell me what the hell you need." Fury swarmed through him, buzzed in his head like a nest of mad hornets. "I said the damn statement can wait. You're shaking. For God's sake, sit down."

When he reached out to take her arm, she jerked back, her chin snapping up, her shoulders hunching. "Don't touch me. Just...don't." If he touched her, she might break. If she broke she would weep. And weeping, she would beg.

The words were a knife in the gut, the deep and desperate blue of her eyes a blow to the face. Because he felt his fingers tremble, he stuffed them into his pockets, took a step back. "All right. Sit down. Please."

Had he thought she wasn't fragile? She looked as if she would shatter into pieces with one hard thought. She was sheet pale, her eyes enormous. Blood and bruises marked her face.

And there was nothing he could do. Nothing she would let him do.

He heard the distant wail of sirens, and footsteps from behind him. Cade, his face grim, walked to Grace, tucked a blanket he'd brought from the house over her shoulders.

Seth watched as she turned into him, how her body seemed to go fluid and flow into the arms Cade offered her. He heard the fractured sob even as she muffled it against Cade's shoulder.

"Get her out of here." His fingers burned to reach out, stroke her hair, to take something away with him. "Get her the hell out of here."

He walked back into the house to do what needed to be done.

The birds sang their morning song as Grace stepped out into her garden. The woods were quiet and green.

And safe. She'd needed to come here, to her country escape. To come alone. To be alone.

Bailey and M.J. had understood. In a few days, she thought, she would go into town, call, see if they'd like to come up, bring Jack and Cade. She would need to see them soon. But she couldn't bear to go back yet. Not yet.

She could still hear the shots, the quick jolt of them shuddering through her as Jack had taken her outside. She'd known it was DeVane and not Seth who had met the bullet. She'd simply known.

She hadn't seen Seth again that night. It had been easy to avoid him in the confusion that followed. She'd answered all the questions the local police had asked, made statements to the government officials. She'd stood up to it, then quietly demanded that Cade or Jack take her to Salvini, take her to Bailey and M.J.

And the Three Stars.

Stepping down onto her blooming terraces, she brought it back into her head, and her heart. The three of them standing in the near dark of a near-empty room, she with her torn and bloody dress.

Each of them had taken a point of the triangle, had felt the sing of power, seen the flicker of impossible light. And had known it was done.

"It's as if we've done this before," Bailey had murmured. "But it wasn't enough then. It was lost, and so were we."

"It's enough now." M.J. had looked up, met each of their eyes in turn. "Like a cycle, complete. A chain, with the links forged. It's weird, but it's right."

"A museum instead of a temple this time." Regret and relief had mixed within Grace as they set the Stars down again. "A promise kept, and, I suppose, destinies fulfilled."

She'd turned to both of them, embraced them. Another triangle. "I've always loved you both, needed you both. Can we go somewhere? The three of us." The tears had come then, flooding. "I need to talk."

She'd told them everything, poured out heart and soul, hurt and terror, until she was empty. And she supposed, because it was them, she'd healed a little.

Now she would heal on her own.

She could do it here, Grace knew, and, closing her eyes, she just breathed. Then, because it always soothed, she set down her gardening basket, and began to tend her blooms.

She heard the car coming, the rumble of wheels on gravel, and her brow creased in mild irritation. Her neighbors were few and far between and rarely intruded. She wanted no company but her plants, and she stood, her flowers flowing at her feet, determined to politely and firmly send the visitor away again.

Her heart kicked once, hard, when she saw that the car was Seth's. She watched in silence as it stopped in the middle of her lane and he got out and started toward her.

She looked like something out of a misty legend herself, he thought. Her hair blowing in the breeze, the long, loose skirt of her dress fluttering, and flowers in a sea around her. His nerves jangled.

And his stomach clutched when he saw the bruise marring her cheek.

"You're a long way from home, Seth." She spoke without expression as he stopped two steps beneath her.

"You're a hard woman to find, Grace."

"That's the way I prefer it. I don't care for company here."

"Obviously." Both to give himself time to settle and because he was curious, he scanned the land, the house perched on the hill, the deep secrets of the woods. "It's a beautiful spot."

"Yes."

"Remote." His gaze shifted back to hers so quickly, so intensely, he nearly made her jolt. "Peaceful. You've earned some peace."

"That's why I'm here." She lifted a brow. "And why are you here?"

"I needed to talk to you. Grace—"

"I intended to see you when I came back," she said quickly. "We didn't talk much that night. I suppose I was more shaken up than I realized. I never even thanked you."

It was worse, he realized, that cool, polite voice was worse than a shouted curse. "You don't have anything to thank me for."

"You saved my life and, I believe, the lives of the people I love. I know you broke rules, even the law, to find me, to get me away from him. I'm grateful."

The palms of his hands went clammy. She was making him see it again, feel it again. All that rage and terror. "I'd have done anything to get you away from him."

"Yes, I think I know that." She had to look away. It hurt too much to look into his eyes. She'd promised herself, sworn to herself she wouldn't be hurt again. "And I wonder if any of us had a choice in what happened over that short, intense period of time. Or," she added with a ghost of a smile, "if you choose to believe what happened, over centuries. I hope you haven't—that your career won't suffer because of what you did for me."

His eyes went dark, flat. "The job's secure, Grace."

"I'm glad." He had to leave, she thought. He had to leave now, before she crumbled. "I still intend to write a letter to your superiors. And you might know I have an uncle in the Senate. I wouldn't be surprised, when the smoke clears, if you got a promotion out of it."

His throat was raw. He couldn't clear it. "Look at me, damn it." When her gaze shot back to his face, he curled his hands into fists to keep from touching her. "Do you think that matters?"

"Yes, I do. It matters, Seth, certainly to me. But for now, I'm taking a few days, so if you'll excuse me, I want to get to my gardening before the heat of the day."

"Do you think this ends it?"

She leaned over, took up her clippers and snipped off wilted blooms. They faded all too quickly, she thought. And that left an ache in the heart. "I think you already ended it."

"Don't turn away from me." He took her arm, hauled her toward him, as panic and fury spiraled through him. "You can't just turn away. I can't—" He broke off, his hand lifting to lie on the bruise on her cheek. "Oh, God, Grace. He hurt you."

"It's nothing." She stepped back quickly, nearly flinching, and his hand fell heavily to his side. "Bruises fade. And he's gone. You saw to that. He's gone, and it's over. The Three Stars are where they belong, and everything's back in its place. Everything's as it was meant to be."

"Is it?" He didn't step to her, couldn't bear to see her

shrink back from him again. "I hurt you, and you won't forgive me for it."

"Not entirely," she agreed, fighting to keep it light. "But saving my life goes a long way to—"

"Stop it," he said in a voice both ragged and quiet. "Just stop it." Undone, he whirled away, pacing, nearly trampling her bedding plants. He hadn't known he could suffer like this—the ice in the belly, the heat in the brain.

He spoke, looking out into her woods, into shadows and cool green shade. "Do you know what it did to me, knowing he had you? Knowing it. Hearing your voice on the phone, the fear in it?"

"I don't want to think about it. I don't want to think about any of that."

"I can't do anything but think of it. And see you—every time I close my eyes, I see you the way you stood there in that hallway, blood on your dress, marks on your skin. Not knowing—not knowing what he'd done to you. And remembering—half remembering some other time when I couldn't stop him."

"It's over," she said again, because her legs were turning to water. "Leave it alone."

"You might have gotten away without me," he continued. "You took out a guard twice your size. You might have pulled it off without any help from me. You might not have needed me at all. And I realized that was part of my problem all along. Believing, being certain, I needed you so much more than you could possibly need me. Being afraid of that. Stupid to be afraid of that," he said as he came up the steps again. "Once you understand real fear, the fear of knowing you could lose the most important thing in your life in one single heartbeat, nothing else can touch you."

He gathered her to him, too desperate to heed her resistance. And, with a shuddering gulp of air, buried his face in her hair. "Don't push me away, don't send me away."

"This isn't any good." It hurt to be held by him, yet she wished she could go on being held just like this, with the sun warm on her skin and his face pressed into her hair.

"I need you. I need you," he repeated, and turned his urgent mouth to hers.

The hammer blow of emotion struck and she buckled. It swirled from one of them to the other in an unbridled storm, left her heart shaken and weak. She closed her eyes, slid her arms around him. Need would be enough, she promised herself. She would make it enough for both of them. There was too much inside her that she ached to give for her to turn him away.

"I won't send you away." Her hands stroked over his back, soothed the tension. "I'm glad you're here. I want you here." She drew back, brought his hand to her cheek. "Come inside, Seth. Come to bed."

His fingers tightened on hers. Then gently lifted her head up. It made him ache to realize she believed there was only that he wanted from her. That he'd let her think it.

"Grace, I didn't come here to take you to bed. I didn't come here to start where we left off."

Why had he been so resistant to seeing what was in her eyes? he wondered. Why had he refused to believe what was so blatantly real, so generously offered to him.

"I came here to beg. The third Star is generosity," he said, almost to himself. "You didn't make me beg. I didn't come here for sex, Grace. Or for gratitude."

Confused, she shook her head. "What do you want, Seth? Why did you come?"

He wasn't sure he'd fully realized why until just now. "To hear you tell me what you want. What you need."

"Peace." She gestured. "I have that here. Friendship. I have that, too."

"And that's it? That's enough?"

"It's been enough all my life."

He caught her face in his hands before she could step away. "If you could have more? What do you want, Grace?"

"Wanting what you can't have only makes you unhappy."

"Tell me." He kept his eyes focussed on hers. "Straight out, for once. Just say what you want."

"Family. Children. I want children and a man who loves me—who wants to make that family with me." Her lips curved slowly, but the smile didn't reach her eyes. "Surprised I'd want to spoil my figure? Spend a few years of my life changing diapers?"

"No." He slid his hands down to her shoulders, firming his grip. She was poised to move, he noted. To run. "No, I'm not surprised."

"Really? Well." She moved her shoulders as if to shrug off the weight of his touch. "If you're going to stay, let's go inside. I'm thirsty."

"Grace, I love you." He watched her smile slide away from her face, felt her body go absolutely still.

"What? What did you say to me?"

"I love you." Saying it, he realized, was power. True power. "I fell in love with you before I'd seen you. Fell in love with an image, a memory, a wish. I can't be sure which it is, or if it was all of them. I don't know if it was fate, or choice, or luck. But it was so fast, so hard, so deep, I wouldn't let myself believe, and I wouldn't let myself trust. And I turned you away because you let yourself do both. I came here to tell you that." His hands slid down her arms and clasped hers.

"Grace, I'm asking you to believe in us again, to trust in us again. And to marry me."

"You—" She had to take a step back, had to press a hand to her heart. "You want to marry me."

"I'm asking you to come back with me today. I know it's old-fashioned, but I want you to meet my family."

The pressure in her chest all but burst her heart. "You want me to meet your family."

"I want them to meet the woman I love, the woman I want to have a life with. The life I've been waiting to start—waiting for her to start." He brought her hand to his cheek, held it there while his eyes looked deep into hers. "The woman I want to make children with."

"Oh." The weight on her chest released in a flood, poured out of her...until her heart was in her swimming eyes.

"Don't cry." It seemed he would beg after all. "Grace, please, don't. Don't tell me I left it too late." Awkwardly he brushed at her tears with his thumbs. "Don't tell me I ruined it."

"I love you so much." She closed her fingers around his wrists, watched the emotion leap into his eyes. "I've been so unhappy waiting for you. I was so sure I'd missed you. Again. Somehow."

"Not this time." He kept his hands on her face, kissed her gently. "Not ever again."

"No, not ever again," she murmured against his lips.

"Say yes," he asked her. "I want to hear you say yes."

"Yes. To everything."

She held him close in the flower-scented morning where the stars slept behind the sky. And felt the last link of an endless chain fall into place.

"Seth."

He kept his eyes shut, his cheek on her hair. And his smile bloomed slow and easy. "Grace."

"We're where we're supposed to be. Can you feel it?" She drew a deep breath. "All of us are where we belong now."

She lifted her face, found his mouth waiting. "And now," he said quietly, "it begins."

* * * * *